The Paradise Tree

By
Christopher Steele

My Gifto
Class of 1990

Janury 2010

Thank you...

to Anne Rugani for her help and insight.
to Z, who always encouraged this type of behavior.
to Chris Baty and everyone at *The Office of Letters and Light*. This book would not exist without NaNoWriMo.
to Matt Wiest for his encouragement.
to the Area 3 Writing Project.
to Sue Thomas and the Zoë Barnum Fellowship for the gift of time.
to everyone at the Vermont Studio Center.
to Ed and Evon for, well, everything.
to Zoe and Ethan for everything else.
And
to Elizabeth for making my heart beat fast, and for all those hours and days and weeks and months. You and me. Any day.

For my parents,
who taught me to value the people around me
and to laugh at myself.

Chapter 1

When Manny Montay arrived at the Riordan Home for Boys in November of 1993, Pete O'Boyle had already been a resident for a year and a half. Born 90 miles south, in the San Francisco Bay Area, Pete was 13 that fall, having come to Riordan himself in the summer of the previous year, after several suspensions from school and a few entanglements with police. His aunt, a large, kind woman in her late forties, had no children of her own. And after two years the responsibilities associated with the care of a troubled teenager had proven beyond her.

Eventually, she had gotten to the point where she had taken as much as she could from her dead sister's son and had told him patiently and plainly that she couldn't do any more for him, and that she was going to find someplace more suitable. Aunt Marjorie had brought him to the Riordan Home for a series of interviews, the culmination of which had been a final trip north with two suitcases and his Wilson baseball glove. She'd left him at the Home in late June, a week shy of his 12th birthday.

Pete liked his Aunt Marjorie, and had been upset when she told him she wanted him to live at Riordan for a while. He knew he'd gotten into a lot of trouble, and had done some bad stuff, but he'd always been nice to her. She was his Mom's sister, and as such, the only other remaining piece of Lilly O'Boyle's life. He hadn't been especially close to his aunt before his mom had died, but she'd taken care of him since, always trying to help him when she could. But he also knew he'd caused trouble for her by getting into stuff at school and with the police, so even though he was unhappy, he wasn't mad at her. More than anger, it was fear he felt in the move to Riordan, something he never would have admitted to anyone.

Nestled above the towns of Glenn Ellen and Sonoma in the heart of California Wine Country, the Home was named for the Most Reverend Patrick William Riordan, Second Archbishop of San Francisco. Founded by Father Michael Fitzpatrick in 1953, the enterprise began with a pilot program in Santa Rosa: one house, three staff members and eight troubled boys. The home moved over the Sonoma Mountains in 1958 to a hillside plot of land donated to the Catholic Church by the Quinn family, whose eldest son was in seminary at the time and would eventually become the sixth Archbishop of San Francisco. Once established in the Valley of the Moon, the Home grew quickly, and by 1964 was comprised of five cottages housing over sixty boys between the ages of nine and 17.

By the mid-1980's, Riordan Home had grown to include seven cottages, a nine room dining hall and kitchen, a school, a gymnasium and pool, an industrial arts shop, a large administration building, an infirmary and dental office, a permanent priests' residence and, at the center of it all, the 500 seat Notre Dame Chapel. By the time Pete and Manny arrived, the Home's population was just shy of 100 boys.

Adapting to life at Riordan hadn't been bad for Pete. He'd come near the beginning of the summer session, when most of the boys were gone on home visits. Because only a fraction of the boys were on campus they were all consolidated into two cottages: the older kids were together in St. John's while the younger kids were at the top of the hill in Mt. Olivett. As an almost 12 year old, Pete had been assigned to the younger group. The first few weeks went along pretty smoothly and quickly. Since the group was so small for the holiday, staffers from the various cottages rotated through Mt. Olivett and St. John's, giving Pete a chance to meet and learn the names of most of the workers.

He also learned the routine of cottage life, and with it, the routine of routine. After a few months, Pete understood that Riordan staffers had an unspoken mantra by which they lived: *keep the routine*.

Almost every day was a repeat of every other day, with only the minutest of variations. Each summer day followed the same pattern: wake-up and dress, followed by Chores, followed by transition, followed by chapel, followed by breakfast, followed by morning rec, followed by lunch, followed by afternoon rec, followed by free time/work time, followed by dinner, followed by showers, followed by free time/movie, followed by evening prayers, followed by bed. And every day was followed by another just like it.

For the staff, the routine worked. When everything went along with the routine, everything went smoothly. Disruption to the routine meant disruption to everything. And disruption of everything, Pete had learned quickly, meant consequences, usually in the form of cottage work hours.

At the end of that first summer, Pete was moved from his temporary placement in Mt. Olivett to St. Michael's Cottage. After a year there, and another summer on campus after a short and disappointing week home with his Aunt Marjorie, Pete was moved to St. Gabriel's Cottage in August of 1993. Boys moved cottages at the Home based on both age and maturity. The ages of boys in different cottages dovetailed in such a design as to give placement options to staff depending on maturity and personality conflicts. This meant some boys skipped cottages, while others did not. Even though a boy might stay at Riordan for five or six years, he might only move two or three times. St. Michael's housed 12 and 13 year olds; St. John's, 14 and 15 year olds. Sandwiched between, all of the boys in St. Gabe's were 13 or 14 years old.

Pete like living in St. Gabriel's a lot better than he had liked St. Michael's. The main reason was the staff. Each cottage at Riordan had four full time staff assigned to it. They worked two at a time and kind of overlapped by a day when they changed shifts. Of the four staff at St. Michael's, there was only one he liked, and there was one he hated. The cottage supervisor, Ms. Terry, was nice. She worked from Monday to Thursday, and was good to the boys. She was older than most of the staff, and though Pete didn't know for sure he guessed she was about 40, while the rest of people who worked in the cottages seemed like they'd all gotten right out of college. She was firm with the kids when they needed it, but from his first day around her, Pete truly believed she cared about him. Also at St. Michael's was Mr. Banks, who Pete thought was an absolute jerk. Appropriately, he worked opposite Ms. Terry, coming in on Thursday before she left and finishing up on Sunday night before her Monday morning arrival. The two of them worked together for about 5 hours every Thursday evening, and there was always a sense they were just barely being civil to each other.

And it was weird, because Ms. Terry was so nice to everyone else. But then Pete began to notice how staff from other cottages acted around Mr. Banks, and eventually realized something: even though they all worked together, nobody seemed to like him. After a little while of listening to and dealing with him, Pete decided he agreed with Jordi about Banks. Once, after Jordi had dropped an entire tray of Jell-O in the dining hall, Banks had made fun of him the whole way back to the cottage, even telling other staff what had happened. That night, just before evening prayers, when Ms. Handy had asked if there was anything in need of sharing before bed, Jordi had stood up and announced, "Mr. Banks is a complete and total bastard." Because Mr. Banks was black it was hard to tell, but Pete was pretty sure he blushed as Jordi strutted triumphantly away from the circle of boys. What was sure was that Jordi got 10 hours of cottage time and a week of campus restriction for saying it. But every other boy in St. Michael's chipped in to by him a giant candy bar that weekend, when Banks himself took them the local mall in Santa Rosa.

When he'd been in St. Michael's, Pete had once asked Ms. Terry how staff got partnered up. According to her, the supervisor got to pick his or her shift and the other three shifts were assigned based on "program needs." After a few weeks at Riordan, Pete understood "program needs" to mean two things. First, it meant having, as far as he could tell, one good staff on at the same time as every bad staff. So when a sucky staffer, like Banks was on shift, he had somebody cool, like Ms. Handy to balance him out. Second, it meant staffers who didn't get along worked opposite ends of the shift. As far as Pete could tell, the same "program needs" applied in all of the cottages.

Thankfully, there was no one like Banks in St. Gabe's. True, Mr. Weaver was sometimes an idiot, but he wasn't mean spirited like Banks, he just couldn't seem to decide if he wanted the boys in the cottage to be his friends or not. He acted differently depending on whether or not Mr. Johnson, the cottage supervisor, was around. When Johnson was in the cottage with him, Weaver tended to play *Mr. Hardass-Toughlove* with the boys, like he wanted to show his boss he was in control. But when he was alone he acted like all the boys were his pals, until he got pissed. Then he could be a real jerk.

One Saturday afternoon in September, he'd taken some boys down to the athletic field to play touch football. Things had been great until he'd gotten a little competitive, another thing about Weaver the boys had learned to watch out for. They'd only been playing for about 15 minutes when Billy Roberts had accidentally tripped and Weaver had fallen over him and hit the ground. Hard. Weaver was instantly livid with Billy, yelling at him, saying Billy had tripped him on purpose. Pete had seen the whole thing from the other side of the play, and the truth was that Weaver had been completely focused on getting to the kid with the football; he hadn't been watching where he was going, and had been running flat out when Billy had gone down in front of him. It wasn't until Weaver realized Billy had actually gotten hurt in the collision that he stopped yelling. And when he explained what happened to Mr. Johnson and wrote up the Incident Report, he just called it an accident, and never mentioned his accusing Billy of anything. The boys knew, but they didn't say anything because having staff pissed at you was no way to move through the Riordan world. And having the wrong staff pissed at you could be downright dangerous.

Weaver was the weakest link of the St. Gabriel's staff, and as such was dictated by "program needs" to be paired with the strongest staffer: Mr. Johnson, the cottage supervisor. He and Weaver worked together from Wednesday to Friday. From Sunday to Tuesday Mr. Dawson and Ms. Graham were on shift together. But the shifts were staggered so they overlapped. Each of the cottage staff worked a four-day shift. Johnson worked Tuesday to Friday, Weaver was Wednesday to Saturday, Dawson came in on Saturday morning, and Graham woke them up on Sundays. Tuesdays and Wednesdays were shift change days, so the boys saw three staffers each on those days.

When Manny came to St. Gabriel's Cottage, he came into a group that was still getting used to each other. Five other boys had come with Pete from St. Michael's in August. The other five had been in St. Gabriel's for all or part of the preceding school year. The holdovers were all slightly older than the St. Michael's guys, and as a result, slightly bigger. Except in Steve Sengall's case, where slightly didn't come into play. At over six feet, Steve was one of the tallest kids at Riordan. Only about half a dozen Fitzpatrick House guys were taller, and they were all 17 or 18 and going to the public high school off campus.

But the group was beginning to come together a little. There were never actual fights like sometimes happened in other cottages, when the pressure got to be too much and one or two boys snapped. Occasionally people got a little pissy with each other, but the cottage staff stayed on top of it fairly well (when they were around at least).

Overall, the boys of St. Gabriel's were civil to each other, sometimes even friendly. Which is not to say they were friends.

Friends were something few people at Riordan had. All of the boys had come from one sort of family mess or another, and as a result didn't trust anybody very much. Even Pete, who did trust his aunt, found it difficult to have much faith in the boys at the Home. The main problem was that each of them was there for a reason, and those reasons often were the kinds of things that get people to not trust you. But trust or no, companionship still found its way into Riordan life, and there were a few guys Pete hung around with, each with his own baggage in tow. Frankie Baltazar said he was at Riordan because his parents were getting a divorce, and he had stolen money from his mom's boyfriend. Chris Casper didn't talk about why he was at the Home, but it was common knowledge his parents were both speed freaks. They'd come to see him every couple of months, and Pete recognized all the signs. Jordi Melchior had gotten into trouble at school for selling his Ritalin to other kids. One girl had passed out in class and nearly died.

They were all okay guys to hang with, but Pete wasn't sure if they were his friends. He wasn't even sure if he wanted friends here or anywhere. He'd had friends back home, but they were a million miles away now, or they might as well be. When he'd been back home over the summer he'd seen hardly any of them, and the ones he did see weren't allowed to spend time with him because their parents were afraid he'd get them into trouble.

Before Manny arrived Pete had been rooming with Jordi for a couple of months. They got along fine, mostly because they stayed out of each other's stuff, which wasn't always the case with Riordan roommates. During breakfast the day before Manny showed up, the cottage staff told the boys they'd be changing roommates after school. There had been the usual groans from the usual people. Steven Sengall was especially unhappy about getting a new kid.

He'd been in a room alone since the end of September, when his roommate had been transferred up the hill one cottage to St. John's.

Pete hadn't been looking forward to changing rooms either, and had looked around the dining room at the other boys in the cottage, each making secret deals with the devil if he could avoid certain kids. Rooming with Jordi was something he knew and was comfortable with. It would be bad enough if he ended up with Steven as a roommate, but that wasn't the worst possibility. There were a few guys in St. Gabe's who he hated being around at all, and the idea of rooming with them was simply horrifying. His eyes had stopped on their own for a moment on the table where Tony and Malcolm sat. Either of them would be bad.

Malcolm was a lanky black kid with Tourette's Syndrome. Pete had roomed with him for a month at St. Mike's and it had been hell. The Tourette's (which Pete had never heard of before coming to Riordan) was a freaky thing to be around. Malcolm was twitchy. He blinked constantly and was always moving his face, stretching it. He mumbled to himself all the time, occasionally letting a startling curse word drop. The staff let it go. He couldn't help it, they said. But worse than the twitchiness was the bedwetting. Whatever room Malcolm slept in smelled like old piss all the time. Just remembering the smell had been enough to make Pete shiver in his dining hall chair.

Across from Malcolm sat Tony, a big fat kid who liked to purposefully run his belly into smaller kids then yell at them to "watch the hell where you're going!" He followed around after Steven and was the first to join the fun whenever Steven started in on someone. He was a big, fat, pasty-white kid with a shaved head who tried to do everything he could to sound and act like the black kids on campus, or at least like how he thought the black kids on campus should act and sound. Most of the small black population ignored his over the top mannerism, but not all. Pete had once heard Melek

Jefferson say to Tony at rec, out of earshot from any staff, "Hey, Tubby! The way you talk you must be the darkest N----- on this campus." Tony had turned pink at the sound of the laughter from Melek's friends, but that's all he'd done. Melek was from the Fitzpatrick group home; he was 17 and could have squashed Tony like a big fat bug.

Pete's eyes had then wandered to the worst possible scenario: The Rat. Michael Hamm was a short, gaunt kid with small, dull eyes set a little too close together. His face was a thin triangle topped with hair the color of dust. A substantial overbite jutted out above a lacking chin. Pete always imagined he saw whiskers growing out of the small bony nose, completing the rodent look.

The Rat was Chris's roommate and Pete had heard plenty about what a nightmare he was to share rooms with. Chris had told Pete he'd twice come through the doorway to find Mikey Hamm walking away from his side of the room. One of the times the Rat had been stuffing something into his mouth. It had been a candy bar Chris had hidden at the back of his underwear drawer. What had bothered Chris more than the theft of the candy bar was the fact that Michael had obviously felt no compunction about pawing over somebody else's skivvies to do it. But when he told the staff, he just mentioned the candy. Michael had gotten 5 hours work time and had to pay 50 cents out of his own Riordan Account to buy Chris a new Twix.

But more than the theft, Chris hated living with the Rat because he was just *dirty*. "What do you mean, dirty?" Pete had asked.

"You know," Chris had said, scrunching up his face, "just dirty. He never washes his hands. Ever. Not unless staff is watchin' him. He picks his nose and sticks his nuggets everywhere; they're all over the wall by his bed. And he's a total scrounge. I've seen him in the kitchenette when he thinks no one is watching him. He takes food out of the trashcan and eats it." Pete had seen this too. "But the grossest thing is the bugs. The last time he came back from home visit there were bugs all over his clothes. Fleas." Chris had shaken his head, "That kid is nasty."

Pete had steeled himself against the probability of ending up with one of those three. He'd just prayed it wouldn't be the Rat. But on the way out of breakfast, Mr. Johnson had asked him to wait while the other kids left.

"I'm giving you the new kid," Mr. Johnson had said, glancing down at a pile of yellow maintenance request forms in front of him. "He'll be here sometime tomorrow. Today after school I'd like you to move your stuff into room one, by the windows." Pete had been relieved. The new kid might end up being a loser, but at least he wasn't the Rat. Mr. Johnson had looked back up at Pete's relieved face. After a moment he'd smiled. "Afraid I was going to put you with Michael Hamm?" he'd asked.

Pete had been so shocked by the question he'd nodded before he could stop himself. Mr. Johnson laughed. "No. I think Michael could do with an *older* influence. You've been doing well, Pete. I'm giving you this new boy as a roommate because I think you'll be a good example for him. Will you?" Mr. Johnson had looked at him earnestly.

"Yes sir," Pete had nodded. Mr. Johnson was the nicest of the St. Gabe's staff. He was also the Supervisor, which meant this had been his decision, and he probably meant what he'd said to Pete.

Pete had liked the kind words from Mr. Johnson, but had also been excited because Chris, Frankie and Jordi were all safe from the Rat as well, who was going to be paired with one of the older kids who had been in St. Gabe's last year. Secretly, Pete had hoped for Steven or Tony.

In the end, Frankie got stuck with Malcolm and his ammonia cologne. Chris and Jordi were put together. Fat Tony was the unlucky bastard who ended up landing with the Rat.

Chapter 2

As far as Pete could tell, Emanuel Montay was an average kid. At 5'3" he was an inch shorter than Pete, and slighter of build. He had dark eyes above shadowy rings made to seem even darker for his fair skin. His shaggy hair was so black, Pete at first thought it was dyed. He didn't smile a whole lot, but that was normal for the Home. Smiling had a way of inviting trouble, because to staff it looked like you were hiding something, and to other boys it just made you stand out. And standing out was a bad idea at Riordan. But, at first glance anyway, Emanuel didn't stand out. In fact, there was a peculiar way in which he looked like he'd been at Riordan forever. In the plain white-t-shirts he liked to wear and his jeans rolled and cuffed over his Chuck Taylor's, he might have just stepped out of one of the photos on the wall in the Admin building from the Home's early days, instead of arriving on campus the way he did, dropped off by a blue sedan on a Friday afternoon. When Pete asked about the sedan, and the thick-faced black man who had been driving it, Emanuel had just shrugged.

It was Friday afternoon and the cottage was quiet. A couple of kids were down at the gym for basketball practice, a few were playing bumper pool and Nintendo in the game room, and Mr. Weaver had the rest outside working off "cottage time," which today meant pulling weeds around the side lawn and sweeping up the eucalyptus leaves covering cottage basketball court. Pete had seen them working as he and Mr. Johnson had walked Emanuel down from the Admin building with his bags. Pete didn't owe any time on the board in the hallway, and hadn't in several weeks. He knew it was one of the reasons Mr. Johnson had assigned him to be roommate to the new kid.

At lunch, Mr. Johnson had asked Pete to show Emanuel the cottage and hang out with him while he unpacked. In the front of the cottage, Pete had shown him the laundry and kitchenette, the game room and the two boards outside the staff office. One was the Status Board. It showed the names of all the boys, their room assignments, LEVEL, current house chore, and location. All the information was recorded on paper cards slotted into magnets that could be moved around as the status of the cottage changed. In the location column, Matt and Chris had green REC magnets, indicating they were with the recreation staff. The rest of the boys had nothing, meaning they were all in or immediately around the cottage.

"He's my P.O." Emanuel said, opening up the first of two big duffel bags in their room. He read the confusion in Pete's face. "The guy in the car," he said. Pete nodded. He understood about having a probation officer. He had one too; so did half the guys in the cottage. His was a lady named Jenny Martin who came every six months to visit him and check things at Riordan out. She was a tough woman with a New York accent mellowed by 15 years on the West Coast. She'd been the one who'd suggested the Riordan Home to Aunt Marjorie, having had a boy on her caseload there in the mid 80's.

"He a good guy?" Pete asked, unsure how to talk to the new kid. He never was sure how to act on someone's first day at the Home. After all, how do you welcome someone to a place where no one wants to be?

"He actually is," Emanuel said, kneeling down to unzip his second suitcase. "When I got in trouble, he helped."

"What did you get in trouble for," Pete asked. "What'd you do?" He hoped he didn't sound too eager. Some guys liked to talk, even brag about their problems, others didn't.

"Something I shouldn't have," was all he said. Then, as he rummaged through his second bag he said, "Hey, someone's gone through my stuff." Then looking up at Pete, "Do they do that here, too?"

"Yeah," Pete nodded. "It was on one of the forms your P.O. had you sign. They also do it whenever you come back from a home visit."

"Well, at least that won't be a problem," Emanuel said, almost to himself.

"I don't go home a lot either," said Pete. "A week over Christmas, a week in the summer, otherwise I'm here all the time." Emanuel didn't look up, but continued examining the contents of the searched bag. "Anything missing?" Pete asked. Sometimes you could tell about a guy by what kind of contraband he tried to smuggle onto campus.

"No," said Emanuel. "Looks like it's all here." He began emptying the second bag into the drawers beneath the mattress of his bed. It seemed to Pete all the boy owned was jeans and white t-shirts. After a few minutes of silent unpacking, he turned to look at Pete, still kneeling on the floor. "So," he asked, "why you?"

"What do you mean?"

"Why did you get stuck with the new guy?" he asked.

"Oh," Pete said, "well, I guess it's because I've been doing good. I'm a LEVEL 2, which means I have more privileges than most of the kids. It also means I don't get in trouble much."

"Uh huh," Emanuel said. "4 is bad and 2 is better, right?"

"Yeah."

"And you're a 2?"

"Yeah."

"So, why aren't you a 1?"

Pete was surprised at the question. He and Matt were the only two boys in the cottage to even get close to LEVEL 2, and they'd both been there since the beginning of the school year.

"I don't know," Pete shrugged and looked out the window.

"Have you ever made it to LEVEL 1?" the new kid asked.

"Twice," Pete said, a little defiantly. "Last year."

"Was it hard, getting to LEVEL 1?"

"Kinda, I guess."

"Well," said Emanuel, standing up from his now empty bag, "if it's kinda hard, and you've done it before, it seems like you'd know why you're not there now."

Pete felt himself flush, and he looked away again, out the windows and over the property line to the vineyard beyond.

"Hey, Pete," Emanuel said, "listen, I'm sorry man. I didn't mean to be a jerk. I guess I'm just nervous, and when I get nervous I talk a lot." Pete looked back at him, surprised again, this time at the apology. Again, not something one got a lot of at Riordan.

"It's okay," he mumbled, looking toward the baseball mitt atop his dresser. "Forget about it."

Emanuel nodded, walked over to where Pete sat on his bed, and stuck out his hand. Pete looked from the hand to the face of the other boy, trying to figure him out. Emanuel was smiling a little, his thin black eyebrows raised in question. Pete reached out, and Emanuel took his hand and shook it as he nodded and said, "Call me Manny."

Manny was from the central valley, near Sacramento, the state capital. He was two months older than Pete, and would turn 14 on April 23rd. He'd spent some time in Sacramento County's Youth Detention Facility, though for what he did not say, and Pete didn't press. Before that he'd been living and going to school in a town south of Sacramento called Elk Grove.

As he talked, he opened the last of his three bags, this one half the size of the others. It appeared to be full of books. When he saw the surprise on Pete's face, he said simply, "I like to read." He opened the last of the three drawers under the bed, the one closest to the head, and began to fill it with paperbacks, occasionally telling Pete about them. "This one is by a guy named Pratchett," he said of one, holding it up. "It's about this flat planet and the worst wizard in the universe who lives there. Cool." He held up another, "This one's called *Siddhartha*. It's about Buddha before he became Buddha." And another, "This is about a seagull who learns the secret to flying faster than any other bird." With each book he held up, Manny seemed to get more and more excited. All told, Pete figured his new roommate had more than 20 books in the traveling library.

"I guess you do like to read," Pete said.

"Never trust a man of only one book," Manny replied.

"Huh?"

"Something my dad used to say," Manny looked into the drawer of paperbacks. "It's not actually about books though. He said it means, 'don't trust anyone who only believes in one thing'." The he rolled the drawer shut and patted it after it had closed. Then he looked at Pete. "All done," he said. "Want to show me around some more?"

The mention of his father was the only thing Manny said about family at all that day. Pete didn't think it right to ask him anything else. But by the time they went to dinner that night, Pete was sure that he'd lucked out in getting Manny as a roommate.

Manny seemed to fit in well. He'd met everyone in the cottage, and he'd not just met them, but had actually introduced himself to each boy between dinner and lights out, with a handshake and everything. Most of the guys had been a little put off by it, and a few had looked at him like he was crazy. But they all at least shook his hand. Even Tony and Steven had been ok with him. It wasn't until Saturday morning that things got kind of strange.

They were walking back from the breakfast, halfway back to St. Gabriel's Cottage, when an argument broke out between Frankie and his cousin JP. Mr. Weaver, the St. Gabe's staffer who was supposed to be escorting them back from the dining hall, was lingering near the Admin building, talking to Ms. Murphy from St. Matt's. He had sent them on ahead while he flirted.

Like most arguments between residents of the Riordan Home for Boys, this one was about something that would otherwise be inconsequential, even ridiculous. But such arguments are rarely about the subject matter of the moment, but rather concern power and position and the overwhelming anxiety of a place where too many young people are being raised by adults who are not their parents.

In this case, the dispute had to do with ownership of a length of string. Frankie and JP were tugging back and forth on a piece of dirty grey string, alternately saying "Give it back!" and "Le' go, it's mine!" They weren't yelling (that would attract staff attention) but their voices were getting more and more serious: anger was building in them both. Pete and Manny were walking directly behind the cousins, and Pete instinctively began to slow down. He'd been at Riordan long enough to know that interference was a bad idea. Both boys were getting angry, and the last thing another boy should do was get between them. His mom had once told him, "Get between two people who are pissed at each other and you're bound to get piss on you."

But Manny wasn't slowing down; he was actually stepping a little quicker toward the dispute. Pete reached out for his arm, whispering, "Hey man, back off. Don't get in this!" But the new boy either didn't hear him or ignored the warning, because the next thing Pete knew, Manny had put a hand on each of the cousins' shoulders. Frankie and JP had both been so intent on each other neither had notice Manny until he touched them. The cousins jumped in the way of kids accustomed to heavy handed discipline. They looked at Manny in frightened wonder.

For his part, Manny seemed not to notice their expressions. He said, "Hey, I just wanted to suggest..." JP reached up and slapped his hand away and yelled, "GET YOUR FREAKIN' HANDS OFF ME!" Frankie took possession of the string and slipped sideways, away from both Manny and JP, who had now fully turned to face the new focus for his anger. The group of boys had gone silent at JP's outburst, and the only sound for a moment was the pounding of running feet as Mr. Weaver moved to catch up.

"What's you're problem kid!?" JP asked, looking Manny up and down. "You want a little taste?" He was inching minutely toward Manny, who had raised his palms up, and was actually smiling. *Goddamn*, thought Pete, *this kid's gonna get killed.* The rest of the boys sensed it, too. Pete could feel their excitement, their eagerness for violence and pain that didn't involve them. At Riordan, five minutes of something like this was better than watching TV all night long.

"Hey," Manny was saying, surprise in his voice, "I'm sorry. I was just trying..."

"You ain't sorry yet, but you gonna be." JP was almost nose to nose with Manny when the staff member arrived.

"Back off, JP!" Weaver ordered, putting a hand between the two, but touching neither boy. JP raised his chin and jutted out his jaw as he backed away. "Back to the cottage," Weaver said to the group, "Line up silently at the door. And JP, you're in a red chair until I deal with you! Understand?" JP's face tightened and he nodded. Then turned without looking at Manny again and stalked off toward St. Gabriel's. The group, sensing the show was finally over, walked after him, leaving Pete and Manny with Weaver.

As the group rambled away, Weaver turned to look first at Manny, then at Pete. "What happened, O'Boyle?" Pete, still a little stunned by his new roommate's almost suicide, said, "I'm not sure. JP and Frankie were arguing about something. Manny tried to help."

Weaver's eyes darted to Manny. He nodded and said, "Listen Manny, I know you're new here, but there's some things you gotta learn. Couple of guys start to go at it, the best thing you can do is get staff. Don't try to do anything yourself. Understand?"

Pete thought Manny looked confused, but the new boy nodded.

"Okay. Let's catch up with the group." And with that, Weaver hustled away. As he walked off toward the rest of the boys who were semi-lined up and semi-silent at the door to St. Gabriel's, Manny watched him go, an odd look on his face.

"Weaver's kind of a tool," Pete said to Manny. "He can even be an outright prick a lot of the time." The kid seemed all right, but if he wanted to survive at Riordan, he was going to have to learn some stuff. "But in this case, two guys about to go, when he says stay out of it, he's right."

Manny turned his face toward Pete, and when he did, Pete was stuck by the sincerity he saw there. It wasn't something you saw in a lot of faces at Riordan. Manny just looked at him for a moment, and then finally said, "No, he's not." He turned and walked toward the cottage, leaving Pete standing alone, wondering after his new roommate.

That evening, on the way back from dinner, both Mr. Dawson and Mr. Weaver were walking behind the boys, talking to JP and Frankie. Theoretically, they were within hearing distance of the main group, but practically, boys in places like the Riordan Home quickly learn the art of quiet conversation. Pete had spent the day introducing Manny to the various staff members they came into contact with around the dining hall and the rec department. They were walking together again as Pete explained about the school, and gave his opinions about the various teachers. They hadn't talked about the thing with JP since it happened. Pete figured there was no point. A little while at Riordan would be a better explanation of how things worked than he could give. They were talking about one of his favorite teachers, Mr. Nielsen.

"What do you mean he's only got one ear?" Manny asked, fascinated. "How's he only got one ear?"

"Skin cancer," Pete said. "He told us about it last year. You'll recognize him easy because he always wears a hat outside, no matter what the weather is."

"So, if there's no ear, what's…?"

"You're goddamn weird, kid!" came the rushed whisper from behind. Both boys glanced over their shoulders. About 2 yards behind them, Steven Sengall was walking with Tony Bruletti. They were both staring at Manny. Steven, smiling viciously, interested in seeing if he could get a reaction from the new kid, and Tony with the bull-brained expression of someone who just likes to hurt people.

Turning back to face forward, Pete said, "Just ignore him." But Manny kept looking back over his shoulder, his own face a quizzical mask.

"Dude," Pete whispered anxiously, "stop staring." But Manny kept his curious eyes on the boys behind.

"Your mama musta dropped you on your head or something," came the urgent voice again. Pete heard Tony cackle at this, and a few other boys sniggered as well. Some of the more perceptive boys had begun to sense the possibility of blood on the horizon. Several pairs of eyes darted sideways making sure not to miss anything. Manny was proving to be a potential source of serious entertainment.

"Huh," said Manny, in his own whisper. *Oh God,* thought Pete, and looked around again himself. Mr. Weaver and Mr. Dawson were still way behind talking to the cousins, and only making occasional glances at the rest of the boys.

"I'm curious," Manny said, "why would you say that?"

"Cause it's true you little butt wipe!" said Tony, making his first foray into the conversation.

Steven nodded, "Yeah, she musta dropped you on your freakin' head, that's why you're so goddam weird." There was a challenge growing in Steven's voice, whisper or no.

Pete was sure they expected Manny to front up and fight back. They'd even brought his mom into it, something most boys at Riordan didn't do because they didn't want done to them. Instead, Manny did something no one expected.

He nodded and smiled.

Pete felt his eyes widen.

The looks on Steven and Tony's faces changed quickly from the jeering smiles of taunt to the tightened jaws of malice.

"Yeah," Manny finally said, "That must be what happened." Then he turned around and looked forward again, showing them his back. Pete knew this was it. He could see it in the faces of Steven and Tony, and in their bodies. They were going to jump Manny any second.

"Hey guys, wait up!" It was Mr. Dawson calling out to the group. The assemblage stopped in their tracks and turned to face the staff member, all, Pete noted, except Tony, who was still staring at Manny. Manny just looked past Tony, at Mr. Dawson.

When the staff and cousins caught up, Mr. Dawson told the group that Mr. Weaver was going to take a few boys off campus to pick up a movie for the evening while the rest went back to the cottage and showered. All of the boys clamored to go with Weaver, but Mr. Dawson shushed them to silence. "Let's see," he said, looking over the group. "Pete, Matt, and Jordi." There was a lot of grumbling as the three boys began to walk toward Admin with Weaver. "Oh," added Mr. Dawson, "and take Manny with you too."

As the selected boys and Weaver walked back the way they had just come, Pete looked over his shoulder, and saw Tony and Steven continuing to glance at him and Manny.

Pete shook his head. This was just Manny's second day at Riordan, and already there were at least 3 guys who wanted to thrash him. By the morning that number would probably go up a little. Even if there weren't many friendships at a place like Riordan, there were alliances. And Pete knew he had to be careful too, because guys like Tony didn't necessarily mind if other people got in the way of a beating. Pete thought Manny was crazy, but he liked him ok. But like or not, he had no desire to get his ass kicked by association. If Manny didn't want to go along with the way of things at Riordan, that was his lookout alone.

Later, as boys were getting ready for light's out, Pete came into his and Manny's room to find his new roommate sitting on his bed and reading. He seemed to take no notice of Pete, who put away his toothbrush and towel before crawling into bed. On his pillow was a book, one of the several Manny had shown him and talked about as he'd unpacked.

"What's this for?" Pete asked, picking up the book and turning to Manny.

"It's for reading," Manny responded, not looking up from the pages of a book with *The Secret Sharer* printed on the front. When Pete said nothing further, Manny finally put his book down on his chest and looked at him. "It's also a way for me to say 'thank you.'"

"For what?"

"For trying to protect me earlier," Manny said. "For trying to warn me off about Steven and the other one.

Pete felt warming embarrassment creeping up his neck. "I wasn't trying to protect you..." he began to protest, as if trying to protect someone were a taboo. "I just..." But he just didn't know how to explain it.

"It's okay," Manny said. "I appreciate it."

Pete stared at him. "Then why did you respond? You know they're gonna jump you, don't you?"

Manny nodded and smiled in a funny way. "Probably," he conceded. Then he looked past Pete, out the window to the dark vineyard beyond. After a minute he looked back to Pete and shrugged. Then he picked up his book and began to read again. Pete continued to look at him for a moment before sitting down on his own bed. He wondered, not for the first time, why Manny was so different. But, he realized, different or not, the kid was likeable. And he didn't want to see him get smashed up, if for no other reason than because Manny had been nice to him. As he watched his roommate turn pages, completely oblivious to his staring, he humorlessly wondered if Steven might be right. Maybe Manny had been dropped when he was a baby.

Shrugging the thought off, he opened the book to the title page:

**Jonathan
Livingston
Seagull**
a story

Richard
Bach

Wondering at the strangeness of the title, Pete turned to the first page and began to read.

Chapter 3

Sunday morning Ms. Graham woke them up for brunch to be followed by mass. Next to Ms. Terry, the St. Mike's supervisor, Ms. Graham was the nicest person on campus. She was young, short, rounded and blond, and always put Pete in mind of a plush stuffed animal. She often had ribbons or flowers in her hair, and always wore blue. But her inherent softness didn't make her unable to stand up to her charges, though the combination of her demeanor and her partnership with Mr. Dawson meant she almost never had to. Between them they imbued the cottage with so much positive and relaxed energy that there were almost never major blow-ups on Sundays and Mondays, the two days when they were on shift together. Almost all serious resident meltdown came on Fridays and Saturdays. The common denominator in those cases was Mr. Weaver.

After brunch the boys were guided in to the chapel for church. For most Riordan residents mass was the only chance each week to see and be seen by the community. Since mass was always open to the public, a few dozen locals made a weekly pilgrimage to see firsthand the work of the Home and to listen to the priest. Father O'Connell had been at Riordan for a dozen years. Everyone knew he was close to 50 years old, which seemed ancient to Pete, but he didn't look or act old. He liked to joke with the boys and in good weather it was not unusual to find him outside one of the cottages shooting baskets with residents. Mr. Johnson called him the "ageless wonder."

He was the director of the Home, and as such was the final word at Riordan, the determining factor in Home policy. There were others in the power structure: the cottage staff and supervisors, the coordinators, the caseworkers, Dr. Rugani the psychologist and Mr. Goodwin the head of operations. Father O'Connell rarely interfered with the others in the structure. Pete had heard him tell Dr. Rugani that he was lucky, the Home had a staff of intelligent and competent people and the only thing he needed to do to be a good director was stay out of their way.

Even though he had little to no impact on their day to day lives, Father O was a touchstone for the boys. It at first had surprised Pete that the priest called him by name whenever they spoke. Then he'd been amazed to realize Father O knew the name of *every* boy on campus. But it made sense in a way. No boy came to live at Riordan without meeting Father O first. His was the final interview of the lengthy admissions process. And it was said no boy left Riordan without a final meeting, either to receive congratulations and a pat on the back or to get the official boot. Either way, his office was the first and last stop for residents.

Apart from his likeability as staff honcho, Pete liked him as a priest. He was a lot more interesting than the guy Pete had been made to deal with growing up and he gave the impression of really enjoying his faith and his job. After mass even Manny, who'd talked about being Christian "but not Catholic," said Father knew his stuff.

Free time options for boys at Riordan had a lot to do with the Home's LEVEL System. Pete explained to Manny, "Any freedom you have at this place depends on your LEVEL." The staff liked to say one led to the other. *"The choices you make lead to the LEVEL you want; the LEVEL you achieve will lead to more and better choices,"* was printed on blue paper and framed in the T-hall just past the office door, strategically placed, Pete always assumed, so that guys in trouble and waiting outside the office would be forced to contemplate their life choices. He told this to Manny while explaining the LEVEL system and his new roommate laughed.

There were eight different areas in which every boy received a score out of 10 at the end of each day. The average score for the eight became the score for the whole day. At the end of two weeks, the daily scores were added up and averaged. The result was a number between 1 and 10, which determined the boy's LEVEL for the next 2 weeks. Pete thought of it as school. If you averaged 90 percent for the two weeks, it was like getting an *A*. And an *A* equaled LEVEL 1. So an average score between 8 and 9 meant LEVEL 2; a score between 7 and 8 was LEVEL 3; and anything below 7, even if it was a 6.9, meant two more weeks of early lights out and cottage restriction.

And that was why there were so few LEVEL 1 guys on campus. It was just so difficult to maintain. Even one bad score on a single day was enough to screw up a LEVEL 1. And worse, Pete knew from experience that it didn't even take screwing up to have one bad score ruin a day. LEVEL scores was one of the areas in which it was dangerous to have made an enemy of a staff member. While in St. Mike's Pete himself had once contradicted Mr. Banks, correcting him when Banks had been making a verbal report to Ms. Terry about a fight between two boys. In the moment, Banks had said nothing, but later in the evening, he had asked Pete, almost casually, what his LEVEL was. Pete had replied that it was a 2. Banks had looked him in the eye and whispered, "Are you sure about that?"

For the next three days after Ms. Terry had gone off shift, Banks had hounded Pete, jumping on him and loudly correcting him over even the slightest thing. After a couple of days of it Pete finally told Banks to "Go to Hell," for which he'd received 5 hours and three consecutive daily scores of 5 in the "Staff Interaction" category. When the next LEVEL evaluations were done the following week, Pete had dropped to a low 3. When he came on shift a few days later, Banks didn't say anything to him about it, but he did tap the "3" on the board next to Pete's name and smile at him.

By numbers, the largest group in any cottage was the 3s. It was just kind of the default spot where most kids settled. You could be a

3 without trying too hard at anything, as long as you kept clear of fights with other boys and didn't argue with staff. Also, the guys who staff knew were up to something but could never catch ended up spending a lot of time as 3s. And being a 3 wasn't too bad. Being a 3 meant you didn't have to transition in red chairs, and you could breathe for a few minutes between school and working off cottage hours. And even though it wasn't written in the rules, most staff would grant moderate LEVEL 2 privileges to 3s who were having good days or weeks.

The only real difference was that 2s and 1s had much later lights out times. The one thing every Riordan kid wanted was a later bed time. The reason was simple. After dinner and homework, once kids started to go to bed, there was suddenly this moment of freedom the rest of the day just didn't have room to contain. The routine of the day didn't even have room built in for it. But once the 4s started to go to bed at 8:00, followed by the 3s at 8:30, then suddenly the 2s and 1s could watch TV, play games and relax with no other tasks to complete for the day beyond the brushing of teeth.

Boys who either didn't listen or couldn't keep their tempers made up the second largest group: the 4s. This group had the fewest privileges and most restrictions of all. Fours went to bed first. They were not allowed seconds on dessert. Unless they were involved in a sport or with the choir or some other official Riordan function, they were bound to the cottage. They had no break time between getting home from school and beginning work on any cottage hours they owed.

The one thing most 4s hated beyond any other restriction, besides the early bedtime, was transitioning in red chairs. Each cottage had at its front a craft section used in the evenings for homework and almost never for crafts. A built in desk followed the contours of the room and made the whole front end of the cottage into a work area. Before leaving and after returning from anywhere, LEVEL 4 boys had to sit transition. This meant they had to sit silently, without putting their head down on the table, and without reading anything and without making eye contact with any other boys. All while the cottage's other residents went to the bathroom, played in the game room, or headed outside to wait for staff. Even Pete had to admit that it was brutal.

The biggest problem with the LEVEL system was the hopelessness it tended to breed in some kids. Pete had watched Malcolm struggle with being a LEVEL 4 since the previous January, and felt sorry for him. Along with his Tourette's, Malcolm had an amazingly short fuse. And when he got angry he cussed like crazy. And even if the cussing was forgivable because of his medical condition, staff still found it hard to deal with his threats to other kids. He'd even threatened Pete once, had let loose, yelling a stuttering, curse filled promise of injury. All because Pete had asked if he was all right after an outburst at Mr. Dawson.

Just one month prior, in early October, Malcolm had born down. He'd told Pete and Chris he was going to get to LEVEL 2 before Halloween, so he could stay late at the Halloween Carnival the rec staff put on every year. And, of course, Chris and Pete had rolled their eyes at each other as he'd said it. But damned if he didn't make a go of it. With only 4 days to go in the evaluation period, he was looking like he might make it. But then the inevitable happened.

Walking through the dining hall, a younger kid from Mt. Olivett Cottage had bumped into Malcolm and not said anything in the way of an apology. At which point Malcolm let out all of what he'd been holding onto the previous week and a half, shoving the kid and screaming, "W-w-w-what the HELL? S-s-s-say you're s-s-sorry A-A-ASSHOLE! W-w-what's the m-m-m-matter with you?" The kid, scared by Malcolm's height, reputation for losing control, and the freakish sound of the stutter did the worst and most natural thing for a 10 year old boy to do: he giggled. Malcolm's eyes turned into deranged dinner plates, he hauled off and smacked the kid in the head. Even so, he might still have made it, except for the fact that he realized he'd probably blown it, and went on what Frankie later called "a three-day crazy." He not only didn't make LEVEL 2, but dropped himself clear down past 3, landing in familiar territory.

Three days later the new LEVELS came out and it was confirmed that Malcolm would remain a 4. He came out for breakfast the next morning with a gang-style permanent marker tattoo across his knuckles. When he lined up his hands next to each other the letters read "FOUR 4LIF." And he grinned like an idiot, proud of his handiwork. When questioned by staff, he admitted that his "friend Tony" had come up with the idea. Malcolm's knuckles were raw from washing by the time he'd scrubbed off the letters. Tony got 5 hours for his suggestion, then another 5 when he told Malcolm he was going to kick his ass, not realizing Mr. Johnson was right behind him. Not surprising behavior, given Tony was also a well entrenched resident of the land of 4s.

Pete was a 2 and Manny, because he was new, was a LEVEL 0. Zeros were treated somewhere between a 2 and a 3; they were given the benefit of the doubt about some things because staff didn't know them yet, but were kept close on some matters, also because staff didn't know them yet. Because Manny was Pete's roommate and the two seemed to get along well, and because he had yet to show himself to be irresponsible, Mr. Johnson told the rest of the staff that he could be treated as a full 2, provided Pete was with him. So Manny was allowed to accompany Pete on walks around campus without staff, a privilege not usually afforded to new boys.

It was on one of these early walks that Manny began to talk about how he'd come to be at Riordan. They were walking alongside Gihon Creek, where it flowed away from St. Gabe's, down between the rec department and the athletic fields. Neither had spoken much since they'd left the cottage. Pete liked that he didn't feel the need to talk all the time when they were hanging out. There was a comfort and familiarity between them. Pete had no siblings and had begun to wonder if this might be what brotherhood felt like.

After about 5 minutes of quiet walking, Manny said, "You haven't asked me why I'm here." Pete looked at him, but Manny was looking down at the creek as he walked, almost as if he hadn't said a thing. Pete didn't immediately respond. "I mean, you asked me what I did to earn a PO, but not how I ended up here."

"No," Pete said, looking back to his own walking. He liked to walk this stretch of the creek, mostly because other boys didn't frequent the area. Since most boys couldn't roam free he often had the dirt path between the cottage and the 4-H barn to himself.

After a few moments, Manny asked, "Why not?"

Pete shrugged, "I don't know. I mean, everybody's got different reasons they're here. I guess it just doesn't matter. You don't seem too crazy, so I guess it couldn't have been anything too bad."

"I thought maybe it's because you don't like to talk about why you're here."

Pete shot a glance at him. "What're you talking about?"

"I don't know," said Manny, shaking his head. "It's just that everybody in the cottage seemed so eager to tell me their stories, like I was taking a survey or something." He chuckled, "And they were more than happy to tell me why everyone else is in here."

Pete remembered. In the beginning everyone tried to figure out a new kid, tried to learn his story looking for commonalities, as if the shared weaknesses of the past somehow make them instant brothers now. But the weird thing of it was how it did kind of work. Guys with parents who were druggies tended to hang together, as did those who'd spent a lot of time in juvenile hall, though in truth there weren't many of those at Riordan.

"So what did you learn?" Pete asked.

"Kinda more than I wanted to," Manny said. "Some of these guys have been through hard times. Like Michael. Man, that kid's had it tough. Kind of makes me feel bad for him."

Pete looked at Manny in disbelief, "You mean Michael in our cottage? Michael Hamm? The Rat? You feel bad for him?!"

"What do you mean?"

"Guy's a bastard is what I mean!" Pete was suddenly annoyed, but didn't know why. He quickly tried to control himself, and went on a moment later, his voice even again. "He's no good. He's not just the Rat because he looks like one; kid's not right. He's like a rodent. You can't trust him. He's only out for himself."

"Yeah, well, they all are." Manny had picked up several small stones and was now lobbing them underhand into the dark waters of the stream. "I mean, that's what the whole get-to-know-you dance is about, isn't it? "

"What do you mean," Pete asked.

"Well, it's like everyone wants to tell their own story, yeah, but that's not all they're after," he said. "It's all like a spy movie, like they're gathering intelligence against a possible enemy." He looked at Pete, "you know what I mean?"

Pete nodded. He understood exactly. The other thing they looked for in a new kid, besides possible commiseration, was weak spots, things they could use to their advantage.

"And it's not just that," Manny went on. "They're all so eager to tell you everyone else's dirty little secrets too. I must have heard at least three different versions of everyone's life story in the last few days." He gave Pete a sideways glance. "Except for yours," he said. "No one seems to know your story. You haven't told anyone."

"No. Nothing to tell," Pete said. It was mostly true. What was true was that he'd never told anyone at the Home everything. Jordi and Chris knew about his mom's cancer, but no one except staff knew about his father.

His mom had told him only a few things about his dad. Scott Hammet had been out of Lilly O'Boyle's life for 6 months before Pete's birth, and had been killed in a car crash less than a year later. He'd been tall, she'd told him, though there were no pictures around to see it. Lilly said she had burned them all after the break-up, before the crash. But he'd been basically a good man, having never raised his voice or hand to her in the eighteen months they were together.

They were almost to the barn now. Through the trees he could see the bright red from the recent summer's paint job.

Growing up without a father around hadn't bothered Pete. He'd had his mom and her parents, and, of course, Aunt Marjorie. He and Lilly lived with his grandparents until just before his 8th birthday, when his grandmother had suddenly passed away from a heart attack. Pete's grandfather had always been a relatively quiet but friendly man. And it wasn't until after her death that Pete realized all his grandmother had done for his grandfather. She had always prepared his food, done his laundry, driven him everywhere, and held his hand or arm when they were out in public. In all of Pete's memory she had been at his side or within arm's reach. Pete had first heard the word *Alzheimer's*, whispered by his mother some years before, but could attach no meaning to it until she explained why Grandpa had to live with the nice people at the small hospital, the one with all the pretty flowers in the garden.

Pete and Lilly had stayed in the house of her parents, spending months cleaning out the debris of 30 years of constant occupancy. Grandpa passed away before Thanksgiving that year, two days after Vice President George Bush was elected to the top job. Pete hadn't even grown out of the brown suit he'd worn to his grandmother's funeral and so wore it again. By the time the calendar flipped to 1989, life with Lilly had achieved a level of normality it had lacked since before Grandma's unexpected death. They were still seven months away from the first mentions of cancer or leukemia.

"I can respect that." Manny's voice pulled Pete out of his memories.

"Huh?"

"You not wanting to talk about your life," Manny said. "I said I can respect that."

"Oh." Pete didn't quite know what to make of this.

"Actually," Manny looked at him and smiled. "I've sort of followed your example."

"You didn't tell them why you're here?" Pete asked.

"Nah. Why give them what they want?" Manny said. "Besides, you're right, and not just about Michael. They're not trustworthy. Well, most of them aren't. Chris and Jordi, and even Frankie seem like they could be decent guys. Though I think Frankie's still pissed about me getting between him and his cousin."

"He's okay. So are Chris and Jordi…" He hesitated.

"But…?"

"No," Pete said. "Nothing. Just forget it." He turned off the main trail.

"They're good guys, but you don't trust even them? That it?"

Pete felt his neck getting warm again. Manny had a way of needling him. *But*, and Pete was pretty sure of this, *he doesn't mean to needle. He just asks what he asks and says what he thinks.* And this thought was followed up quickly by, *It is gonna get him an ass kicking here.*

"Look, man," Manny said, "I'm sorry. Not my business."

Pete waved the apology off, "Forget it." They had reached the side door to the barn. In his paddock next to the barn, Montecristo, the Home's single aging horse gnawed quietly at a bale of hay. Pete opened the door and he and Manny walked in. Pete saw that the sheep and goats were already in for the evening. Mr. Ramirez had already been and gone for the night. He had wanted to introduce Manny to Mr. Ramirez. He'd try to bring Manny down tomorrow after group.

He showed Manny around and named off the few animals with actual names. The pigs and the sheep were not among these. Mr. Ramirez never let them name the animals they showed for 4-H. It was a bad idea he said, to treat them as pets, name them, and then sell them to their fates. Better to just use their tattooed numbers for ID purposes. He did introduce Manny to Jacob and Joshua, two Nubian goats that had been donated to the Home several years earlier.

Manny, who had never seen a goat in person before, was fascinated by them. "Check out those eyes." He was bending down to look into Joshua's large almost oval eyes. The elongated dash of the animal's pupil followed his movement. "I've never seen eyes like these."

"Yeah," Pete said, "they're weird." He was glad they had left the previous conversation outside. But after a few minutes of looking at sheep and chickens, Manny said to him, "I'd like to tell you something."

"Okay," Pete said, unsure where Manny's tone was going to take them.

"About me and why I'm here."

"All right." The cool of the barn seemed to suddenly disappear, and Pete felt at once nervous and intrigued. Manny was different than other guys he'd seen come in to Riordan and Pete wanted to know his story. But he wasn't sure he wanted to be in a position where he felt like he had to share his. He'd never asked about the history of another boy. Most didn't need asking, they felt a compulsion to tell everybody who'd listen how they ended up at the Home, hoping to come off more normal than they probably felt. And Pete listened because it was sometimes interesting.

"I got into trouble last spring. At my school. See, there was this teacher who'd been giving this kid Andy a hard time. Now Andy, he's just this dirt-poor kid from the old, poor part of town. All the folks who've moved there in the last 20 years like to pretend the poor part doesn't exist, and more that the people there don't exist. But they do, and I went to school with some of them. Kids of farm laborers mostly. Black, white, Hispanic. But this Andy kid hadn't been doing his homework or something, and the teacher, Mr. Brice, he decides to embarrass Andy in class, right in front of everybody. While we're working quietly, he announces that he's going to call the parents of all the kids who haven't been turning in homework regularly and that he's going to do it right there and then."

"So he calls up Andy, tells him to stand in front of the room and asks him for his phone number. Andy doesn't respond, he just looks down at his shoes. Whole class is quiet, everybody staring at this poor kid, me included."

"So Mr. Brice asks Andy for his number again. Kid still says nothing. Brice tells him he's got detention, and then tells him to stay there, still in front of the room while he looks up the number in Andy's file, which he pulls from his desk drawer. Andy's still got his head down; his hair is kinda long, so none of us can see his face. Brice says his name again, but Andy still won't look up. The teacher picks up the phone, and dials the number. Eventually he starts to say something, then stops, and listens. Then he holds the phone away from his ear, so the kids who sit near his desk can hear the recorded voice saying the number has been disconnected. And he's got this sick, evil little smile on his face." He shook his head and looked up at Pete. "How is it only fat men can get such evil little smiles?" He went on without waiting for an answer.

"Now, I look at Andy, and I'm certain I'm not the only one who sees the tear splashes on his broken down Nikes. Teacher says, 'You may be seated now, Andrew,' just as sarcastic as you please."

Manny paused here for a while, looking into the sheep pen.

Pete could barely stand it, now that he was finding out. He asked, "So did you do something to the teacher?"

Manny nodded at the sheep. "Tried to talk to him first. Before Andy's butt was even in his seat I was standing next to Mr. Brice's desk, telling him that what he's done was wrong. That treating a kid like dirt just because of homework was not only stupid, but irresponsible." Manny smiled, this time looking back to Pete. "I think that's when he got mad, when I told him that he'd been stupid and irresponsible." He nodded, the continued, "Anyway, he barks at me to sit down. I tell him he should apologize to Andy. He tells me to either sit down or leave." He stopped, and Pete wondered if this is all there was to the story.

"So what did you do?" Pete asked.

"Went a little crazy; acted like an idiot." He paused for a long time, and Pete was getting ready to prompt him again when he spoke. "I chose to leave the room. But I decided to take his telephone with me."

"His phone?"

"I know," Manny chuckled again. "Dumb. But it seemed like a good idea at the time."

"But how..." Pete started.

"I reached across his desk, picked it up and ripped it out of the wall."

"Wow," Pete said.

"Yep."

"Is that it? I mean, it's vandalism, but it still doesn't seem like very much."

"I'm not sure what my plan was. I was thinking I'd smash his windshield with the phone, and then leave it on top of his car, but looking back that seems like a pretty lame idea," he smiled at himself. "But," he continued, "Whatever my plans were, Mr. Brice changed them." He stood up, and performed the rest for Pete in a kind of pantomime.

"See, I was halfway to the door when I felt him grab my shoulder," he said. "Well, one hand was on my shoulder, and the other one was reaching for the phone. He was yelling, 'Give me that you little bastard!'"

Pete laughed. "He said that?"

"And more. But I held the phone away and turned to face him." Manny turned quickly on his heel, like a gunslinger ready for the draw, right hand clutching an imaginary telephone. "He backed up a little when I turned around. I guess I must have looked pretty crazy by then." He smiled at the memory, but as Pete watched, the smile waned and was replaced by something very different. In fact, Manny's whole body seemed to shift states, and he slid from the gunslinger stance up to his normal height. The imaginary phone forgotten, both hands found their way into the pockets of his jeans. He went on, but in a subdued voice. "Then I yelled something like, 'Here, take it,' and I hurled it at him." He was looking away now, seemingly studying the bales of hay stacked up at the far end of the barn.

"Did you…?"

"Right in the face," Manny nodded, moving left and sitting down on a bench near the sheep pen. "Broke his nose and right cheekbone."

Pete felt his eyes widen. This was the same kid who tried to stop the cousins from having a little stupid argument two days before.

"I didn't want to hurt him," Manny said to the straw. "I don't like to hurt people." He sighed. "But there he was, both hands over his face, blood pouring off his fat chin and already spotting the carpet. And I had this flash, this moment where I knew exactly what to do next. So I stepped forward and kicked him between the legs as hard as I could."

There was silence as Pete let the described images sink in. Manny sat quietly for several minutes. The scratching of chickens in their pens, the wooly coughs of the sheep and the sounds of Joshua and Jacob drinking water filled the quiet barn.

"I don't know if I thought about doing it before I did." Manny finally said. "I like to think that I'm a reasonable guy, you know? That I think about what I do, before I do it? I mean, I knew I wanted him to feel bad like he'd embarrassed Andy. I want to tell you I kicked him because of what he'd done. But I don't think that's the truth. So I won't say it like it is. I think I kicked him because I was angry. And... he was there."

"And I hurt him. He went down hard. At my school the carpet is right on top of the concrete slab. His head bounced off the floor when he hit. I think he may have passed out. I kind of hope he did." And Pete could tell from the way Manny said it that this hope was not because he'd wanted to knock the guy out, but because then at least some of the teacher's pain would be only a blurry memory.

"What happened after that?" Pete asked.

Manny shrugged. "I left the classroom, walked across campus to the office and told them what I'd done." He laughed sadly and shook his head. "They didn't believe me at first. They tried to call his classroom." He chuckled sadly again. "But a minute later they got a radio call from security. One of the other kids in the class had gone for help after they were sure I was gone."

"Brice was in the hospital for a couple of days, and I was in juvenile hall for a bit, while the school district expelled me."

Pete knew he was staring at Manny, but couldn't stop himself. Finally, stunned with the truth of this strange new boy's past, he said quietly, "Holy shit." Manny snorted a tension breaking chuckle. Most of his smile returned.

"So that is my story, Pete O'Boyle. Well, most of it anyway. Do with it what you will." Pete didn't understand him and it must have shown. "What I mean is, if you want to tell people, it's okay. It doesn't matter."

Pete didn't understand why, but he felt hurt by this. "Do you want me to tell people? Is that why you told me?"

Manny looked him in the eyes for the first time since he'd begun telling the tale. "No. That's not why."

"Why then?"

"I'm not sure." Manny glanced toward the goats then back to Pete. "Maybe I just needed someone here to know, and you're the one guy who's been genuinely nice to me. I guess I'm saying I trust you."

Pete looked quickly away from Manny's trust, not wanting to see it. People at Riordan didn't speak of things like this, never admitted to things like trust. Trust was dangerous. Trust was not to be trusted. "We should get to dinner," he said too sharply, checking his watch too deliberately. It was still half an hour until mealtime, but he had to get out of the barn, away from what Manny had just said. "Better if we're early. That way we'll be allowed to travel campus the next time we want to."

Manny nodded and stood up.

As they left the barn, Pete asked Manny why he'd been sent to Riordan after Juvenile Hall. "I mean, they let you out, didn't they?" he asked. "Hadn't you paid enough for what you'd done?"

Manny seemed to consider it as they headed up toward the school and the dining hall beyond. Finally he said, "I don't think it works like that, paying for what we do. I think my dad had it right. He used to say, 'We don't get punished for our anger, we get punished *by* our anger.' I guess I'm just not done paying yet." This idea brought Pete up short. He considered it, looking at Manny, and nodded gravely.

They walked in silence, the slipping sounds of the creek falling away behind them. As the neared the dining hall, Manny said,

"There is more. I may tell you sometime, but if I don't tell you on my own, you can ask." The words were crisp and fragile in the chilling air.

"I'll always answer you anything you ask." From the way he said it, Pete knew he meant it. All the same, he decided to let Manny tell him more when he was ready.

Chapter 4

A week after Manny had given him the book, Pete tried to return *Jonathan Livingston Seagull*. Manny wouldn't take it back.

"It was a gift," he said, not raising a hand to take back the book Pete was holding out to him. They were in the room they shared. It was early afternoon and they were changing out of their school attire into play clothes. Pete had received permission to take Manny up to visit another one of the cottages. In the last week they'd seen four of the other houses. Today Pete was going to take him to St. Anthony's, the youngest cottage on campus.

"But, you can't give gifts," Pete said.

Manny's brow furrowed. "What do you mean? Why can't I give you a gift if I want to? It was my book; now it's yours."

"No, that's not what I mean." Pete realized that Manny just wasn't catching on to how the place worked. "I mean no one at Riordan is allowed to give gifts to another boy."

"You mean like a rule?"

"Yeah."

"Why not?"

"I don't know," Pete said, "I guess they don't want some kid to be intimidated into 'giving' someone his stuff."

"Okay," Manny said. "Yeah, I can see that. But still, I can't take it back."

"What do you mean?" Pete asked. Hadn't he just explained it?

"What I mean is I don't lend books. Once I give a book I can't take it back. It's yours. You can decide what to do with it."

"But what…?"

"Listen," Manny said, "I understand the rule, but it doesn't apply here. If someone asks, you can tell them you're borrowing it if you want. Just as long as you understand you're borrowing it until you decide to give it to someone else."

Manny went back to tying up his Chucks, leaving Pete confused yet again. He carefully tucked the book into his back pocket before they left the cottage.

It wasn't that he didn't want the book. He did. The ever-consistent routine of the Riordan Home didn't leave a lot of time for casual reading, even for a LEVEL 2. And at night, Pete liked to play video games and watch TV. So at first, he only remembered to read the book in the few minutes between brushing his teeth and his lights out time. But as the days went on, he found he was skipping other entertainments at night to first finish then voraciously re-read the book. He knew Manny had seen him reading, but the other boy had never said anything.

Pete had always liked reading in a neutral way, which was to say he didn't mind it if the subject was interesting. When he was younger his mom had bought him a few Judy Bloom books which he'd loved, but in the last few years he hadn't read anything outside of school; for a long time now, reading books had seemed silly, childish. Now, he was re-reading a story for the third time in a week.

The more he read the seagull book the harder he found it to put down. He liked the idea of this seagull doing things because he wanted to do them, not caring when the other seagulls kicked him out of the flock. When he finished the book it had been with a surprising excitement and want for more. He didn't understand why this little book about a bird had thrilled him so much, but there was no denying it had. At some point during the week he had begun carrying it with him. It was a very thin volume and he found he liked having it close.

St. Anthony's Cottage was located midway up the hill, just off the main campus road. Walking on the blacktop from St. Gabe's, Manny and Pete went across the bridge in the direction of the Admin building and chapel, but followed the curve of the asphalt left, away from those buildings and the school, and moved toward the steep uphill portion of the campus road.

On their way up to St. Anthony's, Pete asked Manny about the book, trying not to sound as affected as he was.

"That's one of my favorites," Manny said.

"I know it's about a bird, but it's about more than that, isn't it?" Pete asked hopefully. For some strange reason he wanted the book to be about him.

"Yeah, it's about more. It's an allegory. It is a story about a bird, but it's about how people treat each other, and how people who are different get treated by the community."

"People who are different?"

"Yeah, you know, people who don't do what everyone else does. That's what's so cool about Jonathan. He flies his own way and becomes more than just a gull."

"What did you call it?"

"An allegory. It means something like, 'a story about more than just the things in it.'"

They walked on, passing the infirmary on the right and St. John's and St. Michael's Cottages on the left. Boys were out shooting baskets in front of both cottages. Others were walking with staff members in and out of Admin. Pete said 'hi' and introduced Manny to a few kids he knew. The days were getting a little cooler. A few boys walked by wearing dark blue Riordan sweatshirts. Pete pointed out some of the places he hadn't shown Manny yet. They were back walking next to the creek, following its course in reverse up toward the two youngest cottages on campus.

They were just about to turn off the main cottage road when Manny pointed up the hill and across the road. "What's that cottage called again? I remember it's different, not a saint name, right?"

"Mt. Olivett," Pete said, glancing up. "Younger kids, but not as young as where we're going." He turned back toward the side road and St. Anthony's.

"What's up there?"

Pete stopped and followed Manny's outstretched hand, and saw he was pointing up, past Mt. Olivett, to the top of the hill beyond.

"Nothing. Just the hill."

"Can we go up there?" Manny asked, his eyes on the trees.

"Not without staff," Pete replied. "See the fence?" Low cyclone fencing stretched across the top of campus, just beyond and above where the Olivett lot ended.

Pete shifted his arm to point farther right to the end of the campus road. "And the gate?"

Manny followed Pete's arm right. The pavement ascending the hill stopped just even with the back of the Mt. Olivett blacktop. A metal gate hung at the end of the pavement. Beyond the gate a dirt extension of the road continued up the hill, winding eventually away and out of sight to the right.

"Is it part of the campus?" Manny asked.

"It belongs to Riordan, but like I said, we're not allowed up there alone."

"But you've been up there?"

"Sure," said Pete. "Lots of times."

"What's up there?" Manny stood staring up the hill.

"Nothing," Pete said. "I mean, there's a water storage tank up there, one of the big ones. And a couple of maintenance sheds. Otherwise it's just trees and grass until the far fence."

Manny looked back at Pete. "What's past the far fence?"

"The winery. Well, it's their property anyway, all the way to mountain."

Pete checked his watch. It was almost 3:30. They were supposed to be at St. Anthony's in a few minutes. "Let's go," he said to Manny.

As they walked up the last few yards to St. Anthony's, they saw a half dozen of the young residents spill out the front door and quickly arrange themselves on a grid painted on the cottage blacktop. Manny laughed at the way they scrambled. Pete was always reminded of the old Keystone Cops movies his grandmother had loved. He used to watch them with her all the time when she was alive. One of the scrambling kids yelled, "Hey Pete!" He waved back. As the boys finished sorting themselves out on the grid, a small woman emerged from the cottage and called, "Quiet transition, please." At which the six young boys dropped into immediate silence.

"Hi Pete. Who's your friend?" The woman walked over and stood between where Pete and Manny were and where her charges waited in silence.

"Hi Miss. This is Emanuel Montay."

She stepped over and stuck her hand out, casting her grey eyes up at Manny, "Nice to meet you Emanuel. I'm Ms. Kelly. Are you new to Riordan?"

After a second of silence, Manny found his voice. "Uh…yes, Ma'am." Pete was sure he saw Manny's hand tremble as he put it out to shake with Ms. Kelly. "I've only been here about a week." Manny was going through what most boys did when they met Ms. Kelly. Pete had gone through it himself not very long ago. She was a small woman, a shade under 5 feet and not more than a few inches taller than the very young boys of St. Anthony's, only as tall as some girls half her 22 years. And (and there was no way of getting around this or missing it among the rest of the staff) she was beautiful. She had once told Pete she was half Italian and half Mexican, "Chiquita Salami" she had called herself. All the boys at Riordan thought she was completely hot.

She had dark hair; usually worn like it was today, up in a think ponytail that dropped from the top of her head down to her slender but muscular shoulders, covered up by a Riordan Athletics t-shirt. Pete had seen her hair down only once, but it was a sight he was sure he would never forget, one that sometimes flashed to him in the middle of class at school and made it difficult to concentrate for a few minutes.

"Well," Ms. Kelly said, "Welcome to St. Anthony's Cottage." Pete glanced at Manny, who was trying very hard not to stare at the diminutive staff member.

"Miss," Pete said finally, "Mr. Abrams said I could come up today and bring Manny with me. Is it still okay?" Mr. Abrams was the supervisor for St. Anthony's.

"Yeah," she smiled, "it's fine. Mr. Abrams and Ms. Michaels are inside with the rest of the boys. They're all either working hours or in the game room." I was going to take these guys up the hill for a little while."

Manny seemed to stand up a little straighter. "Up past the cottages?" he asked.

"Correct. It's supposed to rain this weekend, so this might be our last chance to go up there for a while." Pete noticed that the St. Anthony kids behind her were still standing quietly, and he was a little amazed. *Then again*, he thought, *I'd sure as hell do* anything *she asked me to do.* "You want to come with us, or stay with the rest?" Pete didn't need to read Manny's mind on this question.

"We'll come with you," he said, "if you don't mind."

She smiled at him, "You know I never mind having you around, Pete." Her smile made him feel wobbly inside. It always did. "But," she said, "you made the arrangements to come up with Mr. Abrams, so you better check with him. We'll wait here while you do."

As they headed into the cottage, Ms. Kelly safely 10 feet behind them, Pete heard from next to him, very softly, "Wow. She's... wow."

"Dude, believe me, I know." Pete smiled as he opened the door for Manny and whispered to him, "Do you think I come up here because I like hanging out with little kids?"

What Pete liked about Ms. Kelly, other than her being pretty, was the fact that she was so unbelievably real. She was one of the few cottage staff he had never seen yell at a kid. She seemed to be able to get boys to listen and respond to her in ways other staffers couldn't. And it wasn't just because she was pretty. She appeared to care about the boys on campus. Pete knew from overheard conversations that Mr. Johnson had desperately been trying to get her over to St. Gabe's for a while now, but that she liked the little kids at St. Ant's.

Another thing separating her from most of the staff was the way she talked to the boys. She had no trouble being casual with them, talking to them about her life in high school and college. Yet she never tried to be their friend, she was smarter than that. Trying to be buddies was one of the reasons so many kids couldn't stand Mr. Weaver. Because, and it seemed to Pete the boys as a whole understood this better than some of the staff, being friends just wasn't possible. *Might as well ask the prisoners at San Quentin to be friends with the guards.*

But her authenticity didn't diminish her ability to be tough when needed. Pete had personally seen her take a kid down when she had to. It had been over the recent summer, and this kid named Wesley had completely lost his mind because his parents hadn't shown up to take him on home visit (not an uncommon occurrence at the Riordan Home). Wes had been storming around the cottage for five minutes when Ms. Kelly finally told him he needed to either calm down or be escorted to Admin. Wes had gotten right up in her face and stood over her and screamed that she was a bitch and should shut her freaking mouth. And she'd calmly repeated her directive to leave the cottage. She'd simply stood there, facing him while another staff member had called one of the Coordinators to come escort Wes out of the building. She'd stood there and listened to him rage at her, at the world. She'd taken it and done nothing. Until he touched her.

Wes had been about 5'5" and 150 pounds, far larger and heavier than Ms. Kelly's 4'11" and 125. He had finally gone over the edge and given her a shove to the shoulder. Pete had never seen an adult move as fast as Ms. Kelly had. The instant Wesley's right hand made contact with her right shoulder, her hand had snaked up between them, caught his wrist and twisted his body around. Before Wes could even let out a sound she had picked him up on her hip and spun him face-first into the corner behind her, and in the process had readjusted her hands in such a way that his arms were now crossed in front of him and she was gripping his wrists at waist level from behind, one knee up in the small of his back pinning him into the painted plaster corner of the cottage game room.

At first Wesley had yelled and struggled to free himself of the restraint. Ms. Kelly just held him easily, and she talked to him in a soothing voice that matched her flowing beauty. Within 10 minutes Wes had been calm enough for her to release him. He'd turned around and apologized for touching her, then let himself be led to a red chair to wait for the Coordinator to escort him to Admin. After the incident, Wes never raised his voice to her again, and had even gotten five hours for punching another boy in the mouth for making lewd comments about her. That was the type of loyalty she inspired.

As they walked up the Campus Road, the younger St. Ant's boys all clamored around Manny and Pete, anxious to hear about life in the big cottages. Between yelped questions from the little kids, Ms. Kelly asked Manny about where he was from, how old he was, his hobbies. Pete tried to ignore it, but he was forced to admit to himself that he was a little bit jealous. He liked when Ms. Kelly talked to him, and watching her focus on Manny made him feel a little queasy. He tried to distract himself by looking up at the top of the hill and the dull blue sky beyond.

The day was cool but dry and the walking was easy, but Pete knew that when the rains started later in the week, the hill would become treacherous. When the wet came, water flowing down the north and east slopes from the hill's height toward Gihon Creek was hijacked by the muddy ruts in the service lane and emptied onto the Campus Road. Water sheeted down the blacktop all winter long. During wet months boys didn't walk on the road, but instead on wooden steps set into the hill. The steps ran between cottage blacktops up from the base of the rise all the way to Mt. Olivett.

After a few minutes of walking they reached the end of the paved roadway. Ms. Kelly had them stop. "Now remember," she said, and all of the boys were immediately attentive. "We're going to the water tower. We'll climb up the tower and be there for 15 minutes. Then we'll come down the tower and return to the cottage." Pete had heard her break down stuff like this for the Ants before. She'd told him it was a necessity with the little ones. "Are there any questions?" There were none. She led them through a gap in the fence to the right of the large metal sheep gate and up onto the dirt of the service road.

The water tower, not visible from anywhere on the campus proper, was a winding 10 minute walk up the service lane. Pete and his cottage usually made the walk faster, but the Ants had short legs. But then, so did Ms. Kelly. The road actually went more or less west up the side of the hill, curving along the terrain as it did. Eventually, a sharp climbing switchback to the left sent the walkers back southeast and up toward the Hill's summit. Another 75 yards and the ruts of the road let out onto a relatively flat piece of land. A hundred yards ahead the flat rose up gently to disappear under the canopy formed by giant Garry Oaks. Beyond the oaks, the hill dropped again to Mt. Olivett Cottage and the rest of the campus beyond.

"So, wait a minute," said Manny, looking around with a single raised eyebrow, "the campus is over there? Right?" He pointed uncertainly toward the trees Pete was staring at.

"Right."

"Okay, I just get kind of turned around sometimes," he said with a touch of embarrassment.

"Me too," Ms. Kelly said from behind them. Turning her attention to the youngsters, called out, "Slow down, boys."

The Ants, who'd already been running across the dusty hill toward the water tower, suddenly slowed their pace to a quick walk. Ms. Kelly continued to chat with Manny. He'd mentioned reading as a hobby and they were talking about the book he'd been reading last week. She'd read it in high school she said. Pete thought about jumping in and saying something about the seagull book, but decided against it. *But next week*, he thought, *maybe I won't bring Manny with me when I come up to visit Ms. Kelly.* But as soon as he thought it he knew it wasn't true. He knew he was being childish, and that he was only thinking this way because she wasn't focused on him. *Stupid.*

The water tower wasn't a tower as such. The massive green structure sat on the ground and didn't jut up into the sky. It was a large water tank that Pete knew housed not just water, but also Riordan's large well pump. *The world's biggest toilet mint* was how Pete thought of it. But it was big. A staircase spiraled up the side of the tank, three stories from the ground to roof. There was a railing around the edge of the gently domed roof, making it safe for the boys to walk on. In August Mr. Nielsen had brought his telescope from home and set it up on the top of the tank. There was a massive meteor shower he wanted some of his science students to see. He'd even convinced the administration to let a dozen boys stay up really late because the best viewing wasn't going to be until after midnight.

Some of the Ants were already climbing the tower. Ms. Kelly was getting ready to follow them. Pete knew the tank offered a great view of Sonoma Mountain to the west. Unfortunately, because it was situated back from and below the top of the hill and the 75 foot oak trees that lived there, the tower was no good for the view Pete liked the best.

"Ms. Kelly," he asked, "can we go walk through the trees for a few minutes?"

Ms. Kelly looked at the trees, then back to Pete. "Okay for you," she said, "but Emanuel will have to stay with me." Manny looked at her in question. "Sorry." she said. "But you're a new boy, and I can't let you wander off up her by yourself. I hope you understand."

Manny nodded, but Pete could tell he was a little disappointed. He'd seemed jazzed to check out the trees. "No big deal," Manny said after a second. "I wanted to see the view from up there anyway." He stepped past Ms. Kelly and headed up the tower's spiraling steps. She watched him head up for a moment, and then turned to Pete. "Nice guy," she said. And then she smiled at him. "No wonder you two get along." And she was gone up the steps. Pete turned toward the oaks. About halfway there, he heard Ms. Kelly call to him: "Back in 15 minutes, Pete." He turned and waved at her then checked his watch as he headed toward the trees.

On a field trip last year, Mr. Nielsen had brought Pete's class up to the top of the hill for an afternoon. They'd collected various specimens of insects and plants on a kind of biological scavenger hunt. He remembered that the oak trees on this part of the property were not the Live Oaks which grew in mass around the pastures and the 4-H Barn. Mr. Nielsen had identified them as Oregon Whites or Garry Oaks. He said they were a little different than most oak trees because, unlike their cousins, Garrys that grew in close proximity to each other formed a high canopy which gave the area underneath the feeling of cool pillared cave with a very high ceiling. The result was that, even though the sky was all but invisible from the ground, it was relatively easy to see through the wide stand of trees.

Pete was headed to the far edge of the oak grove, the one right above the campus. As he walked he pulled the novel out from his back pocket and thumbed the pages. He loved the view from the edge of the oak grove. There was a high haze in the sky, but the valley floor was clear and bright. On a day like this he should be able to see almost all the way to the Bay. During the summer, it was possible to see light ripple on the waters of the Petaluma River Estuary feeding into the top of San Francisco Bay. It wasn't that he couldn't see the river from the water tower, but he couldn't see Riordan from up there. And, more and more, Pete found, he liked looking down on the Riordan Home. He liked being able to see boys moving around and working their hours and playing basketball.

When he first came to Riordan, he was determined to spend as little time on the premises as possible. He'd even considered making an attempt at getting kicked out. He couldn't understand the boys who acted as if being at Riordan was fine with them, like they didn't care about being abandoned by their families. He saw them as soulless, resigned to the misery of the place. Their attitudes and willingness to listen to staff directives baffled him.

No longer. He had come to be one of those boys he hadn't understood. It had happened recently, sometime within the past half year. The truth was simple: as little as he liked some of what Riordan was, he understood that it was his home now. And, unlike some of his peers, he was at peace with his understanding.

He was thinking about these things as he walked through the oaks and his thinking wandered to the first and only fight he'd been in at Riordan. He laughed at himself, and at the memory of being locked in what at the time had felt like mortal combat with Chris Caspar at the end of his second week. *All because he tripped over my foot in the game room.*

He was pulled out of his memory by a sound off to his right. He stopped and looked in the direction of the noise, which sounded like it had come from a big animal. He couldn't see anything; the hilltop sloped down toward the neighboring vineyard in that direction. Pete changed course and began walking slowly south, trying to find the source of the sound.

He heard it again; a sharp snort. *From what, a horse?* He kept going down the side of the hill, moving now from tree to tree, wondering how a horse had gotten up onto this part of the property. Had Montecristo gotten out of his paddock? It wouldn't be the first time some boy had left the gate open and allowed the aged palomino to wander the campus. Sunday mass had been interrupted once last spring by Gandalf, the rec department dog, barking at the big blond horse on the front lawn of the chapel. But there was no way Montecristo could have wandered all the way up past the cottages without being corralled by someone

He heard the snort again as he came around another wide trunk, and finally caught a glimpse of the animal responsible. This was definitely *not* Montecristo. This horse was huge and black, heavier looking than the Riordan stallion. It was down in the small gully where the fence wound up from the Sonoma Highway to the back of the property past the water tower. It was standing just over the fence, beneath a giant oak. It was not tethered, but was wearing a saddle of dark red. Hanging from the saddle was a tan piece of leather, a long tapered tube, rigid and empty. From movies he'd seen, Pete had a pretty good idea what was meant to fill that tube: a rifle.

Pete could see no sign of a rider. He came around the tree a little more, trying for a better view. He was looking in the shade around the horse, wondering if maybe the rider had gone down injured. From behind him he heard the voice.

"Freeze."

He froze, staring down at the empty rifle holster.

"Turn around, slowly," the voice said.

Pete turned around slowly, putting his hands up as he did.

Standing on the hill above him, next to the last tree he'd used for cover, was a girl. She was older than him, he was certain, but not by much: maybe two or three years. Pete goggled at her. Not because she was particularly beautiful; she wasn't. But she was a girl. And she was holding a baseball bat. She was a girl on Riordan property, and she had him covered with a Louisville Slugger.

"What are you doing?" she asked.

"Nothing," Pete stammered, "just walking."

She eyed him suspiciously. "You running away from the place?"

"No, I'm up here with staff. I'm supposed to be here." Pete realized something. "But you're not. Who are you?"

"You were sneaking up on me!" He saw her eyes flick to the book he held aloft in his left hand.

Pete shook his head, "No. I heard your horse." He slowly lowered his hands, hoping it made him look less guilty. "I was just trying to see what was making noise. It's usually quiet up here."

Her stance softened a bit. She let the head of the bat drop a few inches. She walked sideways down the hill, keeping her shoulders squared to him and maintaining a buffer zone of several feet.

When she was level with him on the hill, she squinted at him and asked, "What's your name?"

Still surprised, he answered without thinking, "Pete O'Boyle."

The girl nodded. She was taller than him. At first he thought her height had been an illusion because she'd been up hill from him, but he could see now that she probably had him by half a foot. She was wearing an un-tucked red plaid flannel over a white t-shirt. Her blue jeans were well worn; the left knee had a small hole in it. The thread sprung hems of the jeans sat atop a pair of dusty silver buckled boots, the rough kind meant for work and riding and not much else.

She lowered the bat finally, letting the head of it come to rest on the toe of her right boot. "What are you doing up here alone? I thought you guys had to be around the teachers, or whatever all the time."

"I am. She's just over at the tower." Pete motioned back towards the direction he'd come.

"So why are you over here?"

"I asked to go for a walk. I'm a LEVEL 2, so she trusts me."

Calmer, with the bat no longer an immediate threat, Pete looked at her. She wasn't beautiful, but she definitely wasn't unattractive either. Her dark hair was cut well above her shoulders, held back from her fair, pale face by a simple silver clip. Light rings ran under her green eyes, making her look tired. He could see no signs of make-up. Small silver hoop earrings were her only visible jewelry.

The flannel was unbuttoned and the t-shirt was snug over her breasts, and ended an inch above the faded denim of her pants. As much as he didn't want to notice, Pete saw smooth pale skin between the shirt's hem and the waistband of the jeans. Residents of the Riordan Home for Boys didn't have much chance to see teenage girls up close, and Pete had to make a conscious effort to look at her face. Which was okay, because she was almost smiling now.

"I'm sorry," she said, "about the bat. I didn't mean to scare you."

"It's okay," Pete said and looked down the hill toward the horse, still grazing under the oaks. The he looked back to the girl. "Who are you?"

"I'm Tabitha," she said. She did not hold out her hand to offer a shake. *But at least the bat's still down.* He looked back at the fence and said, "I'm pretty sure you're not supposed to be here."

She looked at him puzzled for a moment, and then looked down at the horse herself, and the fence she had crossed to get to where she was now standing.

"Oh, yeah," she said. "I'm not." And she began walking down the slope. Pete, still startled from the whole encounter and not knowing what else to do, followed her. She looked back at him with a slightly furrowed brow, but Pete noticed the baseball bat still swinging slowly near the ground.

"How did you get here?" he asked as they neared the fence.

She stopped and looked back at him, "I rode. See the horse?"

"No," Pete said. "No, I know you rode, but how did you end up at this fence?

"Oh," she nodded and pointed beyond the fence, "that's my backyard over there." Pete didn't understand, and it must have shown in his face. She stepped next to him and grabbed his shoulder, turning him slightly to the right. She squatted down so her head was level with his, her shoulder against his and sighted along her arm, which she pointed up and out of the small gully they were in. "See there," she said, pointing to the next tree covered hill. Pete looked, trying to ignore the smell of her. There was a talcum scent coming off of her, mixed with sweat. The sweet talcum smell reminded him of the soap his mom had used.

"Do you see?"

"What am I looking for?" he asked, trying to quietly breathe in as much of her smell as he could.

"The smoke," she said. It was a hazy day, one that brings rain to mind if not to ground. Pete scanned the trees and saw nothing.

"I don't see…" and then he did. Across the gully near the top of the hill beyond, he saw faint white smoke against the growing grey of the sky. Following it earthward with his eyes, he could just make out a few dark straight lines through the branches: part of the hidden house.

"You live there?" he finally asked. Now that he knew where to look, he could make out other shapes through the trees, including the cut of a road which traveled down the side of the hill for a few hundred yards then disappear completely. When she didn't respond, he glanced around at her.

She was looking at him intently. "What?" he asked.

"How long have you been at Riordan?"

"A year and a half."

"Where were you before here?"

"Home. The Bay Area. A place called Redwood City."

She nodded, "My cousin lives down that way. In Woodside."

"Yeah," Pete said. "It's right across the freeway."

Her eyes narrowed and she looked him up and down. Finally she said, "You don't look dangerous."

"I don't think I am."

"How old are you?"

"Thirteen." He looked back at her. "How old are you?"

"Fifteen," she said quickly. Then she smiled. "Well, I will be in a couple of weeks anyway." Her smiled stayed.

Her smile was big and attractive. She had beautiful straight, white teeth. Pete felt suddenly self conscious, standing there on the hill, talking to a girl, with the sweet autumn sky beginning to darken above.

After a moment more of silence, she started again toward the fence and the horse beyond. Pete walked slowly after her, unsure what to say next, but knowing he wanted to say something, anything to keep the conversation from ending. The low fence here was wood, two cross-boards running between posts six feet apart. Tabitha threw one leg over then the other, not looking back at him.

He wanted to make her stay, just for a moment longer. He desperately tried to think of something to say. "What... what's your horse's name?"

"Christabel," she said, sliding the baseball bat into the holster.

"Pretty name," Pete said, knowing exactly how lame it sounded.

She nodded. "Yeah it is, but it's from a creepy poem my dad read in college or something. He named her."

Pete remembered something. "Your house," he said. "Isn't it on the winery's property?"

She turned around and looked at him, her brow furrowed slightly. "Yeah?"

"You live on the winery?"

"Of course we do. It's my family's winery." She turned back to the horse and took something out of a pouch on the saddle. It was an apple. She produced a small folding knife from one of her pockets and quickly quartered the apple then fed the pieces one at a time to Christabel. The horse seemed to positively enjoy this.

"She likes apples, doesn't she?"

"They're her favorite," she said, turning back to face him as Christabel went to work on the last cut of the fruit. "Do you want to pet her?" she asked.

Pete felt the smile drain away from his face. What the fence between them meant was brought home to him. He shook his head, "I can't."

"Why not?"

He put his hand on the fence and said, "If I cross the property line, I get 25 / 60." She didn't understand, he knew, but explaining it was only going to make him feel worse.

"What's 25 / 60?"

He looked down the fence line, in the direction of Sonoma Highway. The geography of the hill made it so the campus proper wasn't visible from here. He looked back up in the direction of the water tower. It too was out of sight. *I could get away with it.*

"What's 25 / 60?" she asked again.

He sighed. He probably could get away with it, but...

But what? his mind asked. *A pretty girl has just asked you to come over the fence and pet her horse!*

No! he told himself, and took a deep breath, looked at her and plunged into it. "25 / 60 is 25 hours of cottage time and 60 days of campus restriction. It's the biggest consequence we can get here."

She nodded. Then she looked down and up the fence line as he had done a few moments ago. "You could get away with it. You know that, don't you?" She was looking at him closely as she said this. He had the feeling she was studying him, like a scientist examining an animal in a cage or some experiment under glass. *Well that's what I am.*

"I'm the only one who would know," she went on, "and I wouldn't report you or anything." He nodded, and looked away, up toward the house on the hill, the house she would ride back to any moment.

"Huh," she said, "you could get away with it, you *know* you could get away with it, but you won't do it. Will you?" He dropped his gaze. She was going to call him lame, or retarded, or a dumb kid or something similar.

Instead she said, "Hey!" He looked up startled. She had a smile on her face, but different than the one from before. This one was not just appealing, but in some way Pete couldn't figure out, it was also incredibly kind.

"What happened there? Why'd you get all quiet?"

Pete could only shrug.

"I think you're smart," she said. "I mean, it's just a horse. And I wouldn't be the only one who knew. You'd know you did it." He nodded, surprised she hadn't just laughed at him and ridden off.

"Thanks," he said, not sure if she'd understand.

She did. She walked to the fence and said, "We should do this right." She stuck her hand out to him, smiled again and said, "Hello Pete O'Boyle. I'm Tabitha Pembrook."

For a moment, he wasn't sure what to do, and stood there dumbly. Tabitha raised her eyebrows and said, "You gonna leave me hanging here, or what?"

Pete recovered with a small shiver, and reached out his hand. Hers was strong and rougher than he expected. But it was also warm. And he stood there thinking, *My hand is 25 / 60, but it might just be worth it.*

"Thanks," he said again, unsure this time why he said it, but feeling like it needed saying. She laughed at him; a small sound of amusement that hurt his feelings not at all.

"You're welcome." She said as their hands parted. Pete dropped his hand to his side. He started to slide it into his pocket, but stopped. He could still feel where and how her hand had pressed against his. He didn't want to lose that yet. He wasn't sure what else to say. She was obviously going to leave, and he wasn't sure how to even say goodbye.

"Good book," she said, and for a moment, Pete had no idea what she meant. His face must have shown it. She pointed and said, "*Jonathan's* a good read."

He looked down dumbly at the slender book then back up at her. "You know this book?" He was incredulous.

She laughed again, "Sure."

He nodded. It was all he could think to do.

Tabitha looked over her shoulder, at the house on the hill then back to him. Her smile had faded. "I've gotta go," she said and walked back to where Christabel had resumed snacking on the grass. She grabbed the saddle horn, stuck her right foot into the stirrup and swung herself up expertly. Once on the horse, she flicked the reins and clucked. Christabel swung her head around and walked over to the fence. Pete was startled and backed up. "It's okay," Tabitha said, "give her a pat." Pete stepped forward and reached across the fence with his left hand, patting the side of the horse's neck, feeling the heavy muscles rippling under the skin.

"Nice to meet you, Pete."

"Yeah," it was all he could think to say. "I mean," he shook his head, "I mean it was nice to meet you too, Tabitha."

"Bye," she said, and tugged the reins, gently turning Christabel away from the fence and back toward the house.

Pete watched her go, watched Christabel bounce along through the high brown grass of the hillside.

He looked at his watch almost absently, and then quickly looked at it again.

DAMN. He was late. Ms. Kelly was going to be angry. He turned and began sprinting back up through the grass and foxtails, but when he got to the edge of the wooded hilltop he stopped and turned around, scanning the opposite hill for one last look at Tabitha. It took him a moment to find her in the dimming November light because she had stopped moving. She had brought Christabel up to the trees lining the driveway to the house, and had turned the horse in profile against the oaks. As he stared, she waved at him across the pocket canyon and he felt his stomach lurch. He waved back. Then he saw her twitch her hands, and Christabel turned away and carried her into the shadows between the trees and out of sight. He breathed deep, then, remembering himself, spun and ran.

Ms. Kelly hadn't been mad, but she had made it clear to him that he needed to be back on time or she wouldn't let him come up with her any more. He'd only been a few minutes late though, and by the time he and Manny had left St. Anthony's and headed back to their cottage she'd been her old self with him, giving him and Manny both high fives. Manny hadn't said a thing, and Pete was wondering if his roommate had noticed him sitting at dinner with his elbow on the table and his right hand lingering near his nose. He imagined he could still smell the sweet talcum from where she had touched his hand.

Later though, when they were sitting in the St. Gabe's game room alone after dinner, Manny eyed him over a game of chess and finally said, "Okay, you've hardly said anything at all since we left the hill. What happened up there anyway?"

Pete hadn't decided what, if anything to tell Manny about his encounter. They weren't friends. There were no friends at Riordan. But, Pete had to admit, there were times when he was with Manny, and they were on a walk, or just talking, when he forgot, just for a few minutes, where they were. And in those moments he believed this boy could be trusted in a way others in this place couldn't be, that he could be an actual friend.

So he told him. Every detail, from her sneaking up on him to the smell of her, to the feel of the muscles in Christabel's neck, to the sound of the apple crunching between the horse's teeth, to her noticing the book, to the wave in the gathering dark. Manny listened all the way through the telling of it, simply smiling, not interrupting once.

After Pete was done, and was regaining his breath from the telling of it, Manny asked, "What do you think she had the bat for?"

This stopped Pete, because he hadn't even considered it. "I don't know. Snakes, I guess."

"Huh," Manny nodded, taking one of Pete's bishops with a knight. "Yeah, that makes sense."

Later, after lights out, Pete fell into a solid slumber. He dreamed the hilltop was an island, and Tabitha rode around it on a giant seagull named Christabel. And she floated and danced through the air, waving at him and blowing him kisses. And the sea around the island was deep and warm and safe. Instead of the Garry Oaks, apple trees and evergreens covered the island. The sandy beaches glittered in the soft sun and he could smell talcum.

Chapter 5

The Thanksgiving break from school, and the accompanying home visit was only four days away when Pete learned he'd be spending the holiday at Riordan.

Mr. Turnbull came down to St. Gabe's after school on the Tuesday before the week-long break began. The boys in the cottage were all talking about their plans to go home and see family and friends. The staff was upbeat as well. Pete had noticed the way staff always perked up a little before home visits. He guessed he understood. After all, they had families they wanted to see, too. But it always kind of made him wonder why they had this job if the only thing they ever got excited about was time without the boys.

He and Manny were in the game room, playing bumper pool on the cottage's small octagonal table. Manny had just won his third game in a row when Pete spotted Mr. Turnbull through the windowed walls of the staff office at the center of the cottage.

"Hey," Pete said, and pointed up at Mr. Turnbull. Manny looked up.

"Wonder who he's here for," Manny said. Mr. Turnbull was the Caseworker they had both been assigned to when they'd come to Riordan and Pete was grateful for his presence at the Home. He'd made things easy on Pete in those first weeks, having taken him off campus for lunch a couple of times, checking in to see if there was anything he needed, and getting messages to Aunt Marjorie. But the best thing he'd done was to take Pete out to play catch. Before coming to Riordan in his late 20's, the tall caseworker had been a professional baseball player, which was enough in itself to make Pete think he was the coolest adult he'd ever met.

Pete watched as Mr. Turnbull spoke with Mr. Johnson, who was sitting in the office filling out an incident report about some gang related attire he'd taken off of JP at lunch. Mr. Turnbull almost completely blocked the doorway of the office, his shoulders left no room for a boy to squeeze around and his clean shaven head was just a few inches from the top of the door frame. Pete had once asked him how tall he was, and in his east Texas drawl Mr. Turnbull had said only, "'bout tall enough." But Pete had found out another way. In his office Mr. Turnbull had one of his own baseball cards. The front of the card showed a 22 year old Mr. Turnbull in his home white Braves uniform, standing on the pitcher's mound at Atlanta Fulton County Stadium, staring into the catcher for a sign.

On the back of the card his vital statistics were listed under his full name: Charlie Turnbull. It also noted his nickname: Chuck "The Truck." The card said he was from Houston, Texas, and had been drafted in 1983 in the 4th round out of USC, where he had been a part of the same team as a skinny kid from Pomona named Mark McGwire and a 6'10" left hander named Randy Johnson. On the back it gave his height as 6' 4", and his weight as 225. Pete thought the card might have been wrong on the small side.

After a few minutes of conversation, Mr. Turnbull looked up and let his eyes scan the cottage through the 360 degree windows of the staff office. Eventually his gaze came to rest on Manny and Pete. He tapped the glass and waved for Pete to come to the office.

"Looks like it's you," Manny said, setting up the bumper pool table again.

When he got around the office to where Mr. Turnbull stood, the Caseworker said in his soft Texas accent, "Hey Pete, could you come up to Admin with me for a few minutes?"

"Sure," said Pete, wondering if somehow he was in trouble. It had been a little over a week since he'd had his encounter with Tabitha Pembrook up on the hill, and in the days following he had expected to get called in by the Coordinators at any moment and given a consequence of some sort. But after a few days had slipped by, he assumed he probably wasn't going to get into trouble over it. Maybe this was trouble finally come home.

After they exited the cottage, Mr. Turnbull took an envelope out of his hip pocket and handed it to Pete. "Open it," he said. Pete did, and inside found a piece of heavy cardboard folded around something. He carefully unfolded the cardboard and came face to face with what many people considered the scariest man in baseball.

"Whoa! No way!" The card was in a protective plastic sheath and taped to the cardboard. "This is awesome!"

"Thought you'd like it," Mr. Turnbull said. "Old Randy had a pretty decent season this year."

Pete looked at the card. "Decent" didn't cover it. Randy Johnson had just come off the best season of his career, having won 19 games and struck out over 300 batters for the Seattle Mariners. The card was from last year and showed the 6'10" pitcher on the mound at the Kingdome, glove raised up to his chin, his lank hair resting on the shoulders of his uniform. In his excitement, it took Pete a moment to notice the signature scrawled across the figure's legs.

"It's autographed!"

"Yep. We'll put it with the rest of your collection in my office."
It was one of the things Mr. Turnbull had done to make Pete's
transition to Riordan easier. Pete had been very worried about his
small card collection, but unwilling to leave it behind at his aunt's.

"Thanks so much, Mr. Turnbull."

"Not a problem," the caseworker said as they walked along to
Admin. "I've been meaning to have Randy send me one for my son
for a while now anyway. I just asked him to send two instead."

It still tripped Pete out that Mr. Turnbull referred to Johnson,
McGwire and Glavine as Randy, Mark and Tommy. He sometimes
wondered if his caseworker missed playing pro ball. *He had to miss
it, didn't he?* But more than once, Mr. Turnbull had told Pete that
shredding his rotator cuff was one of the best things to happen to
him. After baseball, he'd said, he'd found his wife and his real
calling.

Pete carefully re-folded the cardboard and tucked the prize back
into the envelope and handed it back to Mr. Turnbull. They walked
the rest of the way to Admin in quiet, under the threatening sky that
had held off rain thus far but promised a deluge in the coming hours.

After they mounted the steps of the main building, Mr. Turnbull
turned and sat on one of the benches lining the front of the big
covered porch. Pete automatically joined him.

"Pete," the big man drawled, looking down at him, "your aunt
called today."

Oh shit, Pete thought, knowing this could mean only one thing.

"She said she has to work most of next week. Apparently one of
the other nurses took ill, and there's been a scramble to cover shifts."

"So, she's not coming to get me?" Pete knew Mr. Turnbull could
hear the hurt in his voice, but didn't much care. He'd been looking
forward to being away from Riordan for a week.

"I'm afraid not."

"What about Christmas?" Pete asked. "Did she say anything about the Christmas home visit?" He looked at Mr. Turnbull, and knew she had. She had said that she wasn't coming for him then either.

After a moment, Mr. Turnbull said, "She did mention she was going to be on a trip during some of December, but she didn't have the specific dates. Said she'd call me back with them in a few days." Pete could tell from his voice that Mr. Turnbull expected Aunt Marjorie to call back about as much as he expected it.

Pete suddenly felt like he was on the island in his dream, but this time there was no Tabitha and no gull. There weren't even any trees, and the waves of a dark, harsh ocean bit cruelly at the sharpened sand.

"It's not fair," he said quietly

"No," Mr. Turnbull said. "It's not."

"I mean, she sent me here so I could learn to be better, so I could get stuff figured out, and I have, I mean, I've been doing good in the cottage." Pete felt himself sinking into the thoughts he didn't usually let himself think, feeling the things he tried not to feel. "She knows, doesn't she? You've told her how good I've been doing, right?"

"Yes Pete, 'course I have." Mr. Turnbull was speaking in his usual calm tones, his soft southern cadence doing its part to alleviate Pete's growing stress.

It's not fair, Pete's mind repeated. His hands were on his knees, clenching and unclenching the worn denim there. He stared down at the ground between his feet, at the rough aggregate surface of the concrete, river rocks and glass suspended in cement. He stared until the stones in the surface blurred, and grey of the concrete began to darken with his tears.

Mr. Turnbull said nothing. He just sat next to Pete, his elbows on his knees, leaning forward and quietly watching the trees.

Eventually, Pete wiped his eyes with the heels of his hands, and sniffed up the snot that had come loose with the tears. He looked at Mr. Turnbull who was looking away toward where Gihon Creek ran past the small Admin parking lot and down toward the fields.

Pete sniffed again, "I'm sorry," he said quietly.

Mr. Turnbull looked back to him, surprised. "What's that?"

Pete felt the warmth of embarrassment coming on like it always did when he made a fool of himself. "I said I'm sorry."

Mr. Turnbull furrowed his brow and asked, "What on earth for?"

"For crying, it's stupid."

Mr. Turnbull breathed out loudly, and then nodded as if he'd made a decision about something. "Pete," he said, "you have every right to be angry with your aunt."

Hurriedly, Pete began, "But I'm not..." But Mr. Turnbull stopped him with a huge raised hand.

"Just hol' on a sec." The caseworker paused for a moment, seeming to choose how to say what he wanted to say. "Now, I don't know 'bout Thanksgiving. It does seem possible this was a last minute complication she couldn't have foreseen. However, I do have a great difficulty with her choice to not be around during the Christmas break."

He looked at Pete. "I know we've talked 'bout your anger Pete, about how you don't like to feel it. 'Bout how feeling angry makes you feel bad about yourself. And I can appreciate your not wanting to feel anger. I understand why you avoid it."

Pete looked away, toward the dining hall that lay on the far side of the Admin building. He didn't want to hear Mr. Turnbull anymore. He had no desire to think about the things Mr. Turnbull wanted to talk to him about.

"See, the thing is, Pete," Mr. Turnbull drawled on, "sometimes anger is an absolutely appropriate response. When we've been hurt, or scared, getting angry is natural. Heck, it can even be useful sometimes."

Pete wondered what was for dinner tonight. They'd had his favorite sausage for breakfast, and he was hoping for pasta this evening. He tried to not listen to Mr. Turnbull. He'd heard it before, from too many adults. From the school counselor, from the therapist at The Hillcrest Juvenile Detention Facility. Even Aunt Marjorie had tried to tell him the same stuff. Not listening made it simple.

"...know ya can hear me, Pete. I know yer listening. And I know that somewhere inside, in some corner you don't like to admit you have, you are right aggravated with your aunt. I'm tryin' to help you understand: it's okay to feel like that. Keeping it all bottled up does no good for you. And, even though I never had the privilege to meet the lady, I don't think it's what *she'd* want for you."

Stunned, Pete whipped his head around and looked at Mr. Turnbull. *He couldn't mean that. Couldn't be talking about her.* Mr. Turnbull stared at him, not unkindly, and said, "I think your mom would want you to be happy. At least, happy as you can be in a place like this, with what you been though."

Pete felt his face tighten, felt his cheeks get hot. His voice though was icy, "You didn't know her. You can't speak for her."

"Don't mean to," the staffer said calmly, "Just speculatin'. That's all."

"I just..." he stopped, until he was sure he could go on without getting angry. "I was looking forward to it. Even to spending some time with Aunt Marjorie." He breathed deeply, calming himself down. Mr. Turnbull was nice to him, but didn't know everything.

The caseworker nodded, reached into his deep hip pocket and produced a pouch of gum which he silently offered Pete. It was grape flavored Big League Chew, the kind he always had. He'd told Pete a lot of his teammates over the years had used tobacco, but that he thought tobacco was dumb. He'd been chewing Big League

Chew since high school, and it was what he chewed all the way through college ball, the minors, and for his three and a half years in the major leagues.

After Pete had helped himself to a wad of gum, Mr. Turnbull did the same. They sat there in silence for a few minutes, chewing their gum, both working it into something they could talk around. Pete wondered if Manny would be around for Thanksgiving.

Finally, Mr. Turnbull stood up and said, "Wait here a sec, Pete. There's something I forgot on my desk." He walked through the front door of the Admin building and disappeared down the hall. Pete sat chewing his gum on the bench. From the patio cover above came the tapping of the first raindrops of the afternoon. By the time Mr. Turnbull returned three minutes later the clouds had decided to open up.

Mr. Turnbull handed Pete another envelope, this one was lavender in color and addressed to him. There was a cancelled stamp on it and no return address. Not surprisingly, the letter had already been opened: standard procedure for mail at Riordan. Pete noticed the postmark; it said "Redwood City." *Home?*

"Sorry about readin' it," Mr. Turnbull said, "but it's the rule when we don't know who a letter's from." Pete noticed the caseworker watching him carefully. Slightly confused, he turned his attention back to the envelope. As soon as he opened it, his confusion deepened. Before he even reached into the envelope he smelled the sweet talcum scent from within. He tried not to react too much, remembering how Mr. Turnbull was watching him, but he did hesitate for a moment before withdrawing the single folded page.

The letter was the same lavender as the envelope and when he unfolded it the scent was intoxicatingly strong. His head swam back to the hilltop, back to the feeling of her hand in his as he tried desperately to focus his eyes on the words scripted on the page.

November 8, 1993

Dear Pete,

I hope you're doing well. We miss you here. Even though it's been a year and a half since you were in school with us, we still talk about you all of the time.

Everybody misses you, especially Tabitha. She told me about the day you two spent together in the hills last summer and that she wishes she'd had the nerve to kiss you goodbye.

She tries to tell Christabel to mind her own business, but her crush on you has only gotten bigger since you left last time.

We hope we'll see you again soon, but we know it's unlikely. Take care of yourself, Pete.

Come back to us soon.

Yours truly,
    Marilyn

As he finished reading, he felt the caseworker's eyes on him. He examined the letter again, because he didn't yet want to look up into Mr. Turnbull's face. When he turned the page over he noticed a return address, printed on the bottom of the back side of the page.

Marilyn Roberts   2850 Kings Mountain Road   Woodside, CA   94062

"I asked your aunt," Mr. Turnbull said, "She said she didn't remember any of these names, but she also said she didn't know your friends too well."

Pete swallowed and wondered, *Who the hell is Marilyn Roberts?* And, *How can she know about Tabitha?* And, *What does it mean: 'telling Christabel to mind her own business?'*

"Seems like you have a real admirer, Pete."

"Uh, yeah, I guess so."

"You never mentioned her before," Mr. Turnbull said, still watching him closely.

"I..." Pete began. *How do I cover this?* "I didn't know how much she liked me."

"Uh huh." Mr. Turnbull smiled at Pete, but there was something behind the smile Pete couldn't read. "Well, I 'spose now I understand why you were so fired up to get home. You got a girl waitin' on you."

"Yeah," Pete smiled back up at his caseworker, finally understanding the implications of the letter. "I guess I kinda do."

Mr. Turnbull chuckled, "I gotta get back to work, Pete." He turned toward the door. "You don't get too wet going back. Try an' run between the raindrops." He walked through the glass front door of the building and was gone. Pete stood there alone on the porch, listening to the rain dance on the metal above and re-read the line he had almost missed in his initial confusion: "...*she wishes she'd had the nerve to kiss you goodbye.*" He looked from the letter up the hill, in the direction of Tabitha's house, though he knew he couldn't see it from here. By now he knew exactly the spots on campus from which the Pembrook house was visible.

He folded the letter and tucked it under his sweatshirt. He held it in place through the heavy cotton as he ran back to the cottage, his aunt and anger forgotten, raindrops crashing down on his grinning face.

Chapter 6

It was Manny who spotted the code in Tabitha's letter. For all the times he'd read it over, Pete hadn't even noticed it. He showed the letter to Manny while they were getting ready for bed, and Manny read it appreciatively. "Wow," he said, "this is awesome, man." Pete simply beamed, knowing the grin he wore probably looked weird coming from a Riordan kid but not giving a damn. After dinner Pete had figured out the Redwood City post mark, and who Marilyn Roberts must be. And the realization had clarified for him just how clever a person Tabitha Pembrook was. It had been daring to send him the letter, but she had figured out a way to do it without getting him into trouble or letting anyone know she had met him. Thanks to Marilyn.

Manny was sitting on the edge of his bed and had read the letter over a few times before he asked, "Have you noticed this design she made in the margins? The pattern?"

Pete nodded as he put away his toothbrush and paste, "Looks kinda like dice."

"Yeah, but did you notice anything about it?" Manny was turning the paper in his hands now.

Pete could see the back of it and said, "She drew it on the back too, right beneath the return address."

Manny continued turning the paper around in his hand for another 30 seconds, and then he smiled and nodded. "I gotta hand it to her; your girl is crafty."

"What are you talking about?" Pete asked, letting the *'your girl'* slide by comfortably.

Manny held out the paper, "I think you should look at it again."

Pete, who had already committed the entire letter to memory, took it, wondering what he could have missed about the doodles Tabitha had made. He peered at them. Not seeing anything, he began turning the page as Manny had done. He still didn't notice anything at first. Then, suddenly he noticed it. "Oh. It repeats." He looked up. "Is that what you saw, that the pattern repeats?"

Manny, still smiling, shook his head and stood up. He took the letter from Pete and put it on top of his wardrobe. From the top drawer, he produced a pencil.

"What are you doing?" Pete asked.

"Don't worry," Manny said, "when I write I'll write lightly." He turned the paper so Pete could see the letter right side up. "Okay, so you see the pattern." He began to turn the letter counter clockwise. "And you see the pattern repeat."

Pete nodded, but was confused.

"Now," asked Manny, "How many elements art there in the pattern?"

Pete counted. "Seven."

"RIGHT!" Manny exclaimed, and turned the paper over and wrote beneath the pattern on the back.

Marilyn Roberts	2850 Kings Mountain Road	Woodside, CA	94062			
⠦	⠦	⠦	⠒	⠄	⠖	⠒
5	5	5	2	1	4	2

"NO?" Manny shook his head, looking surprised that Pete still didn't get it, and joked, "Maybe I deserve a finder's fee for this." Then he made a final quick mark on the paper and asked, "How about now?"

Marilyn Roberts	2850 Kings Mountain Road	Woodside, CA	94062

And Pete felt his eyes try to exit his skull. "Holy Shit," he whispered. "That's a phone number!"

Manny said, "It is amazing what wonders our eyes will behold if we only allow ourselves to see." Pete looked up at him, a question in his eyes. Manny waved him off, "Just something my dad used to say."

Pete stared back down at what had to be Tabitha's phone number.

"So," said Manny, heading back over to his bed and picking up the book he's started the previous night, "you thinking about making a phone call during rec on Saturday?"

Pete laughed, "You know, I just might."

Manny lay down on his bed and pulled his book up onto his chest. "I'm not sure which was the cleverer trick," he said, "this or the Marilyn thing."

Pete nodded. Coming out of the dining hall after dinner he had looked up in the direction of the Pembrook house and the spot where he had shared his moment with Tabitha. Looking up there brought her face to mind, and her voice. He heard her asking him how long he'd been at the Home, how old he was, where he was from. And then Marilyn stepped out of the shadows for him. Tabitha had told him; *"My cousin lives down that way. In Woodside,"* she had said.

Tabitha had either gotten her cousin to write the letter or had written it and sealed it herself and sent it to Woodside to be relayed back north. Whichever way she'd done it, it had been brilliant.

And then there was the phone number. Saturday. Rec. The only public phone on campus. *Yes.*

During school on Friday, boys began to disappear. They were called out of class by caseworkers and coordinators as parents and guardians showed up to temporarily reclaim them. Pete found it easy to pick out the boys who wouldn't be leaving for home visit. They were the kids who got quieter and quieter with each departure, almost as if they were willing themselves away from Riordan, as if stilling themselves just so would be enough to pass beyond the realities of time and place, and return them to the families who had dumped them then promptly forgotten about their existence.

But today, even though he was indeed staying put for the week, Pete was not one of those guys. Since receiving and decoding the message from Tabitha, he'd been completely content with being at Riordan over the holiday. It would be quiet with most of the boys gone, and he would have the chance to call Tabitha on Saturday from the pay phone in the rec hall. And, Manny would be around too. Pete found he'd become used to Manny, even though the new boy did have an odd way of seeing the world.

The majority of boys leaving for Thanksgiving had departed by Friday night. By the end of the weekend the rest would be gone. Only Pete and Manny would be at Riordan for the whole holiday week. But on Friday night, there were still four other guys in the cottage: Jordi, Frankie, JP, Tony and Steven. Frankie had said that he and JP were getting picked up by his mom on Saturday Morning. Jordi, who was scheduled to go on Monday, had heard Tony and Steven talking about being around until late Saturday or early Sunday. Pete hadn't heard it himself, but it wasn't a real surprise.

Over the past few days he'd noticed the brain trust stopped talking whenever he was around. It wasn't a particularly new trick on their part; they were secretive a lot of the time. Steve liked to think of himself as the ruler the cottage, and as a ruler, felt the need to meet secretly with his chief goon regularly. And Pete, as a LEVEL 2, was a constant threat to them, both as a reminder of the privileges they couldn't keep their lives together long enough to get, and as a potential snitch.

Though Pete wasn't much of a threat to snitch. He'd only ever told on another boy preemptively once, when he'd heard Charlie Hunter tell some boys at Saturday rec he was going to slit Chris Caspar's throat, and had shown off a box cutter as proof of his intent. Pete had waited a few hours, then finally gone to Ms. Terry and told her of Charlie's threat against Chris. Charlie, who'd had a history of violence at Riordan, and a rumored sociopathic route to the Home, had been escorted from dinner that night to a waiting Sheriff's cruiser. The coordinators had ransacked his room as dinner began and quickly found a bag of pot and 3 razor-bladed hobby knives.

Charlie had spent at least one night in the Sonoma County Juvie in Santa Rosa, maybe more. All Pete knew for sure was that he had never returned to the Home. Pete's name had been kept out of it so that no other boys knew he was involved.

The warning caught Pete by surprise. It came on Friday night as he was finishing up in the bathroom after his shower.

He was brushing his teeth and looking in the mirror when he saw movement in the glass. He'd been thinking about his teeth and the game of chess he and Manny were going to play before bed, and was pulled out of his thoughts by the sight of Frankie walking in behind him. In the mirror, he saw Frankie pause for half a step before taking up position at the next sink. His mouth full of toothpaste, Pete acknowledged Frankie's entrance into the bathroom with a nod and slight raise of his eyebrows. Frankie blankly nodded back.

While he brushed he was thinking about how to counter Manny's knights. He knew the knights were why he always lost to Manny. He'd decided he needed to take those knights out as soon as possible if he was going to have a chance at winning.

Eventually, he became aware Frankie was no longer standing next to him. Glancing in the mirror, he saw Frankie looking around the bathroom, checking for feet under the stalls. Pete knew they were alone in the bathroom, so he didn't pay much heed to Frankie's investigations as he bent over the sink to spit. But when he stood back up he saw Frankie in the mirror, standing back near the doorway in the light blue terry cloth robe his mother had sent him back to Riordan with after his last weekend home. He was alternately looking down the hall and back at Pete. Finally Pete registered the look on his Frankie's face.

"What's wrong?" Pete asked the Frankie in the mirror, not yet turning. Frankie put his finger to his lips in a conspiratorial librarian's hush. He glanced again down the hallway, watching for a moment, then looked down at the floor and cocked his head to hear the sounds of the cottage. Pete watched the reflection carefully and listened himself.

Through the echoing hallways, he heard Steven's loud voice and Fat Tony's slow mule laughter coming from somewhere near the front of the cottage. He also heard Mr. Weaver giving JP a hard time about leaving a mess in the kitchenette. After a moment he turned around to look at Frankie head-on. Frankie still had his eyes on the floor, was still listening, holding his finger up in the same librarian pose.

"What is it?" Pete asked quietly, not quite in a whisper. After a moment, Frankie finally looked up at him, but kept station at the door. Never one to hide much of what he was feeling, Frankie looked worried now.

"Be careful, Pete." It was a whisper so quiet that for a moment Pete wasn't sure he'd heard correctly.

"What are you talking about," Pete whispered back.

"They're planning something," Frankie swallowed. "They're gonna do something to him."

Pete didn't feel the need to ask who *they* were. The only people in the cottage who ever made the kind of plans Frankie was talking about were Steven and Tony. Although, if Frankie had heard, it probably meant his cousin was in on it too. But there was another part of what Frankie had said. *They're gonna do something to* him. *Manny.*

"What are they planning?"

Frankie shook his head, "I don't know, but it ain't gonna be good." He shot another quick look down the hall, then turned back to Pete again and whispered, "And it's probably gonna be tonight."

"Tonight?"

Frankie nodded, "Before they leave for home visit."

"How do you know?" Pete asked.

"I just do, man." But Pete could tell Frankie was afraid to say more. Crossing his cousin was one thing. JP was family; he wouldn't seriously hurt Frankie. But ratting out Steven and Tony by name had the potential of being seriously bad for one's health.

"But…"

"No!" Frankie was sounding angry now, and the syllable came out louder than he had intended. He quickly backed into a whisper. "Don't ask me any more. I've told you what I heard."

"Why? Why did you tell me?"

"Because if they come for him and you're in the way they'll go right through you." And then Frankie stepped closer to Pete, halving the distance between them. He looked suddenly too young for the cottage, like one of Ms. Kelly's Ant kids.   And when he finally spoke again, it was in an urgent whisper.

"They'll hurt you, Pete."   And there was pain in his eyes.   Pete saw the trouble there and he was simultaneously touched and angry.

"What am I supposed to do?"

"Tell staff," Frankie said it quickly.   "Tell after the rest of us go to bed.   That way, they won't know you'd been tipped off."

Pete considered it for a moment, then remembered what night it was.

"No," he said.   "It's Friday night."

Frankie looked momentarily confused, but then nodded himself, remembering.   Friday was Mr. Weaver's sleepover and Mr. Weaver was not known for his discretion.   If he told Weaver, Steven and Tony would almost certainly find out he'd talked.

Almost on cue, the voice of Mr. Weaver carried back through the halls of the cottage: "Light's out for 3s and 4s in six minutes."

The sound of the adult voice shook Pete from his consideration of how to avoid an ass kicking for both himself and for Manny.   Then he realized he'd missed something.   He glanced sharply at Frankie. "You haven't told Manny, have you?"   A look of fear and confusion was answer enough.

"Why tell me and not him?"

Frankie swallowed.   "I don't know him," he finally said.   "I know you."

Pete nodded and looked away, back to the mirror.   He saw Frankie's reflection go back to the door and glance down a reflected hall.   Voices were getting closer; the 3s and 4s were slowly making their way down the long hall, back to the bedrooms and the bathroom.

Frankie pulled his head back inside the bathroom for the last time, and whispered, "They're coming."   His reflection moved behind Pete to one of the empty stalls, where he stepped inside and turned to close the door. But before the reflection disappeared, it said, "Watch your ass, Pete. Don't get dead over some new kid. He ain't worth it." As voices drew even with the bathroom door, Frankie closed the stall, and Pete's eyes found themselves in the mirror.

He gathered up his toothbrush and paste and turned for the bathroom door just as Fat Tony came through. Pete looked down as Tony's bovine eyes scanned the room.

"You all alone in here, O'Boyle?" he asked, his chins jiggling as he talked.

"I guess," Pete responded, glancing up just briefly. Tony was still standing in front of the doorway.

"Didn't interrupt you jerkin it, did I?" the fat boy asked before laughing hysterically at his own wit and walking toward the stalls.

Pete made no response and walked out through the considerable space Tony had just vacated. He headed into the hall and back toward his room, hoping Manny would be there.

The hallway was quiet compared to most nights, but it was still the last location of nervous energy for the day as the boys prepared for bed. With just seven boys in the house, only he and Manny would be up past 9 pm.

Frankie and Tony were both still in the bathroom. Jordi was wandering around slowly as he sometimes did at night. He said it was a side effect of the medication his doctor had started him on over the summer. He would amble from one room to the next just looking in, sometimes saying something, sometimes saying nothing. The staff, normally anal about quickly herding the boys into bed, had grown used to Jordi's wanderings, and only re-directed him if he was bothering the other boys, which was almost never. Almost as a rule, he would be snoring in his bed five minutes after lights out.

Currently, Jordi was standing in the darkened doorway of Frankie and Malcolm's room, staring into the shadows. As Pete passed him, he got a whiff of the mixed smells of piss and disinfectant, and he remembered again how gross rooming with Malcolm was.

As he neared the halfway point of his trip, JP and Steven emerged from Steven's room, talking quietly. Steven, who was walking behind, saw Pete coming toward them and immediately closed his mouth. JP was walking ahead of Steven and had his head turned away from Pete. He was still mumbling something when Steven's hand shot out and flicked him in the ribs.

"Oww," JP hissed, grabbing his side, "What the hell you do that for?"

"Hey kid," Steven said to Pete, ignoring JP and talking over his head. JP, who had finally looked around, rubbed his ribs and went quiet.

Pete looked at Steven but didn't respond, and just kept walking toward his room.

Steven looked stonily at Pete and nodded, "Sleep good, kid. Sleep sound."

Pete nodded and looked away. He quickly passed the two boys and walked to his lighted doorway.

Unfortunately, he found the room empty. Manny had already gone up to the front for the remainder of the night. He was probably already setting up the chessboard. Pete sat down on his bed, trying to decide what to do. He didn't want to tell Mr. Weaver. Sure, Weaver would probably stop it, but would undoubtedly tell Steven, Tony and JP that he had a witness who knew what they were planning. Pete had worked hard to stay away from trouble in the past year. The last thing he needed was to make enemies of those bastards.

From the hallway came the voice of Mr. Johnson: "Lights out in one minute." The tiredness was easy to pick out in his voice. As soon as the majority of boys were in bed, he'd be off for the weekend. He'd say goodnight to Manny and Pete, pack up his small bag and head home to see his wife and two sons.

So he didn't want to tell staff, but he didn't want Manny to get hurt. If he couldn't warn staff, he could at least warn Manny. He had to tell Manny. It was the only thing to do. He got up and put his toiletries away and walked out into the hall. Mr. Weaver was already sitting on the stool in the middle of the back hallway, at the top of the T-junction. In the light from the front hallway he was reading something on a clipboard he was balancing on his knee. He looked up as Pete stepped out of the room he shared with Manny.

"Light," was all he said before looking back down at his clipboard. Pete reached back into the room and hit the switch before he went forward. It was quiet in the hall. Not only were there fewer boys in the cottage, but the only roommates left were him and Manny; everybody else had a room alone for the night, so there wasn't any talking coming from the rooms.

Pete walked past Weaver and turned up the T-hall toward the front of the cottage. Mr. Johnson was sitting in the fishbowl office, working on the boys' LEVEL logs. He waved to Pete, but said nothing.

Pete found Manny in front of the TV, watching the Riordan movie. It was one Pete had seen a few years earlier, before his mom had died. He remembered she'd taken him to see it just after he had worn his brown suit to his grandmother's funeral, but before he'd worn it to his grandfather's. It was about a lost puppy looking for its master. Manny had his slippered feet up on the couch. The chessboard was nowhere in sight.

"Hey," Manny said when Pete sat down on another of the couches in the front room.

"Hey," Pete said back, watching the puppy getting help from a duck. He didn't know what to say to Manny. He sat there looking at but not watching the puppy movie for five minutes without saying anything else. He didn't know where to begin, but he had the sense that if he didn't talk soon he might just let the rest of the evening go without saying anything. At a loss for what to say, he finally settled for something just to get himself talking.

"Where's the chessboard?" It was something anyway.

Manny shrugged, still staring at the movie. "I didn't feel like playing tonight. I'm a little tired."

Now or never.

"Manny, there's something I have to tell you about. Something bad."

Manny looked across the sofa at him, "What's going on?"

"I think they might do something tonight," Pete finally said. "Tony and Steven. I think they might try to do something to mess with you tonight."

Manny looked away from Pete, down to the floor. He let his eyes rest there for a few seconds before flicking them back up to the puppy film, then back to Pete. "Yeah. I kind of thought they might do something before they left."

Pete was surprised that Manny both expected it and was being so god dammed *calm* about it. Obviously, some of what Pete was feeling showed on his face. Manny sat up and looked at him. "I guess I've got it coming," he said. Pete felt his eyes and mouth widen. Manny must have noticed he reaction, because he quickly added, "From their perspective, I mean." His brow furrowed and he shook his head.

Pete was a little unnerved by Manny's lack of concern. But overall, he felt better for having told him. But the question still remained, "So, what do we do now? Do we tell Mr. Johnson before he leaves? Do we tell Weaver?"

Manny looked back to the puppy, who was now being assisted by the duck in seeking advice from an owl. After a little while, he frowned and said, "No. We don't tell." He clasped his hands in front of him and drew his legs back up onto the sofa, leaning back once again into the cushions.

Pete was already shaking his head, "No... I think we should tell Johnson. It'd be different if it was just Weaver, but you know Johnson would want us to tell him." He could hear the pleading quality in his own voice and was immediately embarrassed. Manny heard it too.

"Listen Pete," Manny said, putting his clasped hands on top of his head and nestling down further into the sofa, "I appreciate you wanting to look out for me." He chuckled as he said it and looked back toward the puppy film. Part of Pete's mind recoiled in shock: *He's laughing at me!*

Manny was still smiling, still looking at the television. "I mean, I'm touched," he said, and laughed again.

Pete was suddenly angry, at Steven and Tony and JP and Frankie and Weaver. But more than anyone, he was angry with Manny. He had a desire to swing out at Manny himself, to catch his pale chin with a well placed fist.

After a minute, Manny's eyes flicked from the movie to Pete and stopped as they were getting ready to flick back to the puppy. The smile that had been on his face a moment before froze into a worried grimace. His eyes widened and seemed to move all over Pete's face. Pete watched him through eyes he did not remember narrowing set above a jaw he did not remember clenching. Manny was still staring at him, sitting on the other sofa with his hands ridiculously on top of his head, a look of confusion hung on his face.

"What?" Pete asked.

Manny didn't immediately respond, but slowly lowered his hands and pushed himself back up to a regular sitting position. Finally he said, "What just happened there?"

"What do you mean?" Pete asked, glancing back at the television screen. He remembered this movie. He remembered his mom telling him how they made the movie. She had heard about it on the radio she'd said.

"You just kind of froze."

"Did I?" The animals were real animals that had been filmed near each other, and the people who had made the movie had put peanut butter on the roofs of the animals' mouths so they would chomp up and down and look like they were talking. Actors then watched the film and supplied the lines. When they did it all right, the dog and duck and owl all looked like they were having a regular conversation.

"Yeah. You just stopped moving for about 10 seconds."

"I'm fine," Pete said. Then added, "Did you know, when they made this movie…"

"You sure you're okay?" Manny interrupted.

Pete didn't quite know what to do. Manny seemed legitimately concerned. He looked at Manny. "I… don't want to talk about it right now. Just do me a favor and let it alone for now, okay?"

Manny looked as if he had no intention of letting it alone. He looked worried.

Pete looked down and took a deep breath. When he released it he made eye contact with Manny and said, "Please."

Manny still looked wary, but after a minute he nodded. There was silence between them. Pete could tell Manny was just barely holding back from demanding an explanation, but Manny would have to wait. If he couldn't even get the words right in his own head to explain it to himself, how could he explain it to someone else?

His thoughts were interrupted by Mr. Johnson's voice from the hallway. "Good night boys." Pete looked back over the sofa and saw Mr. Johnson standing in the light of the hall, shouldering into a brown leather coat. Pete couldn't bring words up, but Manny saved him.

"Good night sir. Have a good weekend."

He began to wave, and then he looked at Pete. "You all right, Pete?"

Pete mentally shook himself, "Uh, yeah. Just tired, sir."

"You sure?" From the look on the cottage supervisor's face, Pete knew Mr. Johnson wasn't buying his explanation.

"Yeah. Just need some sleep."

"Okay, I'll take your word for it." Johnson's eyes narrowed slightly as if to tell Pete, *I don't really believe you, but you don't usually lie to me, so we'll let it go this time.* Pete kept smiling in what he hoped appeared to be a tired manner. Johnson smiled himself. "See you two on Tuesday."

Manny waved, "Night sir."

Mr. Johnson nodded, then looked down the hall and waved at Weaver. He turned and headed for the door with the final wave. "Night."

The sound of the heavy oak door of the cottage swinging shut seemed to break the moment of heaviness between Manny and Pete. As if to verify this, Manny looked away from the hall and back to Pete, and let out a long breath.

Pete looked away and back to the puppy movie. The duck was in trouble, caught in a box trap, and the puppy and owl were trying to get it out. Pete was looking at the movie, but not watching it. He was suddenly sure he had forgotten something.

"Anyway," Manny finally said, "I don't think they'll actually do anything."

"What?" Pete said, coming back and looking at Manny.

"Steven and Tony. I don't think they'll do anything."

Pete couldn't believe he'd let himself forget about it, even for a moment. "You don't think…"

"No," Manny said. "I mean, sure, they put the word out they're gonna get me, but it's just talk. Probably meant to scare me."

"Is it working?" Pete asked.

"Well, it's distracted me from the pooch movie, hasn't it?" he indicated the television. "But I think they're just looking for someone to not like. My dad used to say that hatred can give meaning to an empty life. I think they're just trying to fill themselves up by focusing their anger on me."

"No," Pete sat up on the edge of the sofa. "What they're going to do is focus their fists on you. They will. Especially because other people know. If they don't do it now, they'll be seen as weak. They have to do it."

But Manny stood up and walked over to turn off the television. As the picture tube flicked off, Pete heard Mr. Weaver whistling as he walked down the hall toward them. A moment later, the voice came from behind him: "Twenty minutes 'til lights out guys."

Manny, who had moved toward Pete's sofa looked up and said, "I'm headed back now, sir."

"And what about you, O'Boyle?"

Pete glanced at the staffer who was looking back down at the clipboard and nodded, "Yeah, me too."

"Okay," Weaver said, not looking up from the papers he was reading. He turned and wandered away into the entrance hall.

If Weaver asked right now, Pete thought, *I'd tell him everything*. With Manny being purposefully blind to the ass kicking he was about to receive, Pete might just have told the staffer about Steven and Tony and all of it. But Weaver would never ask if Pete was all right. That would have required both interest and the ability to read body language. It was common judgment among the boys that Weaver was interested in them and their problems as much as his paycheck and the law required and no further, which didn't involve much time considering feelings or body language. Unlike the cottage supervisor, Mr. Weaver was satisfied with the verbal answers alone.

"Quite a caring guy," Manny whispered chuckling to himself.

Pete was caught off guard and let out a little laugh too, "Yup."

"Come on," Manny said, taking the first few steps toward the hall. "Let's get to bed. I want to rest if I'm gonna wake up pounded." And then he was gone down the hall, leaving Pete still sitting on the sofa staring after him.

Pete awoke with a start. It took him a second to orient himself, and calm his breath. He sat up in bed and looked out the window toward the fence and the darkened vineyard beyond. He couldn't see the moon, but the vines were all bathed in silver. He looked over at Manny, a lump under the covers. On top of his dresser, his alarm clock read 3:56.

He didn't remember falling asleep. He had planned on staying up all night, sure Manny was wrong, expecting shadows to enter the room any minute and start to work on the pile of blankets in the other bed. The last time he remembered checking the time it had been 11:25. He'd been stunned when Manny had fallen asleep less than 20 minutes after Weaver had come back to turn out the lights.

The heat was on and the vent above his dresser was blowing hot air into the room. He listened carefully to the sounds of the cottage. He could hear Jordi snoring softly from across the hall and the distant sounds of the heater coming from on top of the building. Otherwise there was nothing. He shifted up toward the head of the bed and leaned his back against the aging plaster of the bedroom wall. Looking out his window at the vineyard he thought about Tabitha, and the coded message she had sent him. He looked back at the clock and thought, *This is Saturday already.* He smiled in the darkness, thinking about the phone call he was planning on making later in the day. He reached down next to the bed and opened up the drawer where he kept his few important possessions: his baseball glove, a beaten up 1987 Will Clark Fleer card, his grandfather's broken pocket watch and the book Manny had given him.

He withdrew the last from the drawer which he didn't bother to close; this would only take a minute. He opened to the middle of *Jonathan Livingston Seagull* and withdrew the envelope. He opened it, but did not retrieve the letter from inside. It was too dark to read, and besides, he had committed it to memory rendering the actual reading of it almost unnecessary. Instead of reaching into the envelope, he pulled it open wide, put it over his nose and breathed in deeply, letting the intoxication of talcum bring him back to the hilltop, to her side.

Chapter 7

In the morning, Manny said he wasn't surprised there had been no nocturnal attack. Frankie silently poked is head into their room early, even before staff came at 7 am to officially wake them. When he saw Manny and Pete were both all right, the look of concern on his face broke into an embarrassed smile.

Things were calm all morning. Steven ignored them as he usually did. Tony however, kept glancing at Manny then smiling to himself. At least, Pete assumed the smiles were directed inward. All through breakfast, he kept catching Tony looking furtively in the direction of his and Manny's table, then looking away and grinning like an idiot. Just before the end of breakfast, one of the coordinators came in to walk Tony back to Admin where his Mom was waiting.

On the way back from breakfast, Pete admitted to Manny that their behavior this morning, especially Tony's, seemed to support the theory of psychological warfare. Maybe Manny had been right: they had wanted to scare him into thinking they were going to do something.

After breakfast, they spent the rest of the morning helping Weaver and Mr. Dawson with some cleaning around the cottage.

Even though they were working, doing the very types of chores they were often assigned to do while working off cottage hours, there was a completely different feel during home visit work. Pete actually liked helping out when he was around during home visits. The cottage staffers were always a little nicer, easier to talk to, less likely to give consequences. Pete guessed it was because they were suddenly in charge of fewer than half the usual number of residents. They were just looser. Talking about the phenomenon once over the summer, Jordi Melchior had summed up the change in staff demeanor for Pete when he said, "Even Weaver isn't as much of a dick as he usually is."

He and Manny were given the job of washing and folding all of the cottage sheets and towels. They were sitting on the living room sofas, each with a pile of laundry when the call came for Steven to head up to Admin. He was in the middle of helping Mr. Dawson move firewood into the big box behind the fireplace in the living room when Weaver stepped out of the office and told him to grab his stuff and head on up. After passing Steven the message, Weaver headed toward the front door and disappeared from view. So as Steven came around the fireplace to walk through the living room toward the hallway, he was out of staff sight for a minute.

Pete saw him look toward the office, then back over his shoulder to where Mr. Dawson was still bent over the firewood box. Realizing he could be seen only by Manny and Pete, Steven slowed his walk slightly. Pete watched apprehensively. Steven, whose default expression was stony and dark, offered Manny a tightlipped, mirthless smile and pointed at him. Manny watched, a look of curiosity on his face and the beginnings of a question forming on his lips. But before anyone spoke, Steven dropped his hand and let his eyes slide to Pete and his expression shift to one of contempt before resuming his usual quick pace and walking back toward his room.

"What the hell was that about?" Pete whispered to Manny, who only shrugged.

With half of the hundred boys on campus gone, and another 20 or 30 leaving before dinner, life at Riordan shifted dramatically. First of all, LEVEL status became a day to day thing: behavior today earned privileges tomorrow. On the first full day of home visit, everybody got promoted to a modified LEVEL 2. The message from the staff was pretty clear: *you guys all got screwed out of your chance to be home, so we'll try to make life just a little easier for the next few days.* The "modified" aspect of LEVEL status came from the fact that the newly minted 2s didn't get all privileges automatically. Who was allowed to go off campus on trips to the video store, mall or 7-11 was completely a matter of staff discretion. Also, bedtime could be altered at any moment. If some kid started getting goofy during the nightly movie, early bed was the staff's final tool of the day.

Another change had to do with accommodations. In the dining room, as the number dwindled down to the 20 or so boys who would be around for the entire week, the number of cottage dining rooms used shrank. At breakfast on Saturday, all of the rooms in the dining hall were populated if rather sparsely so. By lunch, the 30 boys left were in three dining rooms. By dinner they would be using only 2.

Similar to meal locations, sleeping arrangements also changed during home visit. Because most of the boys were gone, home visits were a time when many of the staff took vacation. To minimize coverage necessary, cottages were consolidated for nights. Boys spent some time during the day in their own cottages, but ended their days by going to sleep in which ever was the "open cottage" for the break. The previous week they had been told which cottages would be open for the Thanksgiving home visit. St. Michael's would house the younger residents, while Pete, Manny and Jordi would be sleep with the older crowd at St. John's.

*   *   *

In Pete's estimation, the two best things about Saturdays were afternoon rec and Mr. Dawson. While most of the cottage staff at the Riordan Home for Boys was in their mid to late twenties, Mr. Dawson was near on to fifty. He'd once told Pete he'd been at Riordan since before a full third of the current staff had been born, including Weaver and Ms. Graham. He was the same age as Father O'Connell.

He'd started out as a cottage worker right after graduating from, what had at the time been Sonoma State College. He'd worked in the cottages for a long time, including four years as Supervisor of St. Mike's, had spent several years working in the rec department, and had even taught English at the Riordan School for 4 years. He was a comparatively short man, standing just a few inches taller than Pete and a few inches shorter than Steven Sengall. His head was bald on top with a short graying ring of fluff running around the back from one ear to the other. He was stocky with a small bulging belly that pressed hard against his always tucked in shirts.

The shirts themselves were interesting. Every one of them had a college logo on it, and they were all the logos of different schools. He had t-shirts and polo shirts and sweatshirts from big California institutions like UCLA, Stanford and UC Berkeley. But he also had apparel from big national schools like Miami, FSU, Duke, St. John's and Purdue. There were even a dozen or more articles of clothing from colleges Pete had never heard of anywhere else. Schools with names like Creighton, William & Mary, UTEP, Mount Holy Oak, Mississippi Valley State and Cañada College. One time, because people in places like Riordan will do just about anything to pass the time, Frankie Baltazar and Chris Caspar counted 37 days on shift before they saw Dawson in a repeated shirt.

Today Mr. Dawson was wearing tucked in white t-shirt with long burgundy sleeves and the words *Foothill Baseball* emblazoned across the chest. As he walked them over to the dining hall for lunch, he told them about his days off. He had taken his eight year old daughter out fishing for the first time and she had caught a 10 inch rainbow trout. And that was the great thing about Mr. Dawson. He was more human than the other staff. Pete liked Ms. Graham a lot, and Mr. Johnson was a solid guy, but talking with Mr. Dawson always felt like talking to a relative; like a grandfather, but one who wasn't losing his mind. He had an easy way about him, and unlike most of the other cottage staff, his usual expression was not one of anger or suspicion, but rather of amusement. Of course, he could turn off the kindly grandfather at a moment's notice and be very serious indeed, but he seemed to seldom have the need. In that respect he was a lot like Ms. Kelly.

After lunch, Mr. Kinnear and Mr. Talan, the rec staff for the day, led the 18 boys past Admin and down toward the playing fields. There would be an hour of organized time followed by a break, and then an hour of free play. And free play time would give Pete his chance to use the phone.

It was a cool, overcast afternoon. The trees surrounding the green expanse of the large field had shed their leaves, which lay in drifts at their bases. The soccer goals were set up for a short field: one net on an end line and the other at mid-field. A half dozen balls lay scattered around one goal. The staff quickly split the boys up into two teams. Pete, who had never much liked soccer and was a lot better with his hands, volunteered to play in goal for his team. Mr. Talan fished two pair of well worn goalkeeper gloves out of his bag and handed one to Pete and the other to Mario Velasquez from St. John's.

The game was fast pace and exciting. The short field meant the ball was never too far from one goal or the other. There were a lot of shots at Pete, who did a good job defending his net. The teams were pretty well matched, but in the end, Mario was just a little bit better. The final score was 4-3, with Pete and Manny's team going down to defeat. Overall, Pete was happy with his performance; he'd made a couple of good saves and had been close on all three of the goals he'd allowed.

After the game, Kinnear took a few boys with him to put away the soccer gear in the gym and Talan walked the rest of the boys up toward the rec hall.

The rec hall was the newest building on campus, having been completed just a few months before Pete's arrival at Riordan. It had been built with money from community fundraising, charity events and a few private donations. It was the pride of the recreation department. Situated just behind the auditorium and adjacent to the swimming pool and outdoor basketball courts, the outward appearance of the building was polished and inviting, with a wall of windows offering a view of the pool below it and the athletic fields beyond.

Inside, there was no shortage of amenities. At one end of the main room there was a separate kitchen with a bar opening out on the hall proper. On the kitchen counter were sodas and pitchers of water and cups. There were also small bags of chips and cookies for boys to snack on. The other end of the building had a large television with a few couches arrayed around it. The middle of the hall was home to four pool tables, two ping pong tables and one table each for foosball and air hockey.

Two bathrooms were situated on the side of the building away from the pool. And it was between the two bathroom doors that a solitary stool stood next to the only amenity Pete was interested in today.

As Pete understood it from his caseworker, the installation of the payphone had been an issue of some serious debate among the staff.

There were apparently many staff members who objected to having a public phone on campus, saying that it would permit uncontrolled communications with the very people in their lives that the boys had been sent to Riordan to get away from. The argument went back and forth for several weeks after plans for the phone were brought up at a staff meeting. Finally, Mr. Turnbull said, Father O'Connell himself made the decision to go ahead with the phone.

Usually during Saturday rec there was a line for the phone. When all hundred boys were around they were split up into four groups, and each had only about 45 minutes in the rec hall. Almost everybody tried to use the phone each week. Today however, with the only boys on campus those unable to see their families, it appeared no one was interested in calling home; the tall stool next to the phone stood empty and the 3-foot square chalkboard where boys kept the phone wait list was silent green.

Pete stood in the center of the rec hall, staring at the phone. Manny stood beside him. He had practiced this a hundred times in the last few days; what he would say, how he would say it. He wanted to be so calm, so smooth, but he knew it unlikely. He'd never had any meaningful conversations with girls. Sure, he'd known some back home, had even met a couple he had liked, but he had never moved on his attraction. Now, standing here with four quarters in his pocket, he felt completely unprepared to dial the phone.

"I can't do it," he whispered to Manny.

"Sure you can," said the other encouragingly, "just dial and see what happens."

"No..." Every possible problem, none of which he had thought about at all since figuring out the phone number, suddenly seemed incredibly likely to happen. What if she didn't want him to call? What if she changed her mind and now wished she hadn't given him the number? What if *someone else* answered? What if he got an answering machine? What if she actually answered and wanted to talk to him? He thought that might just be the worst possible scenario because he had absolutely no idea what to say to her! He voiced this last concern to Manny for the 50th time.

"You'll be fine," Manny reassured. "Remember, she *wants* you to call."

"*But what do I say?*" Pete felt the first vestiges of real panic begin to invade his mind.

Manny seemed to consider this question for a moment before answering: "Ask her why she sent the letter."

Pete nodded and said, "Ok. Yeah."

Manny smiled, adding, "Go for it."

Pete took a deep breath in and let it out slowly, then walked to the phone. He picked it up and heard the dial tone waiting for the number. Still breathing slowly, he pulled a quarter out of his pocket and dropped it in the coin slot. The dial tone hiccupped then went steady again. Without taking any more time to think about it, he punched in the long since memorized number.

The phone clicked and then the ringing began. It rang once. Twice. Three times. At the fourth ring Pete let out a breath he hadn't even been aware he was holding. *She's not home*, he thought, *Thank God…*

Then there was a click and a voice:

"Hello?"

Oh crap!

"Hellooo?"

It was her! It was her! He tried to talk: "Hhhh—." His tongue suddenly felt swollen, like it was filling his entire mouth.

"Is there somebody there?" She sounded like she was starting to get annoyed.

He tried to speak again: "Mmmm—."

"Ok, this is getting a little weird. I can hear you breathing, so either say something now, or I'm hanging up."

Oh God! No! He finally had her on the phone and was going to blow it because he couldn't talk!

"Last chance," he heard her say from across the fence and a million miles away.

"Okay then…"

He imagined he could hear her phone receiver slamming home. *Anything, say anything!*

"Wait!"

There was no response. She'd already hung up; he'd missed her.

He sagged and exhaled deeply. He'd moved to hang up when he heard something out of the earpiece. He pulled the receiver back to his head so fast he smashed his ear against his skull. It was a nasty stinging pain but he fought through it.

"Hello?" he said.

"Yes?" Her voice was guarded. She was suspicious.

Feeling him on the verge of getting stuck again, he blurted out, "It's me."

"Me, who?" she asked.

"Me, Pete." He cringed at how it sounded. *Oh my God, I'm completely lame!*

There was no response.

Pete felt his stomach begin to curl up, sweat sprouted from his brow. Then in a moment and two words, every thing was right again.

"Hey Pete." He could swear he heard her smiling.

"Hi." Relief swept over him.

"Well, I gotta say, you're pretty good Pete O'Boyle."

He laughed and said, "Thanks." *She remembers my name.*

"I was hoping you'd figure it out and call."

"Yeah," he could feel the idiotic grin on his face, but didn't care. He looked at Manny, who gave him double thumbs up and wandered away toward one of the pool tables.

"So," she said, "what do you want to talk about?"

"I don't know." He didn't know what else to say. He had been so excited just to call her; he hadn't spent any time considering what he would actually say. "I just figured I'd give you a call."

She laughed, and he felt again like he was back on the hill.

They talked for as long as they could on Pete's four quarters: almost 13 minutes. She told him about using her cousin to send the letter and he told her about Manny being the one to figure out the telephone code. They talked for a minute about trying to figure out how to see each other again, but stopped when they both realized it might be impossible to coordinate. She told him the number he had called was her room number and that he could call it at any time, day or night. She said her room was on the opposite side of the house from that of her parents' and they couldn't hear her phone ring if the ringer was turned way down. He told her he'd try to call each afternoon this week from rec and would see if there was any way he could arrange a trip up to the water tower.

"I'm going to leave something up there for you," she said. "So if we miss each other, you'll still have something from me."

"What can you leave up there?"

"A surprise," she teased.

"Where will it be? How will I find it?"

"You'll just have to look carefully."

"What do you mean?" he asked with a laugh.

"Just look for something out of place."

"Okay."

There was another pause, but unlike the first painful and awkward gap, this one was full of hope for Pete.

Finally Tabitha said, "I think our time's almost up."

"Yeah, I know."

"Thanks for calling, Pete. I'm glad you did."

"Me too." He wanted to say more, to make the conversation last just a little longer. "Thanks for writing—." There was a click.

"Tabitha?"

A quick series of clicks chimed in his ear and were replaced after a few seconds by dial tone.

Damn.

But still, he couldn't help being happy. He hadn't known what to expect before the phone call, but it had been better than he could have imagined.

He replaced the receiver carefully, almost gently, not wanting to let go of the plastic, warmed by his hand and face. But he did let go, and turned around to look for Manny, spotting him almost immediately for the company he was keeping. It was always difficult to miss a bald, six and a half foot tall ex-baseball player among a roomful of boys; even of he was leaning over a pool table for a shot. Seeing he was off the phone, Mr. Turnbull gave a quick wave to Pete and smiled his lopsided grin, then beckoned him over to join them at the pool table. Feeling like he could beat the world at any game it offered, Pete smiled and headed over.

Chapter 8

Pete knew he was probably starting to bug Manny. For his part though, Manny was nice enough not to rain on Pete's parade, and just smiled and nodded as Pete told him for the fifth time about her plan to hide something for him on top of the hill.

"I mean, what do you think it could be?" Pete asked Manny as they got dressed after showers. They were in their room at St.

Gabe's. Jordi was sitting on Pete's bed, leaning back against the wall with his feet up on the backpack he was bringing to St. John's. He was reading a book Manny had given him. After dinner Mr. Dawson had told them they would be heading up to St. Johns for the evening at about 7:30. The clock on Pete's dresser read 7:14.

"I don't know," Manny chuckled, "But ask me again in three minutes and maybe I'll have an answer for you."

Pete stopped with a blue Riordan Athletics shirt half on, and looked at his roommate, the warmth of an embarrassed smile spreading across his face. "Okay, okay. I'm sorry I keep talking about it. I just can't believe it."

"Its fine," Manny reassured him. "I'm just having fun with you."

"Hell man, keep talking," Jordi chimed in from behind *Siddhartha*, not moving his gaze from the pages. "You've been closer to a girl than any of us since we got back from summer. If I can't get any, at least you should have a crack at some."

"Wow Jordi," Manny said, "I didn't realize what a romantic you are."

"All day long, baby. All day long."

There were only 9 guys staying in St. John's cottage that night: along with Pete, Manny and Jordi from St. Gabe's, there were three younger boys from St. Mike's and three slightly older boys who called St. J's home full time.

Mr. Dawson had informed them earlier as to the sleeping arrangements for the night. Jordi and Manny would be bunking together while Pete was tasked to a St. Michael's boy named Nacho. This news was fine with Pete. Sure, he'd miss talking to Manny as they settled down for bed, but Nacho was a cool kid. He was only eleven, and a little young for St. Mike's. He'd been put there because of a housing crunch in Mt. Olivett, the next youngest cottage. Pete had met him in Mr. Mcleese's art class at school. They got along well enough. And it was always nice to room with someone you knew a little rather than just getting thrown in with a complete stranger.

The staff had arranged for a birthday cake for one of the St. Mike's kids whose birthday it was. The cake was served during the movie Mr. Junn, the St. John's Supervisor, had selected for the night: *Star Wars*. Pete loved the movie. It was one his mom had always liked. In fact it was one of only three movies Lilly O'Boyle had ever bought. The other two had been an old black and white movie called *Casablanca,* and another of Pete's all time favorites, *The Sting*. Pete had seen *Star Wars* enough times to be able to identify almost any scene from just the sound effects and mechanical beeps and blips in the background. He remembered that the three video tapes were in his room at Aunt Marjorie's house. He'd ask Mr. Johnson if it would be all right for him to bring *The Sting* back with him after next home visit.

Nacho had never seen the film before. He sat between Manny and Pete on a couch, leaning forward in his seat, rocking and rolling his way through all of the battle scenes. Manny got a kick out of watching Nacho watch the movie, and kept looking at Pete over the younger boy's head, laughing and nodding.

The other St. Mike's guys sat together, not talking to the others, and the three St. John's guys seemed barely able to tolerate these intruding children. The sat a little apart and behind the other five boys who were watching the film. Pete had heard Jordi talking to the biggest one of them earlier. His name was Teddy Silva. Jordi and he were in the same science grouping at school, but Pete didn't know him. He'd come over the summer with a reputation including rumors of gang involvement. Pete had heard him tell Jordi that he and the other St. John's guys would be gone before lunch on Sunday. Teddy himself had a probation hearing scheduled for Monday and his mom wanted him around the night before to make sure he was cleaned up for the judge.

The two other boys from St. John's had been at Riordan almost as long as Pete. They were one of three sets of brothers on campus, but the only set of identical twins. They were named Alexei and Nicolai Raimanov, but behind their backs, and sometimes to their faces, they were referred to as the "KGB." They were first generation Lithuanian immigrants who preferred each other's company over anyone else's. They didn't talk much except to each other, and then it was almost exclusively in Russian. They could speak English, at least Nicolai could. He and Chris were in the same math class at school, and, to hear Chris tell it, Nicolai spoke English pretty well. Alexei, however, almost never spoke English, preferring to let his brother translate for staff when necessary. The story was their dad had been in the Russian mafia, and had been murdered before they came to America. Like almost all personal histories floating around Riordan, Pete figured there was probably a nugget of truth buried inside all the elaboration.

The only person in the cottage not in front of the television watching the film was Jordi. "Seen it," was all he'd said when Pete asked him if he was going to watch. Instead, he spent the two hours of the movie's run time in the game room, reading.

After the movie, the boys moved to the backrooms and brushed their teeth and got into bed. Mr. Junn came by each room and said goodnight to the boys, reminding them he had sleepover for the night and that his room is the one across from the staff office if they needed anything. He turned out all of their lights.

He was riding Christabel through the hard rain. He was almost to the top of Sonoma Mountain, and up there somewhere, something was waiting for him. Something wonderful. If he could only get through the mist it would be his. He could feel the muscles of the horse beneath him, pulling him onward. The thunder came again, and he could hear his name whispered in its roll. Pete.

Pete.

Pete!

"Pete!" The voice finally jarred him. Christabel and the mountain were instantly gone, replaced by the thin mattress and scratchy cottage blanket. He tried to remember back into the dream.

"Dammit Pete, wake up!" After a moment he realized the demanding whisper was coming from outside his head.

"Whazzit, huh. Wha…"

"Pete, wake up!" the voice hissed again.

Pete felt his eyes fight opening. Finally he managed to win the battle and looked around the still darkened room. He caught site of somebody's clock on the dresser in this unfamiliar place. It glowed a red 2:15 at him. Eventually he found a Jordi-shaped figure at the foot of his bed.

"Jordi?" He was trying to wake up. "That you?

"You sleep like the frickin dead, man!"

"Jordi, what the fff—?" Pete looked around the room and realized Nacho was in the doorway instead of being in his bed. His head cocked to listen for staff. For Pete, the effect was like a dousing of cold water. He was sitting up now, seeing Jordi clearly and noticing the strain on his face.

"Jordi, what's going on?"

Jordi hesitated. Pete guessed the news was not good, thought he couldn't think what would get Jordi to wake him in the middle of the night.

"C'mon, man! What the hell—"

"It's Manny," came the tired reply. Jordi suddenly sounded as if he were going to collapse.

"What about him?" But something in Pete already knew, though his mind could draw no logical connections to explain it happening. *There's no way...*

But Jordi made it plain: "They got him."

Pete and Nacho were in the last resident room at one end of the cottage's back hallway. As he stepped out into the hall Pete saw two heads poking out from a doors just passed, one looking in his direction, the other looking toward the far end of the hall, toward the room where Manny and Jordi had been put up for the night. As he and Jordi got closer he saw the two heads belonged to the other two St. Mike's kids. Of the three older St. John's boys there was no sign. Pete wasn't surprised. *Bastards.*

When he entered the last room he saw Manny lying on the bed closest to the door, his covers pulled up around his neck. His eyes were closed and appeared to be sleeping.

"Manny," Pete whispered.

"Yeah," was the tired response.

"What happened?"

"Nothing to speak of." The voice was matter of fact, almost relaxed. But Pete was beginning to learn how Manny reacted to bad stuff: he just got more calm than usual.

"Hey man, are you okay?"

"Oh, just a little sore. I must have fallen down on my way back from the bathroom," he said. Then added, "And bounced a couple of dozen times." This was followed by a half chuckle which turned quickly into a pain-stifled grunt.

Ouch, thought Pete. *Well, at least he can still talk.* Though that wasn't too much of a surprise. Pete had known they wouldn't hurt his face, they couldn't. Faces were too public, the injuries too easy to spot and impossible to hide. Faces were only ever targets in open fights, ones begun with witnesses, when the dancing kept going until staff cut in and started to lead.

No, when someone went for you like this, in the middle of the night, leaving visible bruises defeated the purpose.

"Where did they get him, Jordi?" Pete asked.

Jordi flinched a little at the sound of his name. "I think mostly in the body. Some on the legs." There was no question as to whether Jordi had been awake for the attack. Of course he had been, at least for part of it. During his third week at Riordan Pete had learned it was impossible to sleep through a blanket party in the next bed.

He'd been awake when four boys had come into his room and thrown a blanket over his first Riordan roommate, Donny Morello. Two guys had held the blanket down on either side of the bed, pinning Donny under it, while the others had swung socks weighted with soda cans. Donny's face had been unmarked, but he'd left in an ambulance with a broken wrist and three cracked ribs. The whole time, Pete had stayed in his bed, peaking out from under the sheets. Just once, before they actually began swinging the socks, one of the attackers had glanced back at Pete's bed, raised a pointing finger and calmly whispered, "Not a freakin' sound, new kid."

"Did they say anything?" he asked Jordi now.

"No."

"Who was it?" Pete asked.

Jordi just shook his head and looked to the corners of the room, away from both Pete and Manny.

Pete nodded. He didn't blame Jordi, didn't think him a coward. He himself had been "unable" to identify Donny's assailants. But he didn't need Jordi's help; he already knew it had to have been Teddy and the other two St. John's guys. He just didn't know why they had done it.

Pete sighed, "We'd better check him out, see if we need to wake Mr. Junn." He turned his attention back to Manny. "Can you get up?"

"I'm all right, Pete,"

"Not what I asked. C'mon, sit up man." He reached down and gently grabbed Manny's shoulder and helped him up to a sitting position. Manny moved slowly, stiffly, sucking his breath in between clenched teeth. He looked at Pete as he came upright. Obviously, he read the concern in the other's face.

"I said I'm all right. No need to go waking up anybody who's still sleeping."

Pete ignored this. "Jordi, turn on the lights so we can see how bad he's hurt."

In the dark he could see Jordi shake his head. "No way man, the rent-a-cop will see it." Pete had forgotten momentarily about the night security person. It was Saturday night; which meant the night security was Earl. Not a rent-a-cop exactly, Earl was actually a retired plumber whose wife, Alicia, worked in the kitchen during the week. He drove around campus in a golf cart during warm weather and in his ancient Pontiac in the cold. In the dark of the night, an unexpected room light could be spotted from across campus. The last thing they needed was Earl spotting them awake and coming to investigate. Pete was considering moving Manny down to the bathroom, where the lights stayed on all night, when Jordi went to his backpack and began rummaging around. He came back with a little key-chain light Pete recognized as Chris'. "He said I could keep it for him until he got back from home," Jordi explained.

Pete pointed the light toward the floor and pressed the button. It was surprisingly bright, but it was also blue. "Don't look into it," Jordi said. "It'll fry your eyes." Pete nodded and asked Manny to show him where he'd been hit. Manny began to protest, but apparently decided against it. He lifted his shirt and exposed his torso from the waist band of his sweat pants to his neck. Pete shined the light at him. Manny's pale skin shone brightly, glowing blue in the darkness. But the reflection was not uniform.

Looking closely, Pete could see faint raised areas that looked purple in the blue light. Each one was vaguely circular, about 2 inches across, with a dark crescent near the center.

There were at least a dozen such marks. Manny was a slender kid with not a lot of fat on him. Some of the marks were over his ribs. Those were the darkest already. Pete knew the color was an illusion of the blue light; the marks were probably still bright red. He also knew that in a couple of days all of the spots would be purple, blue, green and yellow. He remembered seeing Donny after he'd gotten out of the hospital. Almost a week later, he'd still had marks like these, only his had been bigger. Obviously, Teddy and the others hadn't used soda cans.

After a while, Pete said, "I don't know, Manny. Some of these look pretty bad, like they may have broken your ribs or something. Maybe we should wake up Mr. Junn." But Manny was already shaking his head.

"Nothing's broken," he said.

"You're ribs—" Pete began.

"Aren't broken," Manny said. And there was finality to the way he said it.

"How can you be sure?"

Manny sighed, then took a deep breath in, held it for a moment, and then let it out. "Because I can do that. If I had a cracked rib, even a hairline fracture, I couldn't get halfway through a deep breath. Trust me, I know what having broken ribs feels like, and this isn't it."

"How do you know what broken ribs feel like?" Jordi asked.

Manny smiled and said, "Oh, child, if I had a dime for every time I'd been beaten to the point where a hospital visit was debated, well then, I'd probably be able to buy us each a slice of pizza the next time we went to the mall in Santa Rosa." He began to laugh at himself then was reminded by his injuries that doing so might not be the best of ideas. Pete asked him if there was anything he needed, and got him the requested paper cup of water from the bathroom.

After making sure Manny was okay, Pete headed back down the hall and to his own bed. He passed no one in the hall this time. The two St. Mike's kids had apparently lost interest once they figured out nothing else was going to happen. Even Nacho was snoring when he got back to his room. The clock said 2:43 when he laid down again.

Something in the background had been bothering Pete since Jordi had woken him up with news of the attack. He'd not known it was there until he simultaneously realized what it was and figured it out. It happened just as he closed his eyes and decided to try to get back to the dream Jordi had interrupted when —.

His eyes popped open. *Jordi.* Jordi had woken him up. *He had to because I hadn't woken up during the attack.* Then another thought hit him. *Neither had Mr. Junn.* It hadn't occurred to him earlier that they shouldn't have had a choice as to whether or not they were going to tell Junn. He should have been in the back hallway before Jordi had even come to get Pete. *His room is only halfway down the T-hall. There's no way he couldn't have heard.*

Except, Pete knew, there was a way. It didn't make any sense, and he'd have to check with Jordi and maybe Nacho in the morning, but as he lay there in bed, Pete came to a realization which kept him awake and thinking for a long time afterward: even though he'd been pinned beneath a blanket and hit more than a dozen times with something heavy enough to leave 2-inch welts, at no point during the attack had Manny cried out or screamed.

Chapter 9

The next morning was difficult. Not just because of his short sleep, or the resultant headache, but because it was a grand lie all of the boys were telling each other and staff. Right after wake up, Pete went down to check on Manny. He was moving slow, but able to get around okay. When he was sure there was no one else near the room, he lifted his shirt and let Pete and Jordi see the marks in the light. Red and blue flowers were blooming all over Manny's upper body. There were a couple on his shoulders they'd missed last night and Manny said there were also a few on his thighs. He said he hadn't noticed them for the pain in his ribs. They were brutal to look at, and Pete marveled that Manny wasn't yelping with every move.

The bizarre thing though, was every boy in the cottage knew exactly what had happened and none of the four staff members there that morning did. The boys watched each other carefully. Jordi and Pete spent most of the morning before breakfast watching Teddy, Alexei and Nicolai, looking for some kind of sign. The St. Mike's guys weren't sure of the details, but knew enough to stay out from in between the two other groups of boys. For their part, the St. John's guys all ignored everybody except staff and each other. Until breakfast.

Pete, Jordi and Manny had kept up the rear of the procession to breakfast, both to watch Teddy and the twins and to allow for Manny's slightly slowed progress. Campus was still, like it got only on home visit mornings. There was a fog hanging over Sonoma Mountain, tendrils of which worked their way onto the campus itself, cascading down from the water tower.

When they entered the dining room after everyone else, Pete saw that most of the 16 seats were already filled, the extra taken up by staff from various cottages.

The twins sat together at one table and Teddy at another, alone. There were two seats at a table on the far left and another table next to it with an open seat. Pete and Jordi began heading that way, but Manny surprised them by heading to the far right side of the dining room. Before anyone had realized it Manny had walked over to Teddy's table and sat down opposite him. The only person more surprised than Pete and Jordi was Teddy himself. He immediately began looking anywhere except at Manny.

"Pete, Jordi," Mr. Dawson said, "have a seat, fellas."

Jordi and Pete sat down at the open table on the far side of the small dining room. All of the boys were silent and they were all staring, at least obliquely, at the table where Manny sat looking at Teddy and Teddy sat looking at his hands. Since the boys were supposed to come into the dining hall quietly and have a seat until staff directed someone to begin saying grace, none of the cottage workers noticed the obvious silence.

"Pete, would you lead us in grace, please." Pete was staring at Manny, wondering at his insanity.

"Pete?" Mr. Dawson said patiently.

"Huh? I mean, I'm sorry, sir?"

"Grace, if you will?"

"Oh, yes sir." Pete stood and faced the cross on the wall and led the prayer.

Afterward, as platters of food were passed out from a cart which had been rolled in from the kitchen, Pete and Jordi continued to steal glances at the table where Manny and Teddy were eating. They sat in silence, Manny looking out the window at the Admin building with his hands folded in his lap, and Teddy glancing occasionally at the twins, his palms flat on the table on either side of his place setting.

Eventually, a plate of sausage was passed to Manny. Pete saw him take two chunks of the red meat, then offer the platter to Teddy, who until then had still not looked back at him.

"Teddy," Manny said, "would you like some sausage?" Manny hadn't said it loudly, just conversationally, but his voice cut across everything and stopped half a dozen forks in mid air. This time, Pete saw, the staff noticed something, and Teddy was now staring with furrowed brow at Manny, who innocently was offering the white plastic sausage platter across the small table.

Pete saw Mr. Junn, who was sitting with Mr. Dawson, look up in mid-chew. The staff member cocked his head and finished his bite and swallowed. He cleared his throat and said, "Problem Teddy?" Teddy's eyes flicked from Manny to Junn to Manny and back again. "No sir." Then he let his eyes meet Manny's again. He reached out for the proffered platter and the whole dining hall heard him say, "Yeah, okay."

Then Pete saw Manny smile, *genuinely smile* at the guy responsible for the bruises covering his body and say, "No problem."

Teddy's acceptance of the sausage seemed to break some kind of spell, for breakfast proceeded almost normally. The meal became what most of Riordan home visit was about, a time of low pressure, to eat and talk and hang out with staff.

Thirty minutes later, when they had bussed their dishes onto the same cart on which the food had arrived, barely 10 sentences had passed between Pete and Jordi. And it had been mostly due to the fact that Manny and Teddy had been speaking. *To each other.*

Because of the noise of the dining room and the almost 20 feet between their tables, neither Pete nor Jordi had heard the conversation, but they had both watched it unfold. It had started out with the sausage business, but had not ended there. More things had been passed to their table: eggs, toast, hash browns, and separate carafes of orange and apple juice. As Manny finished serving himself from each thing he'd been passed, he would offer some to Teddy, who would either accept or decline the offering.

For Pete, it had been weird to watch, knowing that less than six hours ago the one doing the offering had been at the extraordinarily limited mercy of the recipient. Obviously it must have been strange for Teddy as well. At first, he'd responded to the offered items almost dumbly, semi-grunting his responses. But things had changed when Manny offered him the orange juice. Pete happened to be looking right at them when Manny held out the carafe, so he had seen and heard Teddy say, "No thanks."

Manny had simply shrugged and passed the OJ on to a different table, but the words had had an effect on Teddy. Pete saw him stop: just freeze for half a moment. Then he'd looked at Manny, his brow seeming to knit itself into a question mark. Then Manny had looked back at him, chuckled, and said, "What?" This seemed to have thrown Teddy even further off balance and he'd said something Pete had not caught from across the room. But whatever it had been caused Manny to laugh out loud, which in turn had caused another moment of pause among the boys, all of whom had been wondering some version of *What the Hell is going on here*?

When Pete had looked back at the two, he'd seen them both smiling, and talking in turns, *having a conversation*!

Now, a half hour later, Manny and Teddy had to be asked to hold up their chat so staff could give the schedule for the rest of the day.

Sunday Chapel would be at 10. As usual, mass would be open to the public and boys were expected to be in their church clothes and on their best behavior. The twins were told their mom had called and to be ready for a noon pick up. Teddy got word his ride would be arriving around 11:30. All of the St. Mike's kids would be gone before dinner, leaving only Manny, Jordi and Pete from this group. Tonight they would be moving a little farther up the hill to the other open cottage, St. Matthew's. By light's out, the number of boys on campus would be down from 18 to eight.

"For now," Mr. Junn said, "You'll all accompany staff back to your own cottages to get cleaned up for church. Anything you left or forgot at St. John's can be picked up afterward." Junn stepped back and Mr. Dawson, clad today in a grey sweatshirt with *HUMBOLT* across the front, stepped forward and said, "We need two volunteers to stay and help kitchen staff set up for lunch."

It was a regular request, and, as usual, there were a lot of boys interested in doing the work, not so much for the work itself, but for the change from routine. Seven of nine boys shot their hand up, all except Alexei and one of the St. Mike's kids. Mr. Dawson looked around the room and said, "Ok, how about Teddy and Manny." There were the usual groans of having been passed over while the boys stood to leave the dining room. As he walked out, Pete gave one last glance to Manny, who was already gathering up salt and pepper shakers. Manny spotted Pete's look, then nodded and smiled.

Pete and Jordi were already dressed in their chapel clothes and playing video games in the game room when Manny returned to St. Gabriel's. It was already 20 minutes to 10 when he limped through the cottage door. Mr. Dawson had changed from his college gear into a long sleeved blue button down shirt. He was sitting in the office between the T-hall and the game room with both adjoining doors open. He spotted the limp asked Manny about it. "Just pulled a muscle playing soccer yesterday." Dawson nodded and went back to the medical manual on the desk. Manny looked over Dawson's head and met Pete's eyes. He raised his eyebrows and smiled toward the back hall. Pete, who was in the middle of his turn, passed the controller to Jordi and said, "Finish this out for me."

Manny was sitting on his bed, just pulling on his sole pair of khakis when Pete got to the room. He looked up at Pete and smiled broadly.

"Pulled muscle?" Pete asked with a grin.

"Yeah, I know, pretty lame." He grimaced and added, "My right leg is killing me." He reached down and rubbed his thigh. "Teddy nailed me there a couple of times."

"And this morning you're clearing dishes with him?"

"I know, I know." Manny got up and grabbed a shirt from his wardrobe. "Life is pretty weird, huh?"

"Pretty weird?" Pete was desperate to understand what had happened.

"You know," Manny said as he pulled the shirt on, "Teddy's not a bad guy."

"What?!" Pete clapped a hand to his mouth. He hadn't intended to speak so loudly.

"Don't get me wrong," Manny said, "I think he has the moral compass of a hammer, but I don't think he's actually a bad person."

"He tried to beat you to death!"

"No," Manny waved dismissively. "He loaded up with batteries. Sure, they hurt like hell, but you know it as well as I do: if someone wants to put you out of commission, they go a lot heavier than that."

Pete had to concede the point, remembering Donny and the soda cans. But there was still an important point to be made, an important question needing an answer: "What did he do it for anyway? I mean did you do something to piss him off? Did you even know him before yesterday?"

Manny shook his head. "No. I didn't know him. And he didn't do this for himself. He did it for Steven." He sat down again and began putting on his dress shoes.

"Steven?" It was the obvious answer, but still made no sense to Pete. "I don't think they even know each other. Teddy just got here a couple of months ago. He and Steven have never even been in the same cottage. Why?"

Manny finished lacing the second shoe. "Teddy's in a gang back home in Daly City. Turns out one of his tightest brothers in this gang is a guy named Pepper Sengall. Pepper is Steven's cousin."

Pete felt his mouth drop open. *Cousins.*

"So," Manny continued, "Teddy was just doing right by his friend Pepper by doing a favor for his cousin." He chuckled. "I was just an errand in need of sorting out. Steve needed a message sent and Teddy made the delivery."

"But how do you know all of this?"

"Because Teddy told me." The simplicity with which Manny said this nearly drove Pete insane on the spot.

"He told you? He just *told* you? Why?"

And Manny explained. He'd sat down with Teddy because he'd already suspected the beating had been done on someone else's behalf. After a few moments of tension and the bit with the orange juice, Manny had asked him plainly if Steven had been behind it. Teddy, pointing out there was no way he could ever be caught for the incident, had admitted it freely. Manny had asked him why, telling him truthfully he just wanted understanding and that he wasn't planning revenge, which he thought was a complete waste of time. That's how he heard about Steven's cousin Pepper.

"He told me he respected the fact that I hadn't run to staff and that I had the balls to ask him about it man to man."

"He also told me Steven was a coward for not swinging the sock himself."

"What about the KGB? Why the hell were they there?" Pete asked. "Are they friends with Steven's cousin, too?"

"No. Teddy said they were just doing it to be helpful." He smiled as if this were amusing and not horrifying.

"But he made me promise not to try to get any of them into trouble over it. They were just taking care of something, nothing personal. He has a probation hearing tomorrow about which he is not overly optimistic. He wanted to avoid any negative news from Riordan this week as it might have an unwelcome effect on his chances of avoiding time. He told me anyone trying to screw him around would meet with an accident."

"So he threatened you?"

"Well yeah." Manny was looking in his mirror, running his fingers through his black mop. "But not specifically. And he was very nice about it all."

Jordi showed up a minute later, sent by Mr. Dawson to get them for mass.

On the way up to church, they walked through patches of sunlight beginning to break through the cloud cover. Pete saw other small groups making their way from the various cottages, all heading for convergence at the doors of Notre Dame Chapel.

On the trip up to church, there was no chance to tell Jordi what Manny had learned because it was only the three of them and Mr. Dawson. When a dozen guys were walking together, clandestine conversations were possible, but when the whole group was this small there was just no way to pass information without staff overhearing.

Chapter 10

By Thanksgiving morning, Pete and Manny had gotten comfortable. Pete still hadn't figured out a way to get up the hill and investigate what Tabitha might have left for him, but they'd had a good time none-the less.

After mass on Sunday Pete and Manny had moved their gear up the hill one cottage to St. Matthew's. Sunday's departures had left only eight boys on campus. Monday saw the exit of Jordi Melchior, and on Tuesday Nacho left for the remainder of the week. The final couple of Ms. Kelly's little St. Ant's kids had gone home on Tuesday night. By Wednesday the eight who had been around for dinner on Sunday night had been whittled down to four. Along with Pete and Manny there were two kids from Mt. Olivett.

Willie Preston was one of them. Pete knew him a little bit because they were both a part of Mr. Nielsen's science club. Willie was a talkative kid. A little weird, but overall friendly. He had this crazy thing for bugs. On more than one occasion, Pete had seen him pick up random creepy crawlers to play with. Last summer, while Mr. Nielsen had them all down in past the school looking for examples of different kinds of plants, Willie had come from around the corner of the barn with his hands cupped. Boys had crowded around to see what it was, then reacted by falling backwards to get away as quickly as possible. "Cowards," Willie had said, as the black widow he'd found in a woodpile rose from the well of his hands and walked over the tips of his fingers, gracefully picking its way from one to the next. Mr. Nielsen had managed to get Willie to let the spider go before it bit him.

The other boy was a quiet Laotian kid named Somkhit Lau. He was one of a growing number of Southeast Asian boys who had come to campus over the past couple of years. He had a cousin who was one of the few Fitzpatrick kids staying all the way through home visit. Manny knew Somkhit a little from working with him in the kitchen a few times. He didn't seem very interested in hanging out with Willie or any of them. Before getting picked up on Wednesday afternoon he hadn't said more than 20 words total.

Willie on the other hand loved talking to them. He kept asking how things were different in older cottages. Pete felt compelled to tell the poor kid the truth and say, "Not much." Wednesday's dinner was Willie's last Riordan meal of the home visit week.

As they finished dinner on Wednesday, the coordinator on duty, a thin, salt and pepper haired black man named Mr. Delano, came into the dining hall and told Manny and Pete they would be moving back to St. Gabriel's for the remainder of the home visit. The reasoning was simple enough: since both boys were both from St. Gabe's it made sense they should be in their own cottage as much as possible. After Mr. Delano had left, Mr. Johnson turned to Manny and Pete and asked candidly, "Don't you think they could have figured that out last week? It's not like you two being here over the break was a secret or anything. It's not like they didn't know about it." He chuckled mirthlessly and shook his head.

In his time at Riordan Pete had noticed a disconnect between the cottage staff and the people who worked in the Admin building. Sometimes the staff seemed to kind of forget there were boys around, and would talk openly about frustrations they had with the coordinators or the caseworkers. A lot of time they would talk when they thought the residents weren't paying attention. And a lot of time it happened just like this, only a couple of guys around and the staff member just needing to express what was going on at the moment.

Pete found this all especially weird because almost all of the coordinators and caseworkers had started out at Riordan in the cottages. It was a source of pride among the Admin folks that so many people had made Riordan their home over the years. The divide never made much sense to Pete, but it was real. As he'd heard more than one cottage staffer put it, the people in the Admin building just didn't understand how things in the cottages worked.

The normal routine at Riordan dictated boys went to chapel for morning prayers before breakfast on weekdays and Saturdays.

However, when the number of boys dropped below 20 things were different. Until Thursday, the only time the boys had been in the chapel had been for mass. Instead of going to the chapel for morning prayers, they had simply been doing them while facing the cross above the fireplace in the cottage.

On Thursday however, they would be going back to the chapel for a special Thanksgiving mass. The chapel at Riordan, along with being the geographical center of the campus, was also one of four Catholic churches serving the towns of Glen Ellen and Sonoma. Unlike the others though, Notre Dame Chapel was only a church. There was no church community, other than the residents and staff. There was no traditional parish. Because this was so, mass at Riordan attracted a specific breed of Catholic. The people who came to worship at the Home were people who believed in God and in their Catholic faith. That was all they were there for. There were no socials, no clubs, and no retreat groups. People who came to mass at Riordan were looking for a little time with God, all the other claptrap of organized faith be damned.

A medium sized triangular parking lot sat in front of the Notre Dame Chapel at the foot of the chapel lawn. The Admin building, its facade set at a right angle to that of the chapel formed a second boundary to the lot. The third side was provided by the Gihon Creek and its surrounding embankments, which were steep here at the base of the hill, built up by endless winters of rain surges focused by the gravity of the drop from the top of the mountain. The center of the lot was a large circular planter. Rough hewn rocks surrounded a 20 foot diameter green grass disc. Upon the gently sloping grass mound ornamental hedges had been planted long ago, cultivated and sculpted into a large Letter "R." In the spring the low shrubs sprouted flowers of dark blue, the color of Riordan.

As they walked with Mr. Johnson through the lot, Pete and Manny checked out the automotive population. There were about fifty cars, rides all belonging to locals who came to mass at Riordan weekly. The cars were a mix of vintages and values. Glen Ellen and Sonoma were economic dichotomies; though outwardly both appeared to be villages of wealth. And, indeed, there was plenty of money to be found in the wine, dairy and recreation businesses which made up the lifeblood of the area. That segment of the population was responsible for the Jaguars and BMWs in the lot.

However, for every well off vintner there were a dozen small farmers and ranchers struggling to keep their livelihood. For every Sonoma Mission Inn Resort and Spa there were a dozen small businesses annually staking their existence on the seasonal summer tourism. These accounted for the battered pick-up trucks and sprung station wagons taking up the other spots.

Moving from the growing brightness of the outside world into the dark of the church was always strange for Pete. He felt vaguely bat-like whenever entering the "holy cave" as Chris had once called it. The building was a mystery to Pete. From the outside, it appeared to be a relatively small structure. Looking at it from the campus, one could believe it might be taxed to seat all 100 boys and 75 members of the Riordan staff. Walking through the doors, Pete always imagined he could feel time and space bend, the way it did sometimes in science fiction movies. The interior, with its seating for 500 was simply larger than the exterior should allow. He imagined, were someone ever to check, the dimensions inside the church would measure larger than those outside.

Watching a full crowd exit the building always reminded him of the seemingly innumerable clowns pouring out of the little car he'd seen when his grandmother and mom had taken him to the Ringling Brothers show at the San Francisco Cow Palace. He'd been eight and it was the first time he'd ever been to the circus. Clowns had always been strange to him. He wasn't frightened of them exactly; he just never understood why some people liked them so much. The one birthday party clown he'd ever seen had smelled like a combination of hot sauce and Brut cologne. He remembered that "Bonko" had spent a lot of time talking to the birthday boy's mom who didn't seem to like clowns either.

Inside, the chapel was a simple box, with two rows of pews separated by a center aisle. On normal Sundays the first six rows were reserved for Riordan residents and staff, marked by blue placards set on the pew backs on either side of the aisle. The markers were all identical, each a foot high upper case letter "R."

Today, with most of the boys gone, markers were in place on only the first two aisles. As they walked quietly up toward the front rows, Pete saw there were about a hundred non-Riordan people scattered around the sanctuary. There were several individuals sitting alone, but there were also a number of families, some with young children. But there never were many teenagers. Among Riordan residents, the commonly accepted reason was parents didn't want their sons and daughters near the dodgy influence of the Riordan boys, even if God was also in the room.

A few minutes after Pete, Manny and Mr. Johnson sat down, the last of the residents arrived: three boys and one staff member from the Fitzpatrick House, the group home at the far end of Montecristo's field. The Fitzpatrick guys were a program unto themselves. While the six cottages had boys moving among them almost constantly, the same was not true of the group home. The group home residents cooked for themselves. They ate meals together in their house, not in the dining hall. They all attended or were transitioning to Sonoma High School. All of these things were great, but perhaps the single-most envied aspect of the Fitzpatrick boys' day to day existence was the fact that, unlike bedrooms in the cottages, bedrooms in the Fitzpatrick House all had doors.

A minute after the Fitz kids had taken their seats next to the St. Gabe's guys, a rounded, grey haired woman in a powder blue skirt and matching cardigan arose from the fourth row and made her slow way up to an upright piano set near the side of the altar. She sat down, adjusted her glasses and rested her hands lightly atop the keys. After a moment of preparatory meditation, she began to play a processional hymn.

The boys rose in their places and turned to their right slightly, to see at least part of the central aisle and catch a glimpse or Father O'Connell moving forward toward the altar. Standing there, between Manny and Mr. DeMarcus of Fitzpatrick house, Pete was listening but not paying attention to the music. He was letting his eyes wander over the crowd. He saw a lot of faces he recognized: they were the same faces he'd seen every Sunday since his first at Riordan. Some, he knew, had been coming for far longer.

He spotted a couple of off-shift Riordan staff members in the crowd. As it was with becoming a resident, Pete knew being Catholic was not a contingency of employment. But, because the Home was run under the auspices of the church, it worked out that most of the staff were practicing Catholics.

Father O'Connell was coming up the aisle, wearing red and gold vestments. He was flanked by two altar servers in white cassocks. The servers were both Fitzpatrick guys. Pete casually glanced back from the direction Father O had come. Movement of some sort had caught his eye. Looking, he saw the door swinging shut, while the two people coming in late were backlit by a narrowing bar of the day's strengthening sunshine. As Father came even with and passed the boys, all heads and bodies turned to follow him. But not Pete's. The backlit people had moved to the outer aisle on the far side of the church and taken seats about a third of the way back. Pete couldn't stop looking at them. Even though he'd been temporarily sun-stunned by the light coming in the door, something about the shorter of the two people seemed very familiar.

Pete heard a cursory cough and suddenly realized he was looking the wrong way. Mr. DeMarcus who had done the coughing indicated with a dart of his eyes that Pete should look front to where the big guy was about to get things started. Pete looked forward, squared his shoulders and took a deep breath.

Mass moved quickly. It usually did in winter months. The reason was that the building had a heater to make chill mornings a little more comfortable. Unfortunately, it did not have an air conditioner. In the summer time, when the temperature inside could reach 85 degrees, mass always seemed interminable. Someone had turned on the heater early this morning and warmed the place up just enough for comfort but not enough to induce a massive group nap. Father was at his usual witty, self-effacing best. Pete was always impressed at the way the man could command the attention of people just by being himself. And it was true that Father O'Connell seemed to be the same person all of the time. Unlike Weaver or some of the other cottage staff, the Father O you saw on the Sunday altar was guaranteed to be the same Father O you saw on Friday afternoon.

After the readings and the Gospel, Father stepped up to the altar to bless the gifts which had been brought forward by one of the local blue-hairs As Pete watched the priest hold aloft first the over-sized wafer then the cup of wine, he thought of his mom and of the last boyfriend she had before her death. He was a good guy; a truck driver named Mitch. He was always nice to Pete and seemed to make Lilly happy. One Sunday morning, as Lilly was pestering Pete to get ready for mass, Mitch had wandered into his room. He'd been wearing jeans and a white t-shirt, the tattoo of Wiley Coyote peeking out from beneath his left sleeve. Pete had loved that tattoo. Mitch had come in and leaned against the doorjamb, taken a sip of his coffee and scratched at the week of growth on his chin. "Do you like going to church, Pete?" he asked. Mitch had been raised as an Evangelical Christian, but had, as he often put it, "recovered nicely."

By this point Mitch had been around for the better part of a year. There were still six months to go before he got in his truck and drove away for good.

"I guess so," was how the 7 year old Pete had responded.

"One thing I always liked about the Catholics," Mitch said. "If you gotta sit through an hour of god-talk, you ought to at least get a little snack and a nip from a bottle to tide you over until stopping by the donut store on the way home."

Lilly had appeared behind him in the hallway and had slipped her arms around his waist. "You blaspheming again?" she asked playfully.

"Always. I got a lifetime of being good to make up for, don't I?"

"Well, stop it," she'd teased. "I want my boy to have a sense of God. Don't go jading him too early."

"Hey," Mitch had said, "you get them to start putting cheese whiz on those little crackers and I'll start kneeling myself." Even Lilly hadn't been able to stop herself from laughing out loud at this.

It was one of the memories that always caught Pete off guard. It made him want to smile and weep at the same time. It was his mother happy, as happy as he remembered ever seeing her. She had been in remission for 8 months and was still a year away from the discovery of her final group of tumors. Still almost two years from the final downward turn.

Pete remembered the look on her face when she'd hugged Mitch that day. She had been beautiful in her happiness. She had loved Mitch right until he left, probably even after.

A couple of non-resident members of the congregation had joined Father O on the altar. He gave each of them a crystal goblet full of the blessed wine. He took up a carved wooden bowl and headed to the front of the altar, a Eucharistic minister on either side of him. The congregation stood and the communion procession began.

Along with most of the Riordan staff in attendance, Pete headed out into the aisle. The few non-Catholics stayed in the pews. Among them was Manny, sitting quietly, seemingly staring at nothing, his eyes looking past the wine bearing Eucharistic minister, toward the back of the altar. Right after his arrival Manny had mentioned he wasn't Catholic, he'd been raised in a different Christian faith. Pete had told him he could still receive if he wanted to. Heck, there were a lot of non-Christian boys at Riordan who did. The staff seemed not to be concerned, and Pete had once heard Father O'Connell himself say any boy who wanted to could receive. Some did it just because most did it. But, Manny showed no interest in it at all, not even as a social activity.

Pete followed the Fitzpatrick boys in front of him and, when it was his turn, stepped up to Father O'Connell and received his communion. After putting the wafer in his mouth, Pete turned left and crossed in front of the row of pews and turned up the outside aisle to return to his seat. As he turned the corner, he had a view of the entire church. He looked around the room as he moved back toward his pew, and stopped in his tracks, wide-eyed and stunned.

Coming up the center of the church on the other side of the aisle were two women. The one in back was about 40 with short cropped dark hair. She wore slacks and a tan blazer over a white blouse. But it was the young woman in front who'd stopped him. She was a tall girl in jeans and a light blue sweater. Her dark hair was held back from her face by a simple silver clip. As he watched her, she gave a quick darting glance in his direction, and he was sure there was the hint of a smile there.

"Keep going, O'Boyle." The whisper came from behind him, and Mr. Johnson's words were like a shove to the back. He stumbled forward into the pew, but could not look down to find his footing. His eyes refused to be parted from what they had latched onto. He ran into Manny, accidentally kneeing him in the thigh as he walked back to his seat. The sound of Manny sucking pained breath through his teeth brought Pete out of his stupor. He looked down at Manny, who was trying to get rid of the grimace which had overtaken his face. Pete whispered an apology as he stepped passed Manny and quickly sat down.

As soon as his pants hit the wood of the pew he was looking right, into the aisle where she would any second come even with, and pass him. If he timed it right he might be able to catch her eye. He glanced quickly back and saw she was three pews behind and staring straight ahead. He guessed he had about five seconds until she pulled even, and began counting in his head. At *four* he looked up at the stained glass window on the other side of the church and she passed into his field of vision. She was facing straight ahead still, but she was looking at him, and as their eyes met another sweetly surreptitious grin played across her mouth.

And then she was past him, moving the final 10 feet up toward the altar and Father O'Connell and communion. "Ohhh," he heard Manny whisper from beside him. "Okay." He glanced at him and saw Manny was smiling knowingly and looking after Tabitha as she accepted communion and turned to make her way back to her own seat. Manny looked at Pete and murmured, "Now I understand." Pete couldn't help smiling back. Even when he looked past Manny and saw Mr. Johnson looking at him with a finger to his lips, Pete grinned a silent apology. It took all the will he had in him not to stand and look for her at the back of the building, but he managed to hold off the desire to do so.

Holy shit, he thought looking around. Remembering he was in a church nearly sent him over the edge; he had to stop himself from laughing out loud.

Chapter 11

As was customary, the Riordan boys remained in chapel until the public had cleared out. Normally, individual cottages were dismissed one at a time, but the small number of boys meant they would all be dismissed together. Pete was having difficulty staying seated. He began to wonder what they would give him for bolting right now. Five hours? Ten? *It would be worth it*, he thought, *just to get another chance to see that smile.*

After 3 interminable minutes, the staff released the boys. They all had ten minutes to be back at their respective cottages to change clothes for lunch and rec. Pete all but ran up the red carpet of the aisle, hearing a "Slow down, O'Boyle," from one of the staff. Walking quickly, leaving Manny behind, Pete emerged from the darkness of the chapel into the now bright daylight. He walked to the edge of the concrete walkway in front of the church and looked down across the grass at the parking lot, scanning for Tabitha. He didn't see her. *Damn. Damn. Damn!*

"Hey Pete, come on over here." The voice startled him. He looked over his shoulder to where Father O was standing, still in his red and gold vestments, beckoning. Pete felt himself actually gulp like a cartoon character, because standing near Father, next to what could only be her mother, was Tabitha.

Father O'Connell was still waving him over saying, "There's someone I'd like to introduce to you." By force of will he managed to get his feet to propel him in the priest's direction. He tried desperately not to look at Tabitha.

"Pete," Father O said as he arrived, "I'd like to introduce you to our next door neighbors. This is Evelyn Pembrook." The woman, who up close was clearly Tabitha's mother, extended her hand and gave Pete a surprisingly warm handshake.

"Very pleased to meet you, Pete."

"It's nice to meet you, too," he said lamely, just barely managing to keep his focus on the mother.

"And this," Father O said indicating the object of Pete's thoughts, "is her daughter Tabitha."

With as much control as he could muster, Pete slowly turned toward Tabitha, praying he could keep his face from splitting into a Cheshire grin. Tabitha at least looked as if she was having an easier time holding it together. She offered her hand, and he numbly accepted it. "It's very nice to meet you," she said. Pete nodded, almost forgetting to add the, "You too."

Her hand was cool, but soft, like she had just washed it in a stream. He didn't want to, but he forced himself to let go. It was heartbreaking to do it. Father O began talking again. "Pete here is one of our finest. He's a true example to other boys."

He was embarrassed by the praise, and looked away, not wanting to take the chance of meeting Tabitha's gaze.

"He is," Father O continued. "I think he might be perfect for what you're asking."

Pete looked up at the priest, "Sir?"

"Just a little community service, Pete. The Pembrooks own the vineyard next door, and they've contacted our Development Office about sponsoring some events next year." Pete still didn't understand why he had been called over and said so.

"Well, for example: each year their winery provides a large portion of the sponsorship for the golf tournament." Pete knew about the golf tournament. Everybody at Riordan did.

Though none of the boys were privy to the details, rumor was that the yearly Riordan Invitational Golf Tournament raised more money for the Home than all of the other charity events combined. Working the May tournament was a seriously sweet gig for those boys who were allowed to travel off campus for it. Pete had worked on campus last year, helping set up the gym for the big post tournament dinner and auction. The boys who were selected to work off campus jobs at the actual golf course all came from the Fitzpatrick House and St. Matt's, the oldest of the regular cottages.

"This year," Father O'Connell was saying, "Tabitha is interested in taking an active role in her parent's sponsorship." Pete didn't know what it meant, but it sounded a lot like Tabitha on campus which would suit him just fine.

"I have a community service requirement at school," Tabitha said. Pete looked at her and was a little surprised to see was talking directly to him. "For my religion class we have to do 30 hours of volunteer work in the community." Not wanting to get caught staring, Pete looked up at Father O'Connell and found the priest looking right back at him, his left eyebrow raised a fraction of an inch. Pete noticed the eyebrow and the barely concealed smirk and quickly darted his eyes toward Mrs. Pembrook, who was watching her daughter and smiling.

"Since I have the requirement, and my parents' business works so closely with Riordan," Tabitha was saying, "it makes sense I should be more involved here."

"We were very excited when Tabby came to us last week and asked us to contact you, Father," Mrs. Pembrook added.

"And we were pleased to hear of her interest as well."

This was all fine and good, especially if it meant Tabitha might be on campus occasionally. Maybe there was a way he could volunteer to help out. But he still didn't know what he was doing in this conversation.

"Which brings us to you, Pete," Father said. All three turned toward him now.

"Tabitha will be working with Ms. Muncie to coordinate some of the work the vineyard will be doing with us." Ms. Muncie was a caseworker, like Mr. Turnbull.

Father O continued, "Tabitha and her mother have requested one or two Riordan residents to act as representatives and help her and Ms. Muncie in their efforts."

Pete began to understand.

"They have asked for a couple of boys who are trustworthy and consistently reliable. Obviously, you are at the top of that list," the priest said.

"What will I...? I mean, what...?"

"You won't need to do anything for a while," Father said. "Tabitha has other commitments until after spring." Pete again looked at Tabitha, who nodded.

Ms. Pembrook said proudly, "She's helping with tutoring at the middle school."

Tabitha's eyes widened and rolled. Pete managed not to smile.

Father O put his hand on Pete's shoulder and said, "Ms. Muncie will let you know when we have a better idea what Tabitha's project will be. That is, of course, if you're interested in helping her."

"Are you interested, Pete?"

The question came from Tabitha herself. She was looking at him with almost no expression, save for a slightly raised eyebrow. He had to remind himself to breathe.

"Uh, sure."

Father O smiled broadly. "Excellent."

After a few more moments of chatting between the adults, Mrs. Pembrook stepped away to speak with another woman. Father waved back at one of the churchgoers and excused himself.

Suddenly and against all probability, Pete was standing with Tabitha in front of the chapel. They both looked around for a second before Tabitha said, "Cool." She smiled and kept her voice low, talking so only he could hear her. "I get to talk to you right here in front of God and everybody." She glanced to where her mother was already disengaging from the other conversation, and her smile faded. "Well, not for long I guess." She looked back to him. "Listen, I've left something for you. Up there."

"What is it?"

She smiled. "Find the right tree, find the prize."

"Tabby, we have to go." Mrs. Pembrook walked up. "Pleasure to meet you, Pete."

"Thanks. You too."

Tabitha simply said, "Bye." And they were gone. As he watched them walk across the parking lot Pete had a single thought: *Find the right tree...*

"Tonight?" Manny asked as they changed for lunch and rec. Pete had told him about the entire conversation during their unaccompanied walk from the chapel back to St. Gabe's.

"Tonight," Pete repeated simply. He knew it was stupid. How could he even contemplate doing it? But Tabitha had made it clear: there was already something waiting for him up there. Something she wanted him to have.

"When?"

"I'm not sure," Pete said truthfully. "I was thinking sometime after one would be best."

"What about Earl, or what ever his name is?" Manny asked, grabbing a grey hooded sweat shirt from inside his wardrobe. Pete shook his head, "Tonight it's Roy. Earl drives a Pontiac, Roy's an Oldsmobile man."

"Okay, Roy. Either way. Wasn't it you who told me the 'rent-a-cop' security guys just wander around campus at night, looking and listening for kids to be out and about?"

"Yeah, I did tell you that. So what?"

"So, since there are a grand total of what, seven of us in two cottages now, doesn't that mean he'll spend half the night here and half the night at Fitzpatrick?"

Now Pete smiled. "You'd think so. But on quiet nights Roy likes to find somewhere to cozy down for a nap. We've all seen him crashed out on a sofa at one time or another."

"Sounds shaky to me," Manny chuckled, "but hey, it's your party. So how are we going to get out?"

Pete stopped with his Riordan sweat shirt half on. "We?"

Manny gave a lopsided smile, "Well, yeah 'we.'"

Pete hadn't expected this. "You want to come with me?"

"Of course I do. You have to ask?"

Pete considered for a moment. "It's pretty risky," he said. "Even getting around Roy, we'll probably get caught. I mean, even if we get up there and find whatever she left, we're still probably gonna get caught. Being out at night is an automatic 15 / 30."

Manny grinned again and nodded.

Pete looked intently at Manny. Something he had noticed before he saw again: there was no deceit in those dark eyes, no mocking of his unspoken hopes and fantasies regarding Tabitha, no matter how ridiculous Pete himself knew them to be.

He asked the question then, thought suspected he already knew the answer. "Why would you risk..."

"Because," Manny said. "That's what friends do."

"Friends?" The word sounded strange to Pete, saying it felt like worms on his tongue.

"Yeah," Manny said, "In case you hadn't noticed, I'm you're friend."

Lunch was in the staff dining room. There were already a surprising number of people there when they arrived. About half of the cottage staffers from all over campus were milling around the room, sitting in chairs, or making their way through the buffet line.

When he asked Mr. Johnson about it, the St. Gabriel's supervisor said today was an optional "cottage work day." People could take the day off easily enough if they wanted or needed to. Or they could come in, have a good meal, and then play in a miniature golf tournament at Mission Mini-Golf down Highway 12, all for time and a half their normal pay rate.

As he'd noticed before, the staffers were completely different people when there were only a couple of boys around. The same stern and sometimes unyielding people of a week ago sat about joking with each other and with him and Manny. This was a facet of Riordan he'd never experienced before. Sure, he'd been around a little over summer time, but, except for the first couple of weeks in July when the campus was almost completely deserted, there were still six or seven guys in every cottage; the staff was still outnumbered, and seemed to feel the need to always have their game faces on.

Pete was having a great time. He couldn't believe he'd gotten upset when Mr. Turnbull had told him his aunt wouldn't be coming to get him for the holiday. His anger seemed almost laughable. Sure, there had been the thing with Manny, but even the blanket party seemed to have had an okay outcome (at least as okay as a beating can have). They knew Steven had been responsible, and Manny had even earned the respect of his attacker. If you've got to be stuck in a place like Riordan, it's not a bad thing to have the respect of someone like Teddy.

After they were finished eating, the Coordinator, Mr. Delano came over and told the boys their ride would be showing up in a few minutes. Manny said they didn't even know they were going on a trip. The Coordinator just smiled and walked away.

About 20 minutes later, Mr. Nielsen showed up from out of nowhere. Manny and Pete were sitting together facing the door. A hand clapped down on each of their shoulders causing them both to jump. Looking up, they found Mr. Nielsen standing there and grinning. Pete liked Mr. Nielsen's smile. There was something genuine about the way his bottom teeth were out of alignment from one another. Mr. Nielsen himself joked about having "a European smile."

He was wearing his customary leather bomber jacket over long sleeved checkered shirt, but without a tie today. His wide brimmed waxed leather rain hat was hanging behind him, the drawstring chin thong pressed against his Adams apple.

"Hello, boys!" he said. "You guys got any plans for the next couple of hours?"

"Not that we know of," Pete said. "But Mr. Delano told us to wait for a ride from somebody."

"Ah, the ride. Yes." He smiled broadly again, "That would be me."

"What about rec," Manny asked.

"For today, good sir, I am rec."

"Where are we going?" Pete asked.

"That, Mr. O'Boyle, is for me to know and you to find out." He had them grab their coats and follow him to the parking lot where his 10 year old mini van sat waiting. "Hop in, gentlemen, today's road waits for us."

Today's road turned out to be the stretch of California State Highway 12 running between Sonoma and Santa Rosa, the largest city in Sonoma County. Pete was sitting in the middle row of the van, having let Manny take the front seat. He knew Manny also liked to talk to Mr. Nielsen, and had decided to sit back and just enjoy the ride. And this was a ride Pete liked.

Highway 12 ran the length of the Valley of the Moon, meandering through acres of merlot, chardonnay and cabernet vines. In the late summer, the vines had been heavy with grapes and leaves. The valley looked very different in late November. The sun had completely burned off the fog and mists of the early morning, revealing the valley's winter look. Pete knew a lot people liked the look for the vineyards in the spring and summer, and the bumpy green rows lining the hills. But he liked it now, with its summer coat of leaves and fruit removed. He liked looking at the stark, gnarled twisted bones of the vineyards. They looked dead, so much so that it was difficult to believe they could ever sprout another leaf again, much less produce another million gallons of wine next year. But he preferred to see the vineyards like this. Somehow, it felt more honest to him.

As they drove on Pete watched the fall-dry vines roll past and listened with half an ear to the conversation from the front seat. Mr. Nielsen was explaining the wine making process to Manny. It was an example of what Mr. Nielsen called "practical science," and a lesson Pete had heard before. He let his eyes bounce over the uncountable rows of the vineyards and mind bounce back to what Manny had said in the cottage.

Since coming to the Riordan Home, Pete hadn't called anyone friend. It was a word he didn't have much use for. He was friendly with Chris, Jordi and Frankie, but there was a difference between friendly and friends.

"I'm your friend," Manny had said. And Pete knew it was true; knew it as well as he'd ever known anything. Manny was his friend, and he had a feeling that with Manny, friendship given stayed given. There was a loyalty about him that had taken Pete a while to identify, probably because he hadn't had much occasion to consider loyalty at the Home.

Twenty-five minutes after rolling off of the Riordan grounds, they found themselves in line at the new Santa Rosa Cinema Multiplex. Halfway there Mr. Nielsen had told them they would be seeing a film, but he didn't tell them which film until he had bought the tickets. Though it had come out over the summer neither boy had seen it. Mr. Nielsen had already seen it once but had been looking for a reason to see it again. His wife thought he was a huge geek for wanting to see a movie about dinosaurs a second time. He just laughed and bought a jumbo bucket of popcorn and three sodas.

"Don't worry about it," he said when Pete expressed concern over the cost of the tickets and the snacks. "The movie is my treat, but the popcorn and soda are compliments of Father O."

Coming out of the movie, Pete and Manny couldn't get over how real the dinosaurs had been. "That was awesome!" Pete said. Manny, though not as ebullient, added, "Yeah, I've never seen anything like that before."

Mr. Nielsen said, "No one has. I read an article about the production of the film. Apparently, a lot of the technology used to make the beasts look realistic was actually invented for this movie. From what I read, dozens of groundbreaking computer programs were written to make the creatures as believable as possible."

"Thank you, Mr. Nielsen," Manny said. "We appreciate you bringing us."

"My pleasure, gentleman. My pleasure. Now, let's get you back to Riordan and the awaiting feast."

Thanksgiving dinner at the Fitzpatrick house was awesome. The dinner had been cooked by the boys with help from the staff. There was turkey, dressing, mashed potatoes made from scratch, sweet corn, olives and rolls. Though there were only seven boys left on campus, there were well more than a dozen people at dinner. There were a couple of cottage staffers Pete knew from around, and a few Admin folks, including the on duty coordinator and the Home's psychologist, Dr. Rugani.

Pete thought Dr. Rugani was okay, but a lot of the boys at the Home didn't. The general consensus held him to be weird because he liked people to talk about how they felt.

Father O'Connell showed up after dinner, just in time for Mr. DeMarcus' fantastic apple pie. Father apologized for missing dinner, but explained he'd received an invitation from some retired priests living in the area. One of them was a monsignor who had been the pastor at Father O's first posting twenty-five years before.

After pie, boys and staff drank coffee and hot chocolate, with Father opting for tea. There were ping pong games and a small pool tournament. At some point Manny found a chess set on a shelf in the game room. He and Mr. DeMarcus spent 30 minutes gripped in combat before Manny slipped and left his queen exposed.

By the time they returned to St Gabe's for bed, Pete was tired and stuffed and felt filled up in a way he didn't understand. It had been an almost perfect day. As he readied for bed he withdrew his watch from the top drawer of his wardrobe and hoped for a good night.

Chapter 12

Pete clamped his hand down on his wrist watch after only three beeps. He'd gone to sleep telling himself to get the alarm quickly. As a result he'd slept lightly, waking up several times in the three hours since he'd drifted off sometime after 9:30. He sat up in bed and tried to shake the grogginess away. Manny was a mass of blankets with feet and hands sticking out.

Pete waited for a few minutes, to see if Mr. Johnson appeared in the doorway, checking out the noise from his alarm. He looked down at the watch.

It had been a Christmas present from Aunt Marjorie last year. It had the ability to display the time in three different time zones, a stopwatch and a calendar. It was also bright green plastic with cartoon turtles on the band, solidifying for Pete the certainty that his aunt still believed him to be nine years old. Its hideousness, along the presence of clocks in every room at Riordan relegated the watch to Pete's underwear drawer most of the time. He usually only wore it when he went out on walks and the staff gave him a time limit.

Ugly or not, the watch did have one extremely useful feature: the alarm had a volume function allowing him to set it low enough to wake him but not be heard by the cottage in general.

He swung his legs out of bed and checked the watch again. It had been three minutes since the alarm had gone off, and there was no sign of Mr. Johnson. Smiling, he stood up and started to pull on his jeans.

Twenty minutes later, Pete and Manny were walking wordlessly up the property line between the Riordan Home and the Pembrook estate. When he decided to head up the hill, Pete knew taking the road would be impossible. There was just too much chance of being seen by Roy, the night security guy, or by one of the many cottage staff who lived on campus. However, all along this side of the campus, trees and bushes marked the boundry between cottages and the geometric rows of the vineyard. These were old black oaks, three feet across at the base with waist high shrubs between.

There were more shrubs on the vineyard side of the small fence, and Pete knew that behind the trees and two rows of bushes they could be invisible. But it would mean crossing the fence, and risking 25/60. He just couldn't bring himself to do it. Besides, safely staying on campus beneath the trees and with the moon hiding behind the high clouds, there was little chance of being seen by anyone.

They had each tripped over a couple of roots, but otherwise their trip had been smooth. After the few minutes it took to wake up Manny and get him moving, leaving the cottage had been simple. Since the Riordan Home for Boys wasn't a "locked facility," there were no real bars to exiting the building. Sure, once a boy was outside, getting back in was a problem, given the doors were locked and the windows, though only waist high in the rooms, were almost five feet above the ground outside. But Pete knew there was a 10 foot ladder hanging on the wall of the garden area on the west side of the cottage. One of them could use it to get back into the room, and then the other could return the ladder and be helped into the room by the first.

As they walked through the clouds of their own frozen breath, the campus to their right began to climb away from them, the curve of the foothills rising beneath the cottages while leaving their path at the hill's base. Moving up the gentle slope of the valley, they passed first St. John's cottage then St. Matthew's, both completely dark. As the hill continued to slope and they continued to walk, they went by St. Mike's. A single light burned in a window at the back of the building. Because all of the cottages followed the same configuration, they knew the lit window belonged to a staff bedroom. However, the blinds were drawn and the lighted window was 40 yards away.

Still on plane with the expansive vineyard field on their left, they continued up. After about five minutes of careful walking, the trees lining the edge of campus began to thin, leaving more and more uncovered space between them, and the ground, which had so far been gently rising beneath their feet began to slope dramatically upward. The field of vines on their left, with its countless rows of gnarled, dormant roots, suddenly disappeared along with the trees, giving way to the tall grasses that covered this part of the Pembrook property. And they found themselves walking out in the open along the fence. They passed behind and beneath Mt. Olivett, the last of the cottages. It sat above them on the campus hill, all of its windows dark and lifeless.

And then they were approaching another tree, this one on the vineyard side of the fence, and Pete recognized it with surprise and pleasure. It was the tree where Christabel had been tethered on the day he met Tabitha. He stopped for a moment. Manny sat down against the low fence and massaged his legs.

"How're you doing," Pete asked quietly. It was the first either of them had spoken since leaving the cottage. They were out of sight of any buildings now, so Pete figured a little whispering was probably safe.

Manny nodded in the dark, "Not too bad. Legs are still sore, but they're getting better. The bruises don't hurt anymore, but the muscles still get to aching something fierce."

Pete checked his watch, pushing the button on the side to light up the digital display. It was already almost a quarter of two. It had taken longer to get up here than he'd planned. He knew every extra minute spent out of the cottage made discovery that much more likely. But there was nothing to be done for it now. He'd come out in the middle of the night and was determine to find whatever it was Tabitha had left for him.

Still, there was no reason to stop any longer than they had to. "You ready," he asked Manny?

Manny stood up and shook out is legs. "Good to go."

And, carefully making their way in the dark, they headed up the hill and into the trees.

Their eyes had adjusted well to the dark of the night. But the little illumination offered by the cloud-filtered moon light and the ambient glow from the town below was all but cut out by the high canopy formed by the branches of the big Garry oaks. Once they had stepped into the enfolding darkness, Manny sighed. "Listen Pete," he said. "I don't mean to rain on your parade here, but how are we going to find this tree she's talking about."

In the dark and cold, Pete smiled. He looked east to confirm what he already knew; they were out of sight of the entire Riordan campus now. He rustled around in his pocket for a moment and then said, "Like this."

A burst of blue flashed in his hand and pinned an azure spotlight on the ground between them.

Manny let out a small laugh. "Well done, young Jedi."

Pete smiled again, this time in the blue glow of Chris' mini light. Before waking Manny he'd borrowed it from Jordi's top drawer. "Let's start looking."

It took them nearly 15 minutes to locate the tree, and when they did, it was only after passing it several times. Assuming whatever she'd left would be on the ground at the base of a tree, they wandered the oaks with their heads down, until Manny stopped and took hold of Pete's arm. "Wait," he said. "Point it up there."

Pete let his arm be guided up to chest height, so the beam was pointing at a serious looking oak, four feet across at the base. And hanging on the tree, suspended as if by magic was something plaid. As they walked closer to it they saw it was a shirt. Manny reached out and picked it off the tree. There was a nail driven into the tree. A small headed nail, with a slight indentation in the top. "A finishing nail," Manny was saying, but Pete barely heard. He was staring at the shirt. It looked purple in the sharp blue of the flash light, but Pete remembered what it had looked like in the sun, red over stretched white cotton.

"This is her shirt," he said, reaching out to touch it.

Manny grabbed his hand again and pointed the light up into the tree, directly above them. "Then I'm thinking that might be for you as well."

Pete let his eyes follow upward. At first he didn't see anything except for the shadows of the canopy and the patches of blackened sky peeking through.

Then, just as he was about to ask Manny what he was looking for, he saw it: a dark irregular lump against the trunk of the tree, some 20 feet up.

"What the hell is it?" Pete asked.

"Don't know," Manny replied. "But it's definitely not tree. I think it's some sort of sack. I suppose we'll find out soon enough. Assuming, of course, we can answer the more immediate question: how do we get it down?"

After a while of looking about they finally figured out the mechanism of the item's elevation. A thin rope was looped over the thick branch just above the sack, or whatever it was. The chord was dark in color and its path difficult to follow through the shadows and darkness. Eventually, they traced it to another tree nearby, where it had been tied off to a branch a dozen feet above ground. Dangling from the knot was a short length of the rope, dropping to about nine feet. They each tried several times to jump and grab it, but it was too high.

Finally Manny had Pete bend down and he clambered onto the taller boy's shoulders. With Pete wavering on his toes, Manny was just able to reach up and grab hold of the twine and yank as Pete began to stagger. The knot on the tree gave way and Manny let go as Pete fell beneath him. They collapsed in a heap on the hard, cold ground a split second before the sack met the earth 15 feet away.

Getting up stiffly, they shambled toward the fallen treasure. Manny, who'd hit the ground pretty hard, massaged his shoulder and said, "Hope she didn't leave you anything fragile."

Pete laughed and squatted down for the bundle.

Pete was excited as they gathered the contents of the sack up in preparation for the trip back to the cottage, but his exuberance was tinged at the edges by a growing fatigue. He checked his watch and was shocked to find it was almost three o'clock. *Damn!* He told Manny they needed to get a move on.

They were both tired, their legs rubbery from being up too late and the hike up the hill in the cold, but they were still moving fairly quickly down to the cottage. They were moving in the space between St. Matt's and St. John's when the Admin building came into view, and Pete stopped in his tracks. There was a sheriff's cruiser parked in the lot. A deputy was standing in front of the car, looking up onto the Admin porch where Roy, the rotund night security guy stood. *We're caught; they've noticed we're gone. Shit!*

"I think we're kind of dead," he told Manny.

Manny was watching them too, and shook his head. "No, we're okay. Look, the car's still running, but they always do that. No, if Roy knew we were gone and had called the cops, we'd be seeing a light show, and we're not."

Pete realized Manny was right. The light bar atop the cruiser was dark, and there was no coordinator or Mr. Johnson: just Roy and the deputy. Then Roy said something and the deputy burst out laughing. Not what you see when two runaways have been reported. Still though, best not to waste any more time. The continued their course behind St. John's.

When the Admin building emerged again from behind the cottage, things had changed. The deputy was now standing at the open door of the cruiser, a foot already on the running board. Roy was off the porch, still talking to the cop from over the roof of the idling car, but clearly heading away from the building, moving as he talked, toward the ancient land yacht he drove around campus on cold nights. When he got to the car he was either going to head around the chapel toward the Fitzpatrick House, or he was going to drive the 100 short yards down to St. Gabriel's.

We've been too lucky, Pete thought, and quickened his pace. Manny, despite the obvious pain, followed suit. St. Gabe's was close now, just 50 yards away. They had to grab the ladder from the near side of the cottage then get into the room as quickly as possible.

Just before he lost sight of them behind the cottage, Pete saw the deputy and Roy exchange waves and the deputy slide into his car. As soon as he was sure they were blocked by the cottage, Pete broke into a trot, moving toward the ladder. He grabbed it off its pegs and moved around the corner to the back of the building as quickly as he could. He stopped as the sheriff's cruiser cleared the far end of the cottage and turned away from them, down the campus road toward the Sonoma Highway. Any moment the brake lights would blaze because the deputy had just looked in his rearview mirror and spotted two darkly clad figures silhouetted against the white back wall of the cottage, one of them holding a ladder and the other holding a bag.

But the brake lights didn't flare, and as the cruiser took the gentle bend to the right at the end of the Riordan driveway, Pete and Manny began moving with purpose again. Pete propped the ladder against the window and Manny scrambled up and in with the sack. Pete moved quickly to put the ladder back and had just replaced it on the pegs when he heard the mighty engine of Roy's aged Oldsmobile rumble to life.

OH CRAP! He bolted around back again and actually ran past his own window in his panic, but stopped and went back before he'd gotten past the next room. Manny was at the window with his arm dangling out. Pete reached up and grabbed the sill as Manny leaned out and grabbed at his sweatshirt, trying to help as Pete struggled to get up the wall. For a moment, Pete felt his grip slipping and he was sure he was going to fall and pull Manny out of the window with him. But Manny kept hold of him, pulling him up. Pete desperately tried to get his foot up and hook his heal over the sill.

As he finally did so, Manny's grasp slid from his sweatshirt to his belt, and Pete was hauled into the room, collapsing with Manny onto the floor next to his bed. As they both scrambled to their feet, they heard the rumble of Roy's engine come at them through the cottage, reverberating through the front door, down the T-hall and into their panic. As they tore off their clothes they heard the more ominous silence as the engine was cut off. Pete stowed the sack in his laundry basket under his dirty clothes, and heard the cottage's front door open and close as he moved back across the room.

He barely remembered to close the window before sliding into the ice cold sheets of his bed. He turned over, away from the door and had only just closed his eyes when he heard first the heavy breathing then the heavy footsteps of the security man. There was a brief flare of light as Roy pointed his big Maglite at the ceiling to get a visual on both boys. Then the light went out.

Chapter 13

Friday morning was a drag and a half for Pete and Manny, but the oddity of the schedule helped them out. Even though boys didn't need to be back until two o'clock on Sunday after Thanksgiving, they always began arriving on Friday morning. Because the staff knew that boys would be drifting in all day, there were relatively few things scheduled. So after morning prayers and breakfast in the staff dining room with a dozen staff members, they were allowed free time at the cottage until ten forty-five. As a result of the flexible schedule of the day both boys were passed out in their beds 15 minutes after returning to the cottage.

The slam of the cottage door woke Pete at ten o'clock. Moments after the heavy door rattled the casing he heard the voice of Michael Hamm squealing at Mr. Weaver: "I can't believe I'm back here already! This ain't fair! I didn't do anything! I wasn't even there! And arrest me? What's that about? Freaking set-up's what it was!"

Pete heard, but couldn't make out the muted response from Weaver. *Pretty impressive*, Pete thought. *If I was Weaver I'd yell right back at him.* Whatever Weaver said did not have its intended effect.

"You don't know what you're talking about. Were you there?! Did you see? I don't *think* so!

Another murmur from Weaver.

"Calm down!?" the Rat was almost screaming. Manny's blankets were off his face now and he was listening too, eyes on the ceiling. "Tell me to calm down!? Who the hell are you, my father?!"

There was a pause, during which Weaver mumbled something. Whatever he said was punctuated by the Rat exploding.

"F--- YOU!"

Manny sat up, stared at Pete and whispered, "What did Weaver say?"

Pete, staring at the door with eyebrows up just shook his head.

"You can't freaking talk to me like that! I'll tell Father O on your ass. He'll fire your ass for that. You think I can't, watch me?!"

Now they heard Weaver's voice clearly for the first time. There was laughter laced in as he said, "*Fire* me? Pretty funny Mikey, coming from you."

There was a pause, a silence in which Pete could almost hear Mikey Hamm's mind working to figure out what had just been said. Then he did. *Pop.*

"You're a God Damn bastard!"

Now Weaver was chuckling loudly, "Hey, you're the one who used the word *fire*. It's not my fault if you don't understand irony." Then there was a change in tone from the staffer. "Now," serious Weaver said, "I think we're done here. You want to keep jawing at me, you can just sit yourself in a red chair for the next hour, or until I decide to let you up." There was no response. "Fine then," Weaver said. "Go dump your backpack in your room and come back up here. You've got five minutes."

They heard Mikey come down the T-hall and turn away, toward his room and the other end of the hall. A minute later they heard Weaver call them forward, telling them they had twenty minutes to get ready for rec.

They headed up toward the front of the cottage a few minutes later. As they reached the T-hall junction, the Rat came out of his room, his eyes on something in his hands. He glanced up when he sensed them, a surprised look on his face. Pete noticed his hands had clenched around whatever was in them.

"Hey Mikey," Pete said.

The Rat paused a step and gave Pete a half nod as he slid his still clenched hands into the pockets of his zipped up hooded sweat shirt. He'd gotten his hair buzzed while he'd been home. Beneath his quarter inch hair, his narrow face was a blank page mounted in a book of anger.

"Hello Michael," Manny said from half a step behind Pete.

The Rat flipped up his chin in acknowledgement as his eyes slid to Manny. Then Pete saw him freeze. As he stopped moving his look hardened, his eyes locking onto something past Pete's shoulder. The whisper was deadly. "What you looking at, freak?"

Pete followed Mikey's eyes to Manny's face, which, inexplicably, was a mask of concern. Pete knew what Manny was about to say and could come up with no way to block it.

"Are you all right, Michael?" Manny asked, his raised and furrowed brow expressing a deep concern.

Oh no, not again. Manny was letting the Rat know they had heard at least part of his conversation with Weaver.

Pete looked quickly back to the Rat, and what he saw was not good. The shorter boy had his hands back out of his pockets again, and his fingertips were rubbing against the heels of his hands. His thin face was taught, his close-set eyes bulged and his chinless mouth hung open in a feral grimace.

"What the f--- are you talking about?" he asked in his weasel voice. "What the f--- do you know about me?" as he said this last he began moving forward.

Manny stepped forward too, even now with Pete. "I don't know anything about you," Manny said. "But you look upset, like something's bothering you."

Mikey had been surprised by the other boy stepping forward and faltered for a second, his eyes searching all over Manny's face, looking, Pete thought, for something to bite off when he lunged.

"I'm not trying to mess you around, Michael," Manny said, his own hands by his sides, palms turned toward the Rat. "I'm just wondering if there's anything I can do to help?"

Pete was sure that if the Rat had possessed shoulders to speak of, he would have slumped them at this point. What Mikey did do was close his mouth and narrow his eyes. Pete risked another glance at Manny. As usual, his roommate was all honest eyes and friendly concern, his hands out of his pockets, palms forward. He looked, Pete thought, like a police negotiator approaching the hostage taker in some television show: *See, I'm unarmed and coming in alone. No one here wants to hurt you.*

Pete saw Mikey slide his hands slowly back into his pockets, watched them through the fabric as they seemed to each close over something. Then the Rat let out a long breath and looked away, down at the floor.

"Just leave me the hell alone," he said, brushing past them and scurrying up the length of the T-hall toward the front of the cottage.

"Damn," Pete let out a breath. "I wish you wouldn't do that kind of crap."

But Manny didn't seem to be listening; he was staring up the hall after the Rat.

"Manny?"

Without turning around, Manny asked, "Did you see his neck?"

The question caught Pete completely off guard. "His neck? What about it?" Pete hadn't noticed anything about Mikey's neck. He'd been too busy worrying about Manny's.

"You could barely see it with his sweat shirt zipped all the way up," Manny said, looking around now at Pete. "Looks like a nasty bruise, like maybe someone grabbed him around the neck." Then Manny turned away again to stare down the hall. He mumbled something to himself, but Pete was pretty sure he made it out: "Poor kid."

Mikey wasn't the only early returnee. When they got to the Admin building to meet the rec staff, there were five others who had come back early. They went to the rec hall for an hour before lunch. Pete and Manny played pool. But Pete kept checking out the Rat. He was careful not to get caught staring, but he wanted to see of he could get a glimpse of what Manny had been talking about.

Sure enough, when Mr. Talan gathered them up to go to lunch, Mikey Hamm subconsciously reach up and scratch his neck just below the collar line. When he did, Pete saw the green and blue band wrapping over the top of his right collarbone.

After lunch, Pete tried to call Tabitha from the rec hall, but got her answering machine again. He left a one word message, hoping she would understand how completely he meant it: "Thanks."

On Saturday at breakfast, Manny told Pete he was going to try again with Mikey, see if he could help him. Pete simply shrugged. "Try if you want, but I'm going to pass." Manny said he understood. At rec, while Manny played video games with the Rat, Pete curled up on a couch in the rec hall to read the new Richard Bachman book Tabitha had included in her clandestine care package.

The other things she'd left (candy, a letter and pictures) were stashed in his bottom drawer. The candy was nice. She'd somehow guessed he loved Milky Ways, because she includes two of the giant sized ones, along with a couple of one pound assortment bags. The letter was terrific. It was beautiful in its simplicity. She told him plainly in the letter that she liked him, and wished she could see him more often. In it she asked him to call as often as he was able.

The letter was definitely the best part of the package she'd left, but the pictures were a close second. There were four of them. One was of Cristabel tethered to same tree she'd been tied to when Pete had first heard her snort. Two were vacation shots, Tabitha standing in front of the Golden Gate Bridge and Tabitha looking out over the Grand Canyon. The last was the goofiest and the best of them. It was Tabitha smiling her huge, beautiful smile, with laughter in her eyes. The shot included most of her arm, so it was easy to tell she had taken it herself. The picture had been taken outside. Pete guessed that she must have been standing near her house, because Tabitha was framed in the shot by the oak grove above Mt. Olivett and the Riordan water tower, both visible in the background. He'd gotten into the habit of looking at the picture every night before going to bed.

From time to time as he read during rec, Pete would look up and check to see if Manny was making any progress talking to Mikey. At first the boys just played the game, looking at the television depictions of their rival football teams. After a while, Pete noticed that as they played they were also talking, just a bit at first, still watching their game. An hour later Pete had looked up to find the boys still holding the game controllers but ignoring the paused game on the television. They had been looking at each other, and Mikey had been talking while Manny sat there, occasionally asking a question or offering something, doing just enough so it qualified as a conversation and not just Mikey talking to himself. Pete had to admire Manny's determination. Yesterday, the Rat had told him to piss off but today he'd seemingly gotten the kid to tell him his life story.

"No, not his whole life story," Manny had said seriously, as they got ready for bed on Saturday evening. The cottage was relatively quiet still, with a small compliment of only five boys. "But he told me enough. Besides, I already know a lot of his story from when I first got here."

Pete remembered Manny expressing sympathy for Mikey during his first week, and how he had tried to convince Manny the kid was simply no good.

"The main reason he got sent back early was because there was a fire."

Manny went on to explain: the Rat had been arrested for setting a fire in the yard of a vacant house down the street from his mom's place. He'd been gone from his house for about an hour when he came quickly in the door and headed for his room. His mom had gotten worried when she'd heard the sirens a few minutes later, and when the cops arrived an hour later, she'd apparently let them in and pointed up to his bedroom. The fire had been on Wednesday afternoon. Mikey had spent Thanksgiving in the Napa County Juvenile Hall before being brought back by his step-father on Friday morning.

This wasn't the first time the name Mikey Hamm had been associated with fire. There had been rumors circulating since his arrival at Riordan. He always seemed to be hiding something on him. Whenever he came back from home visit he invariably smelled of cigarette smoke or fuel. Jordi said the Rat *always* had contraband. Sometimes staff found it and took it and sometimes they didn't. When he'd roomed with Mikey previously, Jordi had found all manner of flammables stashed in their room: matches, lighters, hairspray, cigarettes, even rubbing alcohol.

And the staff definitely knew something about it as well. Even before Weaver had made his fire and irony comments on Friday morning, Frankie Baltazar had heard staff talk about Mikey as a fire kid. When they had all been in St. Michael's cottage together, Frankie had overheard a couple of staff member talking about boys. They had been at the skating rink on an off campus trip and Frankie had been behind Mr. Banks and Weaver in line for the snack bar when he'd heard Banks refer to Mikey Hamm as a "God Damned firebug." Frankie had also heard Banks say he'd found lighters and matches in the Rat's suitcase when he had come back from the previous home visit.

The Rat had told Manny he'd been released because the police didn't have an eye witness linking him to the fire. Manny also suspected it had something to do with Riordan. If the cops let him go back the Riordan, they'd be able to find him when and if they needed him.

Manny also suspected Michael Hamm's step-father as having been the one who supplied the bruising. "He didn't say it was him," Manny told Pete, but it was pretty clear his step-dad is not a real nice guy."

Pete listened to all of this shaking his head. When Manny finally stopped, he gave voice to his thoughts. "I don't know how you do it."

Manny, who'd been sorting through his book drawer, stopped and looked up at Pete. "What do you mean?"

"Well, it's like what happened with Teddy," Pete tried to explain. "He'd already laid a beating on you, but you go and get him to explain why he did it."

Manny shook his head, "So what?" He seemed irritated, and Pete couldn't figure out why. He tried to clarify.

"It's just… you don't see a lot of guys sitting down to breakfast with the person who laid a beating on them the night before."

Now Manny just stared at him for a long time. His lips kept pursing and relaxing, back and forth, like he was trying to exercise his mouth. Pete had meant it as a compliment, but Manny's responses were causing him to lose his footing. After almost a minute of silence, Pete asked what was wrong.

Manny slowly shook his head. "Nothing," he sighed. "Never mind."

"Okay," Pete said. But he was confused. Manny was acting more distant than he had ever seen him.

After another minute, Manny said, "Listen Pete, I was right in the middle of telling you something about Michael. Can I finish it now?"

Pete was stung by the way he asked. It was almost cold and it stung. He said, "Right. Sorry." But he felt annoyed. He was trying to explain how cool he thought Manny's ability with people was, but all Manny wanted to do was talk about the Rat. Manny had called him friend, but all he seemed to want to talk about was the twerp of a firebug.

Manny looked at him for another few seconds before shaking his head again. "I think his step-dad did the smacking *before* the fire."

Pete had assumed the hitting had come as a punishment for getting in trouble with the cops. He said as much and asked Manny why he thought the beating had come before.

Manny half smiled and said, "Because I asked him what story he'd told the cops to explain his bruises. He told them he'd been wrestling with some friends and had gotten beat up doing that."

"So? Maybe that's what actually happened." Pete said.

"No," Manny sounded exasperated. "Aren't you listening? I asked him what *story* he'd told the cops."

"Oh, yeah. Right." Pete wanted to be done talking about Mikey Hamm. He looked out the window, into the dark night. A blanket of ground fog had begun to form over the vineyard beyond the fence.

Staring out the window, Pete started to wonder which movie the staff was going to show tonight. They'd rented two, an action movie and a comedy.

"Are you listening?"

Pete was called back from the window. "Huh? What?" He looked back at Manny, who was staring at him with an inscrutable look on his face. "Oh. Sorry, I'm just getting a little tired of talking about him. Can we just change the subject, please?"

"Why?" Manny was clearly unhappy, but Pete felt like he had listened to enough.

"Well, whatever I say, all you want to talk about is the freaking Rat."

"Don't call him that, Pete. You know it's not nice."

It was the voice that angered Pete: the way Manny had said it. It felt like his mother was talking to him again in the way she did when she thought he was making a wrong decision. She'd never come out and tell him he was wrong, but would instead remind him he already knew he was wrong.

"Nice?! I'm supposed to be nice to him now?"

"Why wouldn't you be?" Manny seemed honestly confused.

"Because you don't know him!" Pete almost yelled. He regained control on is voice. "Listen, you're still new here Manny, but I'll say what I've said before: the kid is no good. He can't be trusted."

"I'm not talking about trusting him. I'm talking about acting like he's a real human being for a change. Think about what you call him, all of you. You think he doesn't know what everyone here thinks of him?"

"You don't know..."

"You think I don't know him well enough to be nice to him?" Now Manny was getting angry. "Do you honestly think *you* know him better than I do? Or at all?"

This was going wrong. Pete had just wanted to say something nice, to compliment Manny. He tried one last time. "Listen, when I brought up what happened with Teddy…"

"Will you let the damn Teddy thing go, already?!" The remark shut Pete up. It felt like a cold handed slap.

"I was just…"

But Manny's anger had bloomed in full and he let Pete hear it. "Listen, having breakfast with somebody who beat the shit out of me doesn't make me a hero! And if you don't get that, there's no way you're ever going to understand Michael!"

Pete recoiled at Manny's harsh tone. He couldn't reconcile it with the soft boy who had given him a book, given him other things.

Manny regained control of his voice, but he wasn't done. "You'll never understand him because you can't conceive of the fact he does it every time he's home for a visit. He gets to sit down and eat meals with the man who put that purple collar around his neck and has done worse in the past. It doesn't make him a hero, but it does make him a survivor. You can't understand that, so you can't ever understand him. And if you can't understand him…"

Manny let the sentence die a quiet death and sat down on his bed, apparently drained from his outburst. Billy Roberts, a little tow-headed kid who'd come back from home that afternoon, walked past their room deliberately and looked in, clearly hoping to see some action. Pete made a shooing motion at him and he scurried away down the hall.

Pete stood in the stunned silence of the room, his own anger rising in him like bile. He turned again and looked out into the milky blue of the fog. *Why should I understand him?* His mind screamed at Manny. *Why should I even freaking try? And why do you care so much about him?* He thought these things, but said nothing for a few minutes. *'I'm your friend,'* Manny had said. *Sure, until the most contemptible kid in the cottage shows back up.* Pete knew his anger was getting the best of him, but he let it wash over him. *Because he was* my *friend, not the Rat's!* Then he thought, *I wish the little bastard firebug would just burn himself the hell up.* The image was simultaneously disturbing and satisfying. *Like a good sin.* He smiled inside at the pure hatred of the thing, and then felt immediately sick for it.

Pete was still looking out into the night when he heard Manny stand and leave the room.

Chapter 14

For the next several weeks, Pete and Manny barely spoke. For his part, Pete had decided that if Manny would rather hang out with the Rat, it was fine with him. And Manny, as if to oblige, did begin spending a lot more time with Mikey. Everyone noticed the change. Chris and Frankie began talking to Pete a little more frequently again. And Pete got the sense that they hadn't minded Manny being around, but he had made them nervous.

Jordi, who had spent as much time with Manny as anyone other than Pete himself, asked what had happened, and seemed satisfied enough with Pete's mocking explanation that Manny had "found someone he understood better." Frankie had been the most supportive when he'd said of Manny, "Not like we didn't know he was cracked. Just a little more proof he ain't right." Pete's stomach had turned with sick enjoyment when Frankie had added, "Who knows, maybe Steven was right. Maybe his mama did drop him on his head."

Besides sharing a room, mealtimes were the worst, because standard Riordan policy dictated roommates ate together. Not only was it awkward and uncomfortable, it also emphasized the separation between the two to the other boys in the cottage. Where Pete and

Manny had formerly been the most talkative table in the St. Gabe's dining room, they were now the quietest.

On Sunday, when he returned, Steven seemed to take special note of and pleasure in the division between Manny and Pete. At dinner he'd stopped by Manny and Pete's table, looked at them together and said quietly, "Sorry to hear about your break-up, ladies," before sniggering his way back to his own table. There had been brief eye contact between the roommates then, but it lasted only a painful moment.

After showers, when he was coming back from the bathroom, Pete saw Steven walking away from the doorway to his and Manny's room. He wasn't sure, but the impression he had was that Steven had just come out of the room.

Entering warily, Pete saw a size C battery sitting in the middle of Manny's pillow. Obviously, Steven wanted to make sure Manny had no misunderstandings about who had been responsible for the blanket party. Pete said nothing about the battery to Manny, but later noticed it had been put into the wastebasket in the corner.

The residents weren't the only ones to see the rift between the two boys. The staff noticed as well. Mr. Johnson in particular questioned Pete as to what had happened. When Pete gave him no explanation, the supervisor seemed disappointed.

Life in their room had become an exercise in avoidance. By unspoken agreement they tried not to be in the room at the same time unless they were sleeping.

As far as Pete could tell, Manny spent more time with the Rat than without him, and Mikey spent relatively little time in the office or in a red chair. Pete even heard Mr. Johnson compliment Mikey on the good week he'd had. It almost made him ill.

The shock of it all came a couple of weeks after Thanksgiving. During their Tuesday afternoon group session, Mr. Johnson delivered the new LEVEL report. The usual band of suspects held down the carpet at LEVEL 4. These included Fat Tony, JP and Malcolm, who let loose a string of obscenities and stormed out of the cottage as he did almost every time he got the news he had at least two more weeks of early bedtime to look forward to.

After the laughter at Malcolm's outburst had died down, and Mr. Weaver had left the cottage to keep an eye on him, Mr. Johnson continued the report. Jordi and Chris both barely missed LEVEL 2 because of having gotten in trouble together at school the previous week. Pete and Matt Saxon had both stayed the same at a 2, though Pete could not help noticing he had made it by the slimmest of margins. He couldn't help noticing this because Mr. Johnson made a point of telling him in front of everyone.

The two real surprises came at the end. Mikey "The Rat" Hamm, who had lived as a LEVEL 4 since almost the moment he'd come to Riordan, had achieved LEVEL 2. This announcement was followed with silence. There was a surprised bitterness in this for Pete, but he didn't know exactly to what he should ascribe it. Certainly he couldn't be jealous of a scumbag like the Rat. Other than Pete, the most stunned person in the room was probably the rodent himself. Pete noticed the look on Mr. Johnson's face. It seemed to say, *Yes, we even added up the numbers a second and third time to check.* Out of the corner of his eye, Pete saw Manny give Mikey a congratulatory thumbs-up.

Finally, Mr. Johnson came to Manny. Pete wasn't too surprised Manny was going to get a high status. After all Mr. Johnson had made Pete his roommate for a reason: to start him off on the right foot. But when he made the announcement of Manny's LEVEL, Mr. Johnson revealed that the newest member of St. Gabe's cottage had in fact not made LEVEL 2. He had instead done the near impossible: on his first full LEVEL evaluation period he had gone from a zero to LEVEL 1.

The group was shocked as a whole. They had all expected the weird new kid to get a 2, but the 1 was almost too ridiculous and far-fetched to suggest. After a moment, a couple of guys actually applauded briefly. The clappers did not include Steven, Tony, JP or Pete, who sat stunned at Manny's luck. *That Bastard!* Who'd shown him the ropes? Who'd spent all that time teaching him and making sure he understood how things worked at Riordan, no matter how hard headed a student the kid had been. *If I hadn't been so damned focused on helping him, I probably would have made it this time. That's my LEVEL 1!* He looked away, out the window toward the athletic fields. As he heard Mr. Johnson move on to other business, he was dimly aware of Manny staring at him. He didn't look back.

Afterward, while they were back in their room getting changed for dinner, Manny spoke to Pete for the first time in several days.

"Thank you, Pete."

Pete looked around. He'd heard Manny come in, but had gotten out of the habit of looking at him. It was best just to get out of the room as quickly as possible. Now, Manny was at his wardrobe, hands reaching for his sweat shirt, eyes on Pete, who had not immediately responded.

Manny tried again. "Thank you for all of your help getting me to LEVEL 1."

Pete looked away and thought, *How freaking dare you?*

"Pete, I'm trying here, okay?" Still not looking, Pete thought he heard pain in the voice. *Good*, his mind sneered. But Manny wasn't done. He said quietly, "I owe this to you. You're the reason I did it."

Pete found himself suddenly focusing on the items atop his wardrobe. His baseball glove was there. It needed to be oiled before springtime.

"Come on, man. Don't shut me out, ok?"

He had a bottle of neat's-foot oil at his aunt's house. It was the best for oiling up a glove. He needed to ask her to send it up when she had the chance. Mr. Turnbull would probably help him with the glove if he asked.

"— can't fix this if you won't help me."

Next to the glove was his school binder. He had a letter to Tabitha he'd been trying to write. He wanted to send it to her, but it felt silly, writing her a letter. Try as he might he could think of nothing interesting to write.

"Ok, Pete. Never mind."

Eventually, Pete looked around to find he was alone in the room.

Through the grind of cottage life, the campus was getting ready for Christmas. Maintenance had installed a 20 foot high light cone in middle of the lawn in front of Notre Dame Chapel. It was just a tall high pole with alternating strands of red and green lights leading from the top of the pole down to where they were anchored on a metal ring which lay on the grass around the pole. The whole effect gave it a tree-like appearance.

Each cottage received its own tree during the first week of December to decorate and display in the living room. The previous month, cottage staffers had taken requests out of the Sears Holiday Wishbook catalogue. The Riordan Home bought boys Christmas presents every year and the staff let the boys each make a short list of items all adding up to no more than 20 dollars. Pete had asked for a San Francisco Giants throw blanket for his bed and a calculator so he wouldn't have to keep borrowing the one from the cottage office when he did his homework. The staffers made no promises about gifts other than saying they would make an attempt to honor the requests.

Christmas preparations also extended to school. They were orchestrated in that domain by Riordan's only nun, Jacqueline

Gregory, better known as Sister Jack. She was Pete's religion teacher. She taught only in the mornings, and was not a permanent part of the religious staff at the Home. She was actually assigned full time to St. Clare's in the nearby town of Kenwood. But because of her background as a teacher and her friendship with Father O'Connell, she was on permanent loan to the Riordan home. Each December, the loan seemed as if it worked the other way around.

On Wednesday, the first of December, Sister Jack told Pete's class about all of her plans for the holiday spectacular. The annual Christmas concert was planned for the week before Christmas home visit, as usual. But this year Sister Jack had decided to add a little something extra. The evening would begin with the Riordan Boys' Choir and end with the band. All the boys knew the reason the choir opened every concert was simply to get it the hell out of the way. Even Matt Saxon, who was part of the group, admitted the choir was just flat out horrible to listen to. On the other hand, the Riordan band was surprisingly decent. Last year, Pete remembered, they managed to not quite murder "O Come All Ye Faithful," and their "Jingle Bells" had been better than bearable.

"This year," said Sister Jack, "we will be adding a short Advent Play to our program."

The total lack of response from the room made it clear no one knew what she was talking about. Pete was not surprised. Most of the boys who came to Riordan had little or no religious education before stepping onto campus. Those for whom mass or church of any kind had been a regular part of their lives were a small minority. Pete's mother had made sure he'd been in church every Sunday when she wasn't too sick to take him, and even he had no idea what an advent play might be.

"It's quite lovely," she told them in her cultured voice. Sister Jack was in her forties, and had been working at the school on loan for ten years. Pete didn't mind her as a teacher, but wasn't particularly interested in the religion class she taught. Most days were all right, and she even talked to them about other religions and different branches of Christianity. Though, of course, Catholic was still king. On the days when the religiosity was a little thick, Pete liked to distract himself by imagining ecclesiastical debates between Sister Jack and his mom's old boyfriend, Mitch.

"It is a bridging between two of the most important stories in Christian history," Sister Jack told them. "From the Garden of Eden to the Garden at Gethsemane; from the creation to the crucifixion."

Pete, who was kind of following her, could tell no one else was. Sister Jack apparently could tell too, because she said something a little more concrete for the boys. "It's also where we get the idea of the modern Christmas tree." This at last made an impression on the boys. They might not know from bridges between Old and New Testament, but they could wrap their heads around a Christmas tree.

The tradition, she told them, came from Germany. Advent plays had been popular in many countries, including England and Spain. But it was in Germany the plays had given birth to the Christmas tree. Advent plays would be put on in town halls and churches all over Europe, with variations from country to country and even from town to town.

Among the Germans of the 17th century, the most popular advent play had been one called *The Paradise Tree*. The play was a simple re-telling of the story of Adam and Eve in the Garden of Eden. Traditionally, there would be but three characters: Adam, Eve and the serpent. The set was decorated with only a single prop. A large tree would be brought in and have apples affixed to it to serve as the tree of knowledge for the play. Because there was not an abundance of apple trees in rural Germany, townsfolk had to make due with what they had. And in the German countryside, what they had were evergreen trees.

As Sister Jack explained the history of it, an image began to form in Pete's mind of a stage with a single tree upon it. The tree would have apples, or representations thereof, tied to it.

"But the apples would not be alone," she continued. "There would also be large communion wafers hanging from the tree. For you see, the tree was to represent not only the tree of knowledge, but also the tree upon which the Holy Savior would eventually die for our redemption."

There had been some unsure mumbling at this. Malcolm eventually raised his hand, and through his tic laden voice and twitching mouth said he thought Jesus had died on a cross, not falling out of a tree.

"Indeed," Sister Jack said, "but you see, the cross was made of wood. Therefore referring to it a tree, as St. Paul does in his letter to the Galatians, is perfectly reasonable, is it not?"

The group still had doubts but was wiling to set them aside.

"So, what we get from the Advent play, *The Paradise Tree*," Sister Jack continued, "is an image of an evergreen adorned with red globes and white discs." She looked at the class expectantly, eyebrows raised, waiting for the mental connections to be made. Pete glanced around the room. Sometimes Sister Jack had to wait a while for connections. Then, almost 45 seconds after she had left the idea hanging out there, a young St. Mike's kid completed the circuit for those still struggling: "Hey! That's just like a Christmas tree!"

Pete had to admire the way Sister Jack never said *Well duh!* or barked *No Shit!* at a kid who had taken ten minutes to understand difficult concepts, like Jesus was God's son *AND* human, then announced them as if they were proclaiming a law of nature which had been missed by everyone up until then.

What she said instead was always a variant on what she said now, which was, "Yes Kenny, that's right. It is like a Christmas tree. In fact, the paradise trees from the plays were the first Christmas trees."

Sister Jack explained that after a while, some leaders in the German church had begun to take a dim view of the Advent plays. Perhaps their objections came from the fact the decorating trees at the winter solstice had been happening in pagan circles for a thousand years, and they didn't like the church absorbing pagan ritual. Regardless the reasons, in the early 18th century public performances of Advent plays were banned in Germany.

"But the plays lived on," she told her students in what Pete was sure she thought of as a breathless, hopeful voice.

What happened, she explained, was the German people so loved the Advent plays they brought a part of them into their homes in preparation for Christmas. Long before this, Germans had been using Christmas pyramids to decorate their homes. The pyramids were actually more like table top carousels adorned with angels and other religious symbology. The decorations' platforms were mounted on a central shaft so as to spin freely. A propeller was mounted atop the shaft, and candles were arrayed around the carousel. When the candles were lit, the heat generated by the flames would move quickly upward, hitting the propeller's sloped blades and cause them to move, turning the carousel along with them.

When the advent plays were banned many people took the central symbol of the plays, the paradise tree itself, and brought it into their homes. Thus began almost a century of German living rooms with paradise trees and Christmas pyramids side by side.

"Eventually," Sister Jake said, "the two traditions were combined, when the candles from the Christmas pyramid were placed onto the branches of the tree."

After acknowledging the argument from several student that putting lit candles on a dead and drying evergreen was not the best idea, and pointing out the candles had evolved into the lights on a modern Christmas tree, Sister Jack showed them some pictures of what the trees had looked like. Actually they were pictures of paintings. When she had finished showing the slides she told them, "Now, while Mr. Shaw in the woodshop has agreed to construct a large tree for our show, he will need us to create some ornamentation."

As a cast, Sister Jake had elicited the help of three Fitzpatrick boys to play the roles of Adam and the serpent and to narrate. She said a young woman from St. Francis High School had agreed to perform as Eve. They had been practicing their parts for weeks, she said. They would be ready, but it was up to this class to supply them their paradise tree. She set them to work constructing paper-mâché apples and large cardboard communion wafers, traditional decorations for the play.

Chapter 15

Two weeks after they had stopped talking, Manny and Pete were sharing their room in almost complete silence. Manny was still spending a lot of time with Mikey Hamm around the cottage. But he had made other friends at school as well. Pete had even seen him deep in conversation with Malcolm during a couple of recesses. Pete himself had been moving on as best he could, but was having a difficult time of it, he was still so angry. With Manny. With Mikey Hamm. With himself.

Pete didn't like being angry. His mother had always said it was his one weakness, his anger.

"But you've got to learn to forgive people," she'd said to him. It had happened weeks after Mitch had left for the last time, and Pete had still been living and breathing the fury and hurt born the moment the Peterbilt truck had rolled away from the house the final time. She had found him in the backyard, behind the massive redwood tree that dominated not only the O'Boyle's property, but the two adjacent lots as well. He'd been crying when she'd tracked him down. Crying and cursing Mitch.

"It wasn't anyone's fault, Petey," Lilly had said, sitting down next to him against the fibrous husked bark of the redwood.

"He left because he didn't want to be with us," Pete had said through tears. "He should have wanted to be with us."

"He did want to be with us." She had reached an arm around him and had stroked his hair away from his eyes. "He did. But he has things to do in this world and he has things in his life that draw him away." She had continued to stroke his hair.

"He made a promise," Pete had sulked. Then with more anger: "He promised he wasn't going to leave."

"I know, sweetie. I know. He said he'd stay, but now he's gone. Staying angry at him won't get him to come back. So that leaves us with only one choice: we've got to forgive him."

"Forgive him? After he lied?" He had been so angry. "Never."

Lilly had signed deeply then. After a long time she had finally said, "Pete, I want to tell you something, and I want you to listen carefully until I'm done." She had stopped then, and for a moment he had been sure she wasn't going to say any more. Then she began. "You put so much on the people around you. You expect so much from everyone. It's not fair of you." Pete had looked at her in shock. "Now, hang on," Lilly had said. "Let me finish."

He remembered leaning back against the tree again, leaning against her a little as well.

"It's not that I want you to expect less from people, Pete. I don't." She had hugged him then. "I like that you demand a lot from the world. It's just... not everyone can meet your expectations all the time."

"I know that," he'd said softly.

"Yet you get so angry whenever you feel like someone's let you down. And it's not like you hide your disappointment, it's right there on your face and in your words. It can be tough on those of us who let you down."

"So what am I supposed to do?" he had asked her. "Am I just supposed to accept it when someone lies to me?"

"No, baby. But you've got to learn to forgive people."

She had sighed again before continuing.

"You've got to understand, there will be people who let you down and disappoint you and fail to do what they said they will do. Lord knows I'll be one of them. And it's okay to be upset or angry or mad at people for those things."

"But at some point your anger is going to stop being useful. Anger's like that. Full and righteous and clean one minute, then trapping, suffocating and corrosive the next. And you never know when it's going to happen. There aren't always warning signs."

"If you don't learn to forgive now, Pete I'm afraid you'll end up with a permanent anger. And that kind of anger can eat up lives whole. That anger doesn't let you forgive anyone for any sin. It's what stops people from forgiving themselves."

Pete had heard her, but hadn't been ready to absorb her message. Since his mother had spoken those words Pete had wished countless times he'd been able to. Because he knew she'd been right. Unfortunately, it had taken her death for him to realize it.

On the third Friday in December, just three days before the Christmas Concert, Pete was sitting in the craft section after school reading a book when Chris and Jordi came in and told him what had happened in math class. Pete was in algebra, while most of the other guys in the cottage were in the Math 2 class at the school.

During some independent work time, Manny had been helping Malcolm Patty with some basics when Fat Tony waddled over and sat down at the table. Chris and Jordi, who had been working together at the next table, told Pete they'd heard the whole thing.

"So Tony starts in on Malcolm about being a twitchy kid. He said something like, 'Maybe if you're brain wasn't so messed up with the twitchies you wouldn't suck so bad at math.'"

Chris told Pete that Mr. Jensen, the math teacher, had been working with a group of boys across the room when this had been going on.

"So what did Malcolm do?" Pete asked. Malcolm's rants were legendary, especially after someone made fun of his Tourette's Syndrome.

"Nothing." Jordi told him.

Pete was stunned by this, but Chris went on to explain how Manny had started in on Tony before Malcolm even had a chance to get out the first *F* of his customary 'F--- you.'

"So, Manny's looking down at the math," Chris continued. "And without even looking up he says, real quiet, 'Now we all know Malcolm has a medically diagnosed condition which is no more his fault than the color of his skin. And yet you choose to make fun of him, which I find interesting.'"

"He said that?" Pete asked.

"Almost word for word," Jordi confirmed.

"Then what?" Pete looked at them and both boys were smiling.

"Then Manny looked up."

He'd looked up at Fat Tony and said, as near as the boys could reconstruct it, "The kid has an honest to goodness disease with a medical name and everything, and you choose to make fun of him for it. So, tell me Tony, what disease do you have? You got a case of cerebral cellulite, or what?"

Fat Tony had become instantly livid and growled, "Screw you, freak. I ain't got no disease."

"No," Manny had said. "Maybe not yet, but judging from your current spherical form, I'm willing to bet money heart disease and diabetes are probably in your personal crystal ball."

Both Chris and Jordi were having trouble getting through the story without laughing. "But the best part," Jordi said, "was when Manny had to explain to him what spherical meant, and tell him 'cerebral cellulite' was like calling him a *fat head*."

"He explained it?" Pete was incredulous. "He actually *explained* how he was insulting him?"

Jordi was having a difficult time talking, but finally managed: "It was *god damned* beautiful!"

"Then what happened?" Pete was getting frustrated, but still enjoying the way Chris and Jordi were laughing at Fat Tony.

"So," Chris continued, "Tony yells, 'I'm gonna kick your freaking ass, kid!' And Manny says back to him, just as calm as toast, 'Kick away man, just as long as you don't sit on me.'"

Pete was stunned. "He actually said that?"

"Bet your ass he did!" Chris was near tears with laughter.

"Wow." This sounded like a different Manny, one he'd only ever heard about in a story. Pete felt his stomach tighten. It was hard to believe Manny had only been at Riordan for about six weeks. Hard to believe the conversation in the barn during which Manny had told the story about his teacher had been only a month ago.

"So, now Mr. Jensen is on it," Jordi continued the narrative. "He runs over and gets between Tony and Manny. And Tony is standing now, face all red and sweaty, threatening to pull out Manny's throat. But Manny, he's still just sitting there, looking up at Tony. He ain't smiling or frowning or nothing."

"Just as calm as toast," Chris said again.

"Mr. Jensen finally gets Tony out the room, and then everyone starts to talk at once, most of them telling Manny 'good job.'"

"And what did Manny say?" Pete asked, not realizing how hungry for information about Manny he had become until he said it.

Chris and Jordi had begun to compose themselves. And now they both got strange looks on their faces. "Nothing," Jordi said. "That's the weird part. He didn't say anything else. Not even when the coordinator came in to get him."

Pete contemplated this strange person who had entered his life and then virtually exited it again. *He said he was my friend*, he thought, *and then he threw me over for the god damned rodent. Screw him!*

Word got around before dinner: Manny had received five hours of school detention for insulting Tony, and Tony had received 10 hours for threatening to thrash Manny. Further, the rumor was if either boy continued in the dispute, a loss of the Christmas home visit could result. Pete couldn't quite see how that was a threat to Manny, who had said often enough his move to Riordan was as good as permanent.

But the most immediate result of the confrontation was Tony Bruletti's departure from St. Gabriel's Cottage. Tony never returned to the cottage after school. Manny had come in with Mr. Turnbull just before dinner. As they were finishing the meal, Mr. Johnson told the boys Tony was being moved up the hill to St. Matthew's. He explained the move had been considered for a while. Tony was, after all, older than most of the boys in St. Gabe's, and had already been there more than a year. "This change was coming soon enough," Mr. Johnson said as they finished off their desserts. "Today's events have just moved up the timeframe a little."

Of the boys in the cottage, only Steven and JP took the news quietly. The rest of the boys were barely able to contain their joy. Malcolm, who had been Tony's target before Manny had drawn the fat kid's fire, actually applauded before being silenced by a glare from Mr. Johnson. Almost all of the boys were happy about the turn of events. The only who weren't, Pete noticed, were Steven, JP and Manny.

Every time one of the other boys threw Manny a thumbs-up, or a congratulatory look, Pete couldn't help but notice how accepting the thanks seemed to pain him. It annoyed Pete more than a little. Manny was the cottage hero, having single handedly rid them of Fat Tony and done it while publicly ridiculing him. It was a masterful accomplishment, and he seemed to accept praise for it like he was being thanked for peeing on the carpet. Pete simply didn't understand it.

On the way back from dinner, Mr. Johnson caught Pete and asked him to walk slowly back to the cottage so they could talk as the others walked ahead. The rain which had been threatening all week had begun to drop softly as a fine mist, whispering wetness over everything with virtually no sound. As they walked behind the other boys, Mr. Johnson told Pete he was going to make a change. "Tony's departure leaves Michael without a roommate."

Oh, great, Pete thought. *Now I finally* will *end up getting stuck with that god damned kid!* The last thing he wanted right now was to be roommate's with Manny's new buddy. He sighed, figuring he had nothing he could do other than tell Mr. Johnson he understood and it would be fine if he moved into the Rat's nest of a room.

"Well," Mr. Johnson continued, "Michael's been doing pretty well lately, and I don't like the idea of him being alone."

Here it comes.

"So I've decided to move Manny into room five with Michael."

Pete's acceptance was halfway up his throat when it lodged.

"I've already talked to Manny about it, and he said he'd be okay with the change." Mr. Johnson looked sideways at Pete. "I know things between him and you haven't been real good the last couple of weeks."

Pete was suddenly two people, walking side by side. The one to whom Mr. Johnson was talking nodded in silence and looked from the ground to the cottage ahead. The other version of him screamed and raged, grabbing his chest and hair, anything to hold on to himself as he struggled not to vomit.

"This might be good for you two," Johnson was saying now. The second Pete's bowels were cramping up and he became aware he was probably going to be violently sick from both ends. The first Pete just nodded again.

"And with the way things have gone for Michael, I think having them room together can only benefit him."

The second Pete began taking phantom swings at first Johnson then at itself. The first nodded still again.

"Thanks for understanding Pete," Mr. Johnson said. "I know this leaves you solo. But I figured you've kind of earned a break from someone else in your space."

The first Pete glanced sideways at nothing for a moment, then looked up at Mr. Johnson and smiled a tight smile.

"Thank you, sir."

That night, Pete lay awake in his bed for a long time. The sound of rain on the flat cottage roof held no solace like it usually did. The echo of the raindrops seemed all the louder for the emptiness of the room.

'I've already talked to Manny about it, and he said he'd be okay with the change.'

"Good riddance," Pete said quietly to the emptiness. Eventually he rolled onto his side and passed into fitful sleep. When he awoke in the morning, his pillow was damp, though he had no memory of having cried in the night.

Chapter 16

Before dinner on the following Monday, Pete dressed for the Christmas concert. He was to be an usher, escorting members of the public to their seats in the auditorium. He'd been given a dark blue tie by Sister Jack. Mr. Weaver had tied it around his own neck and slipped it off and given it to Pete. Now Pete was standing in the bathroom straightening the tie in the mirror. After dinner the rest of the boys would be coming back to the cottage, but those who were ushers or otherwise involved in the production would be heading directly to the auditorium to help with setup and receive last minute instructions.

He looked in the mirror. The tie looked good, finally straight after ten minutes of goofing with it. He looked in the mirror above the tie. He had not been sleeping well, and the face in the mirror showed it. He wet his hands under the tap and rubbed a spare amount of water over his face, rubbing it in and massaging his temples.

At dinner he sat alone and ate silently, stealing what glances he could at the table across the dining room where Manny and Mikey the Rat had eaten seventeen meals together since becoming roommates last week. *No,* Pete corrected himself, *eighteen now.*

Halfway through the meal, Sister Jack materialized wearing what looked to be a new jacket and skirt of dark blue. A large silver cross hung from her neck. She spoke to Mr. Dawson briefly then asked Mikey to follow her.

After eating, Pete and Matt Saxon walked over to the auditorium, converging there with the thirty or so other boys involved in the show in varying capacities. The interior of the hall was decorated festively with wreathes hung at regular intervals around the walls and wrapping paper and bows on all of the doors, making each one look like a present. A few boys were moving among the three hundred folding chairs, placing a simple program on each metal seat. Pete noticed one of program distributors was Mikey Hamm. The Rat seemed not to notice him, which was just as well as far as Pete cared.

He found Sister Jack at a lectern which had been set up off to one side of the stage and was given the task of setting up a table for the donation box by the front door. One thing about Riordan, they never held an event without a donation box or two handy. Sister Jack told him where to find a tablecloth in the backstage storage closets. As he walked away Pete heard her call, "Michael, come here please," and saw the Rat look up and begin walking toward her.

Directly behind the stage there was a large open area for storing big props and for performers to gather before heading onstage. Behind that was a long hallway running from one side of the building to the other. Off of this hall there were entrances to the two classrooms at the back of the theater building. One served as home to the Riordan band; the other was Mr. Ramirez's 4H classroom. Opposite the classrooms were six side-by-side walk-in closets for general theater storage.

Pete was in the closet nearest Mr. Ramirez's room sorting through boxes of old props and costumes looking for the white lacy tablecloth Sister Jack had assured him was in here somewhere. It was difficult work. The closets had been built as places to store things, not to find them. A single naked bulb provided meager light by which to look and the doors had hydraulic springs designed to pull them closed, cutting off light from the hallway.

He'd been rummaging around for nearly ten minutes when he heard people talking in the hall. He couldn't identify the individual voices, but he knew the tone of conspiracy well enough from his time at Riordan. He stopped searching and listened.

"When's he gonna do it?" one asked.

"Sometime tomorrow, he says. At school."

"No way," the first voice was confident. "He ain't gonna do shit at school. He's not gonna do it where everyone can see him."

The second voice wasn't so sure. "I don't know," it said. "He's still pretty pissed off. He says the kid's mouthy, and that he plans on beating on that mouth."

"He better be careful," the first voice intoned. "Nobody knows that kid's story. He's not too big, but he looks like he might be able to handle himself. And besides, Tony's so goddamn fat he practically gets in his own way when he tries to hit someone." Both boys laughed at this.

"Yeah, were you there when he —" The stop was abrupt. Pete tensed.

"You hear something?" The voice in the hallway was cautious now.

"Yeah. In there."

Oh shit. Pete looked for someplace to stash himself. There was no where to go. He faced the door and prepared to explain he hadn't been listening, he'd just been looking for a table cloth. As he thought about reaching up to extinguish the light, he heard a sound through the wall to his right, from inside the next closet over. Then one of the voices from the hall boomed. "What the hell are you doing you little piece of crap?" He heard a mumble, the sound of a smaller kid trying to explain something. He heard the landing of a blow and an accompanying grunt from the smaller kid.

"Now get the hell out of here!" The retreating sound of small footsteps was drowned out by the laughter of the two voices in the hall. Then the laughter itself drifted away, back up the hall toward the band room.

In the dimly lit storage closet, Pete exhaled the breath he hadn't been aware of holding and blinked. He silently went to the closet door and opened it. He looked around the door and saw two boys turn the corner and move toward the front of the building.

His mind was busy as he went back to searching for the tablecloth.

At 6:50, the auditorium was filling up with people. Most of the cottages were already there. Only St. Gabe's was yet to arrive.

After eventually finding the tablecloth in the closet and bringing it to Sister Jack, Pete had spent the next 30 minutes directing traffic in the hall, telling cottage staff where each house was assigned to sit, escorting visitors to their seats, and pointing the way toward the restrooms. He'd done this on a kind of autopilot.

What he'd heard in the closet was pulling at his thoughts. He was moving around the room, walking people to their seats, pointing the way across the yard to the school bathrooms, smiling at visitors. But inside he was a pool of pain. He needed to tell Manny. That was certain. He was still furious with Manny, but Tony was dangerous. He'd come to accept Manny wasn't his friend anymore, if he ever really had been, but the kid would have to listen about Tony.

The boys from St. Gabe's Cottage arrived five minutes before the seven o'clock curtain. Pete was escorting a couple of blue hairs from the local community down to some open seats near the front, and so was unable to catch Manny before the show. After seating the old ladies, Pete returned to his post by the back of the auditorium, where Sister Jack had told him to remain until at least 7:15, to help direct any late arrivals to their seats.

With nothing to immediately do, Pete looked over the room. The members of the choir were all sitting together off to the left of the stage. They were wearing their blue and gold church vestments. Pete had to smile. The choir in their Sunday finest always looked like a flock of slightly confused macaws.

To the right of the stage sat the members of the Riordan band. There were about 20 of them in all. From having heard them before,

Pete knew they were a group of widely varied musical experience, some having played their instruments since they could sit up, others having played their instruments seemingly since the week before last. They had no group finery, but were instead dressed much like Pete himself, wearing their church pants, their best oxford shirt and a tie, most of them loaners supplied by Sister Jack. They didn't match, but they were at least dressed similarly.

The stage itself was a low one, only a couple of feet off of the floor. Like the floor, it was constructed of a blond wood that had seen its fair share of polishing. Pete had heard Mr. Phillips, the principal of the Riordan school, used to put boys who violated school rules to work hand polishing the floor and stage of the auditorium. Apparently though, the practice had been discontinued some years earlier when a few boys had been caught "huffing" the noxious floor polish to get high.

The front of the stage was visible, and was where the choir would stand while doing bad things to good music. The rear of the stage was hidden by the heavy blue curtain, behind which was the tree Pete's class had decorated.

He was staring at the curtain, thinking about the paper-mâché apples the class had made and painted, when movement caught the corner of his eye. Someone was coming in the door. He surveyed the room and spotted seats for singles, couples and groups of four and five. This way, when he saw how many were in the group he would be able to take them right to a location with enough seats. Confident that he was ready to assist any group, he turned to the door, saw two women and said, "Right this w—." But no more would come.

Standing just inside the door with the slightest twist of a smile on her face was Tabitha Pembrook. He stammered for a moment longer, until he was saved by the unlikeliest of people. Ms. Pembrook stepped from behind her daughter and extended her hand.

"It's Pete, isn't it?"

Pete's eyes snapped from Tabitha to her mother at the sound of his name.

"Uh, mm. Uh, yeah. I mean yes, it is." He reached up and took the offered shake.

"I'm Evelyn Pembrook. We met after mass a few weeks ago."

"Yes Ma'am," he said, trying not to sound like a preschooler. "I remember."

She made a nodding movement which Pete interpreted as her being pleased he recalled their previous meeting. "And of course," she turned to Tabitha, "you remember my daughter Tabitha." Pete looked to Tabitha, whose smile, he noticed, and been replaced with another, very different smile. This one was pleasant and warm, but in a distant way. But the other had been one of familiarity. The other smile had been meant for him alone.

"Hello," he said. She made no move to offer her hand; both were buried deep in the pockets of her blue fleece vest.

"Hi," she said.

"Hello," he said. *Again*, he realized. He stammered, but she smiled, showing only hint of the warmth she had just moments ago, but a hint was more than enough to help him relax.

They stood there in silence for what must have been only seconds, but on this cold winter night it felt to Pete like a long warm stretch in the middle of July. It was certainly long enough for Mrs. Pembrook to feel the need to bring Pete back to the present, by saying, "Soooo, do we just sit anywhere?"

"Oh. Yeah, sorry. Please follow me."

As he turned to lead them down the aisle to a couple of open seats near the front, he thought he saw Evelyn shoot a bemused smile toward Tabitha, who had again retreated to her neutral face.

He walked them to their seats, not daring to look back at her as he did so. As it was, he seemed to be able to see her in front of him even now. He'd looked at her for less than a minute but he was willing to bet he could describe her appearance in detail.

Her hair was not pulled back tonight but instead hung in short waves framing her pale face, focusing an observing eye on her soft cheeks and the way the longest of her hairs just seemed to tickle the side of her neck. She was wearing a fitted long sleeved white shirt under the zipped up powder blue fleece vest. Her pants were a chocolaty brown, the hems of the legs gathered slightly on the leather tops of square toed dress boots. There were heels on those boots. He'd not actually seen the heels, but she was even taller than when he had seen her at Thanksgiving. When he'd looked into her eyes this time, he was sure he'd had to look up a little more.

They reached the seats he had selected for them and he moved aside to allow them passage into the aisle. Mrs. Pembrook stepped past him first. Then Tabitha stepped by and he was transported again to the hill above the cottages and their first meeting. The sweet talcum scent she wore took him there. As she was about to sit, she turned to him and smiled, fully now, her mother behind her. Obviously she wasn't worried about anyone else seeing her. Then, she furrowed her brow in mock seriousness, suppressing laughter as she did so, and said, "Thank you, Pete." Then she sat.

He wanted to say, *It was my pleasure*, or *It was nothing*, but knew if he tried anything even semi-difficult he'd throw up, so he went with a classic: "You're welcome."

He turned and started back up the aisle, when he realized his fellows from St. Gabriel's were seated just across the aisle and a few rows back. And every single one of the boys was staring at him, some with their mouths wide open. Jordi was smiling broadly and holding up a thumb. Steven's usual purposefully blank expression had been replaced by one of confusion. Chris and Frankie had goofy grins on their faces. He looked down the row at them and began to smile himself, until his eyes fell on the only boy from his cottage unaffected by his triumph. Manny was sitting at the far end of the row, unsmiling and looking down, seeming to read his program. Pete felt the unformed smile shrivel and the warm feelings seeing Tabitha had brought evaporate like water on hot metal.

Other than Manny, every boy in his cottage and, now he looked around, most of the boys from the other cottages seated on that side of the auditorium, were staring at him with admiration and envy. They had all seen the brief moment he and Tabitha had shared, all seen her smile at him. And they were all looking either happy for or jealous of him. But not the one person in this place who had ever called him "friend." No, he was deliberately looking away, and not even doing a good job of pretending to be interested in the program. Pete felt his face tighten down and his mood sour. He finally pulled his eyes off of Manny and walked up the aisle, shaking his head.

At 7:04, Sister Jack grabbed the microphone from the lectern and walked in front of the stage. She thanked all of the guests and visitors from the community, pointed out the new choir robes paid for by last year's holiday concert fundraising, and encouraged the audience to continue "supporting Riordan with your time and energy." She then introduced the choir for their five songs.

The best Pete could have said about the singing group was the music teacher had decided they should only do four songs and no one had told Sister Jack. So listeners finished the fourth song and were able to think, *Well at least there isn't a fifth one of those.* Pete thought it was probably for the best; he was sure there was no way they'd be able to top the massacre of "The Little Drummer Boy" they'd just vomited out.

After the choir left the stage to what was in Pete's estimation, far more applause than deserved, Sister Jack got up to introduce the Advent Play. She gave the same brief basic history lesson as she had given in class, adding only, "This play in particular is the direct reason why we all have Christmas trees above the gifts in out homes."

The lights of the hall dimmed and the heavy blue curtain parted to reveal the paradise tree Mr. Shaw had built and the boys in Pete's religion class had decked. Mr. Shaw had done a fine job with the tree. Though Pete knew it was only painted plywood held together by braces and plates, in the footlights of the stage it was a spreading apple tree, complete with apples and communion wafers. Ten feet tall, the tree's spare branches were given life by the delicate greenery Mr. Shaw had added. Soft red and green lighting added to the illusion of the tree's authenticity.

With the opening of the curtain had also come music, soft and instrumental, flowing through the hall's speaker system. It reminded Pete of a ballet he had once watched on PBS.

He was being pulled in by the airy music and the strange realism of the tree when Adam and Eve entered from the left side of the stage. They were dressed in white Roman-style togas. Neither wore shoes and the head of each was adorned with a simple wreath. They walked hand in hand, passing the tree and then stopped mid-stride, pausing in tableau.

"Adam" was Greg Potter of Fitzpatrick House. He was a tall and pale, with the beginnings of a beard on his chin. But the Riordan Home knew Greg. If it had just been him on stage, not a single boy would have been paying attention. But attentive they all were, because of "Eve." The girl was relatively tall herself, but still came well short of Greg's 6'4". And she was attractive. Not in the Ms. Kelly (oh-my-God-I-can't-breathe) kind of way, but she was definitely striking. Even Pete, who still had a nose full of talcum, couldn't help but notice it. Besides being tall, she had cascading black hair which curled softly against her bare shoulders. Her features brought to mind pictures he'd seen in his civics book, of ancient Egyptian queens, and for a moment he imagined her hair up in a headdress and her profile on a coin.

Standing in the back of the hall, looking at the Riordan boys leaning forward to watch "Eve," Pete was reminded of the racing commercials he used to hear on the radio during Giants games, when the announcer would scream, "SUNDAY! SUNDAY! SUNDAY!" and tell listeners they'd pay for the whole seat but would only need the edge. Pete glanced at the program he'd picked up and saw that "Eve" was Michelle Samonek, a sophomore at St. Francis, a private Catholic high school in Santa Rosa.

The booming voice caught a lot of people by surprise.

"And God said to Adam and Eve, 'Eat of anything in the garden, but not of the tree of knowledge. That tree and its fruit are forbidden. Hear me in this, my only requirement of you.'"

The boomer was Chris Rose, another Fitzpatrick guy. Pete knew him as one of the funniest boys at Riordan. Rosie, as he was known, was famous for his ability to imitate the voices of almost any male staffer on campus, including a dead-bang impression of Father O. It was always weird to hear the voices of Mr. DeMarcus, Mr. Turnbull and the Father emanating from the stocky boy with the wavy blond hair. Pete had never heard him use his voice like this, but it was convincing. You could almost believe he had spent the afternoon in prayer, just so he could get the sound of God's voice down in order to reproduce it for the stage.

The play continued with Rosie providing both narration and character voices when necessary. Greg and Michelle drifted around the stage for a bit and were once again admonished to stay away from the tree before Greg wandered off stage.

There was a change in music and the green clad serpent (Michael Olivarri from Fitzpatrick House) popped out from behind the wide trunk of the tree and spoke through Rosie: "Why do you listen to God? He only wishes to deny you understanding."

The story was nothing new for Pete, but he found himself held, and not just by the beauty of "Eve." Seeing the play acted live was enthralling. The simplicity of the staging and story only made the experience more absorbing for him. By the time the Lord gave the couple their walking papers, Pete was fully into a story he'd heard more than a hundred times, and was sad to see the play end, which it did to massive applause from the community members present and from the residents. People actually began to rise from their seats to leave and it took Sister Jack on the microphone to remind the audience the band was yet to play.

Perhaps it was because the Advent play went a little long, perhaps because she knew there was no reasonable way they could successfully follow it, but whatever the reason, Sister Jack decided to hold the band to two songs instead of the planned four.

By the time he stepped out of the auditorium into the cold night, Pete was feeling a little dizzy. The performance had ended at 8:30, and it was now close on to 9:00. Sister Jack had asked him to stay to help with the cleanup and Mr. Dawson had given permission. The two songs from the band had been mercifully quick, and the audience had been appreciative, though Pete was sure the final applause would have been a lot louder had the program ended with the Advent Play.

As the bulk of boys had headed off for their cottages and Pete received several more questioning and envious glances, he had noticed Tabitha and her mom still in their seats. Then as he'd walked through the emptying rows collecting discarded and forgotten programs he noticed they were gone. He'd scanned the auditorium but his eyes found only boys and volunteers. *Damn.* He'd missed her. He'd hoped to have had another chance to see her, maybe even talk to her. He'd started to sag until he'd remembered the smile from earlier in the evening. The memory of the smile had propelled him through the clean-up, all the while sporting a dopey grin of his own.

Now, however, walking back to St. Gabe's he felt the lightness Tabitha's smile had caused begin to dim, remembering what lay ahead. He didn't want to talk to Manny, but knew he had to. If Tony was in fact going to jump him it could be bad for Manny. Yeah, Tony was fat, but he was also really strong. Pete had no doubt a motivated Tony could do some serious damage, and Manny had provided him with plenty of motivation.

When he returned to the cottage boys were watching the last half of a movie they had seen the beginning of that afternoon. Because of the Christmas show, all bedtimes had been pushed back, 3s and 4s were all still up. Pete asked Ms. Graham if he could go back to his bedroom and change into his night clothes and get ready for bed. She waved him on with the proviso he be back up front for evening prayers in 15 minutes.

Pete pulled off his tie as he headed toward the back of the cottage. It was unusually quiet for the night before a home visit. Pete guessed this was due as much to the coming day of departure as anything else. Mr. Johnson had said almost everyone leaving for vacation would be heading home after school tomorrow. The only exception was Malcolm who would be spending an extra night and leaving on Wednesday morning. That meant of all the boys in St. Gabe's, only Pete and Manny would be staying at Riordan through the home visit.

Pete, who just four weeks ago had been thrilled at the prospect of spending the whole of Christmas break at the Home was now dreading time stuck here with Manny. He'd called his aunt from Chuck the Truck's office on the previous Wednesday to see of she could please come get him for just a couple of days, but she'd told him she would be traveling with some friends through New Year's Day, and she was sorry, and did he get her Christmas gift yet. He would have been mad at her if his upset hadn't already been engaged elsewhere.

He reached the end junction in the T-hall and headed left toward his single room. He tossed the tie on the bed and grabbed his bathroom stuff, throwing a towel over his shoulder as he headed down the hall to the toilet. With everyone up front watching the movie, the bedrooms were all dark. As he neared the lit doorway of the bathroom he started to think about Tabitha again and how great it had been to be around her for a little while. Maybe after home visit he could organize a trip somewhere and arrange for her to meet them. It was one of the benefits of being a LEVEL 1 or 2: he could, with staff permission and help, request and plan an off campus trip for either recreational or educational purposes. Last year in St. Mike's, he'd planned trips to a couple of baseball card shops in Santa Rosa. *Maybe we could arrange to meet at the mall.* This thought brought a smile to his face as he stepped around the corner into the bathroom and nearly collided with another boy.

"Whoa," Pete began as he sidestepped the other, "Sorry—." He looked down at the boy as he addressed him and he realized it was Mikey. Immediately he stiffened and stopped talking. The Rat's beady eyes went as wide as they could, and her stared up at Pete.

After a few dragging seconds, Mikey managed a wheezy, "Hey."

Pete gave only half a nod back. He had never liked Mikey, had never spoken to him much. He'd never had need or desire to be in the boy's company for an entire conversation. Their interactions had always been short, terse and marked for Pete by an urge to get as far away from the other kid as quickly as possible.

Right now he just wanted to keep thinking about Tabitha. He didn't need Mikey Hamm ruining that too.

He looked past Mikey now and stepped around him, into the bathroom. He was past and hanging his towel on a hook next to a sink when he heard something mumbled behind him. He looked up into the mirror. The Rat was staring at his back with an intensity that in another time might have frightened Pete, but now only irritated him. He looked away from the scrawny apparition in the mirror and fished in his bathroom bag for his toothpaste.

"I said you should be nicer to people." This time the rasp was loud enough for Pete to hear. He looked up into the mirror again. Mikey met his eyes in the reflection. Pete saw anger in those eyes. *You're pissed at* me? He turned and faced the anger with some of his own.

"Get lost." His voice was low and deliberate. He wanted to say it slowly so the half-wit could follow.

Mikey stuck his hands in the pockets of his jeans and stuck out his almost chinless jaw.

They stood there staring for almost half a minute, the flame of something beginning to burn between them. Pete had meant every word he had said to Manny about Mikey. He was as filthy and nasty a human being as Pete had ever personally known. And he was not to be trusted. Not with information, not with food. Not with friendship. *And this is what Manny chooses for his best buddy.*

Pete snorted out, as if trying to clear his nose of the smell of the kid, and began to turn to face the mirror again.

"Don't you turn your back on me." The voice was a harsh rasp, gravel rubbed insistently on slate.

Pete stopped and looked back at Mikey, whose eyes were blazing now.

This kid, Pete thought. *This miserable excuse for a bastard is who he chooses? Well FINE!*

"You know what, Rat?" Pete saw him wince at the name. *Good.* Stepping forward, Pete stooped down to look Mikey right in the eye. "You, and your new buddy, can both just bite me."

Now Mikey's eyes flared and he reached up with his skinny talons and grabbed at Pete's throat. Pete pulled back and out of his reach. The little kid came forward, hands outstretched and clutching at Pete's shirt. Surprised at the other boy's tenacity, Pete slapped at the wiry arms and shoved him sideways.

Mikey staggered but kept his balance and launched himself back at Pete, who fended off the scrabbling hands. With a slap to Mikey's forearms, Pete spun the other boy half about. And as Mikey began to turn, Pete saw the fury in his eyes and had time to think only, *I've got to end this.* And the Rat regained himself and jumped again, hands high and aimed for the throat, Pete dropped low and shot an awkward punch toward the boy's exposed midsection. As his fist made contact with Mikey's narrow belly, Pete felt fire across his cheek.

Mikey let out a raspy grunt and crumple in midair. He hit the tile floor with a loud slap, and lay there gasping. Pete crouched for a moment, catching his breath, eyes flitting between Mikey and the tile floor between his own feet. Now Pete heard feet in the hallway, and someone entered the bathroom as he saw the first blood drop explode on the tile between his shoes. Manny now came into his field of vision, crouching down at Mikey's side putting a hand on the fallen kid's back.

Pete stood up and looked at himself in the mirror. One of Mikey's ragged, chewed up fingernails had gouged his cheek and the blood was running now. He watched in the mirror as a fat drop hit his white oxford shirt, bouncing across the surface of the cotton and leaving a red tracer down his chest. He grabbed the towel from the hook, dampened the corner under the tap and held the cool wet terrycloth to his wound.

In the mirror, he saw Manny help Mikey to his feet and turn him toward the door. Without a word or a look back, he guided the crumpled boy into the darkness of the hallway, leaving Pete to stare at himself in the harsh fluorescent light.

*   *   *

With a few minutes of direct pressure, Pete managed to stop the bleeding. When he inspected the cut he saw an inch long squiggle running from just below the corner of his left eye. It looked as if someone had used a hobby knife to carve a little tilde down his cheekbone. He wrapped his white shirt inside his towel and put them in the bottom of his laundry basket. He made it up to the front of the cottage for evening prayers just as Mr. Dawson was heading backrooms to fetch him.

"Good Lord, Pete! What happened to you?"

Pete had planned this out already. "I was reaching into my wardrobe to find my slippers and I caught my cheek on the hinge." It was a believable story. The staffers had the same crappy Riordan furniture in their rooms as the boys. Sooner or later, everybody scraped themselves on the protruding hinges. The staffer gave him a disinfectant swab and some ointment to go beneath a plastic bandage.

The boys were already assembled for prayers when Pete was finally done being treated. He walked in and took an open seat next to Billy, who smiled dumbly at him. Mikey and Manny were sitting together on a couch across the circle. Mikey was looking down at his feet and Manny was staring at Ms. Graham, who led them through their nightly *Our Father*, *Hail Mary* and *Act of Contrition*.

After the prayers were done, and the LEVEL 3s and 4s were in bed, Pete was sitting in the game room, re-reading the copy of *Illusions* Tabitha had given him. He looked up when he heard the door open. Manny came in and selected a bumper pool cue from the rack on the wall.

Pete looked through the windows of the game room to the front room beyond. Ms. Graham was watching television in the living room with Matt Saxon. Mr. Dawson had left a few minutes before to run some requisition forms over to Admin.

Pete looked back to Manny, wondering who would speak first. Whatever happened between them though, he had to tell Manny about Tony. *Maybe I should just tell him now,* he thought. But Manny beat him to speaking.

After sinking a few balls, Manny leaned back against the table and finally broke the silence: "You shouldn't have hurt him."

Pete looked up. Manny wasn't looking at him but was instead looking through the glass at the darkened living room beyond. Pete bristled, "I'm getting a little tired of hearing people tell me how I should be tonight."

"What I'm saying," Manny began again, looking toward him now, "is that you didn't have to hurt him."

Pete felt his eyes narrow and his jaw clench. "Are you defending him?" He asked the question quietly, and the quiet was echoing.

"I'm just saying he's a lot smaller than you and—."

"And nothing," Pete cut him off in a snapping whisper. "That little son of a bitch came at *me*. What was I supposed to do, reason with him?! In case you haven't noticed, the Rat isn't big with the sharing and the talking things out."

Manny looked away. He started to say, "Maybe next time you could try —"

But Pete had heard enough: "Maybe next time you can both just kiss my ass." Ms. Graham's head hadn't turned toward them, but Pete's voice was still low. He seethed. *Screw you!* All thought of telling Manny about what he's heard in the theater dissolved like smoke. In its place came something darker: *I hope the fat bastard thrashes you!*

Still looking away, Manny said, "You don't understand him, Pete. You can't." He sounded tired.

"What I understand is he cut me with one of his claws tonight, and we were lucky we didn't get caught fighting!"

"He didn't mean to hurt you," Manny said, shifting his seat against the pool table, eyes on the floor now.

"And just how the hell do you know that?" Pete sat forward on the low couch now, his book forgotten in his hands. "You weren't even there when he went for my freaking throat. He's a damn animal! That's what I understand, and I think it's time *you* understand it, too." Pete was done. He stood up and moved to the game room door; when his hand touched the handle Manny spoke again.

"You don't understand, Pete. You just can't," Manny repeated.

"Well, maybe not," Pete whispered over his shoulder as he opened the door, "but you haven't exactly tried explaining it, have you?" Feeling the heat rise in his cheeks, he walked out and went back to his room.

Pete got into bed and turned out his reading light. He curled himself over on his bed and looked out the windows of the cottage to the darkened world beyond. He looked at the window he and Manny had come through the night they'd gone up the hill. The night they had been friends.

Screw you, he thought again, and had a momentary dark joy at the thought of Manny getting what he deserved from Fat Tony. Sleep for him was a long time coming and it came with no rest.

Chapter 17

"I'm going to send you up to see the nurse this morning, Pete."

They were heading into the dining hall for breakfast. Mr. Dawson had called Pete up to the cottage office while the boys who were leaving for home visit had been doing their last minute packing. He'd made Pete show him the wound.

"I'm okay, sir." Pete didn't want to go see the nurse, especially with an actual wound. She had a tendency to poke at things that hurt. One time last year he had fallen into the Gihon Creek and put a fair cut in his knee. She had poked and prodded at the thing for twenty minutes of cleaning. Pete didn't know if she was unaware doing stuff like that hurt or if she just had the secret mean streak he kind of assumed most medical people possessed.

"Now I'm sure you're fine, but I'd feel a lot better if Ms. Belz took a look at it."

Sure you'll feel fine, Pete thought. *Yours won't be the cheek she's scouring with a wire brush.*

Mr. Dawson told him a pass would come down to the school for him. "It looks a little red around the edge. She should clean it up so you don't end up with an infection. Who knows what might be on one of those hinges."

The mention of infection made Pete realize Mr. Dawson was right, but not for the reason he suspected. Mikey was undoubtedly a Petrie dish of infectious diseases and the damage had been done by his knife-like fingernail. Probably better to have it expertly scrubbed, even if it did hurt like hell.

At least school would be relatively painless today. Because most of the kids on campus would be leaving in the afternoon, school had been scheduled as a half day, with the boys going to shorter versions of all of their classes before being let out for lunch and released from school completely until after New Years. Mostly it would be teachers finishing up projects they had been working on and giving out revised term grades. They wouldn't even be dressing for PE, but would instead be in the rec hall for 30 minutes of pool and ping pong.

Breakfast was French toast. Pete ate with Mr. Dawson while the staffer filled out a medical appointment request. Today he sat with his back to the other side of the dining room and to Manny and Mikey. He hadn't spoken with Manny at all since leaving the game room the night before. They'd made eye contact in the hallway this morning, Pete walking toward the bathroom and Manny exiting it with his toothbrush and towel. At first Manny hadn't met his eye, but did glance quickly at Pete before disappearing into the room he shared with Mikey.

The Rat himself avoided making any eye contact. *So much the better*, Pete thought. He'd slept poorly and this morning he was feeling it. He'd woken up tired, still angry at Manny, but mad at himself too. He knew he should have told Manny about what he'd heard backstage, but the boy's defense of Mikey had been completely out of line. *If you know what's right, you gotta do what's right.* It was his Mitch's voice inside his head. Pete remembered hearing him say it in explanation of something they'd seen on the news a few months before his final trip out of the driveway.

Apparently some guy had broken into a cosmetics laboratory in Los Angeles and freed a few hundred test animals. The news footage showed him in handcuffs, being let to a police cruiser, but his head was up and he was yelling with a smile on his face. The news showed a spokesman for the cosmetics company talking about the care they took for their test subjects and fringe animal rights groups. Mitch had shaken his head and said, "A lesson Pete: If you know what's right, you gotta do what's right. Whatever the cost."

And sitting in the dining hall, finishing his breakfast, Pete knew Mitch was right. Even though Manny was wrong, Pete still had to tell him.

"You and Manny still not talking?"

The question startled Pete. He looked up to see Mr. Dawson glancing from him to the world past Pete, where Mikey and Manny were eating.

Pete shook his head. "No."

Mr. Dawson smiled kindly and nodded. "Ok. I won't ask, but if you want to tell me I'll listen."

"Thanks, sir, but I don't want to talk about it."

Mr. Dawson shrugged, "Your call."

Ten minutes later, Pete was hanging out on the black top between the dining hall and the school. He was listening to Jordi and Chris argue about some damn thing and watching the St. Anthony's kids play Riordan Ball. It was a version of foursquare with slightly different rules. The Ants played it almost every morning before school. Across the yard he spotted Manny talking with Mikey and Matt Saxon, though it looked as though the Rat was working on his listening skills because he didn't seem to be saying a word.

Fat Tony wasn't anywhere to be seen. Probably in doing a kitchen clean up job.

He was still angry at the way Manny had defended Mikey the night before, but knew he should get it over with and tell him. He started to move.

"Pete."

He turned to see Mr. Dawson coming down the steps from the dining hall. When he got close he said, "I just saw Ms. Belz in the staff dining room. She'd like you to come up right now so she can see you before parents start arriving. She has to spend a lot of time talking to parents on home visit days. I'll walk you up so you won't need a pass."

Pete glanced toward Manny and shrugged. It would have to wait. He turned back to Mr. Dawson. "Okay."

"All done. How does it feel?"

Like you enjoyed that! Pete thought, wincing inwardly. The sting of the antiseptic made the wound feel fresh again.

"Fine," he said.

"Well, leave the bandage on until you wake up tomorrow, then let it breathe a little. Put some antibiotic ointment on it after you bathe for the next few days."

"Do you think it will leave a scar?" he asked.

"I doubt it," she replied. "It looks like you and Mr. Dawson cleaned it out pretty well last night, so I shouldn't think it would."

"Thanks, Mrs. Belz."

"My pleasure," she said, then hesitated a moment before continuing. "Pete, can I ask you a question?"

"Sure."

She cocked her head slightly to one side and asked, "How did you get hurt?"

"What do you mean?" he said, knowing his face gave him away.

She smiled. "Well the hinge is a reasonable explanation, but I know what a cut like that looks like and this is a different kind of wound."

Pete slumped a bit. He had no desire to have the details of his confrontation with Mikey brought to light. The more he thought about the fight this morning the worse he felt. He didn't regret defending himself, but Manny may have been right: he might have been able to get out of it without punching the skinny kid.

"Do you want to tell me what happened?" the nurse asked.

He swallowed. "No. Please, Mrs. Belz, it was an accident. The person who did this didn't mean to. We were just playing around and I got hurt, really."

After a few moments of looking him over, she nodded, but her face said, *Okay, but only as long as you understand I don't believe you.*

It was good enough for Pete. He stood up out of the chair and asked, "Am I all done?"

Her look changed into a suspicious smile, "Yeah, you're free to go. But let me know if you'd like to tell me what happened."

He nodded and left the exam room. Mrs. Belz's assistant, Doris, was sitting at the reception desk and smiled up at Pete, "Bye dear."

"Bye," Pete said and reached for the door. His fingers had just begun to curl around the wooden handle when the door was ripped open and out of his grasp. Pete stepped back as the light from outside was all but blocked by the huge form of Mr. Turnbull. The caseworker was turned sideways and coming through the door. The way his arms were reaching back, Pete had the impression he was carrying something, but the massive body blocked whatever it was. Mr. Turnbull paused when he saw Pete, and he looked down as if he didn't recognize the boy.

Just visible past Mr. Turnbull, Dr. Rugani, the psychologist, was holding open the door. Pete was confused until Mr. Turnbull came all the way in the room and turned. Then Pete saw the person walking next to the caseworker, the person Chuck the Truck was supporting. The face was streaked with blood, one eye already beginning to close with swelling. The other eye was open and just visible through low hanging black bangs. Pete's stomach hardened into a solid ball when he saw the eye. Between the bruises, the lips of the face parted to form a perverse smile. Blood shone brightly on white teeth. From the smiling lips, Manny's voice came quietly, yet inexplicably conversational: "How you doing, Pete?"

Mr. Turnbull was calling Mrs. Belz. Doris was already up out of her seat and coming toward Manny with hands outstretched. Dr. Rugani had his hands on Pete's shoulders now and was saying something. Mr. Turnbull turned and walked/dragged Manny across the floor to the same exam room Pete had just left.

Now Pete was being guided outside into the crisp December air. Dr. Rugani's hand on his shoulder moved him from the Infirmary out to the main road and pointed him down the hill. The frost of his breath in the cold morning air left a disappearing trail as he walked down toward the school, not hearing the assurances or questions from the psychologist.

Pete was the first boy into the rec hall for PE. It was his third class of the day and his first with Jordi or Chris, and he needed to talk to them. Mr. Mcleese told him today would be free play within the hall, he could choose his game. He went over to the sofas by the television to wait for the others.

He had heard varying descriptions of the attack from a dozen different boys in his classes, all claiming to have been right there when it had gone down. Teachers tried to quell the talk as best they could, but fights, especially those resulting in blood and serious injury, were containment defying topics.

Some said words had flown before blows. Others claimed it was a jumping, plain and simple. One kid from Mt. Olivett even said Manny had thrown the first punch, but after Pete had asked him if he'd seen it himself, the kid admitted he hadn't, but had been told by someone who swore it was true. Pete needed to hear about it from someone reliable. And though he had told Manny there was no one at the Home he trusted, he was coming to understand he had been deluding himself.

Because there were people he trusted. Despite his protests to the contrary, Chris and Jordi and Frankie were his friends and had been for a long time. And right now he wanted to hear the story from them. He needed to talk to friends.

Boys trickled in during the passing period. Chris and Jordi arrived together a couple of minutes after Pete and hurried over to the sofas when they spotted him. They wore identical masks of concern.

"Did you already hear about it?" Chris asked before even sitting down.

"Yeah. But everyone saw something different. I don't know which story to believe. Did you guys see what happened?" They both nodded and Jordi's eyes drifted toward the floor. Pete could see he was watching the whole thing again.

"Tell me."

It turned out their version most closely matched the one Pete had heard from Nacho during Math. Manny had still been talking to Matt and Mikey right before the first bell rang. After Pete's departure with Mr. Dawson, Chris and Jordi had begun drifting across the blacktop, both because their first class was in that direction, and because they needed to ask Frankie a question to settle their argument. Frankie had been talking with his cousin on the periphery of a group of JP's friends, including Steven, Teddy and Fat Tony.

"I saw it right before the bell," Jordi said. "Steven looked at his watch and said something to Tony. Then he looked around for staff." Pete didn't need to ask how Jordi knew staff was what Steven had been looking for; the furtive eye darting of a boy checking staff whereabouts was all too recognizable at the Home. "Then he said something else to Tony, and Tony started moving toward Manny and the others."

Chris picked up the narrative. "Matt and Manny kind of had their backs to him as he came up, but not the Rat." Pete noted the anger in Chris' voice. "No, not the Rat. He saw the whole damn thing coming and didn't do shit to stop it." Chris shook his head.

"He did say something," Jordi said. "Right before Tony got there, Rat said something to Manny. Don't know what it was, but he was looking past at Tony when he said it."

"I didn't see that," Chris said.

"Then what happened?" Pete asked. But he already knew enough from Nacho's telling of it.

"Bastard nailed him right in the back of the ribs is what happened." Jordi said. "Just as the bell started to ring, he got to Manny. Matt almost warned him in time but was too late. Tony cracked him one in the ribs and Manny went to his knees." Jordi cringed at the memory and shook his head. "And once he was on his knees, man, he was done."

Pete had a mental image of Manny on his knees, fire coursing through his ribs, Fat Tony's ham like fists raised above.

"Matt was about to jump in," Jordi said, "but Jeremy Temple stopped him." Pete nodded. Jeremy was Matt's cousin. He was older, having just moved to the group home this past October. He hadn't yet started at the high school and was still attending classes at the Riordan school.

"What about Mikey?" Pete asked.

"The brave hero?" Chris spat. "Little bitch bugged out as soon as the first punch landed." He shook his head. "Freaking RAT! All that Manny's done for him, as nice as he's been to him and he pusses out the first chance."

Pete found himself touching the bandages across the gash in his cheek, remembering the Rat was capable of some damage. But that had been one-on-one, he told himself. Even Mikey wasn't stupid enough to get between Fat Tony and his mark.

Chris looked around the room, as if he was looking for Mikey, despite the fact he was in a different class this period.

After a few moments, Pete felt the need to press the story onward. "What happened after Manny went down?"

Jordi stood silent for a few moments, and Chris brought his eyes back to the sofa and looked down at his folded hands.

"After he went down," Chris said, "there was like... a moment of quiet." Jordi nodded and looked away.

Pete nodded too. He knew the quiet the other boy was describing. It was the same quiet that came right after someone cussed at staff, like the time everyone in the cottage stopped what they were doing to find out if Malcolm had actually just called Weaver a 'little bitch monkey.' But Pete knew, like Malcolm's moment, which had stretched just enough for everyone to notice the silence, Fat Tony's fists could only stay up in the air for so long.

The beating had been brief but savage. Chris had counted at least five punches landing before Fat Tony himself had been taken out.

"And it was weird," Chris said. "He just disappeared." Though they had only been a dozen yards away from the fight when the ambush happened, by the time Tony had started dropping clubbing blows onto the grounded Manny, the crowd had thickened. So when Tony's shaved head dropped from view they had no idea what had happened. Then, where none had been moments before, suddenly cottage staffers were everywhere around the blacktop, working crowd control and pushing the gawkers off toward their classrooms.

When the crowd had thinned enough for them to catch a glimpse, Jordi and Chris had seen Fat Tony face down on the ground, only his massive belly and forehead touching the pavement. His arms and legs were held up behind him, pinned by Mr. Banks and another staffer. "He looked like a fat, hogtied rocking horse," Jordi said, but even he didn't laugh at the otherwise comic image.

"What about Manny?"

Chris shook his head. "I thought he was dead at first. He was just lying there, bleeding. Not moving." Pete's imagination wouldn't let him away from the image of Manny, broken on the grayed asphalt. Having seen him bloodied in Mr. Turnbull's arms was somehow not as bad as hearing the beating described.

*　　　*　　　*

Though he had no appetite, Pete was the first boy to the St. Gabe's dining room for lunch. Besides Manny, several other boys were gone, having already disappeared to their home visits. In fact, dozens of boys had already left campus, and the whole of the dining hall was practically deserted and the collective sound of the campus meal felt muted and mournful to Pete. Of the St. Gabe's boys, only Jordi, Matt, Billy and Malcolm were still around. Mr. Dawson had moved the small tables together and the six of them ate around a single family sized table. There was a minimum of conversation and for a long time no one spoke about the morning's events.

Finally, Matt Saxon asked where Manny was, if he was okay. From the look on his face it was obvious Matt felt guilty about not having helped Manny before things had gone bad. But Pete didn't blame Matt. *No,* he told himself miserably, *it wasn't Matt's fault.* Mr. Dawson answered only that Manny was going to be fine. Chuck the Truck had taken him to Kaiser Hospital in Santa Rosa to see a doctor. As he pushed macaroni and cheese around on his plate, Pete wondered if Manny would be back tonight. He hoped so, but was sick at the thought of trying to explain, to apologize for not having warned him.

After being prodded by Mr. Dawson to eat something, Pete managed to choke down about a third of his lunch, but passed on dessert. He spent most of his time staring out the window, toward the Admin parking lot, where a sheriff's cruiser was parked. Jordi had seen the car and its massive occupant arrive during second period while he had been waiting in the Admin lobby to talk to his caseworker. It had been nearly 2 hours and the car was still there.

The cruiser wasn't alone. There were a lot of extra cars in the lot belonging to parents picking up kids for the holiday. Pete imagined the Admin staff was probably doing some impressive tap dancing trying to explain away the police presence to moms, dads and legal guardians. He'd witnessed enough pick-ups to notice a trend of parents being really critical about every little thing at the Home. It always struck him as strange that parents would complain persistently, and sometimes loudly about the Home, but would invariably bring their kids back at the end of home visit. The cop car had to be a major topic of conversation this morning.

Pete spent the better part of the late afternoon alone in the living room of St. Gabe's, watching the road. The extended afternoon rec had crept past slowly after lunch, boys disappearing as the day progressed, coordinators and caseworkers stepping into the rec hall and plucking students away to bestow them upon waiting parents and relatives. As more and more boys departed, Pete found himself again wishing he was going home as well. He'd called Tabitha at rec but had gotten her answering machine.

Now, sitting in the living room of the cottage waiting for dinner, he stared down the length of the Riordan driveway. For almost two hours he'd been looking down the road, impatient for the return of Mr. Turnbull's big red Bronco. In his lap was the book Tabitha had given him. He ran his thumb over the edge of the pages, listening to them ripple and zip.

As he watched the road, he thought back over the last two months since Manny's arrival. He let himself relive the strange relationship which had developed between him and the other boy. He still knew so little about Manny, and what he did know often confused him. What he was beginning to understand though was what made Manny different than the rest of the boys at the Home, why he stood out. It took him a while to be able to name it, and realizing what it was only made Pete feel worse. He had spent so much time angry with Manny for taking up with the Ra— with Mikey, he had not been able to see what his friend had done for the sad kid. The change he had wrought in Mikey had been almost mind boggling, from his LEVEL change to his school work to his general demeanor, Mikey had been almost transformed through Manny's efforts.

But, and here was the thing, Manny's efforts hadn't even been that great. He had simply been kind to Michael Hamm. He had talked to the kid, had listened to him, encouraged him. And such was Manny's gift, what made him different: he was genuinely a good person.

Pete could not believe it had only been three and a half weeks since Manny had accompanied him up the hill to retrieve the gifts left there by Tabitha. Three and a half weeks. Mr. Nielsen had once told the class that during its year long orbit around the sun, the Earth travels 10 million miles in one month's time. So much had happened in these last three and a half weeks. For the first time in his life Pete imagined he could almost feel those millions of miles taking their toll.

Fat Tony was gone. Mr. Johnson had told Pete when he'd come on shift after rec. Tony been taken to juvenile hall for assaulting Manny and breaking his probation. The supervisor wouldn't venture a guess as to whether Tony be returning the Riordan Home, he said he'd seen kids come back after doing worse and kids remanded for doing less. Pete himself thought it unlikely they'd see the fat kid again. Though they were far from friends, having lived in close proximity for a year and a half was enough for boys to pick up each others' stories. Pete and everyone knew enough about Tony to know Riordan had been a last ditch effort by his mother and P.O. to try to keep him out of permanent trouble. The common assumption among the boys of St. Gabe's was that Tony's attack on Manny would prove too vicious to be ignored by probation officials or a judge.

As the light let itself out of the day, Pete stayed where he was, watching he road and thinking of Manny.

*   *   *

Chuck the Truck showed up during dinner. Pete was eating in the staff dining room again, along with the other two dozen boys still on campus. They had been told they would all be returning to their own cottages, and that all cottages with at least two boys would be open for the night and consolidation wouldn't happen until tomorrow evening.

He had regained some of his appetite and was eating alone when Mr. Turnbull showed up and came over to him. The caseworker told him Manny was back on campus and was being checked in through the infirmary. He would meet them back at the cottage afterward. When Pete asked how badly Manny was hurt, Mr. Turnbull hesitated for a moment before speaking, then finally said, "He's banged up purty good. Got an eye patch over his left, and he's kinda medicated." Pete shook his head in question.

"He's got a couple broken ribs to go along with his shiner," Mr. Turnbull said, "so the doc gave him some codeine to take the bite outta the pain." The man smiled wanly. "Ole Manny tried to convince the doc he didn't need the pain meds, said he preferred not to have them because they tend to knock him flat. But the doc said nonsense, and made him take the first one there in the office." The caseworker raised his eyebrows and nodded, "Manny does know himself, though. Got to give him that. He all but passed out on the way back here because of the meds. Doing better now though. But I got to give him another pill before he sleeps, so you may hear him mumbling to himself like he did all the way back here in my truck. At least he did promise the doc he would ask for another pill tomorrow if he is hurting still."

Manny was already at the cottage when Pete and Ms. Graham returned. Mr. Johnson was working in the staff office while Manny was sitting at a table in the living room picking at half of a turkey sandwich. A brown bag from a local deli and a large fountain soda also sat on the table. When he noticed Pete walk in, he looked up through his one good eye and smiled, repeating the last thing Pete had heard him say: "How you doing, Pete?"

Mr. Turnbull showed up just after 8 pm to give Manny his last dose for the night. Manny offered only minimal protest before downing the pain drug along with some anti-inflammatory pills for the swelling. And there was a lot of swelling. After he'd finished eating the half of the sandwich he wanted, Manny showed Pete the bruise on his back, from when Tony had sucker punched him and cracked the two ribs. Pete thought the bruise looked like Australia. Manny studied the swelling in the mirror and had said he thought it looked more like Borneo.

While Manny's shirt was up, Pete had been able to see small shadows of older bruise, all but faded on Manny's chest. He'd mentioned this to Manny who had said the doc had asked about them too, had wondered at their origin. Manny, who'd seemed lucid despite Chuck the Truck's warnings, said he'd told the doc "mostly the truth" about the blanket party, only brushing up against a lie when he'd suggested the guy responsible had been expelled from the Home.

Beneath the patch, his left eye was all but swollen shut. According to Manny, the doctor had said he didn't get enough injuries like this one. When Pete asked what the hell he was talking about, Manny explained the doc had indicated the damage was ugly and extensive, but looked to be mainly cosmetic.

As they sat and chatted, Pete felt himself double again, like he had the night Manny had moved in with Mikey. But this time, the second Pete wasn't made up of rage, but of guilt instead. He couldn't bring himself to tell Manny the truth about his role in the beating. And why should he? He had Manny back! Despite the horrors of the morning, and the anxiety of the afternoon, things had turned out ok: Manny was going to be all right, Fat Tony was gone from Riordan (probably for good) and Pete had his friend back. It was like they had just been up in the oaks on top of the hill last night. For the first Pete, the one not comprised of guilt over his inaction, life was feeling good and right again.

But the second Pete knew he should tell Manny the truth. *He deserves the truth.* And Pete also knew instinctively that Manny would probably believe he didn't withhold the information willfully, that he hadn't wanted this to happen. But it didn't make beginning the conversation any easier. How could he even bring it up? Did he ever need to? Things were better between them now; they were back to where they had been before their falling out over Manny's growing friendship with Mikey. He didn't want to take the chance of Manny blaming him for the attack.

Pete knew he would ultimately have to tell Manny what had happened, about knowing of the attack beforehand. *When he's feeling better,* Pete thought. *And after he's off the meds.* There was no rush. He could tell him after Christmas.

Chapter 18

By Christmas morning, Manny was medication free, but Pete could tell he was still feeling pain. They were sharing a room in the Fitzpatrick House where they'd been for the previous two nights. The group home had palatial appointments compared to the regular cottages: the furniture was newer, the carpets had thick padding under them and the rooms themselves even had doors. And, instead of a large communal bathroom with stalls and a bank of showers, the homes had four individual bathrooms like in regular homes, each with a toilet, a sink, a shower and a door.

Manny was still moving gingerly around the room in the mornings, but now he was making jokes about it, as opposed to the first couple of mornings when he'd woken groggily and couldn't think or focus for several minutes. In fact, the first morning they had been in the Fitzpatrick home it had taken Manny almost five minutes to snap out of his stupor and remember where he was.

At breakfast in the staff dining room, there were only six boys and only two staff, Mr. DeMarcus, who had spent the night with them in the Fitzpatrick House, and Ms. Kelly, who came in midway through the meal, ruffled Manny's hair and winked at Pete. She was dressed more formally than they were used to seeing her, in dark slacks and a cream colored sweater. Her hair was down today, making it almost impossible for Pete to take his eyes off her. As she served herself from the buffet table, both Pete and Manny watched her every move. With her back to them, her hair spread across the shoulders of her sweater like dark chocolate on vanilla ice cream. Both boys quickly shifted their eyes back to their plates right before she turned back to them. Loaded up with eggs and sausage, Ms. Kelly stopped at the coffee urn before coming to sit with them.

"How's the eye?" she asked as she dove into her eggs.

"Getting better," he told her. "I get it checked out again on Monday. I should be done playing Blackbeard after that."

"I don't know," Ms. Kelly said through a bite of sausage, "the pirate thing is a good look for you. You look like the comic book character, Nick Fury agent of S.H.I.E.L.D.."

She obviously saw the look of disbelief on both their faces and laughed: "What? A girl can't know comics?"

Later, when Ms. Kelly excused herself to get more coffee, Manny asked Pete, "Did you know she was into comics?"

"No," Pete said.

"Wow," Manny laughed, "and I thought I was in love with her before."

*   *   *

After breakfast Ms. Kelly walked them down to St. Gabe's to change for 11:00 Christmas Mass. While Manny took advantage of the quiet to catch a shower, Pete laid his pants and shirt out on his bed, next to the new fleece San Francisco Giants blanket, his Christmas gift from the cottage staff.   He let his eyes drift to Manny's gift: a small battery powered book light. The light was on top of Manny's current read, *Stranger in a Strange Land*.

He'd asked Manny what the book was about. It sounded like an adventure story of some kind, maybe a person going somewhere he doesn't belong. Manny said sort of, it was about a human raised on Mars who comes home to find he doesn't fit in. Pete decided he might like to try it out after he finished the book his aunt had unexpectedly sent him for Christmas. She'd also sent along a note apologizing for her absence over the holiday and explaining Mr. Turnbull had suggested a book might make a good gift this year, evidence suggested Pete had taken an interest in reading. In the note she went on to describe getting a recommendation from the sales clerk at the book store who had suggested what he considered the perfect book for a 13 year old boy: Stephen King's *The Gunslinger*.

At 10:40 Ms. Kelly ushered the clean and neatly dressed boys out of the cottage and toward the chapel. Based on the number of cars in the parking lot, Pete was expecting a crowd when they stepped through the doors at the back of the sanctuary, but he was still surprised. It was common knowledge the chapel had seats for 500, but after a quick glance Pete guessed there were close to 100 people standing along the back wall.

Because the Home was all but empty of boys, there were no pews designated as reserved for them. But Ms. Kelly walked them to the left side of the last row where Mr. DeMarcus had saved three seats.

From where they were sitting, Pete had a view of the whole congregation, or at least of the backs of most of their heads. He saw Mr. Nielsen and his wife several rows ahead of them. Mr. Nielsen was hat free of course, and Pete noticed again how his missing ear made him look slightly lopsided. In the crowd Pete saw several other Riordan staffers, some alone, others with partners and families. He kept looking, hoping he'd be able to find Tabitha in the crowd. When they'd talked briefly the previous week, she'd said her family was coming to mass and to look for them near the middle of the right side of the church, that they almost always sat on that side. He was looking there now and not seeing her. He figured she was over there, just behind someone. He kept looking, hoping to find the right sight line.

He was still looking to the middle right of the crowd when Manny nudged him and whispered, "Other side. Two rows up."

Pete let his eyes travel back several rows from the middle of the other side of the large room. After a desperate moment of silently cursing Manny for messing around with him, he found her, right there, almost straight across the church. She was wearing a teal cable-knit turtle neck sweater. It covered her neck up to her ears, which were visible thanks to another of the simple silver hair clips she favored. She was alternately talking to the person next to her and peeking around the room. On her far side Evelyn Pembrook sat in the end seat of the wooden pew. She appeared to be reading the liturgy book while Tabitha continued chatting with a man whose back was to Pete.

He kept staring at her, willing her to see him. And almost three minutes later she did. While the man was speaking, Tabitha's eyes slipped past his shoulder and found Pete. He was sure she momentarily sat up a little straighter, and her conversation partner must have sensed it as well, because as Pete felt the smile coming to his face, the man cocked his head and said something to Tabitha.

Then he turned his head to follow her gaze. Pete whipped his eyes forward, finding Mr. Nielsen's one good ear and locking onto it. But he knew he'd been caught.

Once mass had begun and he could see both of their profiles virtually side by side, Pete had no doubt as to the identity of the man.

After the service, Pete lingered on the periphery of the milling crowd, watching hopefully for a chance to talk to her, but she stayed with her mom and dad, chatting with other families on the chapel steps. Finally, as Ms. Kelly nudged them toward the cottage to change for Christmas at the Nielsen's, Pete made eye contact with Tabitha. He was about to look away for the last time when she turned suddenly and shot him a darting smile. Thought it was hardly a smile at all, her lips having barely moved. But the warmth flowing out of her eyes in that half heartbeat of stolen time was the distilled essence of smile. And it was his. He turned and walked toward the cottage, imagining her eyes following him.

Shortly after returning to the Fitzpatrick House following Christmas dinner, Pete fell into bed ready to sleep until New Year's Eve. They'd had another spectacular holiday feast, this time at Mr. Nielsen's house, and Pete was being quickly enveloped by a rather pleasant post meal warmth spreading outward from his full belly. It had been a great day. Mr. Nielsen had gone non-traditional and had bar-b-cued amazing baby back ribs. And Mrs. Nielsen had outdone herself on the side dishes and desserts. The only thing missing from the day had been a chance to speak to Tabitha. Seeing her at mass had been great, but it would have been nice to talk to her. Pete smiled at the memory of the moment their eyes had met.

Manny walked slowly in from the bathroom and lay down gingerly on his bed. "Wow, talk about some great pie."

"I actually had the chocolate cake. It was like a super dense coco brick."

Manny chuckled, "Yeah, I had a bit of that too. Mrs. Nielsen kept pushing food at me. Like she thinks food helps with bruising."

"Does it?"

"Well, breathing doesn't kill me like it did a few days ago, but it still does hurt a lot, and I don't think I'll be running in rec for a while."

"How's the eye?" Pete looked at Manny, who tilted the eye patch up and blinked away from the light.

"Not too bad. Sensitive though, the light really makes it water." He rubbed the eye gently before replacing the patch. "I see the doc again in a few days."

"Good." Pete's response was reflective of his mood. Manny was back. He'd seen Tabitha. Hell, even his new Giants blanket had him feeling the old Christmas spirit. He felt light, in spite of the heavy meal. Leaning back on the bed, he had a flash of memory from long ago, from a Christmas when his mother was alive. She had been halfway through her first round of chemo therapy then. Her hair was mostly gone and she had taken to wearing knit beanies of varying color and design. On this Christmas she had been wearing a blue one with white snowflakes. They had sat around Grandma and Grandpa's living room tossing a squishy purple ball back and forth all morning, for hours it seemed. And they'd just hung out and talked. Pete didn't remember what they had talked about, but he remembered the feeling of that morning. She had been getting better. The scary time had passed. They were going to make it. Grandpa had cooked his special sourdough waffles.

Then just as quickly, he flashed to her propped up in a big bed, a different knit cap this time: a white one with red tulips. Her hands were folded in her lap, the I.V. lines snaking across the cheap bedspread. She was smiling at him sadly, saying she understood. And he was walking out of her room for the last time. He'd been so angry with her, had told her he was tired of her being sick, that he wasn't coming back to the hospital anymore, that he wouldn't come back again until she was better. And he'd kept his word. He'd gone with Aunt Marjorie back to the house that had once belonged to his grandparents and had not seen his mother again. Even at the funeral two weeks later the box had been closed.

"Pete?"

At the funeral, adults simultaneously felt compelled to speak to him and been unable to come up with anything to say. During the wake at his aunt's house, one of Lilly O'Boyle's acquaintances, a pleasant enough woman named Daphne, had found herself foundering in an attempt to talk to the son of her dead friend and had tried to make him feel better by telling him his mom had been depressed for a while, but had really started fighting again in the last week. "She told me," Daphne had said, "she was fighting for you, for her beautiful boy." And in a last ditch effort to make the conversation comfortable had added, "Wasn't that sweet?"

"Pete?!"

He had nodded, agreeing silently that it was sweet his mother had tried to fight the cancer off for her thankless son who had walked out on her, who had selfishly stayed away from her.

"Pete!"

He blinked several times and turned to see Manny sitting up watching him.

"Huh?"

"You did it again?" Manny sounded upset. "What the hell, man?"

Pete was suddenly sitting up too, hotly embarrassed. "Nothing. I'm ok."

But Manny wasn't taking it. "No way, man. Not this time. What happened?

"Nothing, really." He looked away from Manny, inspecting the closed door of the room closely. From the corner of his eye he could see Manny still staring at him.

"It was nothing," Pete repeated. "It just... kind of happens sometimes."

"*What* kind of happens? You're not answering me." Pete understood now: what he'd first heard as anger was actually worry. And it was genuine, which made the whole thing somehow worse. He waited before answering, too long for Manny's liking. "This is the second time I've seen you lock out like that. What was it?"

Pete sighed. Manny was right, he should tell. "It's just..." but how could he explain what he didn't completely get himself. He looked at his friend, found something there in Manny's gaze he could hold on to and tried again. "I get angry," was all he said at first.

If Manny had said something stupid in response, like *"So do I,"* or *"Yeah, who doesn't?"* then Pete would have been able to ignore the compulsion to keep speaking. But now he felt the edge coming up and he wanted to keep going. And Manny gave him no reason to pause or second guess. He just sat looking at Pete, radiating waves of concern. Pete took a breath, and started again.

"Mr. Turnbull calls them my 'moments.' They usually only happen when I'm angry at myself or somebody close to me." He felt his hands twisting the bedspread.

"They started a little while after my mom died. My aunt was the first person to notice." He thought of his aunt, of the way she sometimes fussed over him. It wasn't her fault her sister had died and left behind a burden. For all of her frustrating traits, she'd done her best for him.

"She tried to take care of me, she really did. But I did a bunch of stupid stuff. I started staying out all of the time, cutting school. I got picked up by the police a bunch of times for loitering during school hours and being truant. That's when my aunt started to get upset, when the cops started showing up at her hospital with me in the back of the car." Pete looked to the bedside table, at the book his aunt had sent him. He needed to thank her for it.

"Eventually," he finally went on, "I got into real trouble."

Manny simply watched and listened.

"This guy I hung with sometimes, Davey Levasseur, one night he broke into the shop at this little nine-hole golf course near my aunt's house. I was with him. I didn't do anything. I mean I waited outside, but I hid in the bushes; I wasn't a lookout or anything. But he gave me half the cash out of the register." Pete remembered counting the money, all $142.00 of it. He'd stashed it in his underwear drawer behind the dress socks he'd worn to his mother's funeral. Every dollar was still there when the balding detective had shown up three days later.

"Davey got pulled in by the vice principal for something else, and they found the money on him. He gave me up." Manny was still listening, nodding at the right times. Pete kept talking.

"Because my aunt was working night shifts at the hospital and couldn't keep track of me, and because I'd gotten into a bunch of trouble at school, I had to spend a few nights in juvie." Pete smiled humorlessly. "The judge said his main concern was my 'lack of parental supervision.'" He remembered the gut punch of the comment, and how the judge had immediately realized the painful truth of what he'd said. He looked up at Manny, and saw he understood, too. "So, probation. Aunt Marjorie was freaked. She wanted to take care of me, but she'd come to realize she couldn't. My P.O. came up with Riordan as an answer."

Pete felt himself suddenly nostalgic for his aunt's house. He'd never considered it his home, but now felt his thoughts drawn there. The window of the room he'd slept in overlooked a park. His mom used to bring him there to play when they visited his aunt.

He knew he had drifted and looked at Manny, to find him still listening intently. He went on.

"About two months after my mom died, my aunt took me to the doctor. She thought I was having seizures. I told her I was fine, said I just kind of got lost in my thoughts, that was all. But she'd seen enough epileptics to know seizures can look all kind of different ways. And I wasn't completely aware of them. Apparently it had happened several times without me knowing it. She told the doctor what she'd seen me do, the way I... she told him about it. He looked me over, ordered some blood-work, and made me get a CAT scan. Didn't find anything wrong. He suggested I talk to one of the hospital's shrinks."

"After one session, the psychiatrist said I was suffering from stress, brought on by my mom's death. She told my aunt that with counseling, the behavior she'd witnessed might fade over time."

Pete paused. Manny was nodding, but his brow was furrowed, a question forming there.

"What?" Pete asked.

Manny said, "I get stress as an explanation, but why does it only happen with anger? Or do you not know?"

Pete stared at Manny for a long moment, and then said, "You told me something about it, when you first got here. You said, 'we don't get punished for our anger, but we get punished by our anger.' Is that what you said?"

Manny nodded.

Pete nodded too. "I don't think its one or the other, I think both are true. And it's not just about getting punished; I know what anger costs."

He breathed deeply again. "You know my mom died of cancer."

Manny's face tightened a little. "Yeah, you told me."

Pete sniffed, then told the worst truth of his life. "I let her die alone." He looked at Manny then quickly looked away. He felt the first tears well in his lower lids and knew he needed to finish this. "I was mad at her. She'd had cancer before and gotten better. She wasn't getting better and I got mad at her for it." He told Manny of his refusal to go to the hospital in those final days, even when Aunt Marjorie had told him he *needed* to come.

"At first, I thought she'd died because of me. But I know now that's wrong. The cancer was just too much the last time. My being in the room with her for the last week wouldn't have stopped the cancer from killing her." He sniffed again, feeling the tears run down his face and wiping them away with his hand. "But if I'd been there, she would have died knowing I loved her." He felt the sob welling. "But she didn't know. I didn't get the chance to tell her. All because I was mad." The sob broke and washed over him. He pressed the heels of his palms into his eyes and sobbed again, and again, and again.

After several minutes, he reached down for the towel he'd left next to the bed after his morning shower, grabbed it and wiped the tears and snot from his face and hands. When he'd finished sniffing his way to composure, he looked up and saw Manny staring back at him through red-rimmed eyes.

Pete felt more collected and finished what he had begun. "It took me a long time to know why I get those moments. But knowing doesn't make it any better. Mr. Turnbull tries to help, but every time he tells me my mom knew I loved her, I want to scream at him. She couldn't have known because I didn't tell her. She may have known the week before, but she didn't know the day she died. She didn't know in her last moments."

Pete looked up again. Manny cleared his throat and asked, "Did she love you at the end? When she was in the hospital, and she knew she was going to die, do you think she loved you?"

Pete felt like he'd been slapped and whispered, "What?"

"Did she love you?" Manny asked again. Clearly he'd been affected by Pete's story, but his tone was matter of fact. Pete felt his jaw open. *Did she love me?*

Manny nodded, "Of course she did. And you know it. Not because her friend told you she was fighting for you, and not because Mr. Turnbull told you she did. And not because she told you herself before you left the last time. You know it because she was your mom, and she'd shown you every day of your life."

Pete felt the tears threatening again.

"She knew you loved her the same way." And Pete knew Manny was correct, but saw his friend took no pleasure in being right. "She probably understood why you stopped coming to the hospital better than you."

Pete sniffed some more, considering what Manny had said.

"So how did it happen this time," Manny asked. "Just a few minutes ago you looked as happy as I've ever seen you."

Pete nodded. "I had a kind of memory slip. I was thinking about this really great Christmas after my Mom first got sick. Just thinking of being with her. Then I slipped ahead to the hospital, walking out on her, and I felt it all again."

"But it doesn't happen all the time? I mean, you got plenty pissed at me last week, after the thing with Mikey, and you didn't have one, a 'moment' I mean." Pete admitted they were inconsistent and the only thing he knew for sure was they seemed to occur less frequently than they once had. But he conceded that it was hard to know for sure since he didn't always notice them himself.

He also said he'd never had a moment in front of any other boys, and he didn't know why he'd had them in front of Manny.

Manny's soft laugh broke the tension. "Well, I guess I'm the special one."

Pete smiled through the embarrassment of the whole thing then said, "Yeah, I guess you are."

*   *   *

On the Monday after Christmas Manny went to the eye doctor in Santa Rosa and came back without his patch. The good news was the doctor had told Manny and Mr. Turnbull that the eye itself, though still obscured by swelling, looked like it had sustained no permanent damage.

Pete had of course seen the extent of the damage long since, but it was one thing to get a quick glimpse of the eye and a completely different thing to see it constantly. Every time he looked at Manny, he could imagine Fat Tony's meaty fists pounding into his friend and he felt sick for it. But he couldn't think of a way to even begin telling Manny the truth. Not even when Manny noticed he was upset. When Manny stood up from the table after dinner and gritted his teeth against the pain of his broken ribs, he saw Pete wince and asked what was wrong. Pete played it off as best he could, saying he just wished it hadn't happened. In reality, he felt his stomach fill with acid and bubble mercilessly.

Chapter 19

The rest of the Christmas home visit passed uneventfully but for one major exception: Pete was finally able to talk to Tabitha in person again.

In happened on the Sonoma town square. Ms. Kelly, Mr. Weaver and Mr. Dawson were on duty with the half dozen boys on campus on New Year's Eve. Mr. Weaver offered to take the two oldest of the residents to Santa Rosa for a film to give them a chance to get away from the younger kids for a few hours. Mr. Dawson took charge of the two St. Anthony's boys, bundled them up and whisked them off for a crisp wintery walk down to the 4-H barn. After the other staffers had departed with their charges, Ms. Kelly looked at Pete and Manny and declared with a sly smile: "We need some hot chocolate."

Fifteen minutes later they were in a Riordan Home van with 20 dollars the coordinator had given Ms. Kelly out of the petty cash box. They were bundled up against the cold, a necessity in many of the Riordan vans, whose heaters worked intermittently at best. The only van available to them today was a prime example: a donated short-bus style school bus someone in maintenance had decided to paint olive green. Some of the staff called it the "Green Meanie," after the characters in the old Beatle's movie, but many of them referred to the van the same way the boys did: Green Weenie.

Outside, the day was all crisp winter blue sky, and according to Ms. Kelly, a perfect day for a huge cup of hot chocolate. "Especially if Riordan is buying," she joked.

After buying their hot chocolates and donuts at a coffee shop on the square, Ms. Kelly gave Pete and Manny leave to walk around on their own for a little bit. It was a holiday and the square was busy with tourists browsing craft booths which were usually only set up on weekends. While Ms. Kelly sat in at a table outside the coffee shop sipping her coco, Pete and Manny wandered across the street and onto the square proper.

They browsed tables of silver jewelry, blown glass and hand carved trinkets. Manny saw a table of books beneath a banner reading "Friends of the Library $.50 Sale." He wandered off to browse titles and left Pete to peruse hand carved wooden crafts. He was checking out a beautiful bamboo cribbage board that reminded him of the one on which his grandma had taught him to play when he felt a tap on his shoulder and turned to find himself looking slightly up into the green eyes of Tabitha Pembrook. Below her bright eyes, a broad smile completed the vision.

"Hey, Pete O'Boyle." The voice stunned him.

"Tabitha!"

"Glad you remembered." The smile was still there, rivaling the blue sky for beauty.

"What are you doing here?" he asked.

"Just hanging out. I'm meeting some friends for lunch at the Cheese Factory. But I came down early to browse the jewelry and to pick up some stuff for my dad."

"Your dad wants some jewelry?" Pete was still too astounded to think beyond each word.

She laughed. She had a great laugh. "No, he doesn't need a necklace or anything. He asked me to grab some things off his desk at the shop." She pointed to the eastern side of the square. Pete turned to look, and there, next to the movie theater where he and the St. Michael's boys had seen a Christmas play last December was a building he had never noticed before. It was an older building of dark stone with an understated sign over the double glass doors that read:

> **Pembrook Vineyards est. 1889**
> **Tasting Room & Shop**

There seemed to be a constant stream of people going in and out.

He turned back to Tabitha and smiled, "Oh."

"So what about you," she asked. "Still trying to earn your 25 / 50 or what?"

"25 / 60. And no, I'm here with staff." He pointed back toward the Green Weenie and Tabitha's gaze followed to where Ms. Kelly was still sipping from her mug and glancing up toward them occasionally.

"Wow," Tabitha said, "she's gorgeous."

"Yeah," Pete said, then quickly realized his mistake as Tabitha shot him a darting look. "I mean… uhhmmm, she…."

Her laughter caught him off guard. "Oh, Pete. Don't worry about it. She *is* gorgeous."

He felt his shoulders slump. "Uhh, ok."

"Relax Pete," She said in a quite voice, no longer laughing, but smiling intently. She stepped closer and almost whispered, "You're doing fine."

"I am?" He felt woozy, like he might fall down at any moment.

She reached and put her hand on his arm above the wrist. Through his sweatshirt he could only feel vague pressure, but he could see her clean, unpolished nails there on his arm. After a moment he realized he was looking down at her hand and quickly raised his eyes. She was smiling still, almost laughing again, but he knew instantly she was not laughing to make fun of him, but because he *was doing fine*. Suddenly buoyed, no longer feeling faint, he grinned an idiot's grin, and felt her fingers slide down his arm and briefly grasp his hand before releasing. Her eyes darted over his shoulder and she said, "We've got company."

Pete, drawn out of the brief moment of fuzzy headedness her touch had brought on, turned to see Manny standing about 10 feet away looking sheepish. Everything about him screamed, *Sorry Dude!*

Pete smiled and made the introduction he'd been longing to make. As he did so, he caught sight of Ms. Kelly, who was no longer sitting back and sipping her hot chocolate, but instead staring across the square, a question forming on her brow, her head cocked slightly to one side.

They managed to find a bench near a stump so all three could sit and talk together. Many took the single seat of the stump. Pete made a mental note to thank him later. Tabitha sat close to him on the bench, not touching, but not far from it. They sat and talked and laughed. It was the most time Pete had ever spent with Tabitha, but

Manny's presence detracted from it not at all. In fact, Pete hadn't been able to shake his idiot grin since Tabitha's touch had put it on his face, and he sat now, listening to Tabitha tell Manny about the winery, school and her parents.

"My dad caught you looking at us in church," she laughed. Pete remembered. "He asked if I knew you and I told him about Father introducing you to me and mom."

For his part, Manny listened and asked questions. And again, Pete was impressed by his friend's ability with people. And Tabitha talking to Manny gave Pete a chance just to watch her smile and laugh. He leaned back on the bench and continued to grin as he watched his friend and his... and Tabitha talk. The fact he didn't know how to refer to Tabitha, even in his own mind didn't bother Pete in the slightest. He was trying to figure out how he might be able to see Tabitha again before home visit ended when she asked Manny a question.

"So, what about you? What are you're parents like?"

The question was asked with a smile, but was not greeted with one. Interested in the answer to one of the many question he had never himself asked Manny, Pete looked at his friend and watched a smile slide into pain. Manny's eyes dropped away from Tabitha, who suddenly looked frightened. Pete sat forward and Tabitha said, "Manny, I'm sorry if —"

But Manny, still looking away, waved her off, "It's all right."

Pete stared at Manny and had started to ask of he was ok when Manny, still looking down, spoke.

"They're dead," he said simply.

Pete's smile evaporated. "What?"

Tabitha said, "I'm — I'm sorry."

Manny was looking down at his hands. "It's no big deal." Then he stood, exhaling against the pain in his ribs as he did. When he had made it all the way up he said, "I think I'll go back and look at the books once more before Ms. Kelly tells us it's time to leave."

Tabitha looked now to Pete, clearly pained, apology in her eyes.

"You never mentioned..." Pete said. "You never told me."

"No. I never did." There was no apology in his voice.

Too stunned at first to move, Pete now jumped to his feet. "But, why didn't you? Why didn't you tell me?!" Pete demanded, immediately regretting his tone.

Manny, who had begun to turn away, stopped. He let out a deep breath and turned to face Pete and met his eyes now. He looked suddenly exhausted, the dark rings beneath his eyes even more pronounced for the crisp bright day. He made no move to speak, so Pete began to ask again: "Why didn't —"

Manny cut him off quietly: "Because." For a moment it seemed he would say no more. Then he added, "Because, you never asked, Pete." Saying nothing else, Manny turned and walked away.

Tabitha stood up next to Pete and watched Manny walk away toward the library table. "I'm so sorry, Pete." He felt her hand take his, but he registered it without joy, and felt a flash of annoyance at Manny for robbing him of that joy.

He felt her hand slip from his and she said, "I have to go."

He looked at her and followed her gaze to a red top-down convertible pulling into a parking stall in front of the cheese shop. In it, bundled against the cold were three high school aged girls.

He turned back to her and was surprised when she embraced him and quickly kissed his cheek. Not knowing what else to do, he embraced her back, feeling awkward, but also at home and strangely sad. Over her shoulder, he saw Ms. Kelly stand up quickly and begin making her way across the street into the square. The staffer's look had shifted slightly. From the distance Pete could not read her face clearly, but thought she looked angry. Tabitha seemed to sense their time was short. The embrace became a momentary squeeze and she whispered in his ear: "Take care of him, and call me when you can." Then she released him and hustled away toward the Cheese Factory and her lunch with her friends.

"Okay O'Boyle, fess up." Ms. Kelly was glancing at him in the passenger seat as she drove. Manny was sitting silently in the back. He hadn't said much since wandering away from Pete and Tabitha. Pete's flash of anger had dissipated and he was worried about Manny, but it would have to wait. Ms. Kelly was insistent: "How in the *hell* do you know Tabitha Pembrook?"

"Miss?!" Pete was honestly shocked at her talking that way. He'd never heard her cuss at all.

"Don't you *'miss'* me Pete. You know that girl, and she *obviously* knows you. And there is no reason you should know each other." She was smiling, Pete saw, but she also looked suspicious, ready to sniff out a lie if he tried to tell one. So he tried not to tell one, not exactly anyway.

"I've met her after mass a couple of times," he said. "Father O introduced me to her and her mom." Which was true, technically. He just left out the fact that the introduction had been redundant. Ms Kelly seemed to sense an underlying deception in his explanation.

"At mass," she repeated. "Yeah, sure. That's why she kissed you."

Pete was reasonably certain Ms. Kelly had a good idea there was more truth he wasn't telling. He didn't want to lie to her, and for her part she didn't seem inclined to make him do it, for she asked him no more questions about Tabitha.

Regardless of her doubts though, Pete still felt like he owed something to Ms. Kelly. She had given him and Manny almost 20 minutes on the square after Tabitha had shown up. Regardless of whatever doubts or questions she'd had, she'd not moved to gather them until Tabitha had embraced him.

*   *   *

Because there were only a few boys around, and the vacation days had no reliable structure, Pete was only able to call Tabitha once during the rest of the home visit, and that ended up in another awkward and embarrassed message on her answering machine. After he left it he became immediately convinced Mr. or Mrs. Pembrook would hear it. Manny, who gave the impression he was getting better by the day, told him not to worry about it, she had a phone of her own in her own room and her parents probably didn't spy on her.

As for Manny, Pete's feelings ebbed and flowed. When he had asked on the square why Manny hadn't told him before about his parents, the answer at first hadn't made sense. *Because, you never asked Pete.* He had at first raged privately, *Why would I have asked!?* Then he remembered what Manny had said to him after explaining how he'd ended up at Riordan.

There is more, he had said that day in the barn. *I may tell you sometime. But if I don't tell you on my own, you can ask. I'll always answer you anything you ask.*

How could he have sat there and listened? How could he not have said anything about his parents when Pete told him about his own. It was something they had in common; something they both had experience with.

There were other guys at the Home and in St. Gabe's who had lost a parent. Matt Saxon's mom had died when he was 4. He barely remembered her, he had said. Malcolm Patty's father had been shot and killed by police during a drug bust when Malcolm had been in second grade. Malcolm never talked about his dad except once in group when he explained Tourette's is hereditary and his father had also been afflicted with the disease.

But with both of his parents dead, Pete had been unique at the Home. And now he had company. It left Pete confused. Why would Manny not tell him after hearing about Pete's own parents?

They didn't speak the rest of the day. Manny spent the afternoon and evening reading a book he had picked up at the book sale on the square. Pete had hung out with the St. Ant's kids. Only after lights out, when they had been lying in the dark of their shared room in the Fitzpatrick house and Pete's anger was resurfacing, did Manny speak to him again.

"I owe you an apology, Pete." After pausing, apparently to give Pete a chance to say something and hearing nothing, Manny continued. "I wanted to tell you earlier, especially when you told me about your mom. But I guess I wasn't ready then. Heck, I was almost as surprised as you to hear me talk about it. But, today I was ready to talk about it a little, even if I didn't know it until Tabitha asked me the question."

Pete suddenly felt the sorrow in Manny's voice. He remembered the first time he had talked to anybody at Riordan about his mom's death. The boy, long since gone from the Home (and, according to overheard staff conversations, a current guest of the State of California on drug and theft charges), had sniffed once, loudly and dismissively, and said, "Sucks man. Did she leave you any money?"

"What I'm saying," Manny whispered, "is I'm sorry. I should have told you."

In the dark, Pete felt his anger drain away again only to be replaced once again by guilt over his own secret.

"It's ok," He said. "We're cool."

There was a distinct sigh from the other bed.

"Thanks."

Chapter 20

Winter break ended on the first Sunday in January. All of the boys were back in the cottage except for two.

Official word had come on the day after New Years: Tony Bruletti would not be returning to Riordan. Mr. Turnbull had come down to tell Manny. Chuck the Truck had represented Riordan at Tony's hearing in Santa Rosa and reported the judge had called the attack on Manny the final straw for Tony. He'd given the boy a chance, the judge had said, and the boy had wasted it. Tony's probation had been revoked and he had been sentenced to a six month stint with the C.Y.A. Hearing the news, Manny had only shaken his head and looked away.

Of Mikey Hamm there was apparently no news. Even staff seemed surprised when he didn't show up by dinner on Sunday evening. Pete couldn't help but be annoyed when he noticed the worried look on Manny's face when Mikey's absence was commented on by a few of the boys on the way to the dining hall. But his annoyance didn't last long. He didn't let it. He was just too glad to be on speaking terms with Manny again.

After dinner on Sunday, Mr. Dawson called Manny and Pete into the office and said it looked like Mikey would be gone for a little while and Mr. Johnson had decided to move Manny back in with Pete, if it was ok with both boys. Since Mikey's status was indefinite, the duration of this move would be as well. Pete said he was ok with the move and was relived and happy to see Manny smile and say, "Thanks a lot, Sir." Pete helped Manny move his stuff back down the hall before lights out.

Near the end of the first week back from Christmas news came of the Rat's incarceration. Weaver told them about it during group on Thursday afternoon. Mikey had been arrested for burning down a new house in Napa on Christmas Eve. According to Weaver, the house was empty and waiting to be moved into. There was no word on when, or even if Mikey would be returning to Riordan.

Pete didn't get the fire-bug thing. He had melted his share of army men by dousing them in modeling glue and striking a match, and he'd even fried a few ants with a magnifying glass. But he had never been careless with the flames. He'd always done it in the middle of his aunt's backyard, on the pink concrete of her patio. She'd had a big potted plant as a center piece of the patio. On the few occasions when Pete had felt it necessary to cremate some soldiers, he had moved the pot aside by a few feet, fried the green guys, then slid the plant back after scraping the cooled plastic puddle up with a shovel.

But Mikey was different about fire. He liked flames. It seemed he came back from every home visit after getting into trouble over starting a fire or being caught with the means to do so. Chris, who had roomed with Mikey briefly a year before, had once told Pete the Rat always had some kind of fire gear with him. He'd been caught with matches and lighters a dozen times at Riordan. Last spring he'd come back from home with a couple of road flares hidden in a rolled up pair of pants. Jordi said he'd even heard Mikey had shown up from home limping, claiming he'd been hit by a car. Finally, staff had pinned him down and gotten him to give up the massive Roman candle he had taped to his leg. Like all of the incendiaries he smuggled onto campus, staff had confiscated it immediately and assigned the appropriate consequence. His desire to burn was the reason Mikey spent life in a constant state of trouble.

Strangely though, Mikey had never actually burned anything at Riordan. Pete guessed it had something to do with Father O'Connell. For some reason, the priest seemed to have a special place in his heart for the little psycho. Pete had seen them walking together many times. Jordi said it must have been in O'Connell's vows to take pity on hopeless cases. Regardless of the reason for the priest's attentions, he was the one staffer on the campus the Mikey listened to unquestioningly. And there were few automatic expulsion issues at Riordan. Starting fires was one of them. Father O had been a chaplain in the Navy, had worked on submarines. A small fire, he'd said many times, was enough to kill a whole sub. And playing with fire was a sure way to find yourself kicked out of the Riordan Home. Even messing with fire alarms or extinguishers could earn you 15 / 30.

But, even if he had never been caught striking a match on the campus, Pete knew Mikey's obsession was totally real. He had seen the kid get into the fires they burned in the cottage fireplace on winter nights. Pete had seen him on many a night, staring through and into the flames, his weak chin hanging slack. It was the attitude some boys adopted when they saw hot girls during trips into town, unable to look away for the beauty of the thing, but afraid to be caught. When Pete had been young, his mother had sometimes complained she had to call his name a dozen times to break him away from the TV's hypnotic hold. Watching Mikey in front of a fire gave Pete an idea about what Lilly O'Boyle might have meant.

Manny took the news about Mikey better than Pete had expected he would. He was clearly bothered to hear Mikey was in juvie, but when Pete mentioned it to him, Manny's only response was to say, "It could be worse. I honestly expected a lot worse."

Steven Sengall came back from home visit with a new swagger and a new tattoo, though the tattoo was not shared with staff. They did notice his new attitude. Pete saw Mr. Johnson and Mr. Weaver talking together quietly and watching Steven. None of the boys talked about it, but they all felt the difference in Steven. If he hadn't already been six three, Pete might have thought he'd actually grown.

After dinner on the night Steven returned, Pete had walked into the bathroom and seen Steven with his shirt up over his head looking at his back in the mirror. He had furtively glanced at Pete then relaxed when he'd realized it was just another boy and not staff. As Pete had walked to the stall he had glimpsed "*VIX* " in the mirror.

"I don't get it," Manny had said later in their room. It was just before lights out and Manny and Pete were folding their laundry. "What's 'vix' anyway?"

"No. It was in the mirror," Pete explained. "What it said was 'XIV.' Fourteen."

"Oh, right," Manny said, putting a stack of shirts in his wardrobe. "Stupid of me. Fourteen. Norteño."

"Yeah. Looks like he got himself all official, but there's more. When he had his shirt up I saw what must have been 20 bruises."

Manny was down on his knees, stowing the last of his laundry in his bottom drawer. He looked up at Pete. "So what happened to him? A blanket party on home visit?"

"I don't think so," Pete said. He finished packing his pants into the drawers beneath his bed. "From what I've heard, guys trying to get into gangs sometimes have to get the hell beaten out of them. It's like some kind of ritual beating."

"And so violence begets violence begets violence."

"How's that?" Pete asked.

"Nothing," Manny said. "Just…" then he paused, and looked up at Pete. "Just something my dad used to say."

Pete looked back at Manny and felt a lump rise in his throat.

"Oh."

Pete didn't ask Manny anything more about his parents. He thought about it and almost did. He knew Manny would tell him if he asked. He also suspected Manny wanted to talk about it. But he let a lot of things stop him from asking, not the least of which was the lingering guilt he felt about the attack. He still thought about telling Manny the truth, but it seemed the farther they got away from the incident the more difficult it was to tell. At first he waited because he wanted to make sure Manny was all right. Then he waited because he wanted to give Manny a chance to get back to normal after his injuries. Then he became afraid of what Manny might say, how he might react. And now, near a month afterward he had no idea of how to even begin explaining how he knew and why he didn't tell.

For the most part, he had allowed himself to forget he'd even known. Fat Tony was gone for good and Manny had mostly healed. There was only a blue shadow around his left eye now, and his ribs had healed sufficiently to enable him to make the walk up the hill to visit Ms. Kelly without pain. And the simple truth of the matter was this: absolutely no one had any idea Pete had known about Tony's plan. How could anyone? He'd been alone in the closet. Even the boys who had been talking about what Tony was planning hadn't known he was there. If he had done it right away, telling Manny wouldn't have been a big deal, but because he'd had to wait, telling him now wasn't an option. Or a necessity.

Chapter 21

At the end of January, Mikey the Rat returned to the Riordan Home and was roomed up with Malcolm Patty.

From the moment he walked into the cottage, it was clear to Pete and Manny he had not been on a vacation. He had the remains of a bump above the hairline of his newly shaven head. Pete judged it had been around for a while as it had drained to blacken both of Mikey's beady eyes. If possible, the damage to his face made him look even more animalistic. "Like a beaten stray," he said to Manny that evening as they got ready for bed.

"Well," Manny had said, "if he is what you say, so are we all. You and me included."

Pete was struck by the way Manny tossed his description of Mikey back at him, and felt his face get hot. Manny must have seen his anger rise, because he said, "I'm sorry Pete, but that was something you didn't need to say." He sounded, not angry, but annoyed. "Yes, Mikey may be a 'stray,' to use your word, with no real home and nowhere to go and probably no one in this whole stupid world who loves him the way he deserves to be loved. But can you name me a guy here at Riordan who doesn't fit that description?"

"I'm no stray," Pete said. He still felt hot.

There was a few seconds of quiet between them. The sounds of the cottage filled the void. Down the hall, Malcolm was mumbling to himself. Weaver was giving Jordi crap about not cleaning up in the kitchenette.

"I never said you were," Manny said after a minute. "It was your word, not mine. I only mean that Mikey is not fundamentally different from you, despite your insistence to the contrary. He's a guy whose life has gone in a way no one should have to deal with. You didn't deserve to have your mom die from cancer. No more than Mikey deserved the abuses of his past. Or his present."

Pete felt himself bristle at the mention of his mom. Manny must have noticed.

"Listen Pete," Manny said in a soothing voice, "I don't want to go backwards here. Just because Mikey is back doesn't mean I'm going to abandon you again. I've thought a lot about how things went bad between us before, and I don't want it to happen again."

Pete was a little startled by what he heard and it took him a moment to identify the cause of his surprise. Manny had just clearly spoken of the fear Pete had been nursing since Mikey's arrival.

"But," Manny continued, "that doesn't mean I'll abandon Mikey either. I feel a responsibility for him. To him."

Pete was confused and it must have shown.

"I can be his friend and your friend, regardless of conventional Riordan Home wisdom. He's not a bad kid, once you get through the crap he's wrapped himself in."

"So what, I'm supposed to be friends with him, after he tore up my face." Pete was surprised at how calmly he asked the question.

"No. But you could think about giving him a chance. He only attacked you because he thought you had been mean to me. He's actually very loyal."

I bet he is, thought Pete. *Like a pet.* "So what exactly *do* you want?" he asked.

"I don't expect you to actually like him. But I would like you to give him a break and not hold what he's done in the past, or what you think he's done, against him."

"But he's the worst guy here," Pete said. "I'm sorry Manny, but he is. Other than maybe Steven, I can think of no boy on the campus I can stand less. It's impossible to get all of the guys here to agree on anything, but if you could hold a vote I'd be willing to bet Mikey would be voted the hands down winner of the award for *Least Liked Boy*."

"Maybe you're right," Manny said. "Maybe he is the least likeable guy on campus. But trust me; likeability is an overrated quality in a man. The most likeable people in the world can also be the most wicked." Manny smiled grimly to himself. "Believe me."

"But, come on man," Pete said, "after what he did to me, how am I supposed to treat him?"

Manny smiled again, this time at Pete, and said, "Treat him like you'd treat me."

Pete shook his head and said, "I don't know." What Manny wanted of him was too much.

"Listen, I'm not asking you to be his best buddy. Honestly I don't think he's capable of having that type of relationship. But I am asking you to treat the guy decently. You are my friend, Pete. The only real friend I've made here, and I'm asking you for your help."

Pete was surprised by the starkness of this and embarrassed by it.

"But, in a way, Mikey is my friend too. It's different than you and me being friends, but he is still someone I need to look after."

Pete nodded. He understood now. Manny had two friends here and he just wanted his friends to be friends, as much as they could be anyway. Pete remembered the legitimate thrill he'd gotten when Tabitha and Manny finally met on the square over home visit.

Manny seeing the nod asked, "You'll help me?"

"Yeah," Pete said. "I will."

Manny, sitting on his bed, exhaled largely and said quietly, "Thanks."

From down the hall came Weaver's voice: "Lights out for threes and fours in two minutes. If you're not going to bed now turn off your lights and come up front."

Both boys stood to head up front. Manny grabbed his current book, *The Magician's Nephew*, and Pete picked up his copy of *The Gunslinger*. As he stepped to the door, Manny said quietly to Pete, "And hey, don't worry. I will be careful with him. I know it's not the same as being friends with you. I know I can't completely trust him." Then Manny stepped into the hallway and was gone up front.

Standing in the middle of the room, Pete suddenly felt like two people again, and the second Pete was kicking him in the gut.

The next few weeks with Mikey were a learning experience for Pete. And by the middle of February, he was surprised to find Manny was right: Mikey wasn't as bad as he seemed. Sure the kid was crude, and at first was deeply suspicious of Pete's suddenly non-stop presence. In those first few days, he wouldn't start a conversation on his own and always stole a furtive glance at Pete before he would answer a question from Manny.

At first Pete thought it comical, like Mikey had anything to say worth knowing. The comedy faded after a day or so, and Pete began to grow annoyed with the checking looks. It was as if Mikey was saying to Manny, *You sure you want this guy here? You sure you can trust him?* And Pete was near through with the whole experiment. He was almost ready to tell Manny he couldn't go though with the Mikey thing.

But after the first week or so Mikey had become accustomed enough to Pete he began talking more often and more freely. And the more he talked the more he had to say. And, strangely, the more he said, the more worth his words took on for Pete. Mikey lived fairly close to the Riordan Home in the town of St. Helena, across the hills in Napa County. He had been born down hear Los Angeles and had moved north after his mom and dad had split up. Mikey said he didn't remember too much about his dad, whom his mom described as a bad guy. Mikey's mom drank, though Pete didn't need Mikey to tell him this, he'd known it from the first moment he'd met him.

One of the things about being raised by a nurse like Aunt Marjorie was a little pop medical education came with the package. Once when they'd been at the supermarket, Pete had asked her what was wrong with a little boy he'd seen playing near the gumball machine. The kid had been scrawny and his eyes had been set too close together. After catching a glimpse of the boy herself, Marjorie had explained to Pete in the car that the kid had F.A.S.: Fetal Alcohol Syndrome. According to Aunt Marjorie an alcoholic mother was the lone path to a child with F.A.S.

No boy at Riordan had ever seen Mikey's mom, but from her own son's description she was horrific. She was the reason Mikey came home from every home visit covered in fleas and smelling like cigarettes. She and her drinking was the reason Mikey could hardly read and had barely any memory. Her choice in men was the reason Mikey came home from every home visit with fresh bruises.

The guy she'd been married to for the past three years was a construction worker named Lou. Lou liked beer and pot and didn't like his step-son very much. According to Mikey, he especially didn't like it when "the cops come around for me." Mikey said Lou not only used a lot of pot, but sold a fair amount out of his mother's garage. And Mikey's combustible hobby brought a few too many police cruisers around the house for Lou's comfort. Mikey said he'd not been to the doctor before coming back, but Ms. Belz in the infirmary said he'd heal up before too long. Of course, he had told her he'd been beaten up by some kids. "I ain't stupid enough to snitch on Lou. You think I wanna take a big fat dirt nap?"

Once he started talking, Pete found it almost impossible to get him to shut up. He was still his usual quiet self around the rest of the cottage, but with Manny and Pete he was what Aunt Marjorie called a "Chatty Cathy." He talked about everything he'd ever gotten into trouble for at Riordan, from fighting to joy-riding one of the maintenance department's golf carts. He claimed he knew how to break into the staff office of any cottage on campus and that he'd done so multiple times. "Nothing to take in there, though. But you can use the phone without nobody listening."

The one thing he never talked about was his relationship with fire. Pete became aware that Mikey always, *always* had means to make fire on him. It didn't matter where they were, or how recently staff had confiscated a book of matches, or how often they searched his stuff, which he said they did at least once a week. After hanging out with him for a while, and paying attention to him for the first time since meeting him, Pete had figured out how he always seemed to have something combustible in his possession.

Mikey had lighters and matches and who knew what else stashed in dozens of hiding places in and around the cottage.

Watching carefully for a couple of days, Pete had seen him hide, retrieve and just check on items in at least 10 different locations. When he could, Pete would check out the hiding places after Mikey had left them. He found individual paper matches pressed between the pages of an ancient *Hardy Boys* novel in the small cottage library. Wedged beneath the top of the seldom used picnic table next to the cottage, Pete discovered a handful of ten inch fireplace matches in a taped up cardboard tube.

In the bushes behind the cottage, he found an old wooden cigar box containing five cigarette lighters: four were of cheap plastic, but one was silver with a gold leaf eagle on the front. Beneath the black plastic bag lining the bathroom trash can Pete found a stash of half-used matchbooks, each with a cover from a different bar or hotel: places with names like *Holiday Inn*, *Spanky's*, *Corner Pocket*, *Red's Recovery Room* and the whimsically named *Friar Tuck's*.

After spying Mikey near the front tire of Weaver's pick-up truck, Pete had investigated and found a magnetic key holder up under the wheel well. Packed inside the black metal *Hide-a-key* box, along with Weaver's spare key, were a dozen blue-headed wooden matches, the kind with white phosphor tips that can be struck anywhere.

His mom's boyfriend Mitch had once told Pete squirrels can't remember where they hide nuts, so they bury them everywhere so they're more likely to stumble across a stash during the cold winter months. Mikey was like a pyromaniac squirrel. Manny actually laughed out loud when Pete said this, and didn't chastise him for the animal comparison, probably because he knew it wasn't intentional or mean spirited. He had suspected Mikey was hiding stuff around the cottage, but had not investigated as Pete had.

"Surprising, isn't he?"

In spite of himself, Pete had to admit Mikey was indeed more than he seemed. There was a startling honesty living in the kid, right along side the deviousness and an impressive capacity for nastiness. A few weeks after his return Mikey even apologized to Pete for the attack before Christmas. "Sorry man," he'd said to Pete out of the blue one evening while the three of them were walking up toward the dining hall. When Pete questioned him, he'd said, "About going for you. Crazy night. I was pissed."

Surprised, Pete had said only, "Ok, yeah. Forget it."

Manny had called him a survivor. Pete supposed it was true, but couldn't decide if the kid was brave or just stupid. The whole matches and lighters scattered around the cottage thing was, in Pete's opinion, a sure fire way to get kicked out. If staff started finding his combustible Easter eggs, they would sure as hell know to whom all the stuff belonged. It was one thing to have a firebug living at the place, but Pete thought the staff would feel a little different if they knew he was constantly armed with the wares to engage in his potentially deadly hobby. And Father O, who was rumored to have gone to great lengths to help keep Mikey out of lock-up this last time, even he would probably toss the kid out on his ass if he found out.

As Pete spent more time with Manny and Mikey, he spent less with Jordi, Chris and Frankie. He'd made an attempt to explain the change to them. When he'd told Jordi that Mikey wasn't as bad as he'd thought the response he got was almost cold. "Whatever, man." Jordi had said. "It's your time. You wanna waste it hanging out with the Rat, it's your business."

Chris and Frankie had been likewise nonplussed by his recent social choices. When he'd spoken to them together their opinions were clear: "I know Manny and you are best friends," Chris had said. "But Mikey-freakin-Hamm? Are you serious?" Frankie had just shaken his head and said nothing.

Even Malcolm, the universally acknowledged biggest freak in the cottage, had opined in the schoolyard that Pete might want to reconsider his choice to spend time with Mikey. Because, as only Malcolm could put it, Mikey was, "N-n-n-not r-right in the h-h-h-h-h-head."

Steven Sengall only laughed whenever he saw the three of them together.

In fact, other than Manny and Mr. Johnson (who said he was glad to see Pete and Manny had gotten past whatever differences had come between them), the only other person to express anything positive about Pete's newfound interest in Mikey was Tabitha, and even she was cautious. "Be careful," she had warned during a rec phone call the week before St. Valentine's Day. "I think it's good you're being nice to him, but it sounds like he could still be dangerous."

He had managed to talk to Tabitha several times in the preceding weeks and had even received a Valentine's Day letter from her via her cousin again. He added it to the assortment of things she'd given him. He kept the stash stored behind his underwear in the bottom drawer of his wardrobe. Included in the collection were the pictures she'd given him, the letter from the package she's left up the hill and the zip top bag with the last of the candy that had been in the sack.

Chapter 22

On the first Friday in March Steven was transferred up the hill to St. Matthew's. The move was a long time coming. Steven was the oldest boy in St. Gabe's, but it was common knowledge he'd been passed over for movement because he was considered immature by staff. But in recent months he had made his case for movement with staff: keeping out of serious trouble and maintaining LEVEL 3 status, even making it to a 2 for a while in September. Steven had been told by staff on Thursday afternoon and had gloated all over the cottage until bedtime. The consensus among the rest of the boys was, "About damn time!" Because, in spite of his efforts with staff, the boys knew he was dangerous, and only Fat Tony's recent departure had curbed his antagonistic and manipulative ways.

The move would be a double jump, with Steven skipping St. John's altogether. He was already in his room packing when Pete walked backrooms after school. The cottage was all but empty. Mr. Johnson and Mr. Turnbull had taken a crew of St. Gabe's boys to the vintage car museum in Santa Rosa right after school. Only Malcolm, Steven, Mikey and Pete were still on campus. Malcolm and Mikey were both on campus restriction, Malcolm because he was a LEVEL 4 and Mikey as a condition of his probation. Pete had planned on going with the group to Santa Rosa, but hadn't felt well most of the day. He'd asked for and received permission from Mr. Johnson to head back to the cottage and try to sleep off the fever he'd started running after lunch. After passing on joining the game of HORSE Malcolm and Mikey were starting on the cottage basketball court, Pete had checked in with Weaver, who was in the staff office filling out behavior logs for the boys and listening to the radio. Weaver took his temperature and gave him two aspirin when the digital thermometer registered 101.4. After swallowing the medication under Weaver's supervision, Pete headed back toward his room.

Steven was putting his bags into the hallway outside his door when Pete hit the T-hall junction. Pete acknowledged Steven's sudden smile with a curt nod and turned toward his room. From behind him he heard a chuckle. He kept walking, not wanting to talk with anyone. The fever, though relatively low, was giving him a wicked case of the chills. He was freezing. He just wanted to crawl into bed and pull his fleece blanket over his head. But Steven wasn't to be ignored.

"I seen you with her."

The voice was quiet, but it was enough to stop Pete in his tracks, literally mid-stride. He turned to see Steven grinning wide and nodding now. "Yeah, that's right. I know you're doin' the wine girlie." The smile became a laugh. "Givin' it to her good."

Pete hesitated, and then said quietly, "What are you talking about?"

"Yeah, seen you talking to her after church a lot of Sundays, too."

Pete felt his head begin to shake side to side.

Steven laughed again, "Oh yeah, good reaction."

Pete's fevered mind raced. *He knows about her... What does he know?* But there was another question carrying all of these others on its back. He managed it in a not quite panicked voice: "What do you want?"

Steven smiled again. "Just to see you twist, O'Boyle. But it's good to know you don't want people to know. Those people are big money for this place. She wrote some pretty sweet things in those letters."

Pete, already feeling frozen, felt his face break out in sweat. The effect was like being caught in an ice storm with wet hair. "Letters?"

"Uh huh," Steven was smug now. "You know, the ones in your bottom drawer?"

"You went through my stuff." It was not a question. Pete was shaking now, though he was unsure if it was from the fever or rage or a combination thereof.

"Yours and your little faggot friend," Steven confirmed. His voice was still low enough Weaver couldn't hear him up front, especially not with the radio going. "He didn't have anything worth a damn. But you had five bucks and candy. Thanks. For the money and the chocolate."

"Why —"

"I was looking through his stuff first, seeing if he had anything worth taking with me. He's been a pain in the ass since he got here. He got Tony kicked out."

"I'll tell," Pete said, but knew he sounded as weak as he felt.

Steven, whose usual bearing included a stoop shoulder slouch, brought himself up to his full six feet three inches. "You do and they'll know about her."

"I'll tell anyway."

Steven smiled again, but this time there was warning in his eyes and his words: "Careful now. Don't get yourself hurt O'Boyle."

"What are you going to do?" Pete demanded. "Fat Tony and Teddy are both gone. You'll have to do it yourself."

"Not a problem," Steven said, taking a step forward and glaring down at him, silently daring him to try anything.

Pete felt himself getting cold again. He knew if he didn't lie down soon he would probably fall down. And now, along with his fever, he was completely nauseous. He felt himself buckle under Steven's stare and he began backing away toward his room. Steven's grin returned, broader than it had yet been. He raised an eyebrow and said, "Smart move, kid."

Pete turned and walked slowly to his room. By the time his face hit the pillow it was wet and salty, tears and sweat mingling and chilling him further.

Pete slept through the return of the rest of the boys and through dinner. He awoke with a start, trembling his way out of a nightmare. He sat up in bed and tried to shake off the confusion that comes from falling asleep during the day and waking up in the dark. The clock read 1:40am. He felt weak and his sheets were drenched in sweat. His fever had broken. He breathed deeply for a minute as his heart slowed. When it had and he was able to breathe normally again, he looked over at Manny, who was his usual jumble of blankets with hands and feet sticking out at odd angles from underneath the ugly striped Riordan bedspread. He watched until he could make out the rise and fall of Manny's breathing beneath the covers.

Pete stood and walked to the bathroom, trying to shake off the dream. He walked down the hall, past the rooms of the other boys. The cottage was quiet, as usual, with only the sounds of soft snoring drifting from some of the rooms.

After returning to their room, Pete sat on his bed and watched Manny again. In the dream Manny had been hurt, calling for help. He had been in a dark place, what light there was had been inconsistent, unstable. Something had been pinning him down; something Pete couldn't identify. In the dream Pete couldn't see himself. It had been like he wasn't there, but at the same time he knew he had been close enough to help but powerless to do so.

In the morning, Pete told Manny about what had happened with Steven. Manny gave his drawers and wardrobe a cursory look through and confirmed there nothing was missing. Pete, who had collapsed the afternoon before without looking through his things finally did so. As Steven had promised, his letters had all been opened and stuffed haphazardly back into their envelopes. Steven obviously hadn't been at all concerned about covering his tracks. Most of the candy was indeed gone as was the small amount of cash he had not gotten around to turning in to the cottage staff. Scattered beneath the letters and candy wrappers were the few pictures Tabitha had given him. He picked them up and gathered them together. He counted them. He counted them again then searched through the drawer, pulling everything out. He barely heard himself saying "No! No! No!"

Manny, who was busying himself with his books, looked up. "What's wrong?"

Pete, convinced now that the drawer was in fact empty sank down to his knees and cast his eyes to the three photographs scattered on the floor.

After lunch, Mr. Dawson led the 10 remaining St. Gabe's boys down to rec. Pete was walking by himself. Even Manny was giving him room. After explaining it to Manny, he'd not said much since realizing the photo was gone. The missing photo was the picture Tabitha had taken of herself. It was his favorite, the one that had been taken specifically for him, the picture of her smiling at him.

As they approached the rec hall, Pete found himself thinking his words were stupid and useless, they were wasted on the mouth-breathers he had to deal with everyday. He was done with words. Just before they entered the hall, Mikey Hamm pulled him aside. Pete, focused on the hall door and what he knew lay beyond it, was stunned to see Mikey in front of him and even more surprised when he realized Mikey had grabbed his arm. "Mikey, what —"

"Don't!" The whisper was urgent, and Mikey's feral eyes darted back and forth. When he was sure no one else was listening, Mikey said, "He'll kill you man. You seen the tattoo he got at home? Not worth it, man. He'll smack your ass down."

"I don't care." Pete heard his own voice. It sounded cold. He *felt* cold. He was bundled up against the winter day but he could feel the breeze through his down jacket. The Rat was bouncing from one foot to the other in front of him, but he was looking over Mikey's head, through the rec hall door, opened now by Mr. Dawson as the boys from the cottage filed in. Pete shrugged off Mikey's hand and walked toward the open door. Compared to the crisp cold of the day outside, the rec hall was stifling. Pete removed his jacket and felt himself break out in a chilled sweat. He was dimly aware his fever was returning, but was focused elsewhere: on a group of boys halfway down the hall, next to a pool table. Manny was suddenly at his shoulder, staring at the same group of boys. "Pete?" But Pete was already moving.

A group of St. Matt's boys were gathered, talking about nothing. Pete walked up to the group and reached up to tap a shoulder. Steven turned around and looked down at him. A smile, the twin of the previous day's spread itself across his wide face. Steven's eyes darted to establish distance from staff. They were standing in the middle of a crowded hall with pool and ping pong and foosball tables creating a landscape that made life difficult for staff. Pete too glanced around. No adults were within 30 feet. Obviously feeling safe enough, Steven said conversationally, "Piss off O'Boyle." This delighted his fellows who responded with snickers and quietly derisive jeers. Pete took no notice but said, "Give it back."

Steven shook his head and turned away. Pete stepped forward, kicked and buried the toe of his shoe in Steven's hamstring. Steven stumbled and cried out as he did. Pete stepped forward again and punched Steven in the kidney. Steven's swinging right hand, moving back in a surprisingly fast arc, caught Pete across the top of the head, knocking him off stride and giving Steven enough time to turn fully. Pete recovered and charged in again, his fists flying for the larger boy's chest and belly. Steven parried the charge, deflecting Pete into the corner of a pool table. The table dug into his hip and spun him around causing him to fall. He dropped to a knee and caught himself on the rail of the table, stopping himself from going all the way to the floor. He turned his head and looked up to find Steven bearing down on him.

The punch felt like the blow of a hammer. It connected with Pete's temple and shot stars bouncing around the inside of his head. He felt his head snap sideways, but his hands held on to the pool table, keeping him there on his knee. He heard staff and boys yelling now, and looked across the table. Adults were running toward him, dodging between boys and lunging around game tables.

Pete gripped the side of the table and began to pull himself up. He turned his head again to Steven. Through the flashes and a rapidly closing left eye, he saw the hand draw up again, back past a furious grimace.

The fist dropped like a piston and pain exploded through his face. He felt himself reel with the impact and was cascaded in fresh stars when his head connected with the floor of the hall. Then Pete was on his back staring up at fluorescent lights. He heard yelling, but could not make out the words. Someone was at his side, grabbing his hand. The lights skipped and winked. He noticed the coppery taste of blood on his tongue. Then the lights went out.

Chapter 23

Pete woke up in the infirmary. He was propped up in bed, on top of the covers. The room was dark but for an outline of light around the door. After a hazy inventory he came to the conclusion he was a physical wreck. His left eye wouldn't open all the way. His mouth and lips hurt when he tried to stretch them. Even his teeth hurt. His head throbbed and he reached around and found a lump the size of a goose egg on the back of his crown. He was drenched in sweat. His fever must have broken again.

He swung his feet off the bed and sat up, and added a case of whiplash to the roster. He was just about to step down to the floor when the door opened. Ms. Belz was surprised to find him awake and made him lie back down. She offered him some water and crackers and told him he'd been in the infirmary since the incident and they were just waiting for him to wake up to move him back to St. Gabe's. Dr. Thomas had been in to check him while he'd been unconscious and had pronounced him knocked cold, but in no distress or danger. The fever was treatable with aspirin and was just the byproduct of a virus. Ms. Belz said the doc had said he'd be back in the morning to check on him.

She checked his pupils with a small light. In the case of his left pupil the checking itself hurt like hell. Afterward she told him he had a mild concussion and a badly bruised face. She gave him a mirror so he could survey the damage himself. It was gruesome. From his left temple to chin his face was a purple and yellow mash. His swollen eye reminded him of the movie *Rocky*.

Mr. Turnbull arrived just after 9 pm to pick up Pete and escort him back to the cottage. Pete was silently thankful the caseworker didn't push him about what had happened in the rec hall. All Chuck the Truck said about the fight was, "We'll have a little talk about it tomorrow, okay?"

At the cottage, the rest of the guys were watching the Saturday night Riordan movie. Mr. Turnbull stopped at the staff office and Pete walked back to his bedroom to change into his night clothes. He was midway through changing when Manny stepped into the room. Pete didn't feel much like talking and Manny seemed to sense it and didn't press.

On Sunday, Pete saw Tabitha at mass. And she saw him. She even came over to him outside of the chapel afterward.

"My god, Pete. What happened?"

They were standing beneath a crisp winter morning. The winds of the previous day had died overnight and given way to a near freezing blue sky.

"Nothing," Pete said. He couldn't explain he'd fought someone over her picture. For some reason Steven hadn't been at mass this morning.

"Are you ok?" Her concern was real, and it surprised him.

"Yeah, I'm ok."

"But what happened?"

"Did something stupid." He smiled at her, winced from the pain of it, but went right back to smiling. "Got into a fight with a guy."

"Why?"

He shrugged, which hurt his neck something fierce. "It doesn't matter," he said. "It was just something dumb."

She glanced toward where her mom was talking to Father O and some other community members. She looked back and shook her head. "We just never have time to talk, do we?"

They were interrupted by the clearing of a very large throat. Pete looked over his shoulder and up into the face of Mr. Turnbull.

"Mornin' Pete," the caseworker said.

"Good morning, sir." Pete felt a moment of panic, which was only made worse when Mr. Turnbull shifted his gaze to Tabitha, inclined his head in greeting and said, "Ms. Pembrook."

Tabitha gave a tight-lipped smile and bobbed her head. Mr. Turnbull looked at them both and gave a little nod, as if a question had been answered. Pete felt his belly leaden.

"Pete, how's about we have that little chat now?"

"Yes sir."

"I'll let you say a quick goodbye. You can meet me in the staff dining room in five minutes."

"Yes sir."

Turnbull turned again to Tabitha and said, "You have a fine morning, miss."

"Thank you."

Mr. Turnbull turned toward the dining hall and whistled as he walked away.

"I better get going, too," Tabitha said. Pete nodded. The end of their moments together always came too quickly.

"See you next week."

"Bye."

She grabbed his hand and gave it a quick squeeze, then was off. Pete watched her walk away for a minute before turning toward the dining hall and his meeting with Chuck the Truck.

He found the Mr. Turnbull sitting in the otherwise empty staff dining room, two ceramic mugs on the table. Pete joined him at his table and sat down to a steaming serving of hot chocolate. The Truck sipped his coffee and said nothing for a few minutes. Pete appreciated the chance to just sit and sip his cocoa, even if the sipping hurt a little. The sounds and smells of the kitchen drifted in to him. Sunday brunch was always one of the culinary highlights in the Riordan week. This morning Pete could smell bacon and his stomach rumbled a bit. He was glad he had the cocoa to start in with.

"How's the head?"

"It's ok. I got a headache. Dr. Thomas is going to come see me later."

"Quite a shiner Steven left you with."

"Yes sir." Something was bothering Pete. "Sir?"

"Yep?"

"Sir, I didn't see him, Steven, at mass this morning. He wasn't with St. Matt's."

"No, he was not. Well noted, Pete."

"Sir, where —"

"Well, as of last night, Steven is no longer a resident of the Riordan Home for Boys."

"What?!"

"Steven is no longer here."

"Why?" Pete was stunned. There was no reason why Steven should have been booted for the fight. Pete had been the aggressor. Sure, Steven had kicked his ass, but Pete had obviously started it.

"The why is not important. Suffice it to say, Steven is gone and will not be back."

Steven was a bastard, and Pete had every reason to hate the guy, but...

"But, sir, he didn't start the fight, I attacked him."

Mr. Turnbull looked at Pete fully. "I'm aware of that, Pete. So is Father O." There was no mistaking the weight of the last, but Pete couldn't worry about the padre right now.

"Yes sir, but, then why was Steven booted?"

Mr. Turnbull looked down into his coffee and seemed to consider something for a moment. Then he looked back at Pete. "Last year, long before you moved into St. Gabe's, Steven was sent home for a month."

Pete remembered. Steven's absence had been speculated upon by the residents. Steven himself had offered no explanations upon his return to the Home, other than to say his temporary expulsion was a load of crap.

"Well," the Truck continued, "before he was let back in, Steven had to make some commitments regarding his behavior and choices. Specifically, he had to promise something to Father O. Well, yesterday after your, uh, altercation with him, it came to light Steven has not kept his word."

Pete didn't understand and said so.

"Steven was affiliated with a gang. Yesterday, after hearing you'd gotten in a few body shots, Doc Thomas asked Steven to remove his shirt so he could check out any possible injuries, see if there was any bruising."

And suddenly, it was clear to Pete. *The tattoo.* Steven had promised Father O he was going to stay away from the gang life. The fresh blue ink between his shoulders was proof he had not.

Pete looked up at Mr. Turnbull and saw from the look on the caseworker's face that something had just clicked home for the

Truck, for he was now smiling ever so slightly. "Knew, did ya? 'Bout the tattoo?"

Pete knew he was caught and simply nodded.

"Well," the Truck said, "Steven resisted removing his shirt, for obvious reasons. Once we got him to take it off he started beggin' for mercy."

The image of Steven pleading was both appealing and troubling.

"After that, things went quickly. Doc told Mr. Delano. Mr. Delano told Mr. Goodwin and Dr. Rugani. Then Father was told."

"Father?"

"The final decision is always his."

Pete nodded, wondering if he too was going to have to plead for Father O's mercy.

"Well, I'll tell you Pete: you surprise me."

"Sir?"

"Guy's twice your size and a gang-banger ta boot. But you don' let that stop you." He shook his head and whistled softly. "You got a yard o' guts son. Doesn't mean you were in the right, o'course. But... still."

Mr. Turnbull didn't have too much else to say. He'd merely wanted to make sure Pete was ok this morning and to let him know about Steven's departure. And Pete was grateful. He remembered how Steven had arranged Manny's blanket party just for smarting off. Steven's leaving meant he probably didn't have to spend the rest of his time at Riordan looking over his shoulder.

Probably.

He thanked Mr. Turnbull for the hot chocolate as the sound of boys entering the dining hall floated into the staff room. He slipped into the hallway and joined the St. Gabe's boys as they walked into the cottage's dining room.

It didn't occur to Pete until halfway through breakfast that Mr. Turnbull hadn't asked him why he had gone after Steven.

*   *   *

Word of Steven's departure was greeted by the boys of St. Gabe's as the grandest of good news. Chris pumped his fist a few times; Jordi and Frankie hi-fived; Malcolm Patty, in his Tourette's gilded excitement yelled, "F--- Yeah!" Even the notoriously even keeled Matt Saxon nodded and said, "Probably best for everyone."

Only two boys in the cottage reacted negatively at all. One of them was Frankie's cousin JP. One was Manny. The departures of first Fat Tony then Steven left JP in a delicate spot. He was now living in a cottage full of boys who knew him almost exclusively as Steven's henchman, who had watched him participate willingly in their harassment. He was not among friends. The other, and for those who didn't know him as well as Pete, the more surprising reaction, came from Manny, who was honestly saddened by Steven's expulsion from the Home.

"He had a chance here, maybe. But now that chance is gone for him." This was said on the way to Wednesday breakfast. It earned a startled glance from JP and a grunt from Weaver, who obviously thought Steven had earned his removal. All through breakfast Pete noticed JP glancing at Manny, his brow furrowed.

And Pete was not the least bit surprised when he saw Manny and JP talking and laughing together at recess the following week. Pete supposed that if Manny was able to find humanity in Mikey it shouldn't be too surprising he could find some in JP.

Chapter 24

The next couple of weeks were a different Riordan experience than what the past months had been. Pete had inexplicably received only 10 hours of cottage time and no campus restriction for his attack on

Steven. Manny suggested perhaps those in power considered the pain of the concussion and black eye a more fitting consequence than not being able to go to the Santa Rosa mall every couple of weeks. Whatever the reason, Pete was still surprised.

He'd had a meeting with Father O a few days after the incident during which the padre had been kind, but clearly disappointed. Pete had apologized for his stupidity, but had demurred when asked for a reason. Knowing that lying to a priest was probably one of the worst sins there was, he nevertheless shaved the truth, saying only that Steven had gone through his stuff and stolen the candy. The director of the Home seemed to accept this in a detached kind of way.

Cottage life settled into a new groove. With the massive drag of Tony and Steven gone from St. Gabe's the staff seemed lighter and more relaxed. Even Weaver was looser, like he no longer felt the need to prove he was the one in charge. When Manny commented on the change in staff demeanor, Mr. Johnson had smiled oddly and suggested it was just the difference between 12 and 10 boys, saying, "A pair of boys can make all the difference in the world." But when Manny speculated some boys could have more impact than others, the Supervisor had raised his eyebrows and smiled slyly.

The results were manifest in the boys. With the constant threat and danger of Steven gone, boys followed the staff example and relaxed with each other. Doing so allowed them to get along easier among themselves and with staff. As a result, daily scores started to go up. And the cottage LEVELS *jumped*. Perennial 3's like Billy Roberts, Chris and Frankie all soared to LEVEL 2 in the first cycle after Steven's departure. Matt Saxon joined Manny as a 1. Even previously buried boys began to extricate themselves: JP and Malcolm both moved out of the land of the 4s, leaving the cottage with no low LEVEL kids for the first time in Mr. Johnson's memory. Pete and Mikey both managed to hang on to their 2 LEVELS. Normally, Pete knew, something like his incident at rec would be enough to doom a guy to LEVEL 4 for a month or more, but the only bad score Pete received all week had been the "Peer Interaction" score for that Saturday. And even then, he'd only been down graded to a five out of 10. Sure it was a lot lower than his normal eight or nine, but he had assaulted a peer whose back had been turned! A zero was what he'd expected to see on the chart, and, he knew, what he'd deserved.

Steven's departure didn't appear to have much of an affect on the broader Riordan community. Pete got hi-fives from a few guys at school, and was appropriately joked about by others. Even Frankie ripped him at recess a week after Steven's removal, saying, "At least you got your ass kicked for a higher purpose."

A strange side effect from the whole affair was that a lot of staff members suddenly wanted to know how Pete was doing, if he was getting along ok, and was he healing up all right? Just about every staff from every cottage seemed to find Pete the week afterward and ask a version of one of those questions. Ms. Kelly hugged him and gently touched his cheek where the swelling was gone, but the coloration was still not right. It almost made the whole getting knocked out worth the trouble.

During the weeks after sustaining his injuries, Pete was pleased to notice a shift in his friendship with Manny. Mikey was with them less and less often. He was still around, still hung out with them some, but Manny was no longer making such an extreme effort to keep track of the kid. When Pete mentioned it, Manny acknowledged he was consciously letting Mikey go. "He's doing fine now. He doesn't need help anymore."

"Does he know that?" Pete asked across the pool table. They were down at Sunday evening rec with a dozen other high LEVEL kids from various cottages. One kid from St. Anthony's was on the phone, and Matt Saxon was playing ping pong with Mr. Talan 30 feet away. The rest of the group was at the far end of the hall clustered around the TVs and video games. Pete and Manny were playing nine ball. Manny had just broken and Pete was moving to shoot.

"I've talked to him about it," Manny said. "I told him I'm proud of him and that he doesn't need me any more."

Pete stared at Manny and again mentally shook his head at the way his friend acted and the fact he got away with it. For a Riordan resident to tell another boy he was proud of him was past ludicrous. It was one of the innumerable paths to a beaten ass and a reputation for being a freak. And yet here was Manny, saying what felt and not worrying about the consequences precisely because he believed what he felt was right and worth saying.

And we're starting to believe it too. He took his shot and missed.

"Anyway, I'm looking forward to less work in the friendship department for a while."

"What do you mean?"

Manny grabbed the chalk and blued up the tip of his cue as he spoke. "Well, hanging out with Mikey was always so much work. In case you haven't noticed, he's not much of a conversationalist. I mean he can talk about stuff, but he doesn't spend too much time contemplating any one subject. Except fire." Manny smiled. "On that topic he could speak for hours, except he *doesn't* talk about it." He shot and missed.

Pete made a couple of balls. Manny took his turn, missed, and continued. "No matter what he's done in the past, I do believe there is some good in Mikey. No matter what he does in the future, I'll still think he's not entirely bad." There was a strange hesitancy to the end of the sentence which made Pete look up from the table. Manny was staring at the cloth of the playing surface.

After a moment, Pete prompted him, "Buuuuttt?"

Manny chuckled and looked up. He sighed. "Make no mistake about it: while I don't think a lot of what he is is his fault, that doesn't change the facts: LEVEL 2 or not, he's still dangerous."

"He's never trusted me. Sure, he's followed my lead and taken my advice on a few things, but I don't think he has any idea how to trust people."

Pete missed his shot and leaned against one of the barstools dotting the hall.

"Of course, I don't blame him," Manny said. "It's not like he's particularly trustable himself."

Pete raised his eyebrows. "So, you *don't* actually trust him?"

Manny gave a tight-lipped grimace. "No way. I wanted to help him, but I never thought it remotely possible I could trust him. Given the choice between his own skin and somebody else's, I think Mikey would be the first person in line to start slicing somebody up."

Pete felt his hand drift up to the place where Mikey had cut him three months and a lifetime ago. The cut was no longer visible, but he could still feel the small scar that had taken its place. He remembered the feeling of his flesh tearing, and he remembered his conversation with Manny afterward: all that was said; and more importantly, what hadn't been said.

Pete nodded and said quietly, "Yeah. You can't trust anybody in this place."

"Well," Manny said, stepping up to the table, "maybe one or two guys."

Pete swallowed and felt the familiar ball drop into his stomach. He'd waited too long; he didn't know how he could tell Manny now. He felt his belly churning around the lead ball of guilt he'd let himself forget about for so long. Manny made his shot then stood up and leaned back against the adjacent pool table. Pete looked at him, knowing he needed to tell, but unsure how to begin.

I heard...

Fat Tony...
I'm sorry...
I knew...

Manny was looking away from him now, down the length of the rec hall, past the boys on couches playing video games, toward the dark windows beyond.

He had to tell. Now. "Manny, I —"

"I want to tell you something." Manny looked at him now, seemingly oblivious to the fact Pete had spoken. Pete was thrown off and hesitated. Manny did not. "There are some things you have the right to know. About me."

"Manny —"

"No, I want to tell you." He was no longer smiling, but neither was he completely frowning.

"My parents are dead. You know that. But I want you to know how."

Pete was totally unprepared for this. Manny on the other hand, had clearly been thinking about it for a while.

"My dad was a Minister. A man of God. No, not a priest, but a minister in our Christian church. In fact, he was *the* minister in our church. We'd moved to Elk Grove when I was four, so my dad could take a job as associate pastor in his uncle's church. A few years later, Uncle Jonas retired and my dad took on the head job." Manny was looking from table to table as he spoke. His eyes would rest on a spot for a few sentences and then slide to the next table.

"He was good. As a preacher I mean." He smiled and looked at Pete for a moment. "You're Catholic, so you may not know what preaching, real preaching, looks like." Pete was not hurt personally by the remark, but did feel a small spasm of defensiveness nonetheless. Manny seemed to sense and explained. "It's just... Catholic priests are all mellow and circumscribed. They hardly ever get carried away." His eyes drifted back to the foosball table. "My dad used to say that religion was supposed to carry you away, that being carried away was the whole point."

"He was huge, six three; like Steven, but a grown man. And he had this great voice. It was a voice that made people want to listen. And when they listened, they *listened*." Pete could hear the naked admiration in Manny's voice. "If dad said 10 volunteers were needed to knock on doors for a cause, he'd get fifty people signing up. When he told the congregation five thousand dollars was needed to retrofit the sprinkler system inside the church, and could they each pinch a penny or two, why, by the next Sunday he'd had donations of more than 20 thousand dollars. I'm telling you, his people would do just about anything for him." Manny smiled at his memories.

"Mom was different from him. She was just as religious. More so. But she wasn't much of a public figure. He wanted her to be; they wanted her to be. And she did some. She attended meetings of various committees and was friends with all the important folks in the flock, but she was never a force in church. I don't recall ever seeing her up in front of the congregation on her own. But, overall, she was just quieter about it." He looked down at his hands, folded around the shaft of the pool cue. Pete saw his brow furrow.

"It wasn't until later I came to understand why she was quiet."

Pete waited. For a moment, Manny stopped with what appeared to be finality. Pete was about to ask a question when Manny started again.

"Mom was quiet because he kept her that way." Manny looked up and must have recognized the confusion in Pete's wrinkled brow.

"Dad was big; mom wasn't. Dad was demonstrative; mom was demure. Dad had a wicked temper; mom learned to be quiet. Dad hit; mom got hit."

Pete felt his eyes widen and lose focus. Small things. Barely noticeable. Dozens of them. He could hear them now, all at once he could hear them.

"I know what broken ribs feel like…"

"Every injury I've had…"

"Not my first trip to the Emergency Room…"

"You can never understand him…"

"Having breakfast with someone who beats you up doesn't make someone a hero…"

Oh god… He looked up and Manny was staring at him.

"Manny… I —." But there was nothing he could think of to say.

Manny frowned and nodded. He looked away. "Yeah."

They sat in silence then. The sounds of the video game and ping pong filling in the gap. Pete's mind was barren. He was in a desolate landscape, groping for anything to help him understand. He should have known. If he'd paid any attention he would have known.

"You couldn't have known," Manny said, and Pete flinched at the way Manny seemed to be answering his thoughts.

"There's a little more I need to tell you." Manny was looking at him again. Pete just barely stopped himself from shaking his head. He didn't want to hear any more.

"Like I said, my dad was good. He knew how to get what he wanted from people. At home, it meant he knew how to control us. And, like I said, he was big. He knew how to hurt people. But he knew how to hide it, and how to make us hide it."

"My mom used to try to explain it away. 'He gives so much to the community,' she would say. 'He just needs us to take care of him.'" He laughed a dry barking sound. "Now, I never could figure out how him threatening and smacking us around was us taking care of him, but according to mom —." He looked away now, down to the floor, his black hair falling in front of his eyes. Through the tendrils Pete could see his wet cheeks reflected by the harsh fluorescents of the hall.

Still looking down, Manny said, "Take a shot."

Pete didn't understand.

Manny looked up with shining cheeks. "The game. Take a shot."

"What? Oh!" Pete hopped from his stool and bent over the table. He hit the cue ball into a random cluster, adding the crack and click of the pool table to the background noise of the hall. He looked down and saw Mr. Talan glance their direction then look back to Matt and their game.

"I was never allowed to get in trouble. Everyone knew who my dad was. He had this amazing reputation in the town. Anything I did to cast a shadow on that was rewarded painfully. I remember, one time in fifth grade I got into a fight with a kid. He'd said something about my shoes; said they looked like I stole them off a homeless kid. So I punched him." Pete was again faced with the picture of Manny doing violence, and again couldn't make images overlay in any sensible way.

"My dad came and claimed me, apologized to the school and spoke all up and down about healing through prayer and searching for forgiveness. He made me sit in the principal's office and write out an apology letter to the kid and his parents."

Manny paused.

"I missed the next week of school because I couldn't walk for the bruising. Dad knew what he was about. He knew he could never hit me in the face, because faces can't be hidden. But long pants never go out of style." Pete realized he'd never seen Manny in short pants, didn't think he'd even seen them in his laundry basket.

"He learned over years of practice how to do maximum damage without breaking anything. Oh, occasionally something would happen. Like I told you before, I know what broken ribs feel like." He chuckled and patted his side. "Now I know again."

Now Manny stood up and moved to the table. He surveyed the balls and potted the seven. *Click.*

"Well, when the thing happened in school, with me and the teacher and the phone, I ended up in juvie for the night. At least it was only supposed to be for the one night. It was the first time anything like that had ever happened. And because I was in custody, dad couldn't get to me."

He made another shot then grabbed the chalk. He didn't mash it onto the end of the stick, but instead gently scraped the tip of the cue with an exposed corner of the grainy blue cube. He took another shot, *click*, and continued his story.

"It was tough, dealing with dad, but we dealt. It got bad sometimes, but I learned to stay quiet and stay out of his way when I needed to. Fear is a mighty teacher. I was able to hide out in my room, or at friends' houses. One thing about being the son of the beloved preacher is that parents are so excited when you want to hang around their house with their kid." He smiled at this, but the amusement he took at the memory was fleeting and the smile faded quickly.

"But she had no escape."

Pete almost asked who she was before he stopped himself.

"She got it the worst. She always wore long sleeves and long dresses. I never remember seeing her in anything else. Even at home, the least she ever wore around the house was a full length robe."

He shook his head, "Nobody can tell for sure what happened. Only they were there in the house, and the neighbors didn't hear anything. Not until the end." *Click.*

"He'd been called by the school, had come in time to see me loaded into the back of the sheriff's cruiser for my ride to juvie. Afterward he didn't go back to work. No one at the church saw him again. His truck didn't show up in the driveway at the house in the evening. It's unclear where he went after about 11:30 that morning."

"He came home late, after midnight." Manny took a deep breath and exhaled slowly. "The police suspect he beat her senseless. She was covered in bruises, her face too. He'd never hit her in the face before. He had been drunk, which was unusual for him. He may have been a man of God, but what he worshipped was control. That was the word he used all the time. It was always about being in control of yourself, of the situation. I suppose you can't be in control if you're plastered."

"Well, control was apparently not on his agenda. Who knows what exactly set him off? It never did take much. Maybe she tried to defend me; maybe she just wondered aloud what would happen to me."

"I want to believe she told him it was over, that I was going to tell the cops everything about him and what he was. But I know she didn't, she was past the point where she might ever say something like that." *Click.*

"Neighbors called the police in the middle of the night. Two gunshots. The first at 4:12, the second less than a minute later. They found him face down on his bed, where they say he probably passed out after laying into her for the last time. He'd been shot twice in the back. Shot with his own gun. The same gun he'd held to her head more than once. The gun he kept locked in a drawer in his desk. He had the only key. She must have gotten it after he'd passed out."

"When they found her she was at the kitchen table slumped over a piece of paper. There was an empty bottle of oxycodone in the kitchen trash. She must have polished the bottle off before shooting him, because by the time the ambulance arrived just after five in the morning she was already comatose. She died later that day."

Almost a minute passed after Manny stopped speaking before Pete realized his mouth was hanging open. He closed it quickly and looked guiltily at Manny, who was still shooting balls and had been during the whole telling of the story.

Pete looked down the length of the hall. The rest of the boys were still playing and laughing about the video game. Occasionally, something exciting would happen and there would be a big group "OHHHH!" Matt and Mr. Talan were still batting the ping pong ball back and forth, but seemed to be doing so in slow motion. Pete marveled at the ordinariness of it all: the way it could go on so normally, as if the world were actually a good place where things like what Manny had described could never happen.

He looked back to Manny, still working the pool table, still shooting and potting balls. Still somehow acting like normal were a real thing and not just the punch line to a bad joke.

Click.

By the time they went to bed, Manny had told Pete the rest too. How the whole thing had gone down on a Friday night and no one had gotten around to telling him until Monday that his parents were dead. How he had been placed into temporary foster care while things were figured out and relatives were contacted. How the state could find no relative willing to come to Sacramento to claim him. All of his grandparents were dead. Uncle Jonas had moved to Florida and died two years before. They eventually tracked down a cousin of his mother's in Los Angeles who had no interest in taking on someone else's 13 year old problem child.

Eventually, he had been brought to court for the assault on the teacher, who had refused to drop the charges, even after Manny's story became more or less common knowledge around town. Manny had insisted his lawyer let him talk to the judge who was overseeing the case. When the judge agreed to hear Manny he had been surprised at the defendant's request for no leniency because of his history. Pete had been stunned by this, pointing out to Manny that the story about his dad would have gotten him out of it. Manny said he knew, but his smacking the teacher hadn't been about his dad. "Well, at least not all about him," he admitted.

The judge had been sufficiently impressed and sympathetic to let Manny off with simple probation. After a few months of bouncing around Sacramento's foster care network his file had landed on the desk of probation officer Louis Montgomery, the man Pete had seen dropping Manny off on his first day in November. After some phone calls, Mr. Montgomery had arranged an initial interview for Manny.

"And the rest is history." Manny looked at Pete and cocked his head. They were sitting on their respective beds, lights out for LEVEL 2s a few minutes away. "You ok," Manny asked. "You've been pretty quiet since the rec hall."

"Yeah. I'm all right. It's just, you know, a lot to take in."

Manny smiled, "Yeah, I know." He sighed then and asked, "Do you understand a little better now? Why it is I have a connection with Mikey?"

Pete nodded. "I do. I didn't before, but I do now."

"I'm glad."

Manny stood to go back up front. As a LEVEL 1 he still had 15 minutes until he needed to be in bed. He grabbed his current book from beneath his pillow. As he headed to the door, Pete remembered something and stopped him: "Hey."

Manny turned, "What is it?"

"You didn't say that thing this time."

"What thing?"

"You know, what you said before: *'That's my story Pete, use it as you will.'*"

"Oh." Manny smiled.

Weaver appeared in the doorway behind Manny and said quietly, "Light's out O'Boyle." Then he disappeared.

"Well," Manny said, "I didn't know you then; didn't know if I could trust you. Now I know. Believe me," he said, reaching for the light switch. "I never would have told you the whole thing unless I knew that for sure. Goodnight." He flicked off the light and left the room.

Sitting on his bed in the dark, Pete felt very alone.

Chapter 25

By Friday that week, Pete still had not found a way to tell Manny the truth. Knowing now, understanding where Manny came from made it impossible for him. He had been ready to do it that day in the rec hall, had steeled himself against whatever Manny's reaction might be. Hell, he had even started to say it! And then Manny had unloaded on him. How could he tell the truth now? How could he add to the pile of betrayal Manny had grown up in?

The answer was he didn't think he could. To tell him now would just stomp on the faith and trust he had put in Pete. And Pete would never do something like that again. Never. So he would not tell. No good could possibly come from telling; he would never tell.

The decision had come as a painful relief, and Pete had spent the next several days coming to terms with it, and trying to forget about it at the same time. He had allowed himself to forget about it several times between the event itself and January. He struggled to get himself back to that, but it was like trying to put himself back into a dream he'd just been woken from.

The attempt to put it out of his mind brought back Mitch and the time he had told Pete not to think of a pink elephant. He'd spent the next hour imagining a cartoon pink elephant, like the ones he'd seen in *Dumbo*, floating through the little hero's dreams. Later when Mitch had asked him how it had gone, if it had been successful, and

Pete had told him, Mitch had chuckled and said, "You can control your mind about as much as you can control your heart. They're both going to do just what they want to, or what they need to."

As Pete worked to earn the trust Manny had put in him and forget the reason it was misplaced, something was happening with Mikey Hamm. Over the proceeding weeks, Mikey had seemed to get Manny's subtle message and had been hanging out with other kids more. He and Malcolm had formed, if not a friendship, a mutual tolerance affiliation. They sometimes played after school and did homework together.

With his sustained success in the cottage, Mikey had even been granted a modicum of acceptance by Jordi, Frankie and Chris. Pete had seen him relaxing and laughing with staff as well. More and more, Mikey Hamm, the "Rat" himself, was behaving like a regular kid. And though Pete wasn't watching for it as he had once been, it appeared Mikey was visiting his hidden treasures with far less frequency.

Then something happened on Monday, the week after Manny had told his story in the rec hall. After school, Mikey's caseworker Mr. Paulino had come to gather him for an appointment up at Admin. He returned near the end of dinner and refused to make eye contact with anyone. The next day, Tuesday, Mikey had gotten up and dressed in his chapel clothes: clean khakis, leather shoes, long sleeve shirt and a blue tie Mr. Johnson had tied for him. He'd left the cottage with a pass before breakfast and the boys had seen him getting into Mr. Paulino green Ford when they'd left the cottage to head up to chapel. He'd not returned until after the 3s were already in bed, and had not spoken to anyone before going to sleep himself. Mr. Paulino had spent 15 minutes in the staff office with Johnson, talking with the door closed.

On Wednesday the change in Mikey was obvious. He barely spoke all day. Even Manny was rebuffed by silence when he had tried to engage Mikey after breakfast. When they asked, Mr. Johnson had said only that Mikey had been at a court appearance the previous day and that it had not gone well.

By Thursday, Mikey was worse, having retreated back into isolation and secrecy. Pete noticed him once again roaming the cottage grounds during free time and checking on his various drop spots and hiding places. Pete mentioned this to Manny and asked of maybe they should tell staff. Manny, not wanting to hoist more difficulties onto the already obviously burdened Mikey, asked Pete to hold off for a few days to see if he might not snap out of it. Pete agreed to this.

On Friday morning things for Mikey were completely back to pre-Manny levels. During cottage jobs Weaver asked Mikey to please re-do the trash can in the kitchenette: the knot hadn't held and the liner had fallen into the can. Mikey threw a bag at Weaver's feet and said quietly, "Do it your damn self."

Pete, sweeping the tile floor of the entryway, stopped to watch. He looked at Weaver and saw the staffer smile wickedly down at Mikey. "Well, well, well," Weaver said. "Welcome back, Mikey. I was wondering where you'd got to."

Mikey fired back something nasty and was confined to a red chair until the group left for chapel 10 minutes later.

By the time they returned from school Mikey had received a school detention from Sister Jack for not listening and had gotten into a fight after lunch with Malcolm. Manny asked Pete to talk to Mikey with him. He reasoned Mikey would listen to the two people he trusted most. Pete agreed and they found Mikey in the garden area next to the cottage. He was just straightening up from apparently inspecting the underside of the picnic table. He startled when he saw he wasn't alone; his eyes darted back and forth between them.

Manny spoke first. "Hey Mikey, can we talk to you?"

Mikey made a non-committal shrug.

"You seem upset since Tuesday. Do you want to talk about what happened?"

Mikey did not answer, but instead plunged his hands into the pockets of his jeans. He looked away to the corner of the cottage yard.

Manny tried again: "C'mon Mikey. We're here because we're worried about you."

Mikey sniffed loudly, but continued to look away.

"Mikey —." Manny stepped toward Mikey.

The kid mumbled something.

"What?" Manny asked stepping closer to him.

"I said 'don't.' Don't worry about me. Just forget it."

"Sorry," Manny smiled. "Can't. We're your fiends. It's part of the deal." Pete heard the sincerity in his friend's voice. Mikey clearly missed it.

"Right! Friends!" Mikey bit the words off, each one of them a separate, bitter statement.

"Mikey, what's wrong? What can we do to help?"

He exhaled again, and Pete heard what to him sounded like a snarl buried underneath.

"Mikey, you can trust us, you know that, right?"

Another shake of the head.

"We know you had a tough time with your court appearance. You want to talk about it?"

"No! Leave me alone!"

Pete didn't consider Mikey a friend, not like Manny seemed to, but he had grown sympathetic toward the kid over the past six weeks. He decided to give it a try.

"Mikey?"

Pete was surprised by the stabbing stare Mikey threw at him, and felt himself recoil. Manny saw it too and looked at Pete, a question in his eyes. Pete looked back and shrugged, honestly not understanding it himself.

Manny looked back toward Mikey, who met his eyes briefly, then looked down and away.

"Mikey? What is it?"

Mikey mumbled something.

Manny reached forward and touched Mikey's arm. "Hey, it's ok."

"Get the hell off of me!" Mikey ripped his arm away from Manny and backed up a step.

Manny held up his hands, palms out and backed off a few steps himself.

Mikey stared hard at Manny, working himself up to something. Then he said:

"You're so stupid, Manny! You think just because you're nice to people, they're gonna be square with you. You're so wrong. Nobody here is worth trusting." He looked pointedly at Pete. "Nobody!"

Pete didn't like the way this was going. Manny had been right: Mikey had come too far for them to let him slip back into what he had been. He took half a step forward and said, "No, you're the one who's wrong Mikey. You can trust us."

Mikey turned on him fully. "You!? You tell me to trust you? Like Manny trusted you!?"

Pete stopped breathing.

Manny looked from him to Mikey and back again. Mikey saw his face, and surprise lit in his eyes. He stared back at Pete. "You never told him, did you?"

Pete's mind stumbled in horror. *He knows! How can he know?*

Mikey saw his reaction and a nasty smile convulsed across his face and was gone.

Pete needed to stop him. *He* needed to tell Manny himself. He couldn't let the Rat do this to him! He started toward Mikey, not knowing what he intended.

Mikey saw him stepping forward and shot a hand out, an accusatory finger pointed at Pete's chest. "You knew." Hand still outstretched, he turned his face to Manny. "He knew, Manny! He knew Tony was plannin' on killing you, but he didn't tell you. He wanted you to get smashed."

Pete looked at Manny. He saw Manny smile and his shoulders slump at Mikey's obviously desperate lie. Then Manny's eyes found Pete's, and the smile melted slowly under the harsh light of the truth.

They stood there in tableau for many moments. Then Manny looked away, shook his shoulders and looked back to Mikey, who dropped his arm, but eyed Pete warily.

"How do you know?" Pete's own voice sounded hollow.

Now Mikey hesitated, his eyes darted between them again. "I was backstage, in one of the closets, getting donation envelopes for Sister Jack. I heard 'em in the hall, two guys talking about Tony going to take Manny out."

Pete remembered so clearly now, *someone in the other closet.*

"They heard me, ran me off." He sneered at the memory. "But I came back. I had to."

Pete felt nauseous.

"I still had to get the envelopes. And when I looked down the hall to see of they'd left I saw you peeking out from the closet next to the one I'd been in. You looked around, like you was doing the same thing as me. Then you went back in."

Pete felt the grey of the afternoon sky close in on him.

Manny walked to the picnic table and sat down. He looked at Mikey, not at Pete, and said, "That's not important right now. We're here to help you."

"Screw you! You can't help me. And I don't want your help anyway. I was fine before you got here. From now on you can just leave me the hell alone!"

Manny looked down and nodded. "Fine. I will." Pete felt the defeat in Manny's voice, and something else. Bitterness?

Manny stood and walked past Pete without looking up. Pete heard his footsteps fade around the front of the cottage.

Pete looked back to Mikey, wanting him dead and doing his best to radiate it.

But Mikey was not to be intimidated and held his stare.

Pete, stripped of his defenses offered up all he could, a weak recrimination: "You knew too. You never told him either." But the accusation was feeble and collapsed in on itself.

"No, I didn't tell him. But he was never my friend, no matter what he thought. Nobody has friends here. You used to know that, Pete. Manny didn't get it then." Mikey suddenly looked pained. "I bet he gets it now."

Chapter 26

The next several days were terrible for Pete. Manny didn't speak to him at dinner that night, barely looked at him even. The few times they did make eye contact, Pete couldn't help but see the disappointment and hurt in Manny's eyes. He could not bring himself to say anything until right before they went to bed.

But when he tried, Manny stopped him with a raised hand and said only, "Don't. Not right now."

Saturday was a day of complete silence between them. From the moment they woke up, through meals and rec and the Saturday night movie, right until Mr. Dawson turned the lights off on him, there was not a single word passed between them. Pete called Tabitha from the rec hall and told her everything. Told her how he'd known and how Manny had found out. She'd comforted him as best she could, telling him Manny was his friend and that forgiveness would come. But she reinforced that Manny had every right to be pissed at him. "You hurt him, Pete. Not because you didn't tell him beforehand, but because you kept living the lie of it." Pete asked her to forgive him and she said, "It's not my forgiveness to give. But I believe you're sorry for it, and I wish I could give you a hug to show you I know."

The next day was Palm Sunday. Chapel was packed for mass. Tabitha was there; Pete caught a glimpse of her through the throng as they exited the chapel but noticed her mother ushering her quickly to their car. He saw Tabitha's eyes searching the crowd but she hadn't seen him before her mom's BMW pulled out of the lot.

Finally, on Sunday night, Pete again tried to talk to Manny. The cottage as a whole was buzzing about the pending Easter home visit. There would only be three days of school in the upcoming week before boys began disappearing for the long holiday weekend. Most of the St. Gabe's guys would be leaving for the duration. All except Pete, Manny and Mikey, who had completely isolated himself again, talking to no one except staff when necessary.

After showers, Pete found Manny in their room, and when Manny didn't leave the room immediately as he had several times over the previous two days, Pete tried again.

"Manny, I want to apologize and explain."

Manny looked at him blankly and said nothing.

"I'm so sorry I didn't tell you. Mikey was right. I knew. I found out that night, right before the play."

Manny sat down on his bed. Pete took it as permission to tell the rest.

"I was still pissed at you, but I was going to tell you. Then I ran into Mikey in the bathroom."

Manny nodded and continued to look at him, but his face was distractingly passive. Pete wished he would smile or frown or do something. His blank expression was disconcerting.

"After Mikey and I fought, and you and I talked in the game room, I was so pissed I walked away without telling. I thought about telling you the next morning, before school, but I had to go up to the infirmary."

"I'm so sorry, Manny. I wish I had told you. You don't know how much I wish I had told you."

Manny sat quietly for several moments. Finally he said, "I believe you."

Pete looked up and felt hope.

"I also believe you wish you'd told me. But that's actually not the point." Manny put his hands on his knees. "Look, I could have gone without my role as a punching bag for Tony, but overall, it was no big deal. Strangely, I'm not even angry about it."

Pete felt his breath coming more easily now; he felt a lightness. Manny was going to forgive him.

Then Manny stood up. "But here's the thing, Pete: I'm not mad you didn't tell me. That's not why I'm mad. What has me angry, almost violently angry, is the fact you kept on not telling me. That you let me believe you were trustworthy. That is what has me upset and disappointed."

"But I was going to tell you, I wanted to tell you."

"No, you didn't." Manny shook his head. "No. If you had wanted to, you would have told me."

"But —"

"No." He put up his hands and shook his head. "Not now. Maybe later, but not now." And again, he walked out of the room.

The three school days passed in blur for Pete, like a movie filmed through a greasy lens. He drifted around the cottage, a ghost witnessing the movements of others, none of whom seemed willing to see him. Mikey was completely solo again. Manny had quickly found another project, and had begun spending a lot of free time with Malcolm Patty. Chris, Jordi and Frankie had stayed away from Pete since Friday. He had not told them about what had happened; he could not stomach the thought of admitting his deceit to them as well. By the time the three of them had disappeared for home visit on Wednesday night, Pete had spoken perhaps two dozen words to them collectively.

After coming back on shift Tuesday, Mr. Johnson had pulled Pete into the office and asked him pointedly what had happened between him and Manny. The change between them had been obvious to Mr. Dawson and Ms. Graham over the weekend and they had left notes about it in the log book asking Mr. Johnson to keep an eye on things. Johnson, always in favor of getting to the bottom of things as quick as possible had decided to do more than just keep his eyes open.

Pete had hesitated before telling Mr. Johnson, but finally admitted his part in Manny's beating. The staff member had been surprised at Pete's story, but had not condemned him as some would have; Weaver would have probably blamed Pete for the whole thing. Johnson had asked Pete if he had apologized to Manny. When Pete explained he had said he was sorry and had tried to explain why he had not told him, Mr. Johnson had clarified his question, "I know you said you were sorry for keeping the truth from him originally, but did you apologize for continuing to hide your involvement from him?" Pete had been forced to admit he had not, and expressed doubts as to whether Manny would listen to him now.

"Well, can you blame him?" the supervisor had asked. "You lied to him Pete, over and over. Every time he trusted you with anything afterward, you were silently lying to him."

Johnson had told Pete it was Manny's prerogative to be angry and hurt, and that Pete could not make things better. He could only apologize and let that be his message to Manny: *I am sorry for lying to you.*

Pete nodded. He knew Mr. Johnson was right and was thankful for him. In a lot of ways Mr. Johnson was like Mitch. Pete envied the staffer's children. Pete stood, but before leaving the office, asked Mr. Johnson about the other matter he'd been worrying on.

"Sir, what's happened to Mikey? You said he had a bad court appearance, but he's still here, so how bad could it have been?"

Johnson had looked at Pete carefully then, and had finally said, "I can't say anything about another boy's personal matters, Pete. I wish I could sometimes, but I can't. If Mikey wants to tell you, it's his choice, but if he doesn't want to, it's not my job to spread his business."

Pete had understood, but found the answer frustrating, so he had sought out the one person he knew would have both personal information on the boys and a total lack of compunction about sharing that knowledge. Mr. Weaver had come on shift Wednesday afternoon, but Pete didn't have a chance to talk to him privately until that night.

The cottage was all but empty, with only Pete, Mikey and Manny left. All of the others were gone on home visit. When the last of the other boys, Billy Roberts had left just after dinner, Pete had thought how great this would have been a month ago, when the three of them had been close and speaking. Now it was well past dinner, and with no one else left in the cottage, the building was almost silent. Manny was reading back in the bedroom he nominally shared with Pete.

Mikey was actually out of the cottage, taking advantage of his LEVEL 2 status and visiting Mt. Olivett Cottage where he had been for his first year at Riordan. He'd asked Johnson if he could go up there to visit Mr. Assad, one of the few staffers he got along with in the whole of the Riordan Home. Johnson said he could and suggested he take some of his stuff up with him. Tomorrow night, they would all three be moving up to Mt. Olivett for the duration of the home visit.

With Mikey gone and Manny backrooms and Mr. Johnson up at the Admin building going over some paperwork with the coordinator, only Weaver and Pete were in the cottage front room. Weaver had put on a video of his own. It was a movie about scientists in a lab under the ocean and these weird alien things they had to deal with. He invited Pete to join him which Pete did. After watching for a while, he asked Weaver if he knew what was going on with Mikey, why he had gone all sullen again.

At first Weaver suggested simply that some boys could handle the pressures of success and being high LEVEL, while some could not. He'd seen it a dozen times, he told Pete: "Kid struggles for a long time, then suddenly, things start to go well, and the kid pops a three or a two. Next thing you know the guy's completely lost it and is back in the land of 4 where he's comfortable."

"But didn't something happen in court last week?"

"Oh, that? Yeah, he found out he's probably gonna get yanked from here."

Pete was surprised. "Yanked?"

"Yep. Kid keeps breaking his probation. He pled guilty to a couple of fires from December. I heard the house fire he started over Christmas did like half a million dollars worth of damage. Looks like the court's finally gonna make him pay for his crimes, instead of letting him stay here and avoid it."

"So where will he go if they remove him from Riordan?"

Weaver shrugged. "Don't know. Youth Authority I suppose. He may end up in foster care at some point, seeing as how his mother can't manage to keep him clean. But before that happens the county will want a bite out of him."

"When is he leaving?"

"Don't know for sure, but he's got a sentencing hearing next Tuesday. Wouldn't surprise me if the court tells us to have him packed on Monday night. They do that sometimes."

Something was bothering Pete now. Just before Mikey returned from Mt. Olivett at 9:30 he asked Mr. Weaver, "Sir, you have any guess as to why Mikey's never started a fire here at Riordan?"

Weaver laughed, "Because he's dumb, not stupid. He knows the second he strikes a match here Father O signs the paperwork to kick his butt out."

"Yeah," Pete said, "that's what I thought." But he was still troubled when he went into the room, where Manny was already asleep.

On Thursday morning the boys walked in silence from cottage to chapel to breakfast in the staff dining room, back to the cottage and then to morning rec. In the staff dining room, the boys had split up: Mikey had sat alone, Manny had eaten with a couple of St. Mike's guys he'd gotten to know at school, and Pete had eaten with Ms. Kelly, who expressed concern at the obvious stress she saw on Pete's face. She'd noted the boys seemed not to be talking again and asked about it. Pete told her things were ok, that Manny was mad at him but he was going to try to fix it.

The rest of Thursday was lost to rec and moving all the way up the hill to Mt. Olivett, for which Mr. Johnson borrowed a Riordan van, not the green weenie this time. The three boys each grabbed a bag with enough clothes to get him through the weekend and piled into the van for the ride up to the highest elevation of the Riordan campus. Driving up the steep road in silence, Pete looked past Mr. Johnson into the trees crowning the hill. He snatched a quick sidelong glance at Manny, who seemed to be looking up into the trees as well. Pete wondered if they might ever get back to where they had been then, back in November when they had trekked through the night to retrieve the gifts from Tabitha.

In Mt. Olivett they were split up and sent to separate rooms, each paired up with a boy from a different cottage. Pete was assigned Room 1 with a fat Asian kid named Bobby Chang. He'd met the St. Mike's kid once and had come away with impression the boy was slow. Mikey and Manny were put in separate rooms at the other end of the T-hall and each given half of the KGB as a roommate. Nicolai was put with Manny and the reticent Alexei was roomed up with Mikey.

After dinner, Mr. Assad offered to take some of the boys with him to pick up a couple of movies. He asked Pete, Manny, Bobby and Tommy McGraw from St. Ant's to come with him. Pete, thanked him, but said he'd rather stay at the cottage. He couldn't help but notice the relief on Manny's face when he told Mr. Assad. Pete was reading in the cottage craft section while Manny and the others were off campus getting the movies. Someone sat down near him, but Pete didn't take notice until he finished the chapter he was reading. When he finally looked up a few minutes later, Mikey Hamm was sitting five feet away, staring at him.

He looked back down, but three minutes later Mikey was still staring at him. Pete was still mad at Mikey. Sure, he knew it was his own fault, what had happened with Manny, but part of him still blamed Mikey for forcing the issue out like he had. He stared at Mikey for a minute, then made what he hoped was a dismissive sound and turned his back, which he knew Mikey didn't like.

"Told you once not to turn your back on me." The voice was quiet from behind him, and deadly serious.

Without looking over his shoulder, Pete said, "Shut up Mikey. Just shut up."

"It was your fault, you know." The voice this time wasn't angry, the tone had shifted neutral.

"He was my friend. I know I said he wasn't, but he was." The voice was sad now, and Pete looked back. Mikey was there, and he was just Mikey, not the Rat. He looked oddly human. Pete noticed for the first time that the features he'd always seen as feral had begun to soften slightly. He looked pathetic, and Pete was angered by his presumption.

"He was my friend first," Pete said.

Mikey nodded, and said, "Yeah, but I needed him more."

Pete thought about this and nodded, "Maybe."

"But he didn't want to be my friend. Not when you were there. But you screwed that up yourself."

Pete nodded again, "I know. But I still wish you hadn't told him like that. I wanted to do it." Pete looked back to his book, but reading was no longer possible.

From behind him, Pete could still hear Mikey's wheezy breathing, but it was several minutes before he spoke. When he did, he sounded strangely subdued.

"I'm gonna be gone soon."

Without turning around again, Pete said, "Yeah, I heard. Tough break."

Mikey's voice was suddenly guarded, "You heard? What did you hear?" he demanded.

Pete looked at him again. Mikey was on the edge of his seat, looking ready to spring. His right hand had dived into his pocket, seemingly of its own will. Pete guessed what might be in that pocket.

"I just heard you might be leaving Riordan, that's all. Your court thing."

"Oh." Mikey relaxed visibly, his hand slowly withdrew from the pocket. His eyes however kept darting wildly toward the staff office where Ms. Dupree of Mt. Olivett sat talking with Ms. Kelly. Pete watched him carefully until Mikey stood up and walked out of the craft section and towards backrooms.

Chapter 27

The next day was Good Friday. Traditionally, Catholics hold the Friday before Easter as the day on which Jesus Christ was crucified, and spend three hours of the afternoon paying respect to the three hours Christ was on the cross. Growing up with his mother Pete always dreaded Good Friday. She used to make him go to Good Friday services at their church, St. Pius in Redwood City. The services were from noon to 3 in the afternoon and consisted of silent prayer interspersed with lectors reading from the Stations of the Cross. As a boy Pete did his best to quietly sit with his mother, but always found it an arduous task. As he got a little older, his mother stopped subjecting him to Friday services and instead let him spend the three hours playing quietly in his room.

Since Riordan was a Catholic institution full of non-Catholic staff and residents, Good Friday at the Home was always a weird day. From talking to some of the more experienced staff, Pete knew Riordan boys used to spend the full three hours in chapel, but as the resident population changed and being Catholic was dropped as a requirement for working there, the Home became more progressive in its approach to the celebration of the Passion. Boys were asked to stay quiet during the three hours from noon to 3. They were not allowed to play outside, watch TV or utilize the game room. They were allowed to read and talk quietly. Most of the 8 boys remaining in Mt. Olivett spent their time sleeping in their rooms. Pete was again reading alone in the craft section. From his occasional glances up, no other boys were visible. He was nearing the end of his book when Manny walked over and sat down. Pete sat stunned for several moments, not knowing what to say. For his part, Manny simply looked at Pete.

Finally, Pete was able to get his lips to form the words they had been longing to speak for the previous week. And once he started talking it seemed like he couldn't stop.

"Manny, I'm sorry I lied to you. I'm sorry I didn't tell you. I wanted to tell you a bunch of times, but I couldn't. I was afraid if I did you wouldn't forgive me. I —"

Manny held up a hand and nodded, "It's ok. I know you're sorry. And I accept your apology."

"You do?" Pete felt the relief course through him like cool water extinguishing the fire of fever. He was surprised by his own reaction and felt his eyes begin to sting as his smile was born and then broadened.

"I do." Manny smiled as well, but he was subdued in his forgiveness. His smile became pained for a moment, and he said, "And throughout all eternity / I forgive you, you forgive me."

Pete's smile softened in confusion and then faded as he realized what was coming next.

Manny nodded, and said, "Yeah. Something my dad used to say."

On Friday night, they sat down in the staff dining room for their final fish dinner of Lent. Unlike the previous week's battered cod and fries, this meal was the best salmon Pete had ever tasted. The sides included garlic mashed potatoes, salad and grilled asparagus. Even the staff complimented the kitchen crew. Ms. Kelly said it was the best Riordan meal she'd ever tasted. She ate with Pete and Manny and expressed happiness that things between them were better.

During dinner, Pete caught a glimpse of Mikey Hamm watching them from across the dining hall. He was eating with Mr. Assad of Mt. Olivett, but seemed to be paying very little attention to his meal.

His eyes kept finding their way back to Pete and Manny. At least, every time Pete glanced in his direction he seemed to be watching them, and the look on his face was not one of happiness.

That night, before lights out, Pete mentioned Mikey to Manny. He told him about the conversation from the previous day. Manny was upset by it. He said Mikey had been right. "Once things between you and I were better, I didn't have need of him any more. Wow. I am the bastard I fear to be. And I never noticed it. Well, I did tell you Mikey was more perceptive than you thought. Apparently, even more than I thought."

Saturday was spectacularly beautiful. Ms. Kelly agreed to take a few of the guys up to the water tower to enjoy the cool sunny afternoon. The Sonoma Valley was green and looked more alive than Manny had ever seen it. He kept talking about how lush everything looked. Pete spent a lot of his time atop the tower looking south toward the Pembrook house, hoping to catch movement through the trees.

He hadn't talked to Tabitha in person since the morning after his beating at the hands of Steven. Tomorrow though, he was sure he'd have a chance to see her. Easter Sunday was one of the biggest deals in the Riordan yearly calendar. Mass would be followed by a community reception in the auditorium. He had hopes of catching a few minutes of conversation with her during the festivities.

After dinner, the boys returned to the cottage for showers and the Riordan movie. Ms. Kelly had picked one of her favorites for the boys: *The Black Stallion*. Pete had seen it before, but Manny had not. The only boy not interested in the film was Mikey. He spent most of his time backrooms, only appearing occasionally to get a snack out of the kitchenette, though Pete did notice him lingering in the hallway near the living room during the beginning of the film when the main character was escaping a burning ship.

Before they went to bed Manny and Pete played a quick game of chess and talked about the upcoming baseball season. Pete was anxious to see how his beloved Giants were going to start the season after their big off-season acquisition: a power-hitting third baseman.

They said good night and both headed to bed at around 10.

Pete awoke to the sound of coughing. He was groggy, and slow to come to, but as soon as he did he knew something was strange was happening. Bobby was coughing and sitting up in bed. It took Pete a minute to realize he smelled something, and another moment for his sleep addled mind to make the connection: smoke.

He sat up in bed and swung his feet to the floor. As he stood, he became aware of a sound: a crinkling coming from the front of the cottage, like a group of gift wrappers were in the front hall crushing heavy cellophane. He'd fallen asleep in sweatpants and a t-shirt. He stood and walked to the doorway. There was smoke in the hall, clearly visible. And there was something else; he could see flickering lights coming from the T-hall. Fire. He ducked back into the room and looked up at the smoke alarm above the door. Smoke was already flowing in the top of the door and coursing over the red plastic alarm unit. Pete ran back to his bed and slipped on his shoes. He could hear the sounds of other boys now, some calling in fear, some asking what was going on. He heard Manny's voice calling out, "Fire! It's a fire! Get outside!"

Bobby was shaking, looking scared. Pete grabbed the front of his shirt and heaved him bodily toward the door. The smoke in the hallway was even thicker now, the sound so loud as to drown out some of the yelling that had started in earnest. Pete turned Bobby right, away from the T-hall junction and out of the emergency door at the end of the hall. There were still no alarms going off. Pete couldn't understand why there were no alarms. He looked at the red fire box next to the green lit EXIT sign above the doorway. It too was bathed in smoke, but not screaming its alarm. Pete heard Manny behind him, "Pete!" He turned to see Manny running, hunched over.

They went together out the exit door and into the fresh air. Manny stood coughing and catching his wind. Bobby was leaning against a tree right at the edge of the drop-off toward the rest of campus; he was shivering in his t-shirt and boxer shorts. A moment later the emergency lights in the cottage blazed to life and Pete heard the cottage alarm's sharp buzzing bursts. Someone had finally pulled the main fire alarm near the office.

Through the door they had just exited, Mr. Assad appeared with a towel over his face. He came out and yelled at them to get around to the basketball courts. Then he plunged back into the thickening smoke. They watched him in the emergency lights go into each room, making his way down the hall toward the open emergency exit at the other end. Pete looked toward the front of the cottage. He saw the windows in the game room flashing orange and black, and from above the cottage an inconsistent glow emanated.

Manny said something above the din of alarm and fire.

"What?" Pete said.

"Did Mikey come out this way?" Manny yelled.

"No, just me and Bobby."

Manny looked worried. "I didn't see him go out the other door either."

"You must have missed him. He's probably over at the basketball courts." Pete was sure he was right. But there was also not a doubt in his mind that Mikey had finally started a fire at Riordan. But the fire seemed to be in the front of the cottage. Probably, he reasoned, Mikey had started the fire up front then left via the big oak front door.

Pete grabbed the freaked-out Bobby by the shirt and led him behind the cottage toward the basketball courts on the other side. Manny walked with him, but stopped about halfway.

"Pete!"

Pete turned and saw Manny standing next to the cottage ladder, propped against the side of the roof. Pete pushed Bobby on and yelled "Go!" when the chubby kid hesitated. Bobby turned away and blundered on past the end of the cottage to the asphalt beyond. Pete could hear the sound of the fire truck now, screaming through the night. Looking down across the vineyard property he could see the approaching lights on Sonoma Highway.

He went back to Manny and said "Come on!"

Manny shook his head. "The ladder," he said.

Pete looked at it, not understanding.

Manny yelled, "I think Mikey's up there. That's why we didn't see him." Then he put his foot on the bottom step and began to climb.

Pete grabbed him, but Manny shook off his hand and went quickly up the ladder, disappearing over the edge. Pete called after him, but he did not reappear. Pete hesitated for a minute. He should go get staff. He should not go up after Manny. Mikey probably wasn't even up there. Pete cursed Mikey and Manny both as he put a foot on the bottom rung. Then, cursing again, he followed his friend up the ladder.

Stepping up onto the roof, Pete was surprised by the smoke. There was far more up here than he would have expected. He looked down the length of the cottage and saw two figures above what he guessed was the staff office, about 60 feet away. Not five yards to the right of them the roof was a churning cauldron of flame. Some part of Pete's mind thought, *the game room is below that.*

Pete called out to Manny, screamed his name, but if Manny heard he made no indication. Terrified, Pete walked carefully forward, trying to stay out of the smoke drifting and billowing across the rooftop. He had to pick his war carefully. Though the roof of the cottage was basically flat, endless pipes, vents and conduits jutted from the surface

Looking down from the roof toward the campus he could see the fire trucks coming up the main driveway now, passing St. Gabe's and the other darkened cottages.

Now he was only 30 feet from them and he could see more clearly. Manny was yelling something and trying to grab Mikey, but the smaller kid was dodging and wielding a burning road flare, the white-hot tip of which left dancing tracers on Pete's eyes.

As he took tentative steps closer, the roof to the left of Manny and Mikey erupted. A single point of light became a spreading circle of flame that went from six inches across to six feet in just a few seconds. Past the new sprouted flames Pete could look down onto the basketball court. He saw the boys from inside and several staff members who had come from other cottages. They were lit with an inconsistent, spitting yellow light. But as he looked down, other colors joined in. The wail of the fire engines was upon them and the first of the huge red trucks pulled onto the blacktop.

Pete could feel the heat from the fire. He was sweating and his clothes were sticking to him. He was only 15 feet from the two other boys now. They were circling around one another, occasionally stumbling on the various pipes and vents projecting out of the roof. Manny was trying to grab onto Mikey and the smaller boy was still dodging and lashing out with the burning flare. Mikey's shirt looked wet, like he had sweat through it. On the roof around them were a backpack and what appeared to be several plastic bottles.

As Pete watched, Manny finally grabbed hold of Mikey's shirt and tried to pull him toward the edge of the cottage nearest the basketball court. Mikey struggled against Manny and eventually jammed the flare into the bigger kid's arm. Pete heard the scream above all other sounds. Manny released Mikey and pulled away, staggering. Pete saw him stumble backwards and catch his heel on a pipe. He fell and landed flat on his back. He hit hard, his head bouncing. Then he was still.

In the flickering light, Pete saw Mikey's face distort into a grimace of shock and pain. He dropped the flare to the rooftop and began backing away. Pete scrambled to Manny and tried to pull him to his feet. Manny was sprawled on the roof and when Pete knelt he felt the heat of the surface pour up through his knee. He looked down at Manny. His burned right arm lay against his chest. His eyes were closed and he was not moving. Pete couldn't make out the burn itself, but this close he could smell the charred flesh.

He looked up and saw Mikey, still backing away, looking down at his own hands and shaking his head. Pete looked past Mikey's legs, at the flaming fissure above the game room, and screamed at him to stop. Mikey seemed to hear, because he did look up, but he kept backing away. Pete yelled again: "MIKEY, STOP!" But, thought Mikey appeared to be looking at him he was not listening. Staring straight ahead, he reached behind his back. When his hand reappeared it was holding another road flare. Staring at Pete and the fallen Manny, Mikey removed the plastic striking cap.

Looking down, Pete saw one of the plastic bottles a few feet from him. He leaned, picked it up and looked at it. It had a familiar shape. It was unmarked; a label had been ripped off. He put the bottle to his face and sniffed. His eyes widened and he looked back to Mikey and his drenched shirt and, Pete now noticed, his wet jeans.

"MIKEY, NO!"

Mikey looked up at him and his face was blazed in the flash of the newly ignited flare. In the brilliant white light, Pete could see tears streaming down the boy's face. The face dimmed as Mikey held the flare out sideways at arms length. Then he slowly raised his arm above his head and it was only a moment before the first glowing drippings hit his shoulders and hair. His scream was high and piercing. He dropped the flare, and collapsed to the roof and tried to stop what he had begun, but it was already too late. Fire raced across his saturated shirt and hair and within moments he was a writhing mass of flame on the graveled rooftop. Pete watched the burning shape of Mikey begin to roll back and forth on the roof in an effort to extinguish the flames. The roof under and around him began to glow, and a gout of flame erupted inches from where he was. As more flame began to leap from the roof around him, Mikey's weight finally broke through the now burning surface and he disappeared from view.

Pete stared after the disappeared body for a moment, lost for action. He looked down and saw he was still holding the empty bottle that had once contained rubbing alcohol. He threw it down and tried again to get Manny to his feet. But Manny appeared to be unconscious. His breathing was shallow and his body was shaking slightly. Pete looked desperately back in the direction of the basketball courts and could not see past the wall of flame and smoke. From behind the wall came the flashes of blue and red.

He tried to lift Manny again. As he pulled him up to a sitting position he saw blood pooled where his head had lain. Pete looked at the roof and in the unreliable light saw a dark smudge on the steel vent Manny had been lying next to. He got up into a squat in an attempt to lift Manny when it suddenly began to rain. Pete looked up into the falling rain and the clear night sky behind it and was confused until he saw the fire fighter descend from nowhere.

Water sprayed from a hose attached to the white metal basket of the cherry picker. The fire fighter directed the stream at hot spots on the roof as the arm from the back of the fire truck lowered him to just above the rooftop. The masked figure exited the basket and ushered Pete in. He picked Manny up like a doll, threw him over his shoulder and was standing in the basket next to Pete in just a few seconds. Pete heard him mumble something and the cherry picker moved up and away from the conflagration.

*   *   *

On the ground, Pete was looked at by one of the paramedics and checked out ok. They were alarmed initially by the blood covering his shirt and hands, then relaxed when they realized it wasn't his. The fire fighters were spread out around the cottage, with hoses and extinguishers.

When they discovered Mikey was still missing they began venturing in to find him. Pete was sitting on the rear bumper of the second fire truck, parked far away from the cottage, right at the base of the grassy hill. A fire fighter had handed him a bottle of water and Ms. Kelly had brought him a blanket and given him a hug before heading back to help wrangle the boys. He was away from the rest of the Riordan folks, who were gathered near the other end of the basketball court, safely sequestered behind a sheriff's cruiser. Between him and the rest of the boys was the ambulance that had arrived at some point during his time on the roof.

Through the open doors of the ambulance he could see both paramedics now working on Manny, stretched out on the gurney. Manny had not moved in the five minutes since they had been brought down from the roof. He watched the quick and deft movements of the paramedics and noticed the way they kept talking to each other the whole time. At the feet of one he could see a pile of discarded gauze wadding, all of it drenched crimson.

After a few more minutes they strapped Manny down. One of the medics jumped out and closed the doors of the ambulance. He then disappeared around the side and in moments the rig was rolling with lights and siren blazing.

As the first ambulance departed a second appeared and pulled in between the fire trucks. For a moment, Pete was worried they were going to make him get in it. He was readying his protests when the paramedics emerged from the back and wheeled the gurney toward the front of the cottage. The fire was coming under control. The roof was no longer burning. A fire fighter was back up in the cherry picker and had been drenching the building since Pete had received his going over from the medic. Through the few windows on this side of the cottage flames continued to spit, but the fire fighters, who had been sprinting back and forth in their heavy coats and helmets, had changed pace to quick walking. Now windows were smashed by axes and hoses were directed in through the broken panes.

From where he was, Pete could not see the front door of the cottage where the gurney had disappeared minutes ago, but he saw it return now, a shape on it. A small shape covered completely with a sheet. The scene blurred in a damp mixture of flame and lights. The different rhythms of the red, white and blue of the sheriff's lights, the blue and red of the truck lights and the red and white of the ambulance melted together as Pete's tears began to fall.

Chapter 28

The sounds of the fire were behind him now. The falling of the water, the shouts of the fire fighters and the sirens still coming from far away, converging on Riordan and Mt. Olivett, were all behind him now. He was walking down from the basketball court, toward the vineyard fence line. Away now from the heat of the fire, Pete walked down into the ground fog.

He walked to the property line and without pausing stepped over the low fence and earned his 25 \ 60. He walked through the valley and the fog, heading down and then up toward the lights of the house through the trees. He walked for a long time, feeling the fog condense on his warm skin, feeling the weight of his sweats, still wet from the hosing down on the roof. He felt the damp material catch on the weeds and grasses, felt the foxtails scrape his bare ankles and lodge in his shoes. He walked. And he felt.

He knocked at the big front door of the house. There were some lights coming from the upper rooms, but none downstairs. Pete wondered for the first time since sitting up in bed what time it was. After a minute he knocked again. The door opened and in front of him was a man in flannel pants and a t-shirt, fleece slippers on his feet. Pete had seen him only once before, at Christmas mass, but even so, up close he looked much younger, like he might be no more than 30. Mr. Pembrook looked at him with more than a little alarm in his eyes, and said, "Yes?"

Pete was bone weary and had only the strength to say, "Tabitha?"

Mr. Pembrook made no move to fetch his daughter, so Pete sat down on a small boot bench next to the front door. He put his face in his hands; he was so tired.

Then she was kneeling before him, in a blue t-shirt and sweats of her own, her hair thrown back in a hasty pony tail. She had never looked so beautiful, and for the first time he was struck by how much she looked like Lily O'Boyle. The same kind eyes, the same curve to the mouth. She put a hand to his face and looked into his eyes. And he let himself get lost in her. She stood, raising him up with her and helped him past her father into the house.

It was almost 5 am when Mr. Turnbull showed up at the Pembrook home. Pete had spent the past two hours sleeping on the sofa with his head in Tabitha's lap, and when he woke up he felt better than he would have expected, until he remembered it hadn't just been a dream. Tabitha hugged him and kissed him before releasing him to Mr. Turnbull's custody. None of the three adults, not even Mr. Turnbull, said a word as Pete and Tabitha embraced at length before he left with the Riordan staffer.

Mr. Turnbull drove Pete back to St. Gabe's. He asked no questions, other than a single check to make sure Pete was uninjured. At St. Gabe's the caseworker let Pete into the dark and empty cottage. He told Pete to shower and get into some clean clothes. Twenty minutes later, Mr. Turnbull led Pete out to his truck. Before getting in Pete looked up in the direction of Mt. Olivett. Though dawn was still 30 minutes away the top cottage was lit up. Huge klieg lights had been set up and bathed the scene in bright white. The tail of one of the engines was visible as were several firefighters walking around the blackened remains of the cottage's near wall. Pete saw the sections of the wall and roof that had enclosed the game room were completely gone, as if they had been bitten out of the cottage by a giant.

On the way to the hospital in Santa Rosa, Mr. Turnbull confirmed what Pete already knew: Mikey Hamm was dead. Manny, he said, was badly injured and being treated for shock. He had not yet regained consciousness. The burn to the arm was bad, but the head injury was worse. It would be several hours before they had anything on the way of a prognosis.

After collecting Mikey's body the paramedics had looked for Pete to make sure he wasn't suffering from any delayed reactions to his ordeal, particularly shock. Only then had it become apparent he had disappeared.

At nearly the same time Ms. Kelly had reported Pete missing to the coordinator and suggested where they might look, Father O had been taking a call from Alan Pembrook, who had reported Pete safe and urged he be left where he was until needed. This last bit of information surprised Pete, but he said nothing.

At the hospital, Pete was fully checked out by a doctor and was pronounced healthy, suffering only from minor smoke inhalation and some small contusions. After getting cleared he was brought in to see Manny.

The sight of Manny might have been troubling or confusing to someone whose aunt wasn't a nurse. His friend was in an oxygen tent. He had a feeding tube down his throat and a ventilator was breathing for him. Beneath the clear plastic of the tent his head was wrapped in so much gauze it looked twice its normal size. His right arm was covered loosely, hidden from view. He looked oddly peaceful to Pete. He looked dead.

Chapter 29

Easter Mass went on as scheduled, though with a far more somber tone than usual. Father O'Connor talked in his sermon about Michael Hamm, the resurrection of the soul and of the forgiveness God has for us all. The community heard the message, looked up the hill to the charred remains of the cottage and wrote fat checks that spilled out of the donation boxes in the back of the chapel.

There were a lot of questions for Pete over the next few days. About Mikey and Manny. About the six or more bottles of rubbing alcohol Mikey had managed to somehow sneak into Mt. Olivett cottage. About the estimated 15 magnesium road flares Mikey had used to start the fire. The police and arson investigators wanted to know if Pete had been in on any of the plan. Did he know how Mikey had managed to remove the batteries from all 16 of the cottage's public area smoke detectors? Did he know how Mikey got into the staff office in the middle of the night to access the crawlspace above the game room where the fire had started?

Pete, accompanied by Chuck the Truck for all of this, told everything he knew. He told about the supplies Mikey kept around St. Gabe's. He told them how Mikey had bragged about the ease of getting into the staff office. He'd had no idea about the rubbing alcohol, the flares or how Mikey had managed the battery trick. Pete speculated some of it may have happened during Mikey's time backrooms on Saturday night, while the rest of the cottage had been watching the movie.

They questioned him about Manny's involvement and the effect his arrival at Riordan had on Mikey. What kind of relationship had they had? Did Manny have control over Mikey as some other boys had suggested? Had they been romantically or sexually involved?

Pete answered these too, to the best of his ability, telling the investigators Manny was simply a good person, that he had looked out for Mikey, had wanted to give him a chance he hadn't had before. Eventually, when he couldn't seem to answer the questions to the satisfaction of the police investigator, he said the guy would just have to wait until Manny woke up.

Aunt Marjorie had shown up on Monday morning to see him. She kissed him and cried over him and, the nurse she was, poked and prodded him to make sure he was ok. She took him to lunch and drove him over to see Manny. On Tuesday evening boys began showing back up after home visit. They had all been notified by phone of the incident, and most had seen news coverage of the event.

The 10 boys who had been living in Mt. Olivett were dispersed to fill vacancies across the rest of campus. Three were moved down to St. Gabriel's, filling the slots most recently occupied by Fat Tony, Steven Sengall and Mikey Hamm. Tuesday afternoon, Mr. Turnbull took him back to the hospital. Tabitha met him there and they went in to see Manny together. She held on to his arm the whole time they were in the hospital and hugged him in the parking lot before getting into her mom's car.

On Wednesday, the rest of the guys returned. Everyone was back by dinner and the buzz of the fire was wearing a little thin for Pete.

After one final time for Chris, Jordi and Frankie, he stopped telling his story; he was just so tired of talking about it.

That night, just before evening prayers, Mr. Turnbull came down to St. Gabe's and stepped into the office to speak privately with Mr. Johnson. When he emerged he sought Pete out asked him to get dressed for a walk up to Admin. When the got into the main building Mr. Turnbull didn't head for his own office, but instead escorted Pete to the second floor, where he'd only ever been twice before, once for his final entrance interview and once to talk about the incident with Steven. At the top of the stairs Mr. Turnbull walked Pete past the empty secretary's desk and through the polished black door into Father O'Connor's office. The priest was indeed there, as was Dr. Rugani, Riordan Home's psychologist. Pete found himself in one of the deep leather chairs facing the big black desk. Father O confirmed Pete's suspicions about this late night meeting.

Pete heard the words and he understood their meaning. But as Father O and Dr. Rugani rattled off things like, "sudden head trauma," "shock," "blood lost at the scene," "complications from the burn," and "fever," all he could think of was Manny would have been 14 in two weeks time. Pete had been trying to find a good book to give him, had been looking for weeks. Now there would be no need to go on with the search.

A funeral mass was held for Manny on the Friday after Easter. In the front row of the church, in the place reserved for family, the boys of St. Gabriel's cottage sat with their backs straight and their eyes shining wet. In the place closest to the aisle, closest to Manny, sat Pete. His left hand rested on his thigh, fingers gently interlocked with Tabitha's. In his right hand was a book about a bird who had soared and changed the way others saw the world.

Source Citation

Four of the philosophical statements Manny credits to his father are in truth attributable to the following sources:

Catholic philosopher St. Thomas Aquinas (1225-1274) warned, "Beware the man of one book."

In his book, *The True Believer*, American philosopher Eric Hoffer (1902-1983) wrote that, "Passionate hatred can give meaning and purpose to an empty life."

Siddhārtha Gautama Buddha (4th century BCE) is credited as saying "You will not be punished for your anger, you will be punished by your anger."

In his poem, "Broken Love" William Blake (1757-1827) wrote, "And throughout all eternity / I forgive you, you forgive me."

Lastly, I must give credit and thanks to Richard Bach (b.1936) for his body of work, especially for the two books Pete reads over the course of this novel, *Jonathan Livingston Seagull* and *Illusions: the Adventures of a Reluctant Messiah*.